THE WINDFALL

A Novel

By CHARLES EGBERT CRADDOCK

1907

CONTENTS

CHAPTER I

Despite his buoyant optimism Hilary Lloyd could but quail as he looked about him. The vast uninhabited heights of the encompassing Great Smoky Mountains, green, purple and bronze, seeming to his theatrical sense magnificently posed against the turquoise background of further ranges, glimpsed through clifty defiles and almost touching the differing translucent blue of the sapphire sky; the river, crag-bound, crystal-clear, with an arrowy swiftness; the forest, dense beyond any computation, gigantic of growths, redundantly rich of foliage, and gorgeous with autumnal tints—all were as revelations to his half-stunned mind. He had never dreamed of the natural wealth, the splendid extent, the picturesque values of this region. His imagination flagged, failed. He was sensible of the strain upon his receptivity to compass the transcendent reality. But whence, amidst these primeval splendours, should materialise the patrons of his little street fair? Its flimsy booths were already rising about the stony expanse of the public square of the town of Colbury, not, in stereotyped phrase, like magic, but with all the laborious accompaniments of hammers and saws, the straining of muscles and patience, the expenditure of profanity and perspiration, and the sound of loud, raucous voices. The tents reluctantly spread their mushroom-like contour, now and again suddenly collapsing from awkward handling or inadequate aid. The manager looked at the few humble toilers with a prescient pang. To be stranded here, on the uttermost confines of civilisation, seemed a disaster indeed of direful menace. He realised his friend's impressions and could have voiced in unison the exact phrase as a heavy fellow of medium height, arrayed in a ready-made suit of a loud plaid, slouched up with his hands in his pockets, and chewing a straw.

"Well, partner, we've done it again!" he said, not without the accents of reproach.

Lloyd obviously flinched at the tone, and his face flushed. It was of a singularly perfect contour and chiselling, according to the canons of art, and in its large nobility of expression it might have served, and possibly had, as a model for an artist's realisation of some high ideal. But there was a most mundane anxiety in his luminous eyes, darkly blue and long-lashed, and the alertness with which they eagerly surveyed the meagre festival preparations gave an accent of the ludicrous to his fine facial suggestions. He was like a man playing the *rôle* of a prince, unstaged, on the bare sidewalk, and his utter unconsciousness and indifference to the effect of his remarkable appearance added to its impressiveness. His hair was fine and light brown in tint, and it shone like silk as he lifted his straw hat and wearily mopped his brow with his handkerchief. He was young, twenty-five perhaps, and very fair of complexion, and the delicate texture of his skin allowed the fluctuating flush of annoyance visibly to come and go in his cheek. He was something more than of medium height, although not notably tall; he was very symmetrically put together, and, while slight and elegant, his movements showed intimations of muscular strength and a swift deftness that implied some special athletic training.

He presently gathered his faculties together and with a desperate courage affected to see naught amiss. "Why, we knew that it was only a country town, Haxon," he remonstrated.

Haxon pushed his wide-brimmed imitation Panama hat on the back of his head, showing in full relief his round red face, beaded with perspiration. He lifted one plump hand with an accusatory gesture toward the infinite stretch of the lonely mountains, and then turned melancholy eyes toward Lloyd.

"Why," Lloyd responded, "what is the matter with the mountains, Hax? I haven't got anything against 'em."

Haxon shook his head dolorously, "A good old country to walk in," he observed, tragically.

Lloyd affected surprise. "Cheese it!" he cried, contemptuously. "With a week to show—we're not stranded yet!"

Haxon's round head wagged to and fro unconvinced. "That railroad agent got us good, Hil'ry," he opined didactically. "We have got time enough to show all right—but nothing to show to."

In truth the prospect was not alluring from a utilitarian point of view. The little brick courthouse, the most considerable edifice in the town, stood in a plot of blue grass, surrounded by a fence of palings, and beyond the paved square without were enough small two-story shops to suggest the intent of the future when the intervals should be built in and the quadrangle complete. To the west the scattered dwellings straggled away along the hilly main street, with here and there a few cottages built on intersecting roadways, which should hereafter develop into cross-streets. But the temple of justice, the stores and the residences were none of them new, and barring a gleam of fresh paint now and again from some cottage out on the hilly reaches of the thoroughfare the town was much as it had been for years, and would be for years to come. There was a wonderful lack of foliage. A few ancient oaks stood in the courthouse yard, and the trellises of vines and low boughs in gardens betokened fruit culture, but along the streets the idea of improvement seemed to find its earliest municipal exposition in laying the axe to the root of every forest tree that had spread its boughs for centuries above the lush spaces now shorn close to give the town room to expand. The landscape, steeped in splendid colour, of infinite vastness, of loftiest heroic

3

suggestion and most poetic appeal, had wrought a surfeit of beauty in the sordid little town, and here, held in the heart of a most majestic expression of nature, there was naught to intimate the contiguity of the heights and the forests save the rare pure air and the fragrance of the balsam fir.

The tranquillity of the sunshine, the bland, suave atmosphere, the benignant breath of woods and waters seemed to impart their languorous lethargy to the inhabitants as well. There was not the frenzied interest in a new project of whatever sort that is the concomitant of enterprise in a live town. The merchants, the clerks, the few lawyers, and the officials of the courthouse noticed with only an episodical attention the preparations to get under way the first street fair which had ever shown its attractions to the denizens of Colbury.

This attitude piqued the curiosity of Lloyd. It nettled and unnerved him. As it fell under his observation in different ways it partook of the nature of those who manifested it. Now it intimated a sort of quizzical contempt, for there is a class of rural wights, who preserve the bucolic species still, always permeated with a disdain of progress, and a distrust of whatever is new to their limited experience. Now it was the outspoken prophecy of disaster.

"Some fools may leave thar harvests ter waggon down from the coves ter see yer show," a citizen suggested. "But a quarter of an eye will do the business, accordin' ter my way o' thinkin'. Ye air goin' ter bide hyar a week, they tell me. Why, man, the bigges' circus I ever see jes' showed fur one evenin', then tucked up its tent an' marched."

"Well, that ain't the style for street fairs," Lloyd explained. "This is a different sort of thing."

"It *is*,—it *is*, for sure, stranger."

4

Though enigmatically expressed, the acquiescence was distinctly uncomplimentary, and Lloyd dropped the topic. He had not come here to exhibit skill in debate, he said to himself, but to conduct a street fair. This, it was evident, would tax his powers. The manager was beginning to realise that he had been victimised in a certain sort by the wily representations of a railroad agent and the summer "cut-rates" in coming to this remote section. The merchants' evident lack of expectation of reaping the golden reward of a "big crowd in town" had a damping effect on the already drooping spirits of the showman. By way of steadying his nerve Lloyd sought reassurance in verifying some of the lures which had led him hither. In the office of the county court clerk, a brick-paved, white-washed apartment in the courthouse, he paid the State and county privilege tax on the show, and after he had taken out his license to exhibit, he courteously presented the officials with free passes to all the attractions.

"I hope you will do well," said the clerk in a tone of condolence.

"I hope so, indeed," returned Lloyd, thinking of the sum named in the tax-receipt. "We expect a good crowd. We have been well advertised throughout the country."

The clerk felt that he had no call to seem optimistic in other men's affairs to the jeopardy of his own soul. He left lying to more amiable wights, and preserved a dispiriting but veracious silence.

"The crops are all laid by," said a pleasant-spoken bystander. "Some folks *may* come down out'n the coves."

"I hear there is a mining camp some miles down the river," said Lloyd hopefully. "We lay considerable on that."

"Convict camp," said the clerk sepulchrally, and the amiable bystander burst out laughing.

5

"Them fellers have season tickets whar they be, stranger," he said. And then he winked hilariously at the clerk, whose funereal aspect brightened dimly at the dreary jest.

The small boy, ubiquitous expression of humanity, was out in force, and underfoot as usual. Every screw that went into the adjustment of the merry-go-round, the wooden head of every dummy horse, the great frame of the Ferris wheel, slowly rounding its circumference high into the air above the house tops and showing the solemn, austere, purpling mountain landscape, suffused with burnished, golden light, grotesquely framed by its towering circle—every detail passed under the personal supervision of the juvenile element of the town, and if the elders lacked interest it was more than atoned for by the frenzy of enthusiasm which possessed the juniors. The rearing of the tall mast, from the summit of which the noted "Captain Ollory of the Royal Navy," according to the florid announcement of the posters—videlicet Haxon, himself, and of what royal navy remains forever unexplained—was to spring into the air and plunge into a reservoir of water below, marked the accession of adult curiosity. This increased to open comment when Haxon himself appeared, cautiously superintending its solid adjustment in the ground, the stretching of the guy wires, the placing in position, at the correct distance, of the great trough of water which was to break the force of his leap from the giddy height of the summit.

The gratuitous advice, freely proffered, and the expressions of wonderment on all sides changed to injurious doubt, as the magnitude and risk of the proposed feat percolated through the densities of the uninformed rural mind. "Jump off'n that thar pole?—*never* in this worl'!" said one of the bystanders. "Onpossible!" commented another. Others opined, "Takes more'n the Street Fair ter fool we uns."

6

"Time come, an' the Cap'n will be tooken with the chicken pip, or the bilious colic, or some disabling complaint an' the defrauded public will be jes' settin' with its finger in its mouth."

If Haxon heard aught of these disaffected remarks he manifested no heed. Silent, surly, he doggedly gave his whole attention to the details on which his life depended. He was well aware that however sparse the attendance at the Street Fair, however disastrous the enterprise financially, the exhibition of his "high dive" must be given, for it was of necessity performed in the open air, and therefore was a free show in the nature of an advertisement.

Lloyd had often heard the cynical remark that the spectators of a hazardous acrobatic feat crowd to see the performer killed, not to witness his triumph, and he was reminded of this as he watched the unsympathetic citizens of the little town and heard their comments and speculations concerning his partner's feat, for Haxon was a half owner of the enterprise. Lloyd deprecated infinitely Haxon's mood of surly disaffection. He knew that it tended to impair the acrobat's nerve and to render his terrible feat doubly dangerous. Haxon, of all men, should cultivate composure, a cheerful and equable state of mind. Lloyd was subtly aware that his partner secretly upbraided him for this unfortunate move, the culminating disaster of an unsuccessful season. For the company to go to pieces at last in the remote wildernesses of the Great Smoky Mountains was indeed the extremest spite of fate, and even speculation shrunk back appalled from the utter blank of the possibilities beyond. The exchequer was almost empty; it was "up to them," as they had said dolorously to each other, to make their transportation back to New York, and they would have been glad of this, even with empty hands as the guerdon of their summer's hard work. And in fact this meant no

7

inconsiderable sum, for in addition to the concessionaries who sold and mended umbrellas, parasols and fans, dismayed inexpressibly by their sudden projection into this primitive community, the owners of the candy-stands and peanut-roasters, the company carried perforce a goodly number of individuals. While there were performers who did double duty in various wise, the "stunts" of the specialists could not be delegated, and this swelled the bulk of the expense accounts. True, Haxon, when his great diurnal feat had been exploited, was wont to array himself in correct evening dress and perform with great spirit on the cornet as the noted soloist, Signor Allegro. The "Flying Lady," when not ethereally a-wing, developed into a ticket-seller of no mean abilities. Even the noted juggler of the company found time to sing tenor in the quartette of the "high-class concert." But for the most part the duties of the others were continuous, and they were restricted to their several stations. Naturally, the freaks—a "Fat Lady," a "Wild Man," and a "Living Skeleton"—dared not court gratuitously the gaze of the public who ought to pay for the privilege of a shock to the nerves, and sedulously secluded themselves in their tents; the kinetoscope must needs shift its scenes unceasingly, and the wild west play which it exhibited reached a conclusion only to begin its active agonies anew; the merry-go-round and the Ferris Wheel were ready to solve the problem of perpetual motion, and throughout all the brass band brayed, in tune by happy accident, or, deliriously indifferent to the laws of harmony, vociferously off the key. But for this microcosm, this bizarre little world to revolve at all, must be attainable the essential motive power, the admittance fee in goodly quantity.

The prospect here had seemed so promising, so reasonable. The company had struggled against the unvarying luck of superior counter-attractions wherever they had gone; to give their show in a locality unused to all diversion, with not a

8

rival in prospect nor even in reminiscence, was a lure not to be disregarded. The lack of an audience in so sparsely settled a community did not readily occur to them; a town, even a little town, implies normally a tributary region of suburbs and farms. The vast uninhabited mountain wildernesses faced them like the land of doom.

Lloyd had had no Scriptural tuition that could remind him of the Scapegoat of the Hebraic ritual, loaded with the sins and the curses of the people and driven into the desert to lose itself in those aridities and die; but could the creature have possessed any sense of its doom and its direful burden, Lloyd might have realised its sentiments, as he gazed appalled upon the infinite stretching of those austere and lofty mountains, which even in the days of the aboriginal inhabitants of the country were called "The Endless." It was not his fault, he said bitterly to himself, his eyes hot as he gazed. The subject had been fully discussed, and all had agreed on the experiment. Haxon, though a part owner of the precarious and ephemeral property, had not made a protest—nay, he had been an earnest advocate of "fresh fields and pastures new." Now Lloyd abruptly reminded him of this, as with a sudden lurch and an exclamation of impatience Haxon snatched the hammer of a workman and with two or three well-directed blows drove home the steel spike that held down one of the guy wires. He looked up, still in his bent posture, from under his frowning dark eyebrows; his round, florid face, that was wont to be so jovial, was all lowering and sullen. His small dark eyes flashed with antagonism and vexation. "Who's sayin' as I didn't agree—eh? Well," as Lloyd made an intimation of negation, "what's gnawin' on ye, then?"

This was evidently no time nor mood for the discussion of the matter, and indeed discussion was futile, a mere waste of words. The die was cast. The Street Fair had met its fate. If

9

the company had been wrecked on a desert island its case could not be more desperate.

Lloyd turned away, looking dully about him. There was scant supervision now necessary—the old routine, practised week after week since the early spring, had grown so familiar to the workmen that the most ingenious blunderer could hardly find a pretext for his activities, and little by little Lloyd's meditative steps took him slowly along the smooth red clay road till presently he found himself on the outskirts of the town and nearing the river. He shook his head gloomily when he stood on the high rocks of the bank and gazing down perceived the course that the road followed through a clifty defile to reach the verge and the ford—there was not even a bridge in this benighted spot, and yet this was a county town! The water was swift, evidently deep—he marked the distance down the stream where the road once more resumed its course on the opposite bank. It obviously took a devious route along the bed of the river, picked its steps so to speak; there must be deep holes, quicksands, pitfalls on either side of the comparatively safe footing of the ford, he reflected. Suddenly he noticed the footbridge; this followed a direct line across the torrent—a trifling, primitive structure, consisting of a couple of logs with a shaking hand-rail, and with the deep, turbulent swift flow of a rocky mountain stream beneath. Once more he dolorously shook his head. Hither must come the patrons of the Street Fair, even now spreading its attractions on the public square to welcome them—not yet a canvas-covered wagon in sight, no horseman, no foot-passenger to tempt the instabilities of the little bridge.

He laid his hand on the rail and as he crossed felt the elastic structure sway beneath every step, while the waters swirled far below. But as he reached the opposite bank and paused for a moment his anxieties were calmed in spite of himself by the sweet peace of the dark, cool solitude; he listened to the ripples eddying about the jagged base of the crags—a sound distinct from the swift rush of the tumultuous currents. It had a secondary tone, seeming keyed higher, a clear metallic tintinnabulation like elfin minstrelsy, barely heard, yet not discriminated by the senses. And oh, the sylvan balm of the air!—it touched so caressingly the forlorn wight's cheek, his hair as he took off his hat, his hot, tired eyes, that he had half a mind to fall a-sobbing on the vague breast of this insensate sympathy. He was comforted in some sort. His lungs, filled and weighted with the soot and smoke and dust of a dozen sordid towns, expanded, drinking in with deep draughts this fragrant elixir that was but the diffusive air. He looked up into the dark green boughs of the giant oaks and beeches, and down again into depths as green, where the crystal-clear water reflected the verdure, leaf by leaf and branch by branch—only on the opposite side of the stream a brilliant section of vividly blue sky was duplicated, flaring out with a flake of cloud dazzlingly white.

So revivifying were these influences that he had a mind for solitude for the nonce. A long quiet walk he thought would restore his composure and steady his nerves. He would compass thus a surcease of the anxiety that harassed him, and by inaction recruit his energies better to cope with his problems. He had a deft, steady, sure step as he took his way along the country road, covering the ground with surprising rapidity, for he was a strong, athletic pedestrian; not that he had ever walked either as a pastime or a profession, but he had done various acrobatic "turns" in his time, and his muscles had served him well. Now and again as he went he lifted his head and looked off through gaps in the foliage at the encompassing mountains, critically surveying them, it might seem, his head discriminatingly askew, his bright eyes narrowing, and it was characteristic of his experience and his

11

limitations that he appraised the value of the landscape, not as scenery nor geographically, nor agriculturally, nor botanically, but simply as it struck the eye for stage-settings. Occasionally as the road swerved he caught a new aspect, and turned himself to face the prospect, holding up both arms to cut off irrelevant details, and bound the picture to the limits of the most effective.

"Gee,—what a flat!" he said once, and sometimes he waved his hands in the air, detaching bits here and there of cliff, or cataract, or bosky dells which he considered appropriate for "wings" or "flies." These erratic attitudinisings might have suggested a doubt of his sanity had there been aught to observe him as he climbed with wondrous activity the steep ascent of a mountain road, hardly more indeed than a bridle path, now about seven miles from Colbury. He saw no living object, save once, high, high in the air above the ranges, a majestically circling bird, whose strength and grace he paused to admire, unaware that it was the distance which so commended the foul mountain vulture; and once, when the laurel pressed close into the road and he heard a step within the dense covert; the next instant a deer bounded out into the path, caught sight of him, fixed his brilliant eyes upon him, and stood petrified with terror for an inappreciable second, holding one forefoot uplifted. Then stamping with all four feet together and poising his antlered head backward in a splendid pose the buck sprang down the declivity, and with an incredible lightness and swiftness disappeared in the densities of the deep woods.

The showman stood in stunned amaze. He had before seen deer—in a disemboweled state and dead as Ariovistus, hanging at the door of a certain restaurant of Gotham that thus advertised its venison, and in the close confines of the zoological display in city parks, but in its natural state, in its

12

native woods it was another creature. He had no dream that a deer was like this.

"Gee," he exclaimed, "I'm paralysed if he ain't the whole show!"

He could have cried out with delight when suddenly the river sought anew his companionship. Down deep in a ravine now it flowed, for he had been steadily climbing, although the zigzags of the mountain road had minimised the slant of the ascent. How darkly cool in its abysmal cliff-bound channel it looked, how melodiously chanting it was as it went. He wondered if he were to cross it again—not at this height, he hoped. But as he progressed ever higher and higher the stream seemed to sink, ever deeper and deeper, and presently the woods intervened to screen it from sight, and soon its voice grew faint as it wandered away till he could barely hear it, still singing, singing as it went, and then he was not sure if the sound were of murmurous waters or the sibilance of the wind.

For the wind was rising, and all the leaves were astir. A thousand voices seemed suddenly to invade the stillness. He wondered to hear a mocking-bird break out in jubilantly brilliant melody—he had thought the species silent at this time of the year; he was acquainted with them as they flourished in cages in barber shops. The trees of the dense woods were as if endowed with language, for he discriminated the difference in the rustling of the varieties of foliage as he passed—a keen sense he had. A tree-toad was shrilling hard by for rain. He could not see the creature; he had no idea to what the voice belonged, so limited was his woodland experience. He only noted the clamorous appeal. He was beginning to be tired. He wondered how far he had come at this brisk pace. Suddenly he fixed the terminus of his jaunt. The road forked at a little distance in advance, and he determined that he would not trust himself

13

to unknown divergences of the main thoroughfare. He slackened his gait as he approached the parting of the ways. On one side the woods grew sparse, showing a deep declivity, a section of valley far, far below, and beyond a panorama of mountain ranges that took his breath away, one above another, one beyond another, tier after tier to the limits of vision. Infinity, that the mind cannot grasp, was here expressed to the eye. The amethystine tints imparted by the western light were upon them, and he knew, therefore, that they lay to the east, but despite the smile of the parting sun a great mass of darkly purple clouds lowered above them, raising a fictitious horizon line almost to the zenith. The wind was a-surge in these clouds and they visibly careened, and collapsed, and filled out anew as if they were sails spread to the fury of a gale, but no token of motion was in the densely wooded mountains beneath them, and only a gentle breeze ruffled the tree tops of the valleys, a silver wake following its invisible passage. On the other side of the road he noted how the timber had been cut away; a cornfield was yellowing in the sun, and at the summit of the slant he perceived, lazily adrift in the air, a whorl of smoke that issued from the crooked and dilapidated stick-and-clay chimney of a little log cabin, almost invisible, embowered amongst the boughs of an ample orchard of thrifty apple trees. Nearer at hand these gave way to peach trees planted in regular avenues and great numbers. In the dearth of manufacturing energies in the region and evidences of any agricultural industry, except of the simplest limits, he was surprised by these suggestions of enterprise and labour. The grassy glades between the rows of peach trees were alluring to the eye; some cereal had been sown and harvested, and in the aisles a lush growth of crab-grass had sprung up, new and thick and green as moss. The peaches had all been gathered, but the graceful lanceolate leaves were still dense upon the boughs, and the somnolent afternoon sunshine here and

14

there flickered through, and lay in long, burnished golden shafts adown the green glooms.

And suddenly he was conscious of motion in their midst. He could not be sure how he had failed to see the figure earlier—or, indeed, had it just come within his range of vision. A girl was standing half in the golden glow, and half in the emerald gloom of the shadow, gazing up wistfully at a bough gently swaying just beyond her reach. As the breeze tossed it, he saw the prize that lured her—a great Indian peach, the last of the season, with all the sweetness of the summer suns, with all the freshness of the summer rains stored within the luscious darkly-red globe. She raised her hand, and made a sudden leap toward it with the lightness, the grace, the agile strength of a deer. The wind brushed the bough beyond her reach, and once more she bounded toward it elastically.

The indescribable grace of her attitudes appealed to the man whose education, and interest, and business in life were pose. Nothing more ethereally dainty was ever exploited before the footlights. He caught his breath, as, realising that she had not perceived him standing in the road, he gave himself up to staring at her, with a vague sense of a discovery growing upon him. Her dress, rustic though it was, impressed him as crudely picturesque. It was of the coarsest yellow calico, and she held up the skirt in front full of clusters of purple grapes, so overladen that the rich bunches and tendrils of vine trailed down upon her petticoat thus revealed, which was of a dark red cotton. A short petticoat it was, and showed her feet and ankles; her chaussure was of the flimsiest,—a pair of old rubber sandals, that, laced with thongs across her red hose, with only a utilitarian intent of retaining them in place, had contrived to achieve a classic effect; these members were so active, so swift and certain, so deftly used, so elastic of muscle as she skipped and leaped,

15

that the idea of the boards was suggested anew—no *première danseuse* that he had ever seen could do a "turn" more daintily. She had all the sportive innocence of a fawn.

A certain difficulty encumbered her. She carried on her head a basket or a piggin, hardly visible so filled it was with grapes, the tendrils and clusters falling partly outside till they touched her thick auburn hair, coiled in a great curling mass at the back of her head. She now steadied this pail with one upheld hand, the arm bare to the elbow, and again she caught at the peach, her fair up-turned face smiling, her brown eyes alight with fun and yet all a-gloat, her full red lips parted over her perfect teeth, and as she danced she sang, or rather panted out, a stanza of a song that seemed inapposite save for the first line, which, perhaps, suggested it to her mind:

> "Oh, shell I git my heart's desire,
> Kind shepherd, tell me true,
> That I may quit before I tire,
> My Kate has many come to sue."
> "Once you fail—'tis talking,
> Twice you fail—'tis mocking,
> Thrice you fail—'tis shocking,
> But a fool will ever play with fire."

Her voice was crudely loud, but so clear. Every tone was so justly true. The enunciation was faulty beyond any power of description, and at first it made him wince, albeit his own capacities for declamation were of no high order. Then her singing struck him as characteristic—good of its kind, but of a kind never classified. He had an instinct for novelty. The second time she sang the stanza, giving herself up with a sort of joyous abandon to the dance, for now she seemed hardly to hope to reach the peach, he was entranced with the picture she presented, the exquisite grace of her attitudes, the incomparable lightness and strength of her dancing, her beautiful, symmetrical form, and the strong sweet melody of her voice as it floated out so richly. He noted the contrast of her slender waist and limbs with the full throat—revealed by the bodice of the orange-tinted calico, the edges of which were turned in at the top for added coolness—the deep chest. With the vocal endowments the build assured the singer.

His interest was as impersonal as if she were indeed a feature of some Thespian exhibition. He had not thought how the scene must end—that if he moved she must descry him standing so near at hand in the road. And in fact he did not move—he was still motionless, spellbound, when a wider circuit of the tree brought him suddenly within her range of vision. She paused so abruptly as to jeopardise the equilibrium of the pail on her head and she lifted her hand to steady its profuse wealth of grape clusters, and thus she stood at gaze, her lips parted, her eyes dilated with astonishment.

He divined her sentiments at the moment of discovery, but he could not understand the facial expression that ensued. Her eyes narrowed with an inimical suggestion, watchful, expectant. Her red lips closed firmly. He had not before noticed how strong of contour was her chin, intimating resolution. He lifted his hat courteously, and waited for her to speak. She remained silent, and there was a moment of vacuum.

Then a sudden sound smote the stillness. A tremendous peal of thunder came from the mass of darkly purple clouds suspended above the mountains across the valley. As he instinctively turned his head, they were rent by a swift zigzag gleam of a sinister whiteness, and again the thunder pealed. The turmoils that had earlier convulsed the clouds had now taken definite direction. The wind was driving them hitherward across the valley, and for the first time in his life he heard the raindrops pattering down upon tree tops two thousand feet below him, while he stood high in the sunshine. One of the sudden mountain storms impended. In another moment, as he perceived, the torrents would be loosed upon them. He was arrayed to simulate prosperity; "out-at-elbows," even in a showman, is a confession of disaster. Had business been good he would have gone far less smart. He had a prudential consideration of shelter.

"Gee! There comes a corker!" he exclaimed. "Could I go to the house, lydy?"

He realised the incongruity of the address with this untutored peasant, but a sense of policy blended with his extravagant courtesy in its application. The "lady" gazed at him with that countenance of severe monition which he hardly understood.

"I was thinkin' ez ye mought ez well," she replied. Her answer was not so ungracious as irrelevant. He was a man of keen intuitions, and he was realising that their thoughts did not meet. She spoke of somewhat else than the storm. He was not a well-bred man in any sense. The impersonations of the stage comprised his tuition of conduct and courtesy, but he had the veneer which even the observation of the customs of gentility afford, the manners of the street, the trains, the theatre, and, as she threw down the bars of the fence and came into the road, he lifted his hat again, and prepared to walk by her side, and proposed to carry her pail. She said nothing. She only gave him a wide, uncomprehending stare, then fell into the road several paces behind him. For his life he could not avoid turning, and slackening his gait, that she might come up alongside.

"Keep right ahead," she said severely, and thus admonished he took up his line of march for the cabin on the hill.

She herded him along as a canine guardian of a flock might regulate the progress of a stray sheep. Once he again stepped instinctively to one side of the path in the expectation that she would join him, but she instantly crossed to the same side, and kept the distance the same between them, some two paces, even when the drops began to fall, and he quickened his gait to a speedy run. Only a short interval elapsed before they were at the bars of the pasture fence, which were already on the ground, and traversing the absolutely bare and hard-trodden dooryard to a log cabin of a most uninviting aspect.

He had scant opportunity to mark its details till he was on the rickety little porch where, looking over his shoulder, he had a cursory glimpse of its stereotyped features—strange enough to him; the wood-pile, situated on a sea of chips; the bee-gums, ranged along the fence; the grindstone; the ash-hopper; the rooting pigs in a corner; the cow, standing in a shed at one side waiting to be milked; a good strong waggon also under that shelter; a bevy of poultry, big and little, pecking about the door; a dozen curs of low degree noisily yelping around him, with so spurious an affectation of fierceness that it could not impose even on a stranger's fears; and a big bulldog, of a most ferocious silence, slowly dragging a block and chain from under the house. Infinitely incongruous the whole seemed with the imperial, august aspect of the purple, storm-dominated mountains beyond and the smiling serenity of the far sunlit valleys, their variant tones of green enriched by the burnished golden afternoon glamours, and by the silver glintings of the river coursing through the coves in the distance. The next moment the clouds fell like a curtain before them all. The thunder pealed; the torrents descended; the dooryard was a network of puddles, and the clamorous beat of the rain on the roof made the room into which he was ushered resound like a drum.

19

CHAPTER II

Hilary Lloyd had never seen aught like this apartment. The beams of the low, unplastered ceiling, brown with smoke and age, were hung with strings of red peppers and bunches of herbs; the two beds, high and plump, were covered with gay patchwork quilts of marvellous design; the vast fireplace—he could hardly believe his eyes when he marked the clay-and-stick materials of its construction—looked as if it had been built by some big bird; the quaint pots, and ovens, and skillets, and trivets ranged in one corner he appraised as cooking utensils, but their like he had never before beheld; for a moment he did not recognise the use of a queer box-like cradle, which a faded young woman, with a snuff-brush in her mouth, was rocking with one foot, delegated to maternal duty, while she sat staring with lack-lustre eyes at the advent of the stranger with the daughter of the house.

"Hi!" he exclaimed delightedly. "Hello, Baby!" He did not wait to make sure of his welcome or for any formalities of introduction. He pounced down on the cradle, yanked out the infant from the coverlets, tossed it up to the ceiling, and then set it on the tall mantelpiece, holding it there with both hands to take a good look at it, while the members of the family stood around in wonder. Whether the child fancied that it had already met the showman and mistook his identity, whether this boisterous method of address accorded with its undeveloped sense of manners, whether the nap to which it had been consigned were compulsory and it rejoiced in its release, it responded genially to the demonstration in the spirit in which this was tendered. It was an attractive object as it sat on the high mantelpiece and flopped its very fat legs to and fro, frankly exhibited by its short pink calico skirt, and laughed widely with two pearly white teeth all agleam in a very red mouth. It had red hair, curling in very seductive ringlets about a fair brow, and its big blue eyes were as merry as a clown's. At every jocose movement of Lloyd's thumbs on its fat stomach, tickling it surreptitiously as he held the child on its perch, it burst into repeated peals of infantile laughter, and no one cared how hard the rain came down, or listened to the thunder roll.

"By George, you're a peach! you're a daisy!" cried Lloyd hilariously.

"Be you uns a family man, stranger?" a high vibratory voice queried, and Lloyd glancing down beheld at one side of the fire an ancient wrinkled face, surrounded by the crinkled ruffle of a great white cap, a venous hand, holding a pipe of strong tobacco at arm's length, and a thin bent figure attired in a blue and white checked homespun gown, with a little red plaid shoulder shawl.

"Good-evenin', madam," he said, snatching off his hat—one hand could hold the baby. "Family man?—*nope!*" he replied emphatically, and he shook his head sagely. "The kind of biz I'm in don't give a feller much chance at the domestic altar—winter and summer, night and day, on the go. As to the lydies—they ain't disposed to marry a man on the road."

He could not understand the appalled pallor that settled on her pinched high-featured face.

"Why n't ye git a better bizness?" she asked, with the plangent cadence of reproach.

He stared, again confronted with that sense of being at once uncomprehending and uncomprehended. "Do I speak the English langwitch, or not?" he said petulantly in his inner consciousness. For the situation fostered doubts.

21

The stress of the obvious misunderstanding placed a period to the carousal with the baby, and he handed the infant back to its mother as he took a tendered chair. The child had no mind to relinquish the gay company it had encountered, and clung to the showman, working both bare feet in the direction of its lackadaisical mother, with a very distinct intention of making her keep her distance, if kicks might suffice. Its strength did not match its resolution, however, and it was shortly consigned to its cradle, where it crawled up out of its coverings, whenever it was laid on its back, yelling vociferously and continuously, save when it paused once or twice to break into a laugh as Lloyd leaned over the back of his chair to snap his fingers at it.

"You have got a dandy place up here," he said by way of making his stay agreeable. "Fine orchard. Must have oodles of apples and peaches."

Again that doubt of the "English langwitch" assailed him. Surely he had said naught affrighting, but there was a look like terror in the old woman's eyes.

"Some o' the trees ain't good bearers," said the girl, speaking for the first time since their entrance. She had bestowed elsewhere her burden of grapes, and she was standing now on the broad hearthstone divested of those picturesque accessories to her costume. Lloyd was conscious of a curiosity concerning her beauty, thus devoid of embellishment, but as he turned to critically scan her appearance his attention was struck by a peculiarity that diverted his survey. She had just been out in the rain—yet how they had both run to reach the shelter before the bursting of the storm! She was evidently wet to the skin, and as she stood on the hot flagstones the water ran off her hair, her hands, her skirts in rills, and the heat of the fire sent the steam ascending from every drenched fold of her garments. Her errand had obviously been a matter of some importance

22

toward which she had had little inclination, for she did not relish her dripping condition, as was manifested in the fact that she was immediately taking down a fresh gown from where it had hung on a nail on the back of a door, and rummaging in a chest for other dry gear. She did not leave the room, however, till a heavy step smote the puncheons of the porch, when she gathered up the fresh garments and climbing a ladder-like stairway to a room in the roof, disappeared in the attic.

She had gone to summon the master of the house on his account, Lloyd realised at length, and with a sentiment of expectant anxiety he turned toward the newcomer, although for his life he could not understand what should require the girl to face a tempest like this to bring the owner to reckon with a chance wayfarer, seeking shelter from a storm. The owner, nay, two, five, a half dozen stalwart men, heavily built, tall, bearded, clad in brown jeans, trooped in, their united tramp shaking the puncheons of the floor like the march of a detachment of infantry. They, too, dripped with the rain, but with more unconcern than the girl had manifested, for they ensconced themselves in chairs, two or three joining the group around the hearthstone, where winter and summer the mountaineer's fire is always aglow, its intensity governed by the temperature; the others leaned back against the wall, their splint-bottomed chairs tilted on the hind legs, all solemnly silent, all monotonously chewing their quids of tobacco, all stolidly eyeing the guest.

Only the eldest seemed to anticipate conversation. Not that he spoke himself, but he fixed his eyes so interrogatively, so coercively on Lloyd's face that the expression betokened a hundred eager questions. An account of himself was evidently in order—but why? Lloyd glanced out of the open door at the glittering, steely, serried ranks of the rainfall, thinking that as soon as they had marched past and down the valley he too would speedily evacuate the premises and see his queer entertainers never again—unless indeed they were minded to patronise the attractions of the great Lloyd & Haxon Street Fair now ready to exhibit in Colbury. The association of ideas allayed a sudden rush of anger which was rising in his consciousness, responsive to the uncertainty of his position, the peculiarity of their manner, the impossibility to compass an accord of comprehension in these simplicities of circumstance. It was stemmed in an instant by the instinct of the showman. Since he was expected by his uncouth host to inaugurate the conversation he would in the interest of the show waive ceremony and essay whatever topic came first to his tongue.

"Sudden storm, sir," he said. "I was out there admiring your fine orchards and it overtook me."

The host's jaw dropped. It was odd that his face could be so expressive, masked as it was by a bushy growth of red beard, evidently once of fiery tint, but now so veined with grey that the effect was quenched to a degree. Perhaps because all its indicia were of the conventional type their significance was easily discerned. His mouth, cavernous amidst the beard, stood open in readily interpreted dismay. His small brown eyes hung with a persistent appeal on the eyes of the stranger. His head bent forward stiffly, with an intent, expectant waiting. He uttered not a syllable.

"Great Scott! They all look as if they had seen a ghost!" thought the amazed Lloyd.

The next moment he felt a sudden touch on his knee, and turning sharply in his chair, perceived the old woman's tremulous claw bespeaking attention as she leaned forward toward him from her chimney corner. Her cap frills quivered in her agitation; her face was deathly pale. "Stranger," she said solemnly, "we make *vinegar*, an' sell it—an' not a thing else. *Vinegar—vinegar*—sell it to the stores in town."

24

Lloyd stared. He felt as if he were in a nightmare. Yet he could recall no nightmare that had ever exerted so great a strain on his mental endowments.

"Vinegar?" he said with a forced laugh. "Well, I don't take much stock in vinegar. I ain't one of the sour kind. Vinegar ain't good to drink. I couldn't pledge your health in that, lydy. With all of them fine fruits I should think you might make something better than vinegar."

The host spoke up acridly.

"Mam," he addressed the old dame, "you jes' hesh up." His voice was husky, as if he spoke with an effort—hasty, as if he scarcely knew what to say.

Lloyd turned upon him with a sudden flare of anger. "I don't want to call a man a cad in his own house," he flamed. "But the lydy will talk as she pleases while I'm aboard. I'd oodles rather talk to her than to you, sir."

The old woman had evidently lost her poise—she cast an amazed, affrighted glance upon her son. Then she clumsily sought to repair the damage that she fancied she had done. "*Dried apples*, stranger, an' *dried peaches*. We uns cut an' sell 'em ter the store—in town. Dried apples an' peach-leather."

"Very praiseworthy. But dried apples ain't the best thing that can come out of an orchard," Lloyd began, but the host cut him short.

"Mam," said the great, bearded giant, anticipating her reply—his face a very mask of terror—"ef you uns don't hesh up——"

"What will you do, eh? Nothing while I'm here," Lloyd blustered. "Why, man, you're a monstrosity. I've a mind to take you off with me!" There was a sudden stir behind Lloyd; he had a vague perception that the five other men were afoot with some intent, which he did not know, and for which he did not care. "I'll put you on exhibition in my show as the 'wild man of Persimmon Cove.' You ain't any more civilised than my big boa constrictor. You ought to draw a crowd all by your lonesome. What sort of behaviour is this for a son?"

"Oh," squealed the old woman savagely, "he is the best son that ever stepped—an' I'll mark the face o' the man who says the contrairy!" She held up her talons tremulously. "The best son that ever stepped."

"Mam," quavered the mountaineer, in despair, "you uns will ruin me bodaciously. Jes' hesh yer mouth an' hold yer tongue, ef so be ye know how."

Lloyd, still seated, looked up wonderingly at the group, now all afoot and gathered about him. He noted that the two younger men presently placed themselves by the door, as if he might make a break for liberty. He was aware, too, for the first time of the number of weapons on the walls. The rifle on deer antlers above the mantelpiece had caught his attention when he first entered, but now he took heed of others here and there sustained in place by pegs driven between the logs. This was not remarkable, perhaps, since there were several men in the family, but he was not used to seeing a living room unite its functions with that of an armoury. He could understand naught of the strange episode, and it had elements and suggestions infinitely distasteful to his predilections. "All I have got to say then is that bad is the best—if that is the best son," Lloyd persisted. "He has got no more feeling than the big snake in my show."

The word, mentioned for the second time, made a definite impression. There was a sudden absolute pause within. The wind outside rose and fell in sonorous gusts above the vast valley. The iterative beat of the rain on the roof was differentiated, in the myriad tentative touches of the drops, from the swirling splash of its aggregations from the eaves. The log on the andirons, long a-smoulder, broke in twain

26

with a dull crash, its two ends falling apart on the piles of ashes in either corner, and sending up a shower of sparks and a cloud of pungent smoke. Even the padded footfalls of one of the dogs were discriminated in the silence as he trotted across the floor and stood at the door, gazing out at the rain for a moment, then with a blended yawn and whine stretched himself to unprecedented proportions and once more came back to lie on the warm hearth, where the group still stood motionless, towering expectantly over the visitor as Lloyd sat in his chair and stared blankly at them all.

"A show, stranger?" the husky voice of the master of the house ventured dubiously. "Be you uns got a show?"

"I have that," Lloyd declared promptly, "and don't you forget it. The Lloyd & Haxon Company. Greatest show on earth! Unrivalled attractions! Flying Lydy, Fat Lydy, Isaac, the snake-eater—eats 'em alive,—Captain Ollory, of the Royal Navy, greatest high-dive artist in the world—daily exhibition free,—finest Ferris Wheel ever seen, Merry-go-round with both saddles and chariots—great musical attractions—quartet of high-class singers, and daily recitals by Signor Allegro on the cornet—brass band concert before each performance—pyrotechnic exhibition at night, free ..." he reeled off this farrago with the utmost respect and seriousness while his host stared in astonishment.

"Stop—stop——" cried the showman suddenly. "I have got some pictorial paper here and other literachure of the company." He drew from his breast pockets some compactly folded posters which when opened out proved to be highly tinted illustrations of these unrivalled attractions. He sprang nimbly out of his chair and began good-naturedly to spread them out on the floor of the cabin at the feet of the old "lydy" who had threatened him with a passage at arms. The others stood around dumbly, doubtfully staring at the red and yellow daubs; even the dogs joined the circle,

27

vaguely wagging their tails and now and then gazing up hopefully into their masters' faces, as if to demand when something in the nature of a banquet would ensue on so much show of interest. One of them, a pointer, suddenly impatient, walked across the paper, leaving on it the imprint of his toes damp from a recent excursion into the puddles of the porch. Lloyd caught him by the nose and lifted him off with one hand. "What d'ye mean by spoiling the portrait of the fat lydy," he said, and dropping on one knee he rectified the damage with his handkerchief.

"Where?—*where*, stranger?" demanded the old woman in a twitter of the keenest curiosity. "Waal, sir!" eyeing the picture, "she is bodaciously broad. Air that thar a speakin' likeness, sir?"

"Honest, she is fat," said Lloyd. "She has to ride in a cart by her lone. But she is a very nice lydy—high-toned. I feel sorry for her."

"Why?" asked the girl, unexpectedly.

Lloyd glanced up doubtfully at her from his lowly posture, then slowly rose to his feet.

"Well," he said, turning his head thoughtfully to one side, as if to scrutinise his impressions, "I always was sorry for freaks. They are always in demand, and they generally earn a handsome salary, but money ain't everything—money can't make people happy."

He stopped short, reflecting that a comparatively small amount would add very materially to his prospect of felicity.

Once more he had a shuddering sense of a venerable claw laid on his arm. The old woman was at his side. "Stranger," she said mysteriously, "ef anybody in town axes you ef we uns make money up hyar on the mounting you kin jes' sw'ar ez ye knows 'tain't true. We uns ain't got nuthin' ter make money with."

Lloyd gazed in amazement at her—then around at the humble place with every evidence of poverty, and to his mind, discomfort. But he could not with civility acquiesce in her statement and he hesitated.

"Mam," her son plained, "ye air wuss than pore, ye air plumb deranged. This hyar man air a showman."

"And I want you, sir, for a freak!" Lloyd declared rudely. "Allow me, lydy, to present you with some free tickets for the show, for yourself and these other two lydies. These will be good for any day and the whole biz, if you can come down to Colbury one day this week." He was shuffling the little blue and red cards in his hands, his instinct being to include the entire family, but a recollection of the acrid remonstrances of "Captain Ollory of the Royal Navy" on the occasion of similar generosities, stayed his hand.

"Naw, sir, naw sir! nare one," the head of the family had found his ordinary sonorous voice. "We may be pore, ez Mam says, but we pay ez we go. We kin tote our end of the log. We'll attend the show—but we ain't wantin' nobody ter gin us a treat."

"Shadrach,—Shadrach," quavered out the old woman in a twitter of anxiety, "whut ye talkin' 'bout. Ye know ye ain't got no money—an' you ain't got no way—no *way*—ter git no money."

"Hesh that up, Mam," the son admonished her, "else you'll go *dee*stracted, and eend yer days with a gag in yer mouth an' tied ter the bedpost."

"Cheese it, I tell you!" Lloyd confronted him angrily. "You will stow your tongue while I'm here or I'll give you what for. I'd floor you anyhow for a nickel, but you are too old for me to touch."

"S'pose you uns try me!" one of the young mountaineers beside the door stepped forth.

He was like unto the sons of Anak, gigantic of build, every movement informed with elasticity and vigour, and the others broke into a great guffaw, so slight by contrast, so girlishly dapper did Lloyd appear, with so rose pink a flush in his cheek as he stood on the hearth. But his eyes flashed at the challenge, and as the muscular young mountaineer approached, carefully eyeing him, he threw off his coat and "bunched his fives" without a moment's hesitation.

The rural giant's lunge was something frightful in its weighty impetuosity. The stranger side-stepped with lightning-like swiftness; his arm flew out in a sudden counter-stroke that landed with an impact like the click of a solid shot; the little cabin shook on its foundations and rang with a clatter that discounted the tumults of the storm as the young mountaineer "went to grass" with a precipitancy that left hardly an available muscle in his whole big body.

There were some capacities for the enjoyment of sport and a sense of fair play in the applause of the others, for Tom Pinnott showed that he was not seriously hurt by ruefully gathering himself together and sitting where he had fallen on the floor, sheepishly laughing and rubbing his shoulder.

"How on yearth, stranger," demanded old Shadrach Pinnott, who seemed to bear no grudge for the several smart admonitions as to his filial conduct which the young showman had administered, "How on yearth did ye ever contrive ter throw Tawm."

"Oh, I have had experience in the ring," said Lloyd, pulling on his coat. "I trained with a good prospect for the light-weight championship, but I gave it up. I don't like to fight. I have got the sand all right, but I have got to get my mad up to fight with any spirit. Now, what I like in a public performance is to show some kind of merit, you know, of fine flavour. I mean something pleasing—that don't hurt nobody, nor leave nobody in the lurch, nor make much of one man to destroy another's prospects. Competitions ain't my lay at all. Now, if I could choose I'd like to exhibit a song-and-dance such as this lydy here was enjoying in the orchard. That would hit the taste of the public, too—to a charm—to a charm."

He wagged his head with the emphasis of conviction. An exquisite bit of rusticity, he felt it to be, as refined, as delicate, as free from the rough edges of common country life, idealised because of the girl's grace and beauty, yet as genuinely bucolic as a pastoral poem or painting. He had begun to ply her with insistence. If the "lydies" would come down he would arrange so that it shouldn't cost them a cent. By fair rights she ought to be paid for dancing and singing, and as she cried out in amazed ridicule of the idea he assured her that in the outside world this happened every day. Ladies received money, legal tender, actual currency, for nothing but singing and dancing. "And few of them can do a turn like you," he declared. But because of his partner—and he paused to disclose to them in a voice of mystery the exceedingly pertinent fact that Captain Ollory of the Royal Navy, whose real name was Haxon, was a partner in the enterprise, and without his consent he dared not offer her money till she had been tried and the public captured.

"Do you think you would be scared?" he asked, ready to reassure the delicate feminine sensibility.

"Skeered o' whut?" she demanded wonderingly.

If she could not instinctively prefigure shrinking from the crowds, from the strange situation, he determined that he would not suggest the poignant anguish of stage fright, and

31

the thought occurred to him for the first time that this was a product of civilisation, the evil of self-consciousness, the prescience of carping criticism or ridicule. He made haste to say that the tent of Isaac, the snake-tamer, where he was wont to "eat 'em alive" was at the other end of the Square from the tent wherein she would sing and dance. True, the "Wild Man" was a close neighbour, but since she was to be in effect for a time a member of the company he would disclose in confidence the circumstance that Wick-Zoo, the Wild Man, was getting to be quite civilised, in fact—in fact—he burst out laughing,—Wick-Zoo was a pretty good fellow. She need have no fear of Wick-Zoo, the Wild Man.

Then he piped up with a very pretty tenor and sang the air which he had caught from hearing it in the orchard, and gave her some points as to the management of her voice to make more of it for the public behoof.

And while the old grandmother listened sharp-eyed and spellbound, the girl, proving docile and tractable, sought to apply his admonitions and criticism, and now and again his dulcet tenor tones rang out to illustrate some axiom. The group of mountain men lingered for a time, but presently drifted out to the rain-drenched porch, where drops still trickled from the eaves. The storm was over; as they gazed out down the valley they saw that it had become all of a luminous emerald green with vast clouds of pearl white vapours shimmering and glistening as the sun smote upon them, floating between the purple mountains near at hand and half veiling the distant azure ranges. A sudden rainbow sprung into the light, spanning the abysses from Chilhowee to the Great Smoky heights, and further down the valley, like a faint reflection of its glories, a duplicate arch was set in the mists beyond. With stolid unperceptive eyes they mechanically dwelt upon the scene—it was to them but the ordinary aspect of life. They appreciated naught of its

32

splendours, its vastness, its pictorial values, its uplifting subtlety of suggestion. It meant to them that the rain was over and that sunset would soon emblazon the west. Cows were to be milked, the stock to be fed, the wood to be cut, and perhaps other duties pressed upon their recollection, for Tom presently said in a low voice to his father, "Granny mighty nigh let the cat out'n the bag."

Shadrach Pinnott warily nodded his head in assent.

Another of his sons spoke up after cautiously listening to be sure that the newcomer could hear naught but his own carolling, "'My Kate has many come to sue!'"

"Ef *he* hed been what Clotildy took him fur the whole secret would hev been out fur true."

The bare suggestion that this danger might have so nearly menaced them put the whole group out of countenance.

"Ye 'low ez ye be sure, dad, ez he air nuthin' but a showman like he say?" asked Daniel, the eldest of Shadrach's sons, a slow, sedate-looking man of thirty years. "Ye 'low he didn't sense nuthin' o' the facts from them words that Granny let fall?"

Shadrach Pinnott's shock head bent in his deep cogitation. "He hed the papers an' the tickets of a showman," he argued. "An' thar hev been word of a Street Fair comin', down in Colb'ry."

"An' he hev got the muscle an' the showin' of a reg'lar prize-fighter," said Tom, the athlete, bethinking himself to rub his shoulder.

"An' lis'n," said the crafty old moonshiner; "he sings like a plumb mocking-bird. In my opinion the whole Revenue Department ain't ekal ter sech quirin' ez that."

33

And once more the dulcet plaint "My Kate has many come to sue," challenged the echoes.

CHAPTER III

For a long time after Lloyd had quitted the place Clotilda Pinnott stood on the porch and listened to his retreating footsteps. An impressive silence had succeeded the turmoils of the storm. No more the echo repeated the sonorous proclamation of the imperious thunder. One could hardly realise how the trumpeting wind had blared through those narrow, deep, mute valleys with their yet more secluded, cup-like coves. The glancing lyrical notes of the rain, falling on the ear like myriads of uncomprehended words keyed to harmony in rhythmic measure, had left but now and again the patter of glittering silver drops from the low-hanging boughs of some moisture-weighted tree. In this quiescence of nature she could mark his progress, as silent, too, she leaned against the post of the rickety porch, her fresh gown of faint blue cotton still distinct in the fading light, so clarified was the air, so pervasive the reflection of the great expanse of the deeply yellow western sky, glowing like burnished copper above the dusky purple mountains that deployed against the horizon line, high above the emerald valleys below. Now she heard the impact of his foot on stone, and again it was the shifting of sand and gravel dislodged by his step that told her he had turned the curve of the road; now she knew he was almost immediately in a line with the house, but nearly a thousand feet below on the mountain side. She was apprised when he passed the chalybeate spring, not indeed by the sound of his tread, for the distance here was too great; some vague reverberations began to issue from the gigantic gneiss cliff hard by that rose

34

austere, grey, columnar, nearly one thousand feet sheer, standing out in half relief from the main mountain mass like a flying buttress of some buried castle in the mythical days of the giants. Its niched and creviced summit was on a level with the cabin perched so high on the mountain side, and now and then a broken vibration betokened the sound of a step below; then came the echo of a voice faintly singing the orchard song. Then silence—a long lapse of time—and still silence.

"He's gone," she said. "He's gone!"

She sighed with a vague languor, an unappreciated pain, and shifted her posture. The tension of her vigilance was relaxed. She stretched up both her arms against the post and dully yawned. Then she looked out at the scene with the effect of observing it for the first time. For a long interval she gazed at the burnished translucent yellow glow of the west that despite its brilliance seemed to diffuse no light upon the world below. Shadows were mustering; the valley beneath could hardly be discerned now, but for the rising of the mists. Their white glimmer among the darker tree tops prolonged the visibility of the forests. Only the horizon line, sharply drawn against the saffron glamours of the heavens, preserved the contour of the mountains, otherwise lost in the dull purplish dusk.

No longer silence reigned. First she heard the tremulous trilling of a tree-toad; a pause ensued in the moist vacuity of the atmosphere, and then came a raucous tentative note of a frog, and presently there sounded a dozen like voices, and now the air rocked to and fro with the strophe and antistrophe of the batrachian tribe, all a-croak by the water courses, and the continuous shrilling of the cicada. All were loud in the calm twilight, so loud that an appreciated sense of silence seemed attendant on the evening star, pellucid, white, quivering in the yellow glow of the west, and the slow dropping of the crescent moon adown and adown the sky.

Clotilda appeared as if she were going to meet it, as she suddenly stepped into the bridle path and began to take her way up the steep ascent of the mountain. A pine tree showed high against the heavens, and as she looked the moon seemed for a time as if entangled amidst its fibrous boughs. Then, as the direction of the path veered, the mystic cresset once more swung against the rich daffodil sky, with opaline glimmers trailing after on all the sea of mist which now submerged valley and forest, still vibrant with the voices of the night; the mist rose above the precipices to the left and tossed its waves, spectre-like, detached, flickering amongst the dense jungle of the laurel growths through which the path had begun to stray. Its trend grew difficult to discern; now it was obliterated, then it reappeared, and again was altogether and finally lost to view. A darksome, dubious way to be sure, and lonelier than aught might express. Even Clotilda lingered, reluctant, perhaps, turning her white face toward the moon, its glamour full upon her pensive pallor. The darkness annulled all else save only this elfin face among the glossy leaves gazing on the magic bow of pearl and loath to quit the light. Suddenly she was gone.

The rhododendron jungle closed about her. If there were ever a path in its densities only memory might discern it, so thick and interlacing were the evergreen branches. Down and down she went, retracing her way, it might seem, and ever and anon parting the redundant dripping boughs to gaze upward at the moon. She evidently steered her course through this sea of leaves by its station in the sky. More than once she deviated from a direct line, but it was an oft-travelled route and she showed no signs of hesitation or doubt. When she reached a moss-covered rock, lying with a score of its unbroken kind in the density of the jungle she

36

seated herself for an interval of rest after her long tramp, betraying not an instant's uncertainty of the landmark. She rose presently, passed between the great boulder and another, impossible to be distinguished from it even in the light of mid-day, stepped down into a crevice beneath them, and vanished from the world.

She had entered an underground passage so often traversed that the gruesome lonely way did not seem long to her, nor more beset with danger than a dark hall of one's familiar home. Her foot struck upon rock here and there where obviously there had been drilling and blasting to remove obstructions to free passage; now and again a wing passed her, and as with a woman's horror of a bat she shrank aside, the uncanny, mouse-like cry of the creature smote the silence with a nerve-thrilling shrillness and she set her teeth in endurance, though all on edge from the repetitious echo. Louder sounds soon caught her attention and these too the echo multiplied. She seemed to hear many voices in the infinitely lonely subterranean reaches of the mountain. At last a vague light began to glimmer dully at the end of a long descent. As she drew nearer and turned suddenly the cavern opened broadly before her and the flash in her eyes was almost overpowering for a moment. She stood still as she always did here, and put her face in her hands to gradually accustom her sight to the transition from intensest gloom to glare.

Yet it was not that the light in itself was so powerful. The glimmer of a tallow dip, however, was adequate to summon glittering coruscations from the great crystals of iridescent calc-spar that studded the ceiling, and the limestone walls reflected the light with myriad sparkles. Their gleaming whiteness was shared by the stalactites which hung down from the roof to meet the stalagmites uprising from the floor, and in the midst of this colonnade of the fantastic sculpture of the waters and the ages—even now she could hear the ceaseless trickle as drop by drop the mountain rill, charged with its solution of lime, wrought out the purpose of creation—the moonshiner had mounted his still. The great rotund copper, standing over the rude furnace of stone masonry, the slouching uncouth figures of the distillers, with their grotesque shadows following them amidst these columns of mystic whiteness, the coiling worm, the big ungainly mash-tubs, the reeking mass of refuse pomace at one side, were all as incongruous with the weird subterranean beauty of the place as some unseemly work of kitchening wrought in the halls of a palace.

And indeed even these uncultured louts could not be insensible of the unique splendours of these surroundings. Unlike the majesty of the mountain landscape, rendered stale by custom, since from birth they had known naught else, this expression of nature was rare and strange, and now and again their minds opened to its aspect.

"I jes' tell you uns, boys," Shadrach Pinnott sometimes remarked over his meditative pipe, "the looks o' this hyar spot air plumb splendugious. Even the parlour in the hotel at Colb'ry ain't ez fine a sight ez this place, fur I hev walked along the front porch thar, an' looked in the door an' viewed it."

The rare qualities of the place aided their appreciation, for though caves, vast and varied, were common in the mountains, and also "rock-houses," as limited grottoes of special geological deposits were called, they were generally of a different formation. This was not a limestone region, and only through some gigantic "fault" of the ranges, bringing diverse and alien strata into juxtaposition this calcareous cavern, these halls of white stone, with their stately colonnades and semblance of statuary and fantastic carvings, became possible. It was not, however, sufficiently rare to render it a curiosity or to lure hither the unwelcome explorer. Along the line of the range, perhaps within the purlieus of the same vast upheaval, a few limestone caves were known to the experience or the tradition of the mountaineers. But it was the only one of which the Pinnotts had knowledge, and they piqued themselves upon the fact that their discovery was not shared. Its existence, so far as Shadrach Pinnott was aware, was absolutely unsuspected save to a few woodsmen like himself whose prowlings amidst the primeval wildernesses of the Great Smoky had led them to these deep seclusions, and these were associated in the profit and the dangers of the illicit distillery. Thrice since the still had been in operation under the white splendours of the stalactitic roof had the marshal's men scoured this region in search of the manufacturers of moonshine whisky—thrice had they ridden away no wiser than they came. Old Shadrach began to fancy his stronghold impregnable, to look forward to a long lease of vinous prosperity. While it might be rumoured that he was concerned in the "wild-cat," he could not be tracked to his lair, and much immunity had made him daring and enterprising.

Even now the girl's entrance remained unnoticed in the vehemence of the remonstrance urged upon him, as he sat on one of the stalagmites that had risen only a few feet from the floor, the stalactite depending from above scarcely reaching the top of his old wool hat. He looked as immovable, as impervious to argument, as if his uncouth figure piecing out the column were of the same material.

"It's a resk—it's a turrible resk," one of the younger men was saying. He had an eager, ardent aspect, unlike the usual mountain type, the dull lack-lustre Pinnott men. He had large, excited brown eyes, and his chestnut hair hung in straight locks to the collar of his blue hickory shirt. His cheeks were red, and now that his blood was up it looked as if it might burst through them. He was tall and agile. He wore his boots drawn to the knees over his brown jeans trousers—there were spurs on the heels and his belt held a pistol. He stood in the flare of the tallow dip glimmering from a low stalagmite which was consigned to other table-like usage and held also a pone of bread, a box of tobacco, a pipe, and an old hat. The others had paused at their labours, the discussion evidently being a matter of special importance, and looked around without other change of posture. Tom Pinnott, stooping to lift a keg of "singlings" to the doubling still, his head lower than the vessel, seemed as if he might have been petrified in that attitude, so little did it seem possible to sustain it by mere muscle.

"It's a resk, to be sure," said Shadrach Pinnott, his face under his shock of red hair as devoid of animation as if it had been carved from a turnip. "But everything is a resk. Livin' is a resk—no man knows what he air goin' ter run up agin pernicious afore night,—but we uns all resk it."

"We uns don't all resk the revenuers though—fur nuthin'," Eugene Binley declared significantly.

It was a word seldom mentioned here—the old moonshiner elected to affect free agency and fear of naught. If he had been asked he would have averred that this place was selected because of its peculiar convenience in getting the gear easily down from the mountains. It had a great shaft-like opening only fifty feet above the valley, and by means of a "rope-and-tickle," as he called it, the kegs and barrels were lowered to a level space in a most secluded nook, whence they could be taken in the midst of the jungle of the laurel and rolled down the incline of a sandy slope, loaded into a waggon on the bank of the river and thence conveyed along the highway under cover of the night to the store of the merchants hardy enough to handle this extra-hazardous

40

ware. Shadrach Pinnott would never have admitted in words the necessity to elude the raiders of the revenue force. He had so long enjoyed safety, ease, the pursuit unmolested of his chosen vocation, that he actually felt well within his rights, and that no interference with him was either justifiable or possible. This immunity had given his courage a tinge of fool-hardiness inconsistent with his age, his earlier devices of precaution, and the terrible and certain penalties of discovery. His character had taken on an arrogance unsuited to a man so obnoxious to the law. He knew, of course, that suspicions of moonshining had clung about his name, but never with aught of proof. The marshal's force came and went, and perhaps he was in their minds merely rated with others maligned by malice without a cause, for except that he was an unusually good farmer, and raised great crops of corn and orchards of fruit, no evidence of illicit distilling could be urged against him. For his crops and fruit, valueless on account of the distance from the rail and the impossibility of such cumbrous transportation with a profit, he could show great droves of well-fed hogs, and they, easily driven through the country, always found a market and brought fair prices. Therefore suspicion on this score was readily evaded, although his detractors significantly averred that hogs are always fattest when fed on distillery mash.

Dangers had grazed him close, however. Once his waggon had been stopped in the road with a barrel of "wild-cat" whisky under a load of goose-feathers. The driver at the approach of a body of mounted men had taken the alarm, cut the traces and fled with the team, and till it rotted the waggon had stood there unclaimed, its ownership unproved, and suspicion could not warrant even the arrest of a man with two good waggons in his shed and feather-beds on every couch in his house. These incidents and their discussion might well sharpen the eyes of the law, and to

Eugene Binley it seemed actually opening the lion's jaws by main force to go to the Street Fair in the dry town of Colbury with a waggonload of the liquid product of the fiery still, under the flimsy disguise of baskets to sell. He had urged this to no avail.

"Them baskets?—why, me an' my industrious fambly hev been weavin' them splints all las' winter," and Shadrach gave a humorous snuffle intended to express the humble, frugal hopes of the worthy poor. Then he broke out into a satirical guffaw.

But the blunt mention of the "revenuers" was more distasteful. He could but feel his jeopardy when it was thus brought before him. Perhaps,—who knows?—now that he was old he regretted his course for the sake of his sons, to whom he must leave so desperate a vocation, so rash an example, so uncertain a fate. The delight of defying the law when the conscience can apprehend no wrong,—for Shadrach Pinnott could never be brought to perceive that he had not an inalienable prerogative to do as he chose with his own, his corn, his fruit, to feed them, to distil them, to export them, for were they not his, had he not wrested them from his own land by the sweat of his brow, the work of his hands,—better men have shared and resisted encroachments, and defied taxation, and risen in defence of claims that the law disallowed and made them law. Of late years he had more earnestly argued this position within himself, and now and again in full conclave as they all sat in the chill white cavern over the coiling toils of the worm, the younger men drinking in his prelections that had the native strength of apple brandy. He was an autocrat amongst them; it was an indignity, an affront, a disrespect to his grey hair and his pre-eminence in his station to confront him, even in warning, with so appalling and degrading a disaster. He retorted instantly.

42

"Waal, the resk ain't much ter be medjurin'," he said. "Folks that ain't so damned quick on the trigger ain't got no call ter be so powerful 'feared."

Eugene Binley winced palpably for a moment. Then his dark eyebrows met above his blazing eyes and the blood surged up from his cheeks to the roots of his hair. His breath came hard and fast. He turned from one to the other as two of the Pinnott sons, taking the word from their father, began alternately to bait him.

"Which air you uns mos' afeard of, Eujeemes—ter stay hyar by yer lone an' let the revenuers ketch ye?"

"Or ter go ter Colb'ry along o' we uns an' hev the sher'ff nab ye?" the other agreeably suggested.

Eugene Binley stood snorting like an angry horse, glancing first at the one with a bag of grain on his shoulder and then at the other with the keg of singlings, as both, half bent, leered up at him from under their shocks of frowsy light hair, their long tobacco-stained teeth all bared in their flouting laugh. His right hand was continually touching the butt of his pistol in his belt, and drawing back as if he found it scorching hot. The old man felt called upon to interfere.

"Leave Eujeemes be, boys," he said pacifically. "'Twon't do ter bait him like a b'ar. Mos' men in the mountings hev killed a man, fust or las', funnin' or fightin'. Eujeemes ain't the fust an' 'tain't likely ez he will be the las'."

"But 't war self-defence," the harassed creature cried out in a harsh, strained voice. He had made this plea often enough at the bar of conscience—his flight had precluded his arraignment at the bar of justice. "'T war self-defence—the world knows it, and the law allows it."

"Then why n't ye leave it ter men, Eujeemes?" Tom's strong back was still bent under the keg of singlings, and his face was still maliciously a-grin. Shadrach could not so easily call off his pack.

This problem of "leaving it to men," the rural synonym of a court of justice, had tortured the hunted fugitive day and night. With the limited mental development of a backwoodsman and the lack of urban or worldly experience he could not measure the unseen forces to which he might consign his fate and thus he resolved and then shrank back, and ventured forth to again run precipitately to cover. What the lawyers could prove and what they could not; how much their own codes constrained them and what they stretched here and let fall slack there; what powers the judge possessed; how grim was the jail; how fell and rancorous were the officers of the constabulary—he could not decide. And thus he lurked here innocent of the crime of which he dreaded to be accused, and by his lurking he became inculpated with the illicit distillery. Now he was doubly amenable to arrest—to escape on one score would convict him on another, and the suggestion that he should leave aught to men had become a nettling taunt. As he remained silent Ben flung at him in antistrophe—"Ef he be so willin' ter leave it ter men why do he shelter hyar with we uns?"

Once more Shadrach sought to interfere, beginning in an unctuous soothing voice—"Stop, boys, stop, boys," when suddenly Clotilda stepped forward into the white lustre of the sparkling walls and the glimmer of the tallow dip. Her presence ended logic. "Why, thar's daddy's leetle gal! How do, Baby. Been singin' an' chirpin' with the stranger man like a grasshopper in August weather."

Clotilda received this simile with a shrug of disdain. She had begun to think exceedingly well of her gifts of singing and dancing and scarcely cared that they should be so lightly and jocosely mentioned. Vanity of all the human traits is the most easily cultivated, and when Eugene Binley, gathering his composure, asked if she were going to Colbury, too, with the others, she replied with a duplicate of the shrug—"Why, 'course *I* be. They air all goin' jes' on account o' *Me*."

CHAPTER IV

An extreme surprise at the good fortune of another is an ungrateful sentiment and must needs be warily expressed. It tends to the suggestion that the reward exceeds the merits in the case, and Eugene Binley by no means commended himself by the astonishment with which he now heard for the first time the extraordinary fact, which Clotilda detailed to him, that her singing and dancing had so entranced the town-man that he had besought the Pinnott family to come to the Street Fair without money and without price, and that there she was to sing and dance for all the crowd to wonder at her gifts and grace.

"That ain't whut the Pinnott men-folks air goin' fur," he said bluntly; "they air goin' ter sell whisky in that thar dry town." And he pointed over his shoulder at a load of splint baskets which several were bringing out of a remote recess, and which were always unused and fresh, kept as a light disguise for a waggon otherwise laden. "It's mighty dangerous," he added. But she made no comment. Presumably she thought the men were able to take care of themselves.

He hesitated for a moment, then recurred to the subject important to none but himself and her.

"Singin' with the stranger-man! I wondered why you uns war so long a-comin' down."

He lifted one hand to that miracle of nature, the snowy stalagmite that expressed the marvels wrought by time, that aggregated drops of water, each with its charge of lime, falling and falling on the floor beneath till the great pillar stood complete. As he leaned thus he looked down reproachfully upon her.

It was hard for her to regain her wonted state of mind. So fluttered, so elated she had been.

"It ain't much later than common," she said absently, fingering a red bead necklace around her throat. He, who knew her simple gauds, was aware that she rarely wore it and accounted it a treasure. He divined that it had been donned to rejoice the eyes of an admiring stranger.

"I s'pose he war all streck of a heap?" he said craftily, his eyes narrowing as he looked intently at her.

"I dunno 'bout that," she laughed coquettishly.

"What sort o' appearin' man war he?" Eugene demanded, arrogating the prerogative of inquisition.

He was not altogether at ease amongst the men, and was sometimes conscious of a disadvantage with them, owing to the anomaly of his position, forced into a crime against the Federal law, of which he became guilty to evade trial for a crime against the State law of which he knew himself innocent. He had not demonstrated any great judgment or capacity in this course, and he knew it affected their estimate. Other men had done more heinous deeds who swaggered openly in the coves. It was in the first rush of terror, the first ill-considered impulse that he had come here, and once entrusted with the moonshiners' secret he could not, he would not draw back. Ill luck might befall them, and here indeed was a danger. The fate of the informer, real or suspected, was a more inevitable terror than all else that menaced him. But he felt all a man's ascendency over the

46

feminine mind, and indeed she divined naught as she replied to his questions.

"Waal, he is just a pretty boy—plumb beautiful! Mighty nigh ez sweet-faced ez any gal."

"I say 'boy'!" he replied incredulously. "They tell me ez he laid Tawm out flat with one lick. Tawm hev been lame in the shoulder ever sence."

"Waal—he is surely strong, though only middle-sized, but mild-eyed—sorter babyfied."

"Shucks! I say babyfied. Waal—all you uns goin' ter the show, an' hyar I be 'feared ter stir,—hid up hyar in a hole in the rocks like a wolf or a painter an' ez ef thar war a bounty on my skelp."

"'Tain't but fur a week—less 'n a week," she urged.

"You uns don't keer—else ye wouldn't go," he said, dropping his voice, and all his heart was in his eyes as he looked down at her.

She had her moments of perspicacity. "Then I won't go," she said, with the facile self-abnegation of one who knows that the tendered sacrifice will not be accepted.

He suddenly came from his negligent posture to the perpendicular, tense and nervous. "Naw, naw—I don't want that nuther," he protested as she had expected.

"I 'lows ye don't rightly know whut 'tis ye do want!" she declared with an air of flouting impatience.

"Yes, I do too—but I couldn't abide ez ye should miss seein' the show—an' mebbe later in the week I'll slip down, too."

A genuinely serious look usurped the feignings of her face. "Better mind, Eujeemes," she admonished him, "ye mought meet the sher'ff face ter face in the street. He be well

47

acquainted with you uns—ye hev tole me that!" She nodded her head with an expression of dreary foreboding.

"Waal," he said desperately, but evidently faint-hearted, "I could leave it ter men."

She looked at him in rising irritation, half minded to withhold the remonstrance that she knew he pined to hear. His own sense of prudence made him yearn for an urgency of caution. But she was yet vibrating with the unwonted excitements of the afternoon, yet aglow with the realisation of an admiration all unaccustomed in its expression and its subject. She was well aware that she had been considered a "powerful pretty gal" throughout the countryside, and though the small distorted surface of a cheap mirror afforded no adequate reflection of her beauty, it was well-pleasing to her untutored eye, and was called into frequent consultation. But this popular repute was an homage shared by a dozen other mountain nymphs, and in more than one instance she was surpassed in public esteem chiefly on account of the tint of her red hair and the tiny freckles here and there marring the exquisite fairness of her face, despite all that baths of buttermilk and May dew could compass.

The incense that the manager offered at her shrine had a new and intoxicating flavour. It was unique, for her alone. It was such as an artist might feel at the first view of some fine example of a great painter's work, or a virtuoso's joy in the discovery amongst refuse lumber of a genuine Cremona. She could not, of course, discriminate the quality of his feeling, but she had never seen a man's face kindle with that impersonal fervour of delight which illumined his when he looked at her dancing pose and listened to the tones of her voice. She had begun to feel very kindly toward one who made her feel so kindly toward herself. Since she had discovered that her father considered it impossible that he could be an emissary of the revenue force seeking the moonshiner's lair, for which she had mistaken him when she had so jealously guarded him to the house that he might render an account of himself to the head of the enterprise, she had given rein to her interest in his personality; she had realised with a sort of wondering pleasure the delicacy, the refinement of the beauty of his face; her heart warmed to the look in his eyes. She had now no doubts of him; that universal attraction which his candid nature seemed to exert on all the world had too its influence on her. She had begun to entertain a sort of veneration for him, his wide experience, his evident singular knowledge of many things beyond her ken—with how few words he had seemed to make her voice, even to her limited comprehension, a different endowment, infinitely sweeter, stronger, with added liberties of compass. She longed even now to try the phrases which he had inculcated, telling her to sing them at short intervals and with due care, to assume her natural beautiful dancing poses, which he had taught her to accent for the greater effect.

The unknown vast world from which he had come had evolved a sudden interest for her; heretofore she had not even bethought herself to be aware of its existence, save as it now and again spewed out the revenue force, with their sombre menace, to be presently lost again in its unimagined turmoils.

Her mind was full of speculations concerning him. He was her first illustration of the gradations of society; he seemed to her a person of vast importance; she had a sort of reverence for the splendours of his calling; he was a showman—a part owner of the great enterprise whose "pictorial paper" he had spread upon the cabin floor, and he had opened to her a world of wonders to contemplate. Her beautiful eyes grew soft and bright with the thought of him.

Her mind longed to follow the trend of these new reflections. She was tired all at once of Eugene Binley's woes. The injustice in his incarceration here in the moonshiner's den was itself like the penance of imprisonment for a crime of which he believed himself innocent. Yet in putting the question to the test he risked more than his liberty—his life itself was jeopardised. His hard case had appealed to her woman's sympathy—the future was dim, veiled, he might not divine the issue of a day. He had had a certain interest for her; he was of a more dashing personality than the duller men she had known. The impulsive temperament that had lured him to his doom had a quality that struck her fancy in dearth of other attractions. He was quick, keen, fiery, and he had a spark of imagination that imparted warmth to others, bare and cold of mental attributes. He had added to his more definite and obvious troubles the æsthetic grief of falling desperately in love, and in a cautious and dubious way she had responded. This was a sentimental result of the privilege of shelter which Shadrach Pinnott had not anticipated, and which he by no means favoured. He had secured for the bare boon of subsistence an additional stalwart worker at the still, and one whose secrecy was pledged for the best of reasons. That Eugene Binley could not venture freely forth like the others, that he was not subject, therefore, to disclose by inadvertence in casual conversation the secrets of the trade, since he saw no one not concerned in the illicit manufacture, gave him an added value to his employer which Shadrach was not slow to appreciate. More countenance than shelter and subsistence he had no mind to afford him. Shadrach had taken no steps, however, to balk the romance thus far. He had some knowledge, perhaps, of the inconstancy of the feminine heart, and relied on this to furnish in due time the solution of the problem, or perhaps like many other people he merely postponed to a more convenient season the guessing of the difficult riddle which circumstance had propounded. Hence, though he now and then glanced askance at the lovers as they stood half in the shadow of the stalagmite, and half in the thin white light of the tallow dip, he said naught to discourage the "fool chin-choppin'" as he denominated their talk, thinking it the course least calculated to do harm. "Lovyers let alone will quar'l enough tharselves ter fling 'em apart. A peaceable disposed person needn't 'sturb hisself ter start a contention jes' ter separate 'em," he argued within himself.

"Leave it ter men?" she was echoing Binley's words dully. "I'd hate powerful ter leave anythink ez I war took up with ter sech ez men."

She gazed speculatively about the place, suddenly illumined with a preternatural brilliancy as Daniel Pinnott flung open the furnace door. All the white colonnades were a-glister with myriads of sparkling points of light. Far, far down the shadowy reaches of the cave they were visible now, with stately arches marking the confines of other and further chambers, unexplored perhaps and of an undemonstrated vastness. The light brought into evidence that peculiar incrustation of the walls of limestone caverns which takes the semblance of flowers, the rough projections seeming roses, lilies wrought in the rock, the similitude being so exact that here and there a flower can be found as perfect of symmetry as if carved by the chisel of a cunning workman. Glimpsed through one of the lofty arches the depending stalactites in a heavy group might have suggested to a cultivated imagination a great chandelier of imposing proportions and thus have heightened the semblance to some stately hall, the audience chamber of a sovereign, the throne-room of the buried splendours of some forgotten magic monarchy. The limitations of Clotilda's experience and mental scope forbade the fancy, but the uncouth forms of the distillers with their slouching shadows, their big hats, their bent postures, their dull lack-lustre faces, their grotesque gestures, gnome-like at their work, seemed indeed at variance with this scene of weird beauty, and little suggestive of those higher attributes of justice, of acumen, of perspicacity. "I'd sure hate ter leave it ter men."

It was the subject in all the world of paramount importance to him, and he was eagerly ready for the discussion of its phases anew. Every point they had often canvassed together with the keenness of a vital mutual interest, and there was naught new to urge. But as he shifted his weight, though still leaning against the pillar, and brought his brows together in a dubitating frown and began, "Waal, now,"—she suddenly revolted from the theme. Her mind, her heart were elsewhere. She hastily interrupted—"Of course, though, it's jes' ez ye think. Mebbe it would be best, arter all, ter leave it ter men."

Adversity is said to be of vast moral value in the discipline of the heart; it is a whetstone to the wits as well. Eugene Binley caught all the sense of dismissal that was in her mind as it unconsciously, insistently reached out for the new thoughts that surged upon it. He was cut to the soul. All that he had was at stake, his liberty, his life, or—if this unavailing seclusion were gratuitous—his restoration to the free, independent, open walks of existence. A terrible doubt beset him. Did she indeed care no longer? Had she ever cared—or was it but an idle whim in default of more serious interest that had lured his heart from him? He could not judge. His head was in a whirl. But remonstrance might avail naught. It was the fact that impressed his mind. He had surprised the revolt of her sentiment—it had been a momentary illumination like that of the open furnace door, now clashed close again, leaving the cave to its dull shadow, the far reaches of dense blackness through distant arches, the dim pure white radiance of the tallow dip, the subdued scintillations of the stalagmitic colonnades, the dull rotund glister of the copper still, the vermicular suggestions of the worm coiled up in the condenser, the intense line of vivid white light that defined the lower edge of the furnace door, the metal fitting ill to the masonry, and thus giving a glimpse of the roaring fire within. Clotilda had turned her face upward toward Eugene Binley, as if waiting for him to speak, but there was within it no light of interest, only dull attention.

He tried the experiment deliberately. "Oh, we uns can't make no decision now, short off; we uns hev been along that road many a time; but we don't often hev news in the mountings. Tell me su'thin' more 'bout the show an' that thar showman."

Her face was suddenly irradiated.

"You uns never hearn the beat in all yer life," she said, her eyes dilated and her head nodding to one side, with pride and delight. "He sung sweeter than any mawkin' bird, but he said ter me, 'Lydy, ef ye'll permit me ter say it,'"—she imitated Lloyd's grave, circumspect manner, "'it's a monstious pity fur yer rare voice an' yer 'strodinary grace in dancin' ter be wasted hyar in this wilderness—would ye consider a proposition ter puffawm in public?'"

She bent forward in such a pretty reverential bow that Tom Pinnott, lying on a pile of sacks of grain,—his shoulder was still lame, and he rested it at close intervals,—called out to the others:

"Look-a-yander at Clotildy. She air mawkin' the stranger-man. It's the very moral o' the critter."

Binley had a vague realisation of the grinning of half a dozen sets of great tobacco-browned teeth among the group that sat around the furnace, perched on kegs or inverted baskets,

53

or sacks of grain. His head was unsteady. His heart beat tumultuously. He hardly knew what was this obsession that had enthralled him. Jealousy he had felt ere this in minor matters, but he had so little conception of the strength of the passion that now, when it grappled with him, he did not recognise it.

"I went straight an' axed dad ef I mought," Clotilda resumed, a little thread of continuous laughter trickling through her words, like a rivulet that cannot stay its joyous course. "I tuk dad out on the porch 'cause he blates so loud whenst he talks—an' fust he said naw, and then when he 'membered 'bout sellin' whisky ter the crowd on the quiet in that dry town, and that folks would 'low ez the family war thar jes' ter view me sing an' dance an' not ter sell moonshine, it 'peared ter him a powerful good excuse ter go."

"Hop light, ladies," sang out Tom, who had a powerful organ in his own deep chest.

But Clotilda put her hands to her ears with a grimace of pain. "I never wants ter hear no other man sing—that stranger's voice was like—like honey. 'Twar so—sweet—soundin'."

Her pensive lids drooped above her great bright eyes and she gave a shuddering little sigh, as if the ecstatic remembrance were fraught with an appreciated pain.

Old Shadrach Pinnott had a sudden monition of business. "That's a fac', boys," he said, taking his pipe from his mouth, "every durned imp of ye mus' be at the tent ter hear Clotildy puffawm—'tis the reason folks mus' understand why we uns all waggon down ter Colb'ry. Mam'll go, an' A'minty an' the baby, all o' we uns will go, an' nobody on yearth would suspicion ez we uns kem fur ennything else than ter hear an' see Clotildy sing an' dance in a public puffawmance."

He puffed his pipe for a few minutes while the others gave varying growls of more or less reluctant acquiescence as they accorded or disagreed with his view of the importance of their appearance as spectators on the occasion. He possibly discriminated this note of dissent, for he remarked presently—"It air sure a powerful oncommon happening— I reckon Clotildy will be the fust mounting gal that ever sung an' danced in a show tent."

"An' she ought ter be the las'," said Daniel Pinnott sourly. He was the conservative one of the sons, a settled married man, and he had the married man's insistent convictions as to the propriety of demeanour and decorous home-abiding fitting for the female sex. He remembered, too, the reach of the long arm of the Revenue Department. Though a volcano may be silent, sleeping, the hot heart of the crater burns with an inextinguishable fire. He did not venture to openly oppose the determination of the paternal autocrat, but he had done his utmost to dissuade the enterprise.

The elder man made no direct rejoinder, but he nevertheless combated this spirit of negation. "Colb'ry hev been mighty dry—sence it's been a dry town," he said significantly, speaking with his pipe in the corner of his mouth. "I reckon folkses' throats thar air about ez dry ez a lime-burner's kiln."

The younger moonshiners eyed the dissentient Daniel with a degree of rancour. "I'll be bound they'll nose out our waggon powerful quick," said Tom. "We'll sell a deal o' liquor, else I'm mightily s'prised."

Old Shadrach nodded assentingly.

"It'll take a heap o' liquor ter git a prohibition town soaked through an' through. We uns hev got a week though ter finish the business. The Street Fair will show fur a week."

"An' I'm ter sing an' dance twict every day," cried Clotilda delightedly. She had listened to the colloquy of the group around the still with a very definite anxiety lest from Daniel's doubts and remonstrances a final abandonment of the

55

project ensue. She now leaned her fluffy auburn head back against the great stalagmite and laughed with a renewal of zest and cheer as she cast up her eyes at Eugene Binley, who still stood beside her looking loweringly down at her.

There was something so aloof, so smitten, yet so menacing in his eyes that her elated spirits suddenly collapsed. It suggested the frightful pathos of a savage animal, sorely wounded and suffering, yet with an unabated ferocity. The very look numbed her joy.

"I be powerful sorry ez you uns can't be thar ter see me," she declared falteringly, suddenly drawn back from her soft conceits of anticipation to this sullen reality.

"Oh, I'll be thar," he protested with a forlorn lame joviality.

"Eujeemes will be afeared ez Clotildy will be gittin' merried ter some o' them town men whilst he be hid out in the mountings. I reckon other folks will be streck all of a heap with her puffawmin' jes the same ez that thar stranger-man," Tom observed as he lay at length.

Tom had but the primitive processes of mind and feeling. He possessed no cultivated sensibilities either for himself or for others, and even his perceptions of policy were rudimentary. The old man, the exemplar of all the distillers, by virtue of his age, his experience, his patriarchal position, struck in abruptly with a sharp reproof.

"Ain't you uns got no better sense an' showin', Tawmmy, than ter be settin' out so brash ter talk 'bout things that ye dunno nuthin' 'bout? Clotildy ain't goin' ter be allowed ter marry nobody till she's twenty, an' she hev now jes' turned eighteen."

"*Twenty!*" exclaimed Clotilda with a sudden revival of interest. "Why, I'll feel so old whenst I'm twenty that I reckon I'll hev ter walk with a stick by then."

"Like the stranger-man do now," cried Tom, the irrepressible. He sprang up and took a few erratic steps along the aisle of the arcade, twirling an imaginary cane, now flinging it jauntily up into the air, now striking it with emphasis on the ground, but a sudden twinge in his lame shoulder gave him pause. He stopped short, with a grimace of pain, seeking to put his hand to it, and then he came heavily enough back to the furnace and sank down on his improvised couch of sacks of grain. "He air a better man than you uns—he downed you uns, Tawmmy," Clotilda exclaimed with such obvious pleasure and pride in the stranger's prowess that Shadrach Pinnott was minded to take reluctant account of the cloud that lowered on the brow of Eugene Binley.

"Shucks," he said contemptuously, "that war jes' sleight o' hand. Them show folks hev l'arned tricks that take the eye. He ain't no spunky fighter sech ez—sech ez—waal, sech ez Eujeemes thar fur instance."

There was a momentary pause, broken only by the muffled roar of the flames of the furnace fire and the trickle of the doublings dropping down from the worm into the keg below.

"You boys mus' be powerful cautious," Shadrach Pinnott presently remarked with a serious thought. "You uns mus'n't talk foolish an' wild. Course Eujeemes ain't got no notion, sure enough, o' goin' ter Colb'ry ter see the show." He hesitated, then spoke plainly and to the point. "I don't want no man along o' me that the sher'ff air lookin' fur." He paused expectant of reassurance.

"I knows that," Eugene Binley answered with a lowering brow.

Shadrach Pinnott expected him to say more. His face, with the pallor that is the concomitant of red hair, bleached yet

57

more by his indoor occupation, was turned with ghastly effect toward the young man who still stood with the girl beside the column. The moonshiner's eyebrows were insistently raised; his eyes had a pointed interrogation; his lips had fallen apart in the stress of immediate anticipation, his mouth showing like a dark hollow in the midst of his great red beard. The pause continued unbroken.

The sound of gentle purling was distinct in the silence. The dripping of the ardent spirits from the worm was hardly to be distinguished from the ripple of the rill of water in the troughs led down from one of the subterranean springs to its mission of utility in the condenser and the big burly mash-tubs, or the occasional irregular trickling from the roof of the drops with their solution of lime charged with the building of the fantastic architecture of the cavern.

"The sher'ff hain't got no call ter meddle with moonshine," Shadrach Pinnott was forced to resume at length. "But ef he war ter hev reason ter s'arch my outfit fur law-breakers agin the State he'd find the liquor an' word would be tuk ter the marshal."

Eugene had his own sullen grievances. He was still a free agent, but at that moment no vague intention of sharing the moonshiners' venture into Colbury had entered his mind. To him it seemed like putting his head into the lion's jaws. He had nevertheless winced from the perception of their carelessness as to his safety, when he had remonstrated against the risks of the expedition which might rebound upon him, and almost equally from their wanton taunts. Now he was indisposed to reassure them in their turn, to set their minds at rest as to the dangers which his presence in Colbury might bring down on them. He said naught, and for the nonce Shadrach Pinnott was at a loss.

By some filial intuition Clotilda divined the emergency, for she was hardly so versed in the exigencies of the hazardous

58

law-breaking vocation as to appreciate it of her own initiative.

"I dunno whut you uns mean by sayin' ye would see me at the show," she said in a low voice. "Jes' now ye war tryin' ter torment me by talkin' 'bout being hid out like a wolf or su'thin' wild."

A casual conversation was in progress amongst the group beside the furnace. Binley lowered his voice to the key of her own. "Do that torment you uns, Honey-sweet?" he asked, lured anew.

She silently cast a glance of reproach at him. Her face was so beautiful with this expression of upbraiding protest—it needed but this touch of sentiment to lift it into the grade of the truly exquisite. He should have been touched by the embellishment which a thought of grief for him had wrought upon it. But he remembered in that moment the stranger's admiration. Doubtless as she looked at him she was conscious of its charm; she gauged its power upon his poor unstable melting heart. All the fascination of her youthful loveliness was no longer a sealed book to her. She had been apprised of its worth even for a public performance. She was now exerting it consciously to make and keep him subject, not to her whim alone, but to bend him to the iron rule of the crafty Shadrach. Eugene Binley loved her after his fashion, but it was not that high, sacrificial passion that annuls self, and fosters faith, and blinds sober reason. If, as he suspected, she loved him no longer; if so soon, so lightly he was supplanted in her heart; if no more his great and troublous trials absorbed her pity and her sympathy, the consciousness would work a metamorphosis in his sentiment. His tenderness would be replaced by revenge; his admiration would resolve itself into contumely; his mistaken faith would evolve deceit. Already on the mere suspicion he was meeting craft with craft. Her upbraiding

59

eyes encountered a look as languishingly adoring as if no divination of her motive informed it, as if this restive, alert, exacting creature were wholly and hopelessly her own. "I 'lowed I'd see you uns—I never said nuthin' ez I knows on 'bout you uns seein' me."

He pushed his hat back on his long, chestnut hair and looked down at her with his large brown eyes luminously watchful as if to minutely descry the effect of his words.

The fascination of the new vista opening in her restricted life, so wide, so long, so variously flowered to one who knew naught heretofore but the wood-pile and the cow pen and the treadle of the loom, filled her every faculty. She longed to be still, to think; she could scarcely affect interest in the distinction he made in his speech—that he should see her but she should not see him—she was eager to have the preparations for the sortie to the cove fairly under way. Nevertheless with the realisation of furthering the moonshiner's plans she kept the wily fish in play.

"What be you uns talkin' 'bout? I reckon I could see you uns ef ye could see me?" she asked, pulling at the strings of dark red beads falling down over the bosom of her light blue cotton gown.

As he shook his head to and fro smiling enigmatically she was so weary of him and his mysteries that the listlessness of her effort at interest could not be kept from her face, and might in itself have intimated her state of mind had he not already suspected it. She bent her face downward as if to escape too close a scrutiny while still, fixedly smiling, he studied its contour.

"I 'lowed ef ye went off an' lef me 'twould plumb kill me, Puddin'-pie," he averred.

"Oh, shucks," she exclaimed, bending her head to pleat a fold of her gown with affected embarrassment.

"An' I 'lowed I'd follow ye, ef I war dead, ez I would of choice while alive; I'd follow ye—an' though ye wouldn't see me my ghost would see you uns."

Her fingers were suddenly still; she looked up at him with a sort of surprised repulsion. His smile was as if petrified on his face.

"Oh, don't," she cried with a chilly disgust. "Ef you uns war dead 'twould be the eend of all on yearth fur you uns."

"How so?—thar is more than we kin see right hyar in this cave."

He took a sort of perverse pleasure in her start of trepidation, in her shuddering doubtful glance over her shoulder down the dim unexplored recesses of the cavern. The furnace door was open now; the fire was to be let to die out, preliminary to the stoppage of the work incident on the trip to Colbury. The beds of live coals cast a wide suffusive light through the spacious, lofty hall wherein they stood; the troglodytic group of distillers still sat by the dwindling fire. Through several of the great arches she could see other vast apartments, all dimly white and with a subdued glister in the far-reaching light. Further still were vague spaces, shadowy and grey, and at the vanishing point of the perspective dusky corridors led to densely black recesses, harbouring who might know what, besides bats by millions and night birds that crept in through some crevice for shelter from the glare of the day. Even now a screech-owl was beginning to send forth its shrill cry ere it sought the outer air and the dim night, and the keen, quavering notes of ill-omen roused all the weird suggestions of the echoes.

"You needn't be afeared, Honey-sweet," he said absently, "Ye won't see me, but I'll see you uns."

There was a pause in which she hardly canvassed what to say—so doubtful, so ill at ease was she.

61

And in that interval a strange possibility had revealed itself to him which he canvassed swiftly with flying thoughts. His cheeks glowed; his wild, restless eyes were ablaze; his breath was quick; he still gazed steadfastly at her as she gazed half affrighted at the familiar subterranean environment dulling gradually as the coals faded and the ash gathered, dulling like the vanishing scene of a dream. He hardly saw her; his every faculty was enlisted in a new theme. It was only mechanically that he repeated thickly, slowly, like the ill-fashioned words of a somnambulist, "You uns needn't be feared. Ye won't see me, but I'll see you uns."

CHAPTER V

When Hilary Lloyd in a flutter of enthusiasm detailed to his partner the fact that he had found a charming new attraction Haxon lowered indifferent. He felt that the show was already good enough for all reasonable purposes.

"I had rather hear that you have found transportation," Haxon said sourly.

"It may help to the same thing," Lloyd argued, bent on keeping up his own and his confrère's spirits. "It may draw more of the country folks. There's a kind of interest in seein' one's own sort perform—if the thing is well done."

As Lloyd went about the square the next day, alert, ready, seeming so capable, so entirely at ease mentally, the flagging spirits of the members of the company were recruited by his cheerful presence, and their secret troublous fears of a desperate stranding in this out-of-the-way corner of the world were exorcised.

It was indeed an humble cause in which to wage so hard-fought a battle. The hopeless courage, the gallant temper, the ingenious expedients, the hearty strivings might have graced a higher plane of achievement. He kept his smiling face, his quiet, serene manner, his courteous suavity to strangers, his unruffled placidity with his employees as uninfluenced as if he did not behold in the immediate future the ghastly vision of the complete collapse and rout of his little force, overwhelmed by a pitiless and grotesque fate. It was ever with him, predominant in his mind. He could not even look at the boa constrictor, which he loathed, without the sardonic reflection how the possession of the reptile would embarrass the holders of the mortgage which their earlier disasters had placed on all the portable property of the show. He had a sensitively organised nature, and it was a positive grief to him that Haxon could not meet their mutual misfortunes in the spirit of good comradeship. Haxon had protested that he did not hold his partner accountable for their beclouded prospects in this last move; nevertheless his sullen disaffection, his lowering silence, his deep aversion to the place and people, his despair that he could formulate no plan of getting away, added a thousand fold to the normal difficulties of the situation, bereft Lloyd of advice and the sense of support, and magnified his fears by the reflection of another's. Lloyd was but a strolling showman, yet he braced his nerves like a soldier in the last charge of a forlorn hope. All smartly groomed as he was, he lent a hand to every need that became pressing as the morning wore on and the preparations for opening the Fair neared completion. He whisked a brisk brush in the lettering of an unfinished sign, while the painter who was one of the clowns in a pantomime "turn" must needs run to paint his face. He wielded a hammer in driving down a tent-peg which the straining of the wind in yesterday's storm had loosened in the ground. He personally supervised the unfurling of the flag and eyed it with a pose of glad satisfaction as it rose to the tip of the tall staff and floated out buoyantly to the soft breeze. He called the bandmaster to account while the instruments were in process of tuning, and himself made sure of a perfect accord, for he had a fine ear. When the first tones of the blaring melody issued upon the air as the military figures with their brazen instruments and tawdry uniforms marched out to make the circuit of the square no one could have divined—as he stood on the sidewalk and watched the pigmy effort at pageant,—the turmoil of emotion in his heart, his racking pity for them, for all the employees, for himself and his partner; his keen sense of responsibility that cut him like a knife; his bruised and desperate hope; his trampled and abased and writhing pride; his awful doubts of the future—oh, that the veil might be lifted one moment, whatever the Gorgon face revealed! Now and again he heard his name spoken as a magnate and celebrity, and was aware that he was pointed out by the denizens of the town to the country folk who had waggoned in to see the show. Certain of the citizens, who had affected to think slightingly of him and his enterprise, were not above sharing the prestige of his notoriety, and the distinction conferred by his acquaintance in the estimation of these rural wights.

These spectators were few, however, chiefly heavy, jeans-clad worthies with their sunbonneted helpmeets, and leading by the hand a goodly delegation of tow-headed olive branches. They all seemed disposed to circle, inquisitively staring, about the tents; not one had yet passed a ticket-seller's wicket. The very signs were alluring to their unaccustomed eyes—the picture of the boa constrictor had a horrifying fascination to a family group who had brought up motionless in front of it, the paterfamilias, chin-whiskered, loose-jointed, his jaws slowly working on his quid of tobacco, his shoulders bent, shortening the set of his

64

brown coat in the back, his knees crooked, drawing the trousers to a generous display of wrinkled, blue yarn socks, a child of two years poised on his elbow, an elder one holding to his hand, two more clinging to his coat tails and the last acquisition, an infant, in its mother's arms.

"M'ria, M'ria," the man exclaimed wildly, "do you uns reckon fur sure that thar sarpient, whut's pictured thar, air actially inside that tent?"

His wife shifted her snuff-brush in her mouth to permit enunciation. "I hope ter the powers they hev got him tied," she rejoined.

Had the worthy couple monopolised the interest of speculation they might have remained indefinitely spellbound, exchanging sapient conjectures concerning the snake, but one of the children piped up suddenly with that juvenile proclivity for the unanswerable. "What be his name, dad?" and the rest instantly chorused—"What be his name?"

"Dunno—the pictur' don't say," the man replied slowly.

This omission might seem a fatal oversight on the part of the managers, but the show had journeyed half over the continent with no sense of aught lacking until a juvenile patron from Persimmon Cove pounced upon the void and would not be denied.

"What be his name?" he cried in the pangs of desperate curiosity, and the others demanded in shrill unison—"What be his name? What be his name?"

"Dunno—let's go in, M'ria, an' ax his name," the head of the family suggested with a frenzied gleam of temerity in his eyes, and, as the spieler at the door saw them approach, he lifted his horn and began to shrill, "Here's Isaac. Come in, come in. He eats 'em—he eats 'em alive," so close on the heels of the plump infant delegation, that it might have suggested cannibalistic tendencies to those uninitiated in the ways of street fairs.

The band, having finished its tour of the square, changed the march to a potpourri of popular airs, and then ensued an interval weighted with silence after the surcharge of sound, when the people began to gather expectantly along the sidewalks; the merchants and clerks left their wares, and stood in doorways or clustered at gaze in second-story windows; the porches and casements of the courthouse were crowded with feminine faces and pretty attire, the society element of Colbury having gathered to this point of vantage from the remoter residence portion of the town. All the air was a-tingle with a nervous sense of expectation.

Lloyd, the victim of suspense, stood on the sidewalk in front of the principal store. Now and then he took off his brown straw hat and fanned with it, his light-brown hair shining in the sun. The pink flush in his cheek had deepened; his long dark eyelashes occasionally rose and fell with a nervous quiver, but otherwise naught betokened the stress of excitement with which he laboured. He did not notice that he had become a mark for the gaze of the village belles on the courthouse balcony—so handsome a man necessarily attracted attention, and the special smartness of the cut of his fawn-tinted suit, his russet brown shoes, the brown four-in-hand tie, and a pink wild aster in his buttonhole differentiated him from the jeans-clad rural visitors, from the clerks of Colbury, and the sedate, black-coated, elderly merchants. The sunlight had that singularly burnished richness characteristic of the last days of summer; a yearning languor of dreams; a longing for repose. A sense of impending rest was in the atmosphere. The shadows were sharp and clearly defined. Far away he could see the blue mountains quiver through the heated air. Nearer at hand they were purple and bronze and deeply green, with here and there on their slopes the sombre shadow of a dazzlingly white cloud, floating high in the sky. He marked how radiant was the fact, how dark and gruesome the similitude to the eye looking only to the earth, and he was vaguely aware of dispensations in life that this resembled. The landscape was cleft in twain by the glittering line of the river, held in deep-channelled, clifty banks, and the circumference of the Ferris Wheel framed the whole, seen through its great circle.

Hardly a movement disturbed the eager expectancy of the crowd gathered in the square; the cries of the spielers were hushed; the peanut roasters, the candy-stands had ceased to vend their wares; the groups attracted by the pictures of the freaks no longer stood to stare; the merry-go-round was still—all waited in blank patience the great sensation of the day. When the band, grouped about the tall mast near the centre of the place, burst forth suddenly with the first sonorous measures of an inspiring melody there was a galvanic thrill as of panic or turmoil throughout the press. A young mule that was new to town and town ways, hitched to the courthouse fence, had borne much exacerbation of nerves that morning in sights hitherto undreamed of, in sounds terrifying and unexplained; he found in this blare of trumpets under his confiding nose the extremest limits of his endurance. He gave one tremendous bound, burst his halter, scattered the meeker palfreys about him, that snorted in scandalised dismay at his conduct, and struggled only to get out of his way, as he galloped through the crowds and across the square, knocking down several men as he passed, and set out at a breakneck speed on the road to the mountains. His owner gazed disconsolately after him, while the half-affrighted crowd recovered its composure in a guffaw at his expense; then, as he muttered philosophically, "Waal, at that gait he'll soon be home," he addressed himself anew to the waiting expectancy, regardless of the problem of transportation which his own dismounted condition presented.

The band, disregarding the commotion, still flung forth its brazen blare of melody, and suddenly a presence threaded the crowd, which every neck was craned to view. A man, bare-headed in the sun, clad showily in pink satin, slashed with dark red, and pink silk tights, with the deft tread of one shod elastically, was passing through the press. Only once Lloyd had a glimpse of the figure long familiar to him, though to have seen Haxon only in street clothes one could never have recognised Captain Ollory of the Royal Navy. As he began to climb the mast, stepping lightly, swiftly, surely, from one steel spike to another, he became visible to the whole assemblage, and, unused to the accepted methods of applause, a cry of gratulation that was half a guffaw of delight broke forth. The acrobat, without the immediate contrast with taller men, seemed of fair height, and the muscle that was suggestive of undue stoutness in his ordinary garb, showed now in full play and athletic symmetry in the thin, elastic silk covering of limbs and arms. He went speedily to the top, and stepped with a deft lightness upon the board that surmounted it, a pitiful square, not more than eighteen inches in compass. He stood for a moment at full height above the quivering and astonished crowd—higher than the tip of the Ferris wheel, higher than the courthouse tower. The band, playing resolutely on, smote keenly vibrant nerves with a sense of discordance. One of the amazed rural spectators, agonised with the strain of the sensation, called out sharply, "Hi, somebody, can't ye make them dad-burned hawns an' accordions quit blating?"

Lloyd glanced keenly about, but the voice could not be located in the crowd. He deprecated aught that might tend to shake Haxon's nerve, aught unexpected, disagreeable, jarring in the stress of the crisis. He knew how far removed from the actualities was the gallant aspect of that richly-bedight figure, the bonhomie of the smile and flourish of salutation from the frightful perch to the humming crowd below. He knew that the realisation of risking life and limb for a meagre stipend that meant bare subsistence was daunting enough to the bravest, but to court this jeopardy for naught, for the amusement of a scanty cluster of country bumpkins, was revolting to any sane man. He remembered anew the cynical saying that the spectators gather to see the acrobat killed, not to witness his triumph, and then came back to him Haxon's sullen complaint this morning that his "turn" was absolutely without compensation—he was convinced that not one-third of the rural crowd would pay their way into a tent. The external aspects and the "high dive," necessarily an outdoor performance and a free show, would satisfy their curiosity, without enriching the exchequer of the street fair company. This state of mind was a poor preparation for Haxon's difficult feat, for it was indeed extra-hazardous, and in several towns in which they had exhibited its repetition had been forbidden by the authorities.

Lloyd was made aware by the shudder, the sibilance of the shivering crowd that the acrobat had moved, and he glanced up wincingly from under his hat brim. Haxon had stooped; he was now in a sitting posture, his feet dangling over the depths below, and the little flat square of wood supporting his weight. He slowly drew from a pocket a large handkerchief, deliberately folded it, and bound it around his eyes, tying it hard and fast at the back of his head. Then, thus blindfolded, he sat on his precarious perch for a moment, dangling his shapely, muscular legs in their pink silk tights. As he started to rise from his posture, a feminine voice from the balcony of the courthouse cried out hysterically: "Oh, make him come down—don't let him be blindfolded!" and there ensued a twitter of derision and admonition among her companions, with gay raillery that she should show herself so "very green."

As Lloyd glanced back at the acrobat, he saw that what Haxon called the business of the "turn" was in progress, and, familiar with it though he was, affected, as he knew it to be, the sight of it made him wince now and sent cold thrills of terror down his spine. The acrobat, clumsily, uncertainly, with all the hesitant motions of the blind, slowly sought to rise, to get his feet once more on the square board on which he now sat. He lifted the ball of one heel to the verge, and sat there thus crouched in dubitation; then slowly, quakingly he achieved a stooping attitude and at last rose unsteadily to his feet, gropingly holding out his hands, now this way, now that, as if he were doubtful on which side of the mast was the reservoir of water below. There was no need of these feints to heighten the temerity of the feat, and Lloyd had always deprecated them. The realism of this affectation of fright, of uncertainty, of hesitation, was so great that its quiver seemed possible to be communicated to the nerves in serious earnest.

Suddenly the acrobat drew himself to his wonted erectness. He stood, for a moment, motionless. Then he leaped, or rather stepped out into the air, still conserving a standing posture; he turned on his back in the instant of descending, and, with an incredible precision of aim, fell into the centre of the tank of water, the impact sending up jets in every direction and spattering the cheering crowd.

All was laughter and good humour. As the round sleek head and the pink doublet, slashed with red, reappeared clambering over the sides of the reservoir half a dozen brawny arms were stretched forth to help the acrobat out. But he sprang lightly past, dripping like a seal, caught a water-proof overcoat from an attendant's hands, slipped it on, and walking with that peculiar deftness appertaining to

70

light, elastic chaussure, his calves and ankles in their pink tights presenting a comical contrast to the overcoat as his feet protruded below, he took his way through the crowd, along the pavement, and in the direction of the village hotel.

Lloyd drew a long sigh of relief. This was well enough so far—but he had an awful premonition that for some reason some day Haxon's nerve would fail him. That accurate judgment of distances would prove at fault. He would miss his calculation by some inconsiderable fraction, and instead of dropping on the elastic surface of the buoyant water he would fall on the edge of the tank, on his back and break it, or on his skull and crush it. This was a life to lead, Lloyd said to himself, a life to lead, but God be thanked its chief trial was over for the day at all events. His consciousness was sore and bruised. He tried to pluck up heart of grace. The sound of the spielers' cries affected him like the commonplace consolations of awakening at the end of a dreadful dream. When he went down to the reservoir he found the groups near it discussing the narrow margin between success and a heart-rending disaster.

"Ef he hed jes' curved a mite to the right or the lef' his spine would hev been splinters," one voiced the opinion of all.

Lloyd was ordering some heavy planks to be laid across the huge trough, the water being some eight feet deep.

"Whut's that fur?" a surly wight demanded, being compelled to give place for the proceeding.

"Some of these underfoot children might come here when nobody is looking and drown themselves."

The man looked at him with a clearing brow. "Fur sech resky folks ez ye 'pear ter be ye air toler'ble fore-thoughted," he said approvingly.

Taking his way back to the sidewalk Lloyd was accosted by an elderly merchant. "The best of your show seems to be free," he said sourly. He had earlier taken occasion to gird at the fair; it was a hindrance rather than a help to trade; it was a novelty, a noisy intrusion, a foolish enterprise, a predestined failure, and he could make no compact of toleration with it. "You ought to remember that thanks are not profits."

"They have no market value, but they are mighty pleasant," returned Lloyd.

"This ain't a paying crowd," the merchant cast his eye disparagingly about. "If business don't improve you and your company won't more than make your keep here." He seemed bent on "rubbing it in."

"We would be glad to do that," said Lloyd in excellent temper. "We thought it was a bigger town—what there is of it seems to be dandy,—and we thought there would be a more populous vicinity. But because we have made a mistake there is no use in sitting down with our finger in our mouth. We are going to give every attraction straight along just as if we were playing to big money."

The sour old man looked hard at the manager; he would fain maintain his caustic admonitions, his disparaging criticism. He hated folly in all its forms; but commercially he felt it to be wicked. A man who wasted money, or fooled it away, he deemed a criminal, albeit not liable to the law. Nevertheless he was mollified in spite of himself.

"Gray," he said to his head clerk, "put up the shutters. All the clerks may go to the fair—and the porter, too—pay his way. We can't do business with this tom-fool street fair gyrating before the door, and we don't want all these hillbillies standing around the counters squirting tobacco juice all over the stock, between the times that they go out to stare-gaze the pictures on the signs. *I* won't house 'em. If they want to see the fair let 'em drop their nickel in the slot, and get the worth of their money."

The closing of this, the principal store in the town, was followed by the placing of other shutters in show windows and the fastening of doors. The chaffering at the counters thus ceasing, the idlers were turned into the street, and here the wiles of the spielers caught them, and soon the ticket takers were busy making change. The tent of "Isaac" was thronged; it is amazing the fascination that the repulsive exerts on the uncultivated mind. Old and young, men, women, and children, yearned with curiosity to see him "eat 'em alive," and a steady procession went in and came out in various stages of gratified disgust. When it was announced that the boa constrictor would be fed on chickens there was a rush for the horrid spectacle, and for a time the peanut roaster and candy stand were dreary and deserted. Wick-Zoo, the wild man, who was caged, half clad in skins, a repellent object of matted hair, and long teeth, and wild eyes, who ran a few steps hither and thither in the restricted limits of his bars, uttering low moans varied now again by a keen, shrill howl, was overwhelmed with visitors until an unlucky episode created a panic amongst them. A mountain woman, young, plump, black-eyed, and with bright rosy cheeks hardly discounted by her pink-checked cotton gown, put a white dimpled hand inadvertently within the bars as she held on to the cage to avoid the jostling of the crowd. It seemed unto Wick-Zoo good and meet to make a demonstration toward the tempting member, and he rubbed his muzzle against it with a jocosity hardly to be expected of a "wild man from Borneo." He was of limited mental endowment, as was natural, and had no prescience of the awful uproar that ensued when the woman screamed that he was snapping his terrible teeth at her, and as she fell back upon the crowd the tent of Wick-Zoo was nearly torn down upon

73

his devoted head before his admirers could fairly extricate themselves. Lloyd, hearing the clamour, came hastily to the rescue, and as he entered the deserted precincts the poor "wild man" hailed him:

"Oh, Beaut, for the love of pity can't you gimme a beer? I'm nigh smothered with thirst."

The happy turn of the tide, the eager desire to make the best of every advantage, the prudent monition that one day is not a week and that the show must live up to its best possibilities, kept Hilary Lloyd a very busy man that morning.

The first check to his hopes came when he encountered Clotilda Pinnott, arrived with all her kith and kin in a big white-covered ox-waggon, to redeem her promise to do a song-and-dance "turn" at the Fair.

CHAPTER VI

The manager did not at first recognise the new star that had arisen in the firmament of the Street Fair, and this was no great wonder. Clotilda Pinnott was standing quite isolated near the intersection of one of the streets with the public square. Near her was the great waggon which had been thriftily utilised to take advantage of the excursion, laden with an immense number of fresh splint baskets presumably for sale; some were hanging all along the sides; others protruded from the white hood at the back; still larger ones were glimpsed through the aperture of the front. One of the team of red-and-white oxen was yet afoot, steadily chewing his cud; the other, unmindful of the diagonal tilt of the yoke which he had thus pulled awry, had lain down on the ground and sleepily eyed the square, with no apparent perception in his dull bovine mind that its aspect was more populous and animated than he had beheld it of yore.

Some half dozen of the dogs had seen fit to accompany this jaunting abroad of the family, and naturally had furnished their own transportation. The pace at which the ox-team had travelled had by no means taxed their brisk energies, but the day was nearing the noon-tide, the September sun was hot, and they too had seated themselves, several under the shade of the waggon, and thence with lolling tongues and small hot eyes they gazed at the commotion, their intentness of observation broken now and then by sudden snaps at flies, and once one, with an air of indignant interruption, dislocated every rule of canine symmetry in the twist he gave his anatomy to get his teeth to bear on the fleas that tormented him. Two evidently had some joke between them, for without warning they occasionally rushed jocosely at each other, the bigger rolling the smaller over and over and tickling and biting him, humorously growling the while, till he whimpered hysterically aloud.

But the girl—Lloyd saw recognition in her eyes which fixed his attention; then he paused to stare wonderingly. "Why, what on earth have you done to yourself?" he broke out in blunt amazement.

Ah, never, never could he have recognised the classic grape-laden canephora of the orchard in the figure that stood before him. Here, here was true rusticity—the other a dream, a poem, some materialised strain from the oaten reed of Theocritus. He had spoken to her then with the deference that befitted the personified poetry of her presence. He now was not intentionally rude, but he was stern, plain, determined. The artistic interests of the promised "turn" were slaughtered.

"How'd ever you make yourself such a jay?" he cried in dismay.

Then he began to perceive in added surprise that she fancied herself arrayed to strike the beholder with admiration and destroy the peace of every man who looked upon her. She stared at him with an amazement that matched his own, so comprehensive that at first it gave no room for anger. As the gradual realisation of objection began to redden her cheeks he made haste to call some good-natured euphemism to his aid, for he would not willingly hurt her feelings.

"Don't you know, child, that 'beauty unadorned is adorned the most'?" he said. "Why didn't you wear those togs you had on when I saw you up in the mountains?"

"Them r-a-ags?" she drawled contemptuously, and with a complacent hand she adjusted the folds of her coarse brown and green mottled muslin, that had at intervals a small egg-shaped pattern in glaring white. It stood out from her heels like a board, so stiffly was it starched. A row of big black beads was around her throat. A yellow sunbonnet, lined with blue, hid all the grace of her head and hair and showed only a moon-like contour of face, and he wondered that he had not before noticed her freckles. And then, worst of all, her shoes. For now her feet were encased in thick red yarn stockings and the stiffest of brogans, several sizes too large.

Lloyd could scarcely stem the flood of despair that surged about him, and the struggle was the more desperate as he perceived how far afield was her complacent mental attitude from any constraint of comprehension. Could he ever make her understand?

"You can't dance in them soap-boxes," he said didactically. "Them shoes won't bend. You can't do nothing but hop— and no bloke is going to pay a red to see a lydy hop. Why didn't you wear the old slippers you had on the other day?"

"Was you uns thinkin' ez I'd 'pear so pore ez ter dance in them old shoes?" she demanded with a flash of the eyes and

76

drawing up her figure with dignity, but alack, a flash, however fiery, from out the blue and yellow frills of the sunbonnet, and the prideful pose of a form disguised by the angular folds of the unyielding fabric that held the starch so stiffly, lost all impressiveness in their disastrous environment.

"I was thinking that same," he retorted unequivocally. He turned to her eldest brother, who had just come up, followed at a little distance by her staring father, and sought to reach here more pliancy of receptivity. "Well, sport," he said genially to Daniel Pinnott, "you see I wanted to show a nymph of the orchard—such as dance among the trees."

The jaws of both mountaineers fell. "When did they dance, stranger?" they uneasily demanded in a breath, as if the mere idea of terpsichorean intrusion among their trees had an inherent disquietude for them.

"Oh, there's no such folks sure enough," Lloyd made haste to explain. "People have pretended that there were spirits of the trees and the like." He hesitated; Shadrach Pinnott's eyes fixed in stultified wonderment on his face were disconcerting. "Of course nobody ever saw them, unless the feller was dreamin' or drunk;"—at the last word Shadrach Pinnott's countenance took on the insignia of comprehension—"anyhow, the book-guys have written a lot of poetry about 'em, and the artist-guys have painted pictures of what they thought these lydies looked like; so when I saw Miss here, dancing and singing in the orchard, she took my eye for a dryad, or oread or a bacchante or some of them nationalities, and I'd like to try the turn on the public—but—" he concluded sternly, "not in them clothes—that's just an everyday Persimmon Cove girl, and no dryad about it."

Clotilda made no sign of relenting, and Lloyd stared disconsolately at her while the slow brains of the two other

77

men turned over his discourse reflectively. "The right kind of glad rags for dancing are never stiff," he urged. "I can't figure out how the lydy managed to stay so stiff and starched these seven miles and more, waggoning down from the mountain. She looks to be just off the ironing-board."

"An' stranger, she *be*," the old grandam's voice broke in suddenly as she hobbled up on her stick. "Clotildy changed into them clothes, under the kiver of the waggin, whenst we uns war about half a mile from town."

Lloyd made a bolt toward the canvas-covered vehicle. "And she has got the same togs along?" he exclaimed. "Three cheers! Three cheers! Get 'em out,—get 'em out. And child, take off your cap or bonnet or whatever that disguise is called—blazes, girl! what *have* you got on your hair?"

Clotilda, overborne by the trend of events and perceiving very definitely that the opportunity for display was lost unless she surrendered her persuasions as to toilette, obediently bared her head to the light, the locks all sleek and smooth and closely banded to her forehead. They were streaked dark and light and glistened when the sun fell upon them. She lifted her hands deprecatingly to her head as he vociferated, "What *is* it that you have got on your hair?"

"Nuthin' but lard," she faltered.

"Oh,—oh—" Lloyd gave a sigh of despair. Then didactically he rejoined: "A lydy who performs in public must be more natural than—than—nature—or seem to be,—which is all the same thing. She can paint her cheeks, which yours don't need—and beautify along natural lines—but no oread that I ever saw billed had a greased head. I take it that this ain't the style among the ones in the mountains, or the boards would have followed the fashion. We will all pray that a cake of tar soap and a pail of river water will wash that grease off. I understand that you are going to camp here a little distance from town," he added, turning to Shadrach Pinnott, and as the mountaineer assented, he continued, "Well, she can go now to the camping ground and get that larded hair washed, and sit in the sun till it dries off, for," declared this disciple of realism severely, "no oread, nor dryad, nor bacchante can do a song-and-dance turn in my show with a greased head!"

Time is a potent remedial agent, and with the aid of tar soap and river water and the benign influence of the sun and the wind it so restored the integrity of Clotilda's locks that when it was almost five o'clock that afternoon and the excitement and interest of the fair had reached the culmination it was announced from the stage of the high-class concert that the next attraction, which was already widely advertised, would consist of a song-and-dance turn by a talented young lady of their own county, Miss Clotilda Josephine Belinda Pinnott.

Lloyd's divination of the value of local interest was justified, for the tent was crowded, and the attractions elsewhere suffered in consequence. Several members of the company left their posts, actuated by curiosity concerning this new feature. The Flying Lady ceased her winged gyrations, since her tent was deserted for the nonce, and came and occupied a back seat, where she looked odd enough, in her short white satin gown, with her illusion scarf and her mechanical wings embarrassing her posture and hanging over the bench, but most of the audience consisted of the rural element with a smaller proportion of the town folks all expectantly staring, anticipating who knows what wonders. The orchestra was in place and the music had been for some moments in full swing when suddenly the curtain drew slowly up showing a stage, dappled with the shadows of peach boughs and calcium light. Beyond could be dimly descried the mountains with sunset on the amethystine slopes and a crimson cloud aloft—this effect had been compassed by the simple expedient of dropping a section of the canvas. The rear of the tent gave on a vacant space above the bluffs of the river; the slight elevation of the stage nullified this interval and thus it was against a background of forests and mountains that the oread came softly bounding on the stage, grace personified, as light of foot, as innocently sportive as a fawn. Her left arm upheld the skirt of her yellow dress, into which she had gathered apron-wise a mass of purple grapes; here and there a cluster with leaves and tendrils fell over against her dark red petticoat.

With her right hand she now caught at a peach on the boughs, deftly interlaced beneath the roof of the tent, and now with a touch she steadied the pail or basket on her head, so overladen with the clusters of grapes that only the contour of the vessel could be descried in their midst. And as she danced she sang, the crude loudness of her voice annulled by the crowd, the space, and perchance a trifle of shyness. But indeed this was not predicable of the gay abandon with which she threw herself into the spirit of the "turn." The lime-light, that simulated the clear and burnished sunshine, showed every perfection of her beautiful face, the soft aureola of her auburn hair, all a fluffy mass, once more, of picturesque disorder; the slender charm of her lissome figure and feet and ankles; the exquisite shape of her arms, seeming in the artificial radiance of an alabastine whiteness. To her voice, like a murmurous rune rather than an accompaniment, for Lloyd was afraid that the unaccustomed adjunct to her singing might throw her off the key, the violins played a gentle pizzicato variant of the theme, of which she had been warned to take no heed, and it was in accord with the effect of the whole performance that, in lieu of the last furious whirl of the danseuse, the usual panting bow, the appealing gesture for the plaudits, the sunlit scene should vaguely vanish, the curtain slowly, softly descending, leaving the oread still sporting in the sylvan shadows amongst the immemorial fantasies of the realms of poesy.

The curtain was, however, ready to rise anew; the manager's touch was on the bell, while the pizzicato theme "Kind shepherd, tell me true," sounded from the violins, and now, to simulate an echo, only one repeated the strain, and again the first and second together, with a note from the viol no louder than a booming bee, and again the faint tones of the single instrument, and then—silence.

It remained unbroken for several minutes, but presently the audience stirred and exchanged comments. There was not the clap of a hand, not a voice raised in applause. Nothing could have fallen more absolutely flat than the whole performance. The musicians, their violins still adjusted under their chins ready to begin anew on the first tinkle of the bell, cast surprised glances at one another, then leered open ridicule, and seeing Lloyd turn away from the hand-bell they lowered their instruments and began to scrape them noisily, changing the pitch and tuning them for a performance in the pantomime tent of a comically illustrated version of "A hot time in the old town to-night."

Lloyd's face was flushed, his jaunty confident expectation wilted utterly. He could not conceive how he could be so far out of touch with the sentiment of others that their appraisement should differ so radically. The value of the "turn" in his mind was not abated one jot by their lack of appreciation; he still thought it beautiful, unique, an exquisite rustic idyl, but he listened with a pained curiosity to the comments on every hand, vaguely seeking to comprehend the reason of this divergence of opinion.

"Warn't them shoes jes' old injer-rubbers?" a country woman was saying to another, with a lowered voice and a scandalised mien.

"I reckon mebbe she don't own no better shoes," her interlocutor of charitable interpretations replied.

"Mought hev been afeard she would wear 'em out with all that prancin' an' hoppin' up an' down," a speculative third suggested.

"Wisht I hed my dime back," a grizzly old malcontent sighed. "Special puffawmance—shucks! I don't see nuthin' special in a mountain gal hoppin' up an' down arter a peach—ye kin see that any day ye look out o' the winder or alongside o' the road."

"Waal, that's what riles me," another of his own sort asseverated. "I can't see the p'int o' that show."

The "stunt" encountered even more than a dull lack of appreciation and disapproval: in one instance Lloyd, looking about with a manager's keen eyes to discriminate effect, detected ridicule, absolute and hearty—a covert ridicule which was to his mind more disparaging to the value of the turn than bluff open laughter. A rural wight, whose intent interest he had earlier noted, was still in his seat, holding his head down till his chin was sunk in the frayed and dirty lapels of his old grey coat. He wore his hat in the tent, the habit of most of the country contingent, and the broad flapping white wool brim almost hid his face, but his bent shoulders shook with convulsive merriment, and again and again he muttered to himself, "What a fool he hev made of her— what a fool—what a fool!" More than once he drew out a great bandana handkerchief to wipe the moisture from his eyes. It was a genuine demonstration of enjoyment of the fiasco as Lloyd, nettled and troubled, could but perceive, for on each of these occasions of the requisition of the red handkerchief the spectator seemed to glance about anxiously over its folds at the surrounding crowd, as if solicitous that his sentiment should not be observed.

The more experienced townspeople had not more receptivity for the subtler elements of the presentation. As the crowd pressed out of the tent, for the special performance had been given a place to itself, Lloyd overheard the comments of one of the village youths, tinged with the contempt always felt by the urban denizens for the dwellers in the mountains and coves.

"I must apologise, Miss Minnie," he was saying to the young lady whose parasol he carried, "for bringing you in here, for imposing on your patience—I thought from the advertisements that this was really going to be something extra."

"She was right pretty," said the young lady politely, trying to seem not to have been so ill-entertained by the performance.

"Pretty?—perhaps—if she were properly dressed—and had had her hair combed—and had sung something new, with snap and ginger in it, instead of the fag end of a drawling old song, as old as Noah."

More than one of the town ladies of mature years murmured in pettish reprobation over her fan to another, "She was real shabby and untidy, wasn't she?" "Perhaps she is poor?" Lloyd heard this excuse suggested, yet once again.

The reply to it stayed in his mind: "*She* isn't poor—old Shadrach Pinnott has the best of all good reasons for not being poor, they say."

The echo of the general rural criticism from persons of local station and presumable propriety and refinement, albeit Lloyd felt their animadversions ill-taken and out of keeping with any artistic perceptions, made him unwilling to retain the position of arbiter in the matter.

It seemed to Lloyd that with his trials, many and various as they were, he hardly needed the added discipline of self-

83

reproach and the fear of having inflicted a disparagement upon an innocent and unoffending soul. He had begun to be so doubtful of himself and the value of his own persuasions that he fairly feared to lay the matter before the old mountaineer and his eldest son. But he had discerned a conservative quality in the serious, steady Daniel Pinnott, and he esteemed himself fortunate in finding the two men together. They were at the camping place they had selected near the town, and although the oxen of the team had been turned out to graze, the waggon stood still laden as he had seen it when in the streets. A fire burned briskly on a rocky space sloping to the river-bank, though amongst the ledges the grass was rank and green. Several great trees, oak, elm, beech, and ash, cast broad shadows from their full-foliaged boughs. The sky, all red and gold in the west, was mottled here and there with purple flecks, and across the blue zenith were two long cirrus clouds dazzlingly white with a suggestion of wings, drooping, folded, not in ill accord with the thoughts attendant on the down-dropping of the vermilion sphere of the sun behind the dark, massive western mountains, and the illuminated, almost translucent aspect of the amethystine ranges to the east. The reflection of the white clouds gave the surface of the river a vivid glint here and there among the rocks that fretted its current. Close to the shore it was smooth, and here the bank was low and shelving. Cows, homeward bound from the range of the woodlands, loitered knee deep in the ripples, now bending a horned head to drink of the crystal-clear water, now in the serene bovine content gazing meditatively, motionlessly, at the illusive apotheosis of the eastern mountains, as ethereal, as unearthly of aspect as a dream of the hills of heaven. There was no glimpse of the town from this point; a slight elevation cut off the view as completely as if this exponent of civilisation were miles distant. Except for the serpentine curves of the road the spot was as isolated as any such sylvan

84

nook on their own mountain. Three sticks and a crane supported a pot over the fire and old Mrs. Pinnott, with a crutch stick, a discerning, excited eye, and a long spoon, bent over to stir the steaming contents. As she caught up her skirts to avoid the flames and circled hirpling about to compass this devoir Lloyd was ashamed to entertain a reminder of Macbeth's witches, whom he knew only in their stage aspect. She did not hail him as "thane of Cawdor" as he passed, but her greeting was hardly less flattering. Mrs. Pinnott had been deeply impressed by the splendours of the Street Fair. There was a pulse within her which beat responsive to worldly glories, and high social preferments, and Lloyd's station in her estimation had appreciated in due proportion. She waved the long spoon at him in the fervour of her congratulation.

"It's plumb beautiful," she opined enthusiastically. "I ain't never seen the beat! I wisht I hed eyes all around my head so ez I mought stare my fill. You—you air a plumb special showman an' no mistake," and once more she bent to the stirring of the pot.

"Now I'll take no denial," said Lloyd, advancing. "You have got to come up to town with me after tea and we will go up in the Ferris Wheel together. That'll be full safe—I'll see to it that you don't fall out. I'll sit by you—the settees are made for two."

"Fine for courtin'," Mrs. Pinnott was airily coquettish. "Some o' them high-steppin' town gals that I see lookin' arter you uns so lovin' this evenin' mought put a spider in my cup, seein' me 'tended by sech a handsome proud-sperited young man."

"Proud-spirited," cried poor Lloyd, with a dreary laugh. "I feel as meek as Moses."

85

Mrs. Daniel Pinnott was peeling potatoes at a little distance, and the baby in a blue calico slip, lying in the grass, kicking up its dimpled pink heels, was consigned to the care of a great cur, that now licked its face and now affected to bite the soft hand which the infant thrust up into his open jaws, and now squealed in shrill pain as the baby fingers pinched and tugged at his defenceless ears with a strength hardly to be expected of such callow muscles.

"Both you lydies must come in time to see the pyrotechnic exhibition, and go through the whole show, and if you bring any money with you I'll hold you up and throw every cent you have got into the river."

Old Mrs. Pinnott inclined graciously to this proposition. She had already paid to see a part of the show and thus satisfied her sense of independence. If the manager were polite enough to favour her with a second view of the scenes which her memory gloated upon with so much delight, she saw no reason why she should deny herself this pleasure. "I be goin' ter stay all night with my niece, Malviny Bostel, her who married a Fenton before she married Bostel—Fenton bein' gone ter glory, pore man! All we wimmen folks, 'bout bedtime, air goin' ter her house fur the night, bein' ez we uns don't favour sleepin' round a camp fire like Towse thar, or the men-folks—thar ain't room in the waggin. An', stranger, I ain't settin' out ter saftsawder you uns whenst I say ez I had ruther go ridin' in that big swing with you uns than ter set in Malviny's 'parlour,' ez she calls it, an' hear her talk so mealy-mouthed, an' finified, an' explain all the town doin's ter her kentry kin—she 'lowed ter me ez she talked through a telly-fun whenst she war in Glaston, an' Rufe Bostel hearn her at Shaftesville, full twenty odd mile off—though mebbe *he* did—his ears air long enough fur anything. He minds me of a mule in more ways than one! Waal, I know fust off ez much about the Street Fair ez Malviny kin tell me, an' more—fur I know her well enough ter take my affle-david to it that she didn't spen' many dimes with you uns. An' I'd be glad ter pass my evenin' somewhar else, so's I kin purtend ter be so tired I can't do nuthin' but sink on my pillow fur my solemn night's rest whenst I git back ter Malviny's 'parlour,' ez she calls it."

"I'll engage that nobody can teach you anything about the Street Fair after I'm through showing you around," Lloyd declared, and mechanically lifting his hat he passed on, leaving her staring after him admiring his grace. "The man's got the manners of a red-bird," she exclaimed enthusiastically.

But Lloyd was ill at ease as he approached Shadrach Pinnott and his son Daniel. The old man stood with the ox-yoke in his hand, half leaning on it as he disentangled a rope that had become wound about it, while his son bent under a bundle of fodder, taken from the rear of the waggon, and was flinging it down on the flat surface of an outcropping ledge of rock near the river, preparing the supper of the oxen. Both mountaineers looked at him with such eager expectant apprehensiveness that the awkwardness of his mission seemed augmented by their attitude. He felt that it was necessary to break the ice at once—in fact he could not be silent before the coercive inquiry of their gaze.

"Did you hear your daughter sing, Mr. Pinnott?" he asked. The surprise, the tension of doubt in the expression of their faces gave way suddenly, with an effect of flouting contempt, as if they had expected or feared to hear something different. Shadrach did not reply. Both seemed absorbed in a silent communion with their own thoughts. Lloyd perceived that what he had said was of such slight importance in their opinion in comparison with what they had in mind that he would have some difficulty in securing and holding their attention.

"It was a good turn—a better song-and-dance I never saw,—but I am sorry I asked her to show. I want to explain to you that I'd rather she wouldn't appear—favour us—again at all."

"Why—why?" There was only curiosity in the old man's tones. The confidence which Lloyd had won was very complete. He suspected no rudeness—he appreciated no lack of tact.

"I feel very responsible for a misunderstanding that has got about," said Lloyd. "I insisted, against her preference, that she should appear in a rustic costume and her soft old shoes. I heard some comments afterwards in the audience. People thought it shabby and inappropriate and disrespectful to the public."

"Them town toads?" said Daniel. "We uns ain't carin' what *they* think 'bout shoes an' sech."

"Call Clotildy—ax the child herself," said Shadrach Pinnott hastily.

She was not far away, filling a bucket with water at the spring which bubbled out from a mass of rocks close by the river side—a clear pool of crystal brown, its depths catching the light like some gigantic topaz. The three men all approached her when her clear answering voice in the evening stillness revealed her presence there. She bent down, sunk the bucket into the depths, then placing it on her head, stood, one hand on her hip, the other lifted to the pail, and waited, motionless, their coming within speaking distance. She was again garbed in her holiday gown of brown mottled muslin, that had so offended the manager's artistic predilections, and once more her feet were encased in the brogans that disguised beyond all suggestion their grace of form and elasticity of fibre. But her hair still showed its soft flaunting auburn hue, and rose in pliant, redundant waves from her

88

brow and was coiled in a great knot at the back of her head. She listened without a word to the explanation which the three men made in disconnected instalments, her eyes turning from one to the other as each successively took up the story. She showed no confusion; her face was absolutely inexpressive. Lloyd began to doubt how he might best reach her understanding. But when she suddenly spoke it was obvious that she had grasped the whole situation.

"The mounting folks purtend ez I ain't got no better shoes—waal, ef they look right sharp ter-night they'll see these, bran new an' middlin' stout." She glanced down at them with the pride of possession. "An' the town folks purtend ter be powerful shocked kase my old calico dress ain't fine enough. Why, they air obleeged ter know ez it air a part of the 'turn' like the peach-tree branches. Nobody gathers fruit and dances in an orchard in thar Sunday-go-ter-meetin' clothes."

Her logic reassured Lloyd as to the merely captious nature of the criticism—he had not insisted on a point that could fairly discredit her in her neighbours' eyes. "But since the question has been raised," he said, "I think we won't have the song-and-dance again."

She withered him with a glance. "These folks can't ondertake ter teach *me* whut's respectable," she said not without dignity. "I'll dance in my old shoes and my yellow calico dress *every* day whilst I'm in town, an' then I'll go creakin' all around in my new shoes an' my new muslin ter show the folks I hev got 'em. I won't allow ez they kin gin *me* the word what air 'spectable."

Then with the utmost composure, her bucket poised upon her head, she took her way past them and shouldered the responsibility herself.

Lloyd was infinitely relieved, but as he walked back toward the town he overtook a man whom he remembered instantly to have earlier noticed—he had been laughing like a satyr at the spectacle of the dancing oread in the show that afternoon. There was something so malicious, so triumphant in the character of his mirth that Lloyd's keen observation might have discriminated its peculiar relish of the girl's failure to win the public favour, even if he had not had the success of the "turn" so much at heart. With his retentive mind he would have remembered the demonstration in any event, but as he passed the man whose face was also turned toward the village he received an unpleasant impression that he had been followed. If this man had gone by the Pinnott encampment along the road, as several others had done, Lloyd argued within himself that he would likewise have noticed the fact; the man had obviously left the town last, and it was certainly somewhat odd that within so short an interval of time he should be overtaken wending his way thither. He was not of the type or station to indulge in a stroll for pleasure or a constitutional tramp. He seemed, moreover, infirm, walking very slowly and he leaned heavily on a stout cane. Lloyd noticed as he passed that the high cowhide boots which he wore had been split by a knife with longitudinal strokes above the toes of each foot, suggesting the torture of bunions. The gray coat loose and long was not of the usual homespun jeans, but of some store-bought fabric, and from the web the nap had so worn that the original texture was indeterminable. The garment boasted few buttons; the substitute of a ten-penny nail was dexterously inserted in the upper buttonhole and an opportune rent in the opposite side. It was frayed and even jagged around the edges, and the trousers of the same goods, loose and bagging about the knees, were in scarcely better repair. His shoulders were bent and slouched, and the coat was either too large at first or had stretched with wear into many rucks and wrinkles. It had suggestions of a miller's habit, for here and there were traces of flour, and the old white wool hat had neither binding on its wide brim nor a hatband.

Lloyd sought to cast off the disagreeable impression. He had naught to hide. He could be followed, if indeed his steps had been dogged at all, only from the idlest curiosity. The rural people seemed in fact so elementary, so primitive, that the showman, himself, might be accounted an object of interest. And even as he thus reasoned he perceived the fallacy, but he had scant leisure to canvass the incident.

CHAPTER VII

Lloyd could not remember an evening in his humble career as impresario that had so strained and racked his endurance. The pyrotechnic exhibition bade fair to be a failure, some of the combustibles having gotten damp in the downpour of rain on the previous evening, and each piece refusing to fizzle or shoot or whirl, whatever its particular method of explosion might be, while all the town gathered and stared, and laughed, and grew indignant, and made sarcastic comments somewhat incompatible with the fact that the fireworks were a free show, and that no spectator was defrauded of his money. Suddenly, after so much futile effort, and without any of the usual incentives, a small waggon which had brought the explosives from the station to the square, was lifted toward the stars in jets of red, blue, yellow, green and white light; rockets were darting, comet-like, hither and thither through the crowd; Catherine wheels whirled; Roman candles blazed; cannon crackers exploded; all in simultaneous clamour and flare. The terrified horse, breaking loose from his harness, set off at a frantic speed, and the driver was thrown to the earth, not dead nor wounded as the men, rushing to his assistance, expected to find him, but powder-smirched, slightly jarred, convulsed with laughter, declaring that his ascension discounted the Flying Lady's jaunts into the air, and showing himself to be very considerably drunk—a state which had not been at all obvious before the explosion.

The crowd's interest in combustibles had very sensibly diminished and when the final balloons had gone wafting away over the dark stretches of the infinite loneliness of the Great Smoky Mountains—to astonish the eyes of some remote dweller therein, knowing naught even of the existence of so sophisticated a fact as a street fair, or perchance to be seen only by a marauding wolf or a crafty fox and seeming to follow with the red eye of menace the beast's pursuit of his prey,—the craning necks of the villagers were tired and the sight-seers turned with ready zest to the merry-go-round, the kinetoscope, the vendors of indigestible edibles, the various show-tents, the revolutions of the Ferris Wheel. The continual ascent and descent of the passengers, swinging in the great periphery, maintained a perennial interest for the public of Colbury. As the wheel lifted its patrons higher and higher into the air it paused entirely now and then, that they might swing gently at a giddy elevation and look away from the town, studded with the lights of the street fair, flaring in the clear, dark atmosphere, and enjoy the far prospect of valley and river and the clifty defiles of the mountains, all an illumined purple and silver in the sheen of the serene autumnal moon.

But even in this simple routine, quiet shunned the harassed manager. The wheel was laden, as Lloyd in his general supervisory duties, strolled up and with his hands in his pockets stood watching its revolution. Every seat but one was filled, and the exclamations of delight and wonder in the voices of children and women sounded pleasantly enough on the air. Suddenly raucous tones from high in the darkness broke forth; a man was thickly protesting fear and anger and contention, and soon his voice rose into sobs and wild cries, infinitely weird and nerve thrilling, sounding from the height and the indefinite gloom, and fraught with unimagined disaster. Amongst the venturesome wights, swinging so high above the earth, the utmost consternation prevailed, and pleas of eager insistence to be lowered and released came from every swing. A halloo of inquiry from the manager below addressed to the disturber of the peace elicited only agonised prayers for succour and cries of pain that rose piercingly into the night. The mystery being insoluble Lloyd's first care was to caution the other occupants of the swings to remain firmly seated in their places and to release them seriatim as soon as the great wheel could complete its revolution. While this was in progress he stood close by, scanning the passengers as one by one they emerged, keenly watching lest the spoil-sport, madman, or victim, who had so signally destroyed the pleasure of the crowd and injured the prestige of the Ferris Wheel, escape undetected in the press. He proved easily enough identified, however, as, still whimpering in the intervals of uttering wild cries, he came to the ground and was seized upon by the stalwart showman.

He had been stabbed, he declared, and he would sue the company. When reminded that he had been in a seat alone, and inquired of as to the perpetrator of the deed he asseverated that when as high as the top of the wheel a stranger had climbed into the seat with him, a stranger of a most terrible aspect. In fact, this terrible stranger looked just like the devil, he solemnly averred, with evident familiarity with the diabolic features. And there, while suspended so high above the world that none could succour him, this demon-man had stabbed him—and he would have damages of the show company—stabbed him in the right side.

93

With the most dismal forebodings, for the man was evidently half fainting and had the pallor of death, Lloyd called the engineer from the little gasoline motor of the wheel to his assistance, and supporting the victim between them they took their way to the drug store on the corner. Lloyd noticed the feeble step of their burden, as his feet half dragged on the ground, and the nerveless languor of his form, and began to fear that he was indeed in bad case. The truth did not even vaguely dawn upon Lloyd until the physician, who had been hastily summoned, looked the victim over and declared that his skin was unbroken throughout and he had never been stabbed.

"Why, what could have been his motive in all this commotion?" asked Lloyd in wonderment.

"Can't you see?" the doctor queried in turn. "He is on the verge of delirium tremens."

As Lloyd stood in the door of the drug store in the light which streamed through the great red and green glass bottles in the windows, that bespoke its functions, he listened to the snickering comments of the men on the sidewalk while they recited to newcomers the details of the incident, and his mind laid hold of certain unexplained points which were most pertinent to its proper comprehension.

"Why, I thought that Colbury was a dry town," he addressed one of the bystanders. "Where do all these drunken men get their liquor?"

"I dunno—*do you?*" His interlocutor favoured him with a facetious wink which was in the nature of things an equivocal demonstration, for as he faced the light of the drug store windows the wink was both red and green.

"Well, the liquor must be pretty cheap to be drunk in such glorious plenty," Lloyd remarked impersonally.

For the crowd was of a grade that has little money to spend, and it would seem that the Fair must needs absorb a good part of it.

"Liquor *is* cheap!—you bet your life," his interlocutor treated him to another rainbow-tinted wink, "liquor *is* cheap,—for Shadrach Pinnott is in town!"

The simple words explained many things to Lloyd's quick perceptions—the waggon laden with baskets to sell, the secluded camping-ground on the river-bank, yet near the town, which was a virtuous dry town with not a saloon open in the place. This surreptitious sale of liquor was doubtless illegal in more than one sense, evading the tax of the revenue law of the government as well as defying the restrictions of the municipal prohibition. He was remembering the occasion of his arrival on the mountain—how the girl had followed him to the house as if she feared his escape; how, despite the torrents of rain, she had sought her father and brothers to submit to their judgment the mystery of his sudden appearance; how eagerly anxious was the old beldame in volunteering to account for their vocation and the use to which they put the product of their great orchards; how obviously relieved they had seemed when they had learned his own vocation. It was all plain, now; they were distillers of illicit whisky and brandy, and they had suspected him as an emissary of the revenue department, a detective, or one of the marshal's men. It was not an unnatural conclusion, perhaps; strangers in those secluded fastnesses, unheralded and without vouchers, were rare and obnoxious to suspicion.

The matter was peculiarly distasteful to Lloyd individually, who was a sober, law-abiding citizen, and in the interests of the Street Fair, specially repugnant. He resented the fact that the enterprising moonshiners should contrive to utilise the presence of his show in the streets of Colbury to share the profits of the occasion with their nefarious and illicit trade. Absurdly enough in view of its humble insignificance Lloyd was proud of his Fair—it was a clean show, he averred; it had no disreputable hangers-on nor traffic; its members worked faithfully for their scanty wages; it lived up to its representations, barring of course the few illusions and devices necessary to heighten amusement. It tolerated no false dealing on the part of its concessionaries toward the unsophisticated and simple population; it was a strictly temperance organisation—the acrobats required sobriety to conserve the control of the nerves, and the other members of the company, hard at work from early morn till late at night, had neither time nor inclination to indulge in the flowing bowl. Lloyd was nettled, even more, troubled, that it should be associated in any way with the risky trade plying on the outskirts of the town. The sudden presence of numbers of intoxicated men could be accounted for by the authorities in no way but by the suspicion of the sly sale of liquor in the Fair itself, or by some surreptitious vendor disconnected with its management. This elusive law-breaker would be difficult to discover, even though he bore the reputation of previous exploits of the kind; the sale of the home-made baskets was a very efficient blind; the spot which the moonshiner had selected was invaluable for his purposes, so secluded, so close to the bank—a sudden alarm and the chaste sylvan waters of the crystal river would be adulterated in a wise never known before, the land flowing with toddy, in lieu of the conventional milk and honey. Lloyd winced as he reflected that he, the manager of the Carnival, had been seen to repair to this spot this afternoon, that he had earlier visited the moonshiners' house, and apparently given them their first intimation that they should attend the Street Fair.

As he still stood on the street corner, looking about mechanically, his hat drawn down over his brow, his hands in his pockets, he was lost in thought and saw naught of the scene before him—the torches in front of the stands of confectionery and the peanut roaster; the electric stars that studded the circumference of the Ferris Wheel; the big mooney lustre of the rows of tents, the flare within illumining the outer aspect of the canvas; the courthouse rising up in the midst, taking on a sort of castellated dignity as its tower loomed in the dim light of uncertainty above; the motley crowd surging hither and thither wherever a sudden commotion gave promise of special attraction or the added sensation of an accident; the straggling glimmer from the lighted windows of the residences of the town along the hillside; and further away the contour of august mountain ranges under the melancholy light of a young moon, little more than a gilded sickle cutting the mists, like the test of the temper of the scimitar of the Orient dividing the gauze veil at a single stroke. He heard naught of the varied clamours of the town—the callow vociferations of the ever-present small boy, the clatter of tongues in conversation and comment, the sudden brazen outpour of tumult when the brass band sent a popular melody pulsing along the currents of the air, the frantic cries of the spielers contending against each other and vaunting their rival attractions. Great favourites these were with the country crowd, and it was a facile laugh that rewarded their pleasantries. Sometimes these verged on hardihood. "Isaac! Isaac! he eats 'em—he eats 'em alive! Come in! Come in, an' see the snake-eater, lady—he eats 'em alive!" Then resounded his rival, "Oh, lady, don't go down there. Come in here and see the Fat Lady—weighs six hundred pounds."

And anon the retort, "Oh, lady, that feller ain't got no fat woman—none but skin-and-bone would look at him. Here's Isaac—worth the money; he eats 'em—he eats 'em, alive."

And once more "Weighs six hunderd pounds—come in and see her tip the beam—oh, lady, don't believe that snakeman. The serpent was ever the snare of the fair sex! That feller is the same one that crawled in the garden of Eden, lady. Come in, lady, and see the handsomest woman of her size in the world—tips the beam at six hunderd pounds!"

Lloyd was deaf to it all. He was still revolving the situation, which was by no means devoid of danger to him. Should the foolhardy enterprise of the moonshiners reveal their infringement of the law and bring down disaster, which could only end in a Federal prison, he might well be involved on the suspicion of connivance and profit-sharing. The truth was that the financial prospect of the Fair must have been greatly ameliorated by the depot of liquid refreshment established on its outskirts. He had not earlier been able to understand the crowd's reinforcement in point of numbers as the day had worn on. He remembered, with a sort of helpless astonishment at the toils of the circumstances as they began to enmesh him, how public he had permitted to be the fact of his acquaintance with these people; the glowing advertisements of the "song-and-dance turn" of Shadrach Pinnott's daughter, which in themselves must have been ample intimation to the initiated that there was something else to be found at the Street Fair as alluring as youth and beauty; the courtesies that he had shown the family as recognition in some sort of the very questionable value of her performance.

He had realised that it was in itself a sort of exhibition, at which he had himself been able to laugh in the lightness of his heart—he had thought it a very heavy heart then, so unprescient had he been of worse troubles to come,—when he had made the tour of the show with the venerable Mrs. Pinnott on his arm, and they had gone up in the Ferris Wheel together. All the crowd below had laughed and guyed the twain, as the mingled fright and ecstasy of the ancient dame sounded on the air while she swayed aloft and clutched her youthful cavalier with a grip of steel. Now and again the listening wights were convulsed with merriment at her pertinent remarks, charged with a pungent old-fashioned native wit, and, when once more on solid ground, the rough but good-natured crowd had given a rousing cheer for "May and December." It was hardly possible that any ascent could be more public.

He was taking himself to task now for his plastic folly. He said to himself that he did not know any other man who would have been guilty of it. The indifference of other men, their surly self-centred natures, their aversion to ridicule, their sense of the value of their own time in rest, if duty did not absorb it, in the luxury of waste, if no dissipation entrenched upon it—all would have protected other men from a situation which had as a sequence menace so serious. Other men might have found a lure in the girl's beauty and thus involved themselves in a troublous association. It was only he, however, who would interest himself in the enjoyment of a funny old crone, by giving her a ride on the Ferris Wheel and a sight of all the wonders of the show, sinking his individuality out of sight, and laughing himself at the crowd's ridicule of the incongruity of the companions. It was no unselfishness, he told himself grimly. He found his own happiness in such ill-advised benefactions. And this fad, that had seemed so simple, so natural, had developed a curiously resilient blow. He could well understand now why the men of the family had no interest concerning the details of the show, and manifested no filial disposition that her narrow, restricted life should be enriched with the sights and sounds that were so much to her wondering simplicity. Overpowered by all they had at stake in their venturesome pursuit of their vocation, in defiance of imminent discovery and the penalties of a long term of imprisonment, they had neither time nor thought for such trivialities as making for her behoof the tour of the Fair.

If a disastrous suspicion of complicity in their enterprise on the part of the management of the Carnival should be entertained by the revenue authorities it would wreck the individuals of the combination beyond all help or redemption, Lloyd reflected. They were strangers, poor personally, and as a company on the verge of financial collapse. Suspicion would mean for them arrest, the jail, utter ruin, for there was no possibility of bail-bonds for stranded mountebanks in a remote and unfamiliar region.

Lloyd staggered under a sense of responsibility. His first impulse was to find Haxon, and in the confidential relations of mutual interest seek some surcease for the terrors that had fallen upon him with fangs that were rending and gnawing at his consciousness. Then he checked himself. No change of plan could be speedily compassed. An itinerant show is an unwieldy device. It was obvious policy that the Carnival should continue the next day without any deviation of plan, until the matter could be canvassed and some decision reached. Haxon's nerve must not be shaken. His diurnal feat, his "high dive," was billed for the morning, and a suggestion freighted with such momentous possibilities would doubtless affect his self-control, his physical poise, and cost him his life. A frightful fate waited on a false step, a trifling miscalculation of distance. Lloyd shuddered at the thought. He had seen Haxon earlier in the evening, and had marked with a sense of gratulation the restoration of the spirits of the acrobat. The improved business of the show, as the day wore on, had revived Haxon's hopes. The company might yet pull through, he thought, making current expenses and transportation. This was the first day, and though he could not discern whence the patrons for the rest of the week were to come, he found a degree of solace in the propitious present, the jollity of the aspect of the square, the flaring lights, the enthusiastic crowds, and all the "turns" were at their best.

With a sigh Lloyd felt that he must broaden his back to the burden. He could carry this weighty secret without a sign till high noon to-morrow, surely. He drew out his silver watch and consulted its dial—he wondered would the course of events change before twelve hours should pass. Still Haxon must not know—the routine could not be altered without suspicion. Lloyd had a keen, intelligent power to appraise cause and event, and he had already noted the sudden fierce temper of rural crowds. He intuitively knew that the public here could not be balked of its sensation with the proffered return of the money at the door, like a metropolitan audience, even if it were practicable. But Haxon's turn was a free show. It was already the inalienable property of the public. A riot might ensue, and in any disturbance disastrous facts might be elicited and precipitate the dangers he feared. Haxon must not know. The crowd must be kept satisfied, and as quiet and orderly as possible until the leap for life was made.

Suddenly Lloyd's heart sank as he wondered why the municipal authorities had not interfered to seek the source of the inebriation of the drunken men on the streets of this dry town. Surely they could not be suspected of standing in with the liquor dealers, or were they even now laying their plans, spreading their snares, waiting for the coming of the revenue force, already summoned, for there were rewards of not despicable sums for the informer.

He was about to start toward the hotel, still lingering in front of the drug store at the corner of the intersection of one of the streets with the square, and he became all at once aware of a covert watchful gaze, that had been fixed on him so long, with such complete immunity by reason of his mental

101

absorption hitherto, that his abrupt turn surprised and caught it. The look came from a pair of dark, bright eyes, under the flapping brim of an old white hat, shown in the flare from the windows of the drug store—young eyes, to his astonishment, for he had fancied that it was an old lame man in the miller's garb, who had "shadowed" him to the Pinnott encampment to-day. He could not be sure of the incongruity, for the man turned his head instantly, and the momentary impression was lost in the turmoil of anxiety, of eager thought, of perplexed fears that filled the brain of the manager of the joyous "carnival."

When one by one the lights of the Street Fair went out, when the town was dark save for the corner lamps at long intervals, when the crowds had vanished and the itinerants had repaired to the little hotel which harboured the better paid, or the boarding-houses where the underlings found refuge, except indeed the "freaks," who from motives of privacy, so essential to their trade, never left their several tents, Lloyd tossed to and fro on his sleepless pillow and canvassed anew within himself the situation, and calculated again the problems of the expense accounts and the gate receipts and the transportation, and wondered if he had decided wisely, and then listened warily to the breathing of Haxon, in his bed on the opposite side of the room, lest the tumult of his wild thoughts might have boisterously wakened the acrobat and defrauded him of his night's rest.

CHAPTER VIII

The morning brought no change in the situation. The sun came grandly up from over the blue and misty mountains, with a train of iridescent and shimmering vapours, and a splendid pageant of clouds, bedecked in red and gold and purple, with scintillating fleckings of jewel-like brilliancy. These were gone, evanescent, before the dew was off the grass that grew all along the sides of the streets, and the sky was densely blue, poised high, high above the lofty mountain ranges, tiers on tiers, that climbed against it as if seeking to reach these spheres of empyreal height. The sunshine was infinitely clear and crystalline. The soft wind had an exquisite freshness and a balsamic tang that the lungs expanded to meet involuntarily as if an instinct recognised its balm of healing.

The breakfast of the little rural hotel, of that peculiar excellence and generous abundance that so often characterise the hostelries in these out-of-the-way places of the South, put new heart into Lloyd, and his hopes were recruited as he went out into the verandah of the hotel lighting his cigar and beholding with benign complacence the array of the Street Fair—the tents, the great circumference of the Ferris wheel, with the mountains framed within its periphery, the merry-go-round, still motionless and vacant as if the dummy horses had just waked up, the humbler employees going hither and thither, on their various duties, getting ready for the day. He did not say a word, for Haxon's mood was so uncertain that it was impossible to know how any casual phrase might affect him. Haxon himself spoke first.

"I suppose I look at that mast every morning with the same feeling that a condemned criminal has for his first glimpse of the gallows," he said bitterly.

Lloyd paused to throw away the match with which he had lighted his cigar. "Gammon!" he exclaimed, contemptuously. "You couldn't be persuaded to cut out that stunt of yours if I begged you for a month." The acrobat's brow cleared, and Lloyd breathed more freely. He had by lucky chance said exactly what Haxon desired to hear. He

103

wished to feel that he acted by his own free choice—that he was not coerced because the hour was set, the feat advertised, and the public waited.

The morning was never characterised by special activity in the Street Fair. The world had all its insistent duties, contending with the delights of sight-seeing. Breakfast was to be discussed, stores opened, the municipal court sessions to be held, the mail to be distributed, and only gradually did spectators begin to gather in the streets, and the spielers to take their stand.

"Only an hour, now,—an hour of life," said Haxon, as the clock in the courthouse tower clanged out its tale of strokes; "when another hour strikes I may be in hell."

Lloyd burst out laughing. "Seem to understand your own deserts!" he cried with a joyous inflection.

And once more Haxon smiled responsive.

Lloyd could not forbear a sigh of relief, and catching his breath it was metamorphosed into a spurious yawn, so fearful was he of shaking his confrère's poise.

The next moment Haxon had forgotten his cold fit of disinclination in sudden overwhelming curiosity. From one of the intersecting streets there rolled into the square one of those vehicles of the region denominated "hacks," strong, light, furnished with a canopy and with curtains for falling weather, and with a brake, regulated by the driver's foot, which the steep slants of the mountain roads rendered imperatively necessary. It was drawn by two strong, well-fed, speedy horses, caparisoned with good stout harness, and gay with red tassels dangling at their heads. It had three seats, and a boot for trunks, and it could hold comfortably nine persons. There were only five passengers, however, and the driver headed straight for the hotel.

The two showmen watched without a word the commotion of the arrival; the porter ran forth with a grin of delighted recognition; the clerk at the desk threw down his pen and issued precipitately on the verandah; nay, the Boniface, himself, outstripped the underling's speed and opened the door of the hack, smiling benignly with the dignity of a portly, affable man, and with so obvious a pleasure that it might seem that he ran an hotel for the fun of the thing.

"Here we are again, Mr. Benson," a lady of perhaps forty-five years of age said agreeably, while Mr. Benson's bald head shone in the sun, and his slippered feet shuffled to and fro as he sought to offer her the most efficient assistance in alighting from the high-swung vehicle.

"Mighty glad to see you all again—fine weather for an outing," he asseverated, still all bland, blond smiles.

The lady was of a slender type, ostentatiously simple, with a black taffeta skirt and a "white handkerchief linen" blouse, speckless, perfect, absolutely plain, with large plaits or tucks, and a broad black belt with a big steel buckle in the back. Her large black hat partly shaded a fair, faded oval face with a crown of blond hair, the sheen of which was fairly quenched by time; she wore a mere thread of a filigree gold necklace about her high collar and on the wrist of one of her delicate, transparent, thin hands, which was without her black silk glove, a narrow gold bracelet with a bangle dangled.

Two young men had leaped out of the vehicle on the other side, while still seated, looking about them for gloves, bags, and small sundries, were two young ladies whose appearance made no pretensions whatever to simplicity. Both were arrayed in the height of the mode, in white embroidered linen suits, one made with a natty short jacket, the other with a stylish long coat; their white lingerie hats were tilted forward, and the embroidered frills gave scant view of aught but fair and delicately flushed cheeks, while at the back of their heads their redundant tresses of brown and gold showed in soft heavy puffs.

"We are simply perishing at New Helvetia," the eldest lady confided to Mr. Benson, "for the lack of something to do or say, or see, and we heard that down here in the 'flat woods' you have evolved a Circus, or Street Fair, or Carnival or something, and it has saved our lives, Mr. Benson. Don't tell us that you are overcrowded and can't take us in, for we don't want to stay over night. You can feed the hungry, surely, Mr. Benson."

"Indeed, madam, we can always do that."

"To perfection," the lady protested, and Mr. Benson bowed and blushed with pleasure, flattered as well he might be.

They were all speedily housed; the flutter of skirts, the swift tread of soft, pliant, well-made boots, and they had disappeared. As the team of the hack trotted off to the stables Haxon beckoned to the negro porter.

There is something very pervasive, coercive, permeating in the influence of cultivation, of fashion, of station in the world of wealth. It had never occurred to Lloyd, so little was he brought in contact with this element, to gauge the lack of refinement in Haxon's endowments or manners till he placed himself in contrast with the newcomers.

"Who are them guys?" Haxon asked of the porter.

The method of address obviously embarrassed the servant. It seemed derogatory to the high estate of these great ones of the earth whom he had rejoiced to serve in their sudden comings and goings. To answer a question which described them as "guys" was in itself an indignity. But he swallowed the affront and replied succinctly—"They are some of the guests what's been stayin' at the New Helveshy Springs in the mountings, sah."

"Thought the springs were closed by this time," Lloyd remarked, and the servant apprehending the observation as applicable to business interests rather than actuated by mere curiosity, replied with a placated mien, "Jes' a few stayin' on, sah—feared ter go home till frost, 'count of de yaller fever whar dey live in Mobile or New Orleans or some o' dem Southern cities. Dey got nuthin' ter 'muse dem at New Helveshy—even de band's gone,—an' dey drive down 'ere wunst in a while." He lingered for a moment, for the satisfaction of possible further queries, but none came and he betook himself within.

Lloyd looked with anxious doubt at the brow of Haxon, seeking to discern and gauge his sentiment, so slight an irritant might now disturb the precarious poise of his equilibrium. But Haxon merely remarked with a sigh, "I wish they were five hundred instead of five."

"Well, there's one comfort," said Lloyd, "the show couldn't be any better if they were five hundred instead of five."

He had struck the wrong note and the discord jangled instantly.

"Well, the railroads don't haul folks on their merits," the acrobat rejoined acridly. "It makes mighty little difference in this cursed hole whether the show is good or bad, if there ain't nobody to see it. I believe you are ambitious of playin' to a cent and a half a day."

The roseate flush on Lloyd's girlish cheek deepened, but it was one of the slow tortures privileged to rack his soul in these days of stress that he was debarred the natural vent of anger. He could not retort, in sheer humanity he could not flame out in petulance at the man whose life was to be placed in most hideous jeopardy in half an hour, balanced on the

107

flicker of an eyelash, lost in a momentary quiver of the nerves. But Lloyd truly felt that his trials increased in a regular ratio with the demonstration of his capacity to sustain them. Sometimes he thought that a sudden sarcasm, an outbreak of the vexation that stirred him might over-awe Haxon, elicit his self-control, and serve really to steady his nerves. It was not an experiment which he was willing to try at another's cost. He braced his own nerves for endurance therefore, and taxed his capacity for expedients.

"Oh, hush," he said, with affected roughness. "You are out of your contract now. You don't know anything about the receipts yesterday—it's all up to me. You are agreed to take no share in business till you've done your leap for the day. Then we'll strike the balance."

A slow smile was dawning in the acrobat's eyes. Business must have been better than he had feared. It is difficult to estimate the number of an ever-shifting crowd. He had placed himself under this restriction that he might have the less strain to preserve his calmness of mind before his leap for life.

Suddenly there issued from the door of the hotel the two young men who had accompanied the ladies from the New Helvetia Springs. They had lighted their cigars, having been debarred that luxury, possibly, on the drive. They drew up two of the many vacant chairs that stood on the verandah and seated themselves near the railing.

"I like nothing better than an old-fashioned *el Principe*," the elder was saying. "It gives a good clean mild smoke. You ought to smoke nothing, though, at your age; your training will go hard with you this fall if you saturate your system with strong tobacco,—then have to leave off suddenly."

It was less the obvious truism than the professional word "training" that caught the showmen's attention. They looked

108

with keen interest at the newcomers. One was much the younger—a tall, blond youth, well-built and muscular, twenty years of age perhaps, fresh, alert, perfectly groomed, glowing with health and bright-eyed vigour. The other had an air of much distinction. He was fully thirty-five, with clear-cut, delicate features, an intellectual face; but with a languid eye; he was tall, exceedingly thin, and very elaborately and precisely dressed in the height of the fashion of the day. Both wore suits of light wool, so nearly white that the faint flecking of brown in one and the broken "shadow check" in the other scarcely impinged on the cream effect. Even their shoes were white. The younger had a straw hat of a natty sailor shape, while the elder wore a Panama hat, and as he lifted it, laying it on the broad rail of the banisters, baring his brow to the refreshing breeze, it became evident that his short brown hair was growing sparse at the temples and a tiny thin space on the top of his well-shaped head threatened a baldness within the next few years. Both were of fair complexion and clean-shaven, and that feature the most expressive of character in a man's face, the mouth, showed without reserve; it was of firm lines in the elder, with a suggestion of uttering not too many nor too lightly considered words, the mouth of a man who was capable of self-control, and had had more occasion for this quality than seemed consonant with the sybaritic conditions of his apparent estate in life. The lips of the youth had joyous intimations—red, elastic, smiling, now widening in a grin of most exuberant mockery as—to be rid perchance of the nicotian lecture—he caught up one of the handbills of the Carnival, which were flying about the town, and his eye fell on an item which titillated his sense of humour.

"Oh, say, Jardine, ain't this rich?" and he read chucklingly, "'Captain Ollory of the Royal Navy, the greatest high-dive artist in the world, will give a free exhibition of his wonderful performance daily.'"

The other smiled with languid amusement. "'The Royal Navy?'—let's see," and sticking his cigar between his teeth he held out his hand for the flimsy sheet. Lloyd felt the blood flare into his face as he watched the eyes of this pampered worldling travel, illumined with lazy laughter, along the lines of the bill which he had written with such eager hope and thoughtful care, and of which he had been so proud until this moment of subtle disillusionment.

"Doesn't say what Royal Navy," Jardine suggested languidly.

"Nor how Captain Ollory—isn't that a delicious name?—happens to cease to sail the seas to dive on dry land for the admiration of the denizens of Colbury and the purlieus of Kildeer County. Isn't it great?" and once more the mobile lips of the youth distended with a grimace of delighted mockery.

A sudden rustle within the hall and the three ladies, fortified by a delicate lunch of a sandwich and a cup of tea after their early morning drive in the mountains, enough to refresh them, but nicely calculated not to take off the edge of their appetite for the one o'clock dinner, issued forth to witness the wonders of the Street Fair, laughing at themselves and at each other that idleness and vacuity in the dreary interval of waiting in the mountains for frost could reduce them to such a kill-time expedient as this.

The younger gentleman could not forbear his gibes. "I have got to recoup myself for not having been in Paris with you and Sister in June," he said to one of the young ladies. "But I should really think *you* would have had enough of sight-seeing for one season."

"I'm sure I'll see things here that never could be found in Paris," she replied carelessly.

The words were trifling, but the voice, so beautifully modulated, thrilled Lloyd; it was so sympathetic of quality, to use a phrase that can but slightly suggest the subtle charm it seeks to express; the very inflection was replete with individuality—it was a voice, an accent altogether new to his experience. He lifted his eyes wistfully toward the group.

The sunlight struck with refulgent radiance on the dense white linen attire of the two younger ladies; they were expanding their white parasols, of embroidered linen like their dresses, this being the fad of the hour, and in the intense light thus focussed the contour and tints of their faces were asserted with a distinctness which the momentary glimpse could scarcely have given otherwise. Both were evidently very young, eighteen or twenty years of age; one was all fair blonde prettiness, with roseate cheeks, and soft pink lips, with blue eyes and golden hair. The face of the other was exquisitely fair, but had no trace of roses, though her delicate lips were of a carmine red; her soft redundant hair was of a pale, lustreless brown; her eyes, of a luminous dark grey hue, were long rather than large, with long dense black eyelashes and black arched eyebrows, and as they caught his glance a deep gravity fell upon them. They held a look of recognition in that momentous gaze. The laugh died out of her face—it was a look as if from another world, another sphere of existence; she might have been a being of another order of creation, so different she was from aught else that he had ever seen; her eyes seemed immortal, like the eyes of a spirit; they searched the depths of his soul—in that moment he knew that she saw him as he was.

It was only for a moment, however; an inappreciable interval of time—the next, she was all smiling ridicule of the Street Fair, of herself and her friends for stooping to glean amusement and excitement in such humble and inadequate wise.

The tread of their white shoes carried them swiftly down the steps of the verandah, and with the younger of the two men they took the lead, while their chaperon followed with Jardine, one of her gloved hands holding the back breadths of her black taffeta skirt to one side, and impressing the calico dames of Persimmon Cove, gazing after her, with their first idea of the possibility of the survival into middle life of the comely, the graceful, and the elegant.

As the group disappeared, or rather as their presence among the ever-shifting crowd was only to be discerned by the glister of the sun upon the white parasols, Lloyd's attention returned so reluctantly to the interests of the present that he had a sense as if he had suffered a lapse of consciousness or was but awakened from the bewilderments of a dream. A vague forlornness waited on the moment. But as his eyes suddenly encountered Haxon's a full realisation of the exigencies of the situation took hold upon him. Haxon's round face was dully red; all the blood had rushed to his head and was pounding at his temples; he was in sudden wrath, and the drops of perspiration stood on his forehead and bedewed his upper lip; his neck looked thick and swollen and bulged in folds above his decent white collar that gave imminent signs of wilting. His small brown eyes flashed and he looked at Lloyd with a rancour that imputed a share of blame.

"Well,—here's a go!" he said, indignantly.

Once more Lloyd spurred up his jaded resources.

"What?—when?—how?" he asked, as if surprised.

"You know you heard them jays——" Haxon paused, fairly sputtering in his indignation, "guying me an' the Royal Navy an' the whole biz. Whyn't you speak up?"

"I—what could I say?"

"Why, you could ha' stopped their mouths—you could ha' told them they needn't stick their faces in it—that I was a

112

better man, navy or no navy, than either o' them—you could ha' told them that they were both bug-house, an' they are,—you could ha' knocked them both down with one hand, and rolled them up together, and dropped them over the side of the porch. If it hadn't been so close on to the time for the dive and the tussle might ha' shook my nerve I'd ha' done it myself."

Lloyd looked at him with an infinite compassion, as he thus worked himself into a red-hot rage. The subjection in which Haxon must needs hold himself to the Moloch-like feat that so jeopardised his life, yet by which he lived indeed, had hardly less constraint for his confrère who so felt for his plight. Doubtless it was this which so sharpened Lloyd's acute expedients.

"Why, I wouldn't have touched them for the world," he declared, and as Haxon gazed at him speechlessly, and curiously, "they had no idea who you are."

Haxon could only lift the handbill and point at the significant words "Captain Ollory—Royal Navy—High Dive;" he did not utter a syllable.

"Well, you ain't labelled—are you? You ain't got a tag marked 'Captain Ollory' tacked on to you anywheres that I can see. They never dreamed it was you—else they wouldn't have said a word. They ain't a rude sort."

Haxon took this in doubtfully, his breath still fast, his face still scarlet and dripping. "I don't know about that," he averred, the insults to the name and the feat he represented still rankling deep.

"I know they never dreamed it—nobody would ever take you for a showman in this world. You look like something in the heavy commercial line."

113

Haxon drew a long breath; he had a sense that this was true, and as the hour for his ordeal was drawing so near he would fain calm himself with the realisation that there had been no insult to be resented.

"You are the image of a drummer of the heavy wholesale lay, white goods salesman, I should say. I don't know what *I* look like," Lloyd declared, "but I am sure they never took you for a showman."

Haxon was reassured. He began to reflect that not even the practised eye of the worldlings could have discerned Lloyd's vocation. Haxon thought indeed that Lloyd looked as much like a man of a high social grade as either of them, though not so smart. He would not have said this, however; he grudged his friend the satisfaction of this flattering theory. Yet not all at once could he quit the theme.

"But what's the matter with the Royal Navy?" he plained.

"It's all right," Lloyd declared.

"If 'Captain Ollory' is such a dead give away as all that, why did you let it go on the bills? I know *I* wanted it——but I did not want to be a laughing-stock when I break my neck."

"Why, Haxon, I'm sure surprised at you——you've bloomed out into such a confounded fool. Of course such people as those know that 'Captain Ollory' is a stage name, and the 'Royal Navy' is to make the country folks stare. They understand that as a little piece of business, and a mighty good little piece it is, too, as you might know by the way they laughed at it. They know that 'Captain Ollory' is a high-class acrobat whose real name doesn't go on the bills, and if they don't know that already they are going to find it out pretty damn quick. I'm blamed if they and their ladies ain't pretty considerable astonished when they see that turn——it's worth forty such fairs, and they jolly well know it."

Haxon had lifted his head; his feathers were gradually smoothing down.

"There's the band now, taking up their positions," Lloyd admonished the acrobat.

Both men gazed down into the square where presently the glitter of polished brazen tubes caught the mid-day sunshine amongst the shifting groups of the country folk. Suddenly the leader lifted his baton—there was a double ruffle of the drums, then the wide blare of the horns surged out, and the illuminated rare air pulsed with the regular throb of the tempo. Haxon precipitately quitted the verandah to assume the pink satin garments slashed with dark red and the pink silk tights in which "Captain Ollory of the Royal Navy" plunged down from the giddy heights in that "high dive" which had so astonished the population of Kildeer County.

The summer tourists, seeking amusement in the unaccustomed paths of the Street Fair, had not prospered. The aspect of the untutored people from the mountains and coves hard by—the jostling, unkempt, jeans-clad men, the slatternly women with snuff-brush in mouth and a wailing infant in arms—so preponderated over the genteeler element of the town that the latter was almost unnoted and ignored.

"Poor humanity," Ruth Laniston exclaimed wearily; "how uncouth, how grotesque it seems when so near to nature's heart."

"How much man has done for man," rejoined her cousin, Lucia Laniston, "in setting and following the fashions."

"Poor humanity indeed," said Mrs. Laniston, didactically, bent on improving the opportunity. "How can you take so superficial a view? As a mere example of the sensate in creation think what a marvellous motive power is expressed in that woman—only a bundle of muscular fibre, but

115

without a conscious effort she moves along this pavement; with an involuntary impulse she sees every item of that garden at the corner—and really those coleus on the terrace are very fine!—think of the curious cerebral processes of her mental organisation———"

"And then think of the curious way her skirt is cut," the irreverent daughter laughed.

Mrs. Laniston grew squeamish presently and balked at the idea of seeing the "freaks." Her interest in "poor humanity" did not extend beyond the normal—she could not abide to view the fat lady, nor the living skeleton, nor the wild man.

"You ought really to see 'Wick-Zoo,'" her son urged her with a twinkling eye. "He is about as wild as I am."

The "snake-eater" was not to be tolerated, and the utmost wiles of the spieler could not lure her party to his tent. The sun was beginning to be grievously hot, and before Haxon had climbed quite to the top of the mast the party had returned to the verandah of the hotel, whence they shudderingly beheld the acrobat's graceful downward plunge.

The ladies had retired within to rest from their somewhat limited exertions and Frank Laniston and Jardine were sitting on the verandah, languidly chatting and observing the crowd in the square, when suddenly they perceived walking briskly toward the hostelry a dripping serio-comic figure, the pink satin garments party invisible beneath an overcoat, below which, however, a pair of stalwart calves encased in pink silk protruded. Lloyd was following and his distinctive face and manner were too individual not to be instantly placed. The tourists had not recognised in the acrobat the respectable commercial-looking figure they had earlier noted with Lloyd on the verandah, but as Haxon marched stoutly up the steps he fixed them with a serious eye and instantly

116

both remembered the man and their comment on the handbill in his presence.

It was young Laniston's instinct to shrink within himself on this discovery; he realised how deeply this ridicule must have cut, with a keener edge that the rudeness was obviously unintentional. His face flushed, his eye faltered, and he hung his head. But Jardine was very much a man of the world. He considered that the matter could not well be mended and hence had best be ignored. He and his friend could not have been expected to recognise the presence of the acrobat and rein their speech accordingly. Perhaps this conclusion was the more easily reached since he himself with his habitual reserve had said little or nothing calculated to offend the sensibilities of the acrobat. He therefore made no sign of a comprehension of the contretemps; he bent his eyes calmly on the sorting of a sheaf of letters which he had just found on inquiry at the post office here. But Laniston, though quick at contention with a fair cause of quarrel, was possessed of the generosities of good-fellowship; he could not disregard the wound which he had unwittingly inflicted and was eager to assuage it. His chair was near the entrance, and thus he accosted the acrobat, as Haxon was about to pass, without seeming to seek an occasion to make the amende.

"I must congratulate you, sir—a more daring feat I never saw," his hearty young voice rang out buoyantly, "and I've seen some good things on both sides of the water. I believe I have the pleasure of speaking to Captain Ollory?"

"No," said Haxon, apparently contradicted by the rills which trickled from his garments as he paused, and the view which the open coat gave of the saturated pink finery and tights, "that is—a stage name."

"Oh, I understand——" Frank Laniston eagerly interpolated.

"Royal Navy—all rot, of course," Haxon stipulated, including Jardine in his explanatory glance.

"But there is no fake about the high dive," cried out young Laniston delightedly.

"Haxon is my name," said the acrobat, flattered and at ease again. "And this is my friend and manager, Mr. Lloyd."

"Happy to meet you, Mr. Lloyd," said Laniston politely as they shook hands. "My name is Laniston." Then with the easy assurance of the very young and unthinking he continued exuberantly, "Let me introduce my friend, Mr. Jardine," with a roguish side-glance at his stiff and reluctant companion. Jardine shook hands, however, with the requisite courtesy, and thus the unlucky episode passed, resulting in naught but the achievement of an informal introduction to the two showmen, which fact, distasteful as it was, did not recur to Jardine's mind until later in the day.

The party from New Helvetia were dining at one of the smaller round tables in the long low room which looked out of several windows on the formal walks and trellised arbours of an old-fashioned flower garden. Here the sunshine was but a drowsy glamour, the shadow of the house and the foliage fell far athwart it, and the zinnias, the gladioli, white and red, the roses and the pinks, made a brilliant display of bloom. The meal was justifying the fame of the cuisine; the breeze fluttered the white jasmine that clambered about the window hard by; there seemed scant need of the punkahs, stoutly pulled back and forth over the three long tables at which the public in general was served. This little round table stood a trifle apart in a recess, which in fact had once been a small room, now thrown into the larger by the removal of a partition. It was sometimes consigned to the use of ladies travelling alone, coming down from New Helvetia to take the train, the new branch railroad having recently reached Colbury; or of some local politician of note,

118

a candidate for Congress alighting here in stumping the district; or of the circuit judge, or perhaps the chancellor holding court in this division; or of some noted revivalist bent on awakening the conscience of a wide itinerary and here refreshing the inner man—always the guests assigned to this table were persons of distinction in their sort, and the board was suspected of furnishing special dainties not served to the general public.

The long tables were very orderly and decorous. Here dined usually most of the young clerks of the stores, a confirmed old bachelor or so, the visiting lawyers and clients from a distance with cases in court, two or three families of the place, the inevitable exponents of "declining housekeeping," a few young unsettled couples, mated but not yet nested, and to-day these were reinforced by the more well-to-do of the country folk attending the Fair. The Laniston party, well content in their sequestered nook and by reason of previous experience accustomed to the situation, now and again cast a casual glance at the long tables, but mostly found the outlook into the fair pleached alleys of the old garden a pleasing interlude between the mountain trout and the saddle of mountain mutton, both the finest flavoured of their kind in the world. The pungent odour of the mint sauce was fragrant on the air; the bees were astir among the sweet peas and pinks in the garden borders; a humming-bird's dainty wings fluttered gauzily among the white jasmine blooms at the window; suddenly the group's attention was recalled by the commotion of a late entrance; the head waiter strode down the room with an air of extreme importance and drew out two chairs at the nearest of the long narrow tables, but on its opposite side.

Mrs. Laniston was electrified when one of two gentlemen, ushered to these seats thus close by, gave a polite bow of recognition toward the table isolated in the alcove. Frank

119

Laniston, punctiliously returning it, felt with the eyes of his mother upon him as if the sins of many sinful years had suddenly found him out. Jardine, with a sense of desperate ambush, formulated in his inner consciousness some hitherto suppressed convictions concerning the "freshness" of the hobble-de-hoy estate, and expressed his feeling of annoyance in a very stiff and formal bow—only vouchsafed indeed lest worse things ensue. Not until after both had spoken did Lloyd bow, and then as stiffly and haughtily as Jardine himself.

"Why, Mr. Jardine, I didn't know that you had acquaintances here," said Mrs. Laniston wonderingly, in a low, reproachful voice and with her eyes discreetly averted. "Who is that tremendously handsome man whom you seem to be keeping to yourself?"

"The stout gentleman?" suggested her son, blushing and considerably out of countenance, but bursting with the inopportune and irrepressible mirth of youth.

"Be still, Francis—of course not. But who was that distinguished-looking young gentleman who bowed directly to you, Mr. Jardine?" she asked.

Mr. Jardine had some affection, real or fancied, that menaced the well-being of his liver, and he had sacrificed to it considerable time in drinking the water of the New Helvetia Springs. While in that region he had contracted an affection, real or fancied, of the heart, the exactions of which would in no wise permit him to depart thence until the Laniston covey should have flown southward. The intimacy which the gradual desertion of the spa had fostered between the few remaining guests, waiting till the fall of frost in their Southern homes should dispel the danger of contracting the yellow fever, that had earlier raged in those cities, had been a favouring element to his attachment, and he had greatly rejoiced in its soft thralls. But now this friendship for the family had placed upon him a certain indirect responsibility in their whimsical, futile outing to the rural amusement of the Street Fair in Colbury. He had, of course, no control of the Laniston cub, nor of Mrs. Laniston, herself. Yet should aught supervene unbecoming or unworthy of the position of the party in any sort, however elicited by their own idiosyncrasies, it would seem that he, experienced, worldly-wise, as he was, should have guarded them from it. He knew that the two Laniston brothers, who had fled from the yellow fever in their city homes only as far as their respective plantations, were infinitely absorbed since the early opening of the cotton bolls and the prospect of speedy shipments of the crop, and glad enough to delegate their family cares, on the theory that Jardine would of course look after anything that Frank could not handle. Jardine lifted his eyes for a moment and observed Haxon's small bright orbs, staring across the long table with the frankest hardihood at the two young ladies, whose fair faces were only slightly shaded by the dainty embroidered frills of their wide white lingerie hats which, for some mysterious reason that Jardine could never fathom, they still saw fit to wear at table. He had a fear that Haxon could interpret perhaps the motion of his lips—then he reflected that the acrobat was not troubling himself to gaze at him.

"That," Jardine replied to Mrs. Laniston with deliberate cruelty, "that 'distinguished-looking young gentleman' is the manager of the Street Fair."

There was a momentary silence.

"Oh, Mr. Jardine," cried Lucia Laniston, "I—do—not—believe—you."

This was the voice that Lloyd had heard on the verandah earlier in the day, low, soft, yet so keyed that distinctness hung on its every intonation—or was it that the distance was slight?—or was it that all space could not have annulled its vibrations to his receptive ear? He could not know what had elicited the words, and his instincts forbade the cool stare of absorbed interest with which Haxon permitted himself to participate in the entertainment of the party at the round table. Lloyd only saw that Jardine's thin cheek reddened as if in surprised annoyance, that he was laughing in mirthless embarrassment, and that Mrs. Laniston was rebuking her niece. "My dear—how can you?—But Mr. Jardine, this does seem impossible."

"I met him on the hotel verandah this morning,—he was introduced to me,—only casually of course."

Frank Laniston had no particular affinity with deceit, but his mother, adoring as she was, had yet her captious and severe traits, and he did not care to take upon himself the onus of having compassed the introduction to the two showmen. He sagely opined that Jardine was better panoplied against her weapons than he—in fact Jardine would not be called upon to sustain her attack. It would be presumed that all his actions were within the limit of the appropriate and judicious, and they would not be questioned. He could not quench the sparkle in his eyes as they met the grave regards of the elder man, on whose shoulders he had shifted the burden of his own cubbish *faux pas*, and he did not realise how little the adolescent type which he exemplified appealed at this moment to Jardine's predilections. Indeed he esteemed Jardine a friend of his own, attached by a perception of his good qualities already budded, and his promise of better still to come, and had no idea that if it had not been for the attractions of one of his feminine relatives he would have long ago been thrown overboard, as it were, and would never have had the opportunity to tie up the straggling, unpruned, untrained vines of his rank, crude convictions to the stanch supports of Jardine's standards. Frank Laniston was one of the conditions of the opportunity to enjoy the society of Miss Lucia Laniston, as was the epidemic of yellow fever raging in the South, and Jardine was fain to submit like a philosopher to the admixture of evils in various degrees with the happiness he experienced in the present, and sought in the future.

"Dear me—you don't say." Mrs. Laniston cast but one casual glance at the subject of the conversation, and then turned to the discussion of her ice cream. She was never the woman to hold on to hot iron when she had once burned her fingers. She had forgotten the man's fine carriage and handsome face before she had finished explaining that this kind of country ice cream, which was frozen custard in fact, figured always at metropolitan hotels as Neapolitan ice cream.

"The Great Smoky ice—how would that read on an up-to-date menu?" suggested Frank, plying his fork.

Mrs. Laniston was not altogether unaware of Haxon's bead-like gaze, and she was disposed to hurry the young ladies through the discussion of their Indian peaches and grapes.

"You will have plenty of those peaches at New Helvetia," she urged.

"But not till to-morrow," said Lucia.

"Let me order the coffee, now."

"For mercy's sake, mamma," the loitering Ruth remonstrated.

"I'm as hungry as a hunter—yet," the brown-haired, poetic-eyed Lucia averred. But she affected no ethereal delicacy or daintiness. She had enjoyed her dinner and meant to finish it with due relish.

Mr. Jardine laughed with unexpected leniency and directed her choice to a great deeply red Indian peach, the biggest, the most luscious in the old-fashioned white-and-gilt china basket.

"I believe the juice in this would fill a cup," she said solemnly.

"No doubt," he assented.

"Blood-red," she looked at it on the spoon.

"A beautiful tint," he agreed.

"And s-s-s-sweet," she fairly kissed it with her delicate, carmine lips.

"Why, Lucia, what a gourmande you seem," said her aunt.

"Bah, all the rest of you are as old as the hills and have got the dyspepsia, except Ruth and me—so you grudge us our good appetites and our nice dinner."

"I'm not old," said Frank with his adolescent laugh, half growl, half chuckle. "I haven't got the dyspepsia."

"No, but you have got the cigarette habit—which amounts to the same thing."

"Coffee, waiter," said Mrs. Laniston succinctly. Not a very wise or witty conversation certainly, but it was not for Haxon.

With the peculiar carrying quality of Lucia's voice every word she uttered was distinct to Lloyd. He could not hear what was said by the others, albeit she spoke no louder. Now and then Frank's facetious growl seemed to slip the leash and a phrase or a laugh became distinguishable. Lloyd had some instinct that stood him in stead for breeding, for tuition, for experience. He would not unduly urge Haxon, but men of their hurried mode of life make swift work of meals and might be called "very valiant trenchermen." They had both finished a repast unusually loitering before the Laniston party had fairly entered upon the fruit course. He

124

threw his napkin on the table and started to his feet ere Haxon's glance of protest could reach him. Then ruefully followed by the acrobat they left the room before the Laniston party could gather themselves together for their avoidance.

A silence ensued at the round table while Jardine leisurely cracked almonds in search of a philopena which he was pledged to eat with Ruth, and Mrs. Laniston trifled with her black coffee.

"Where's your hurry, now, Aunt Dora?" asked Lucia, her eyes narrowing mischievously, and Ruth laughed in delight, growing very alluringly pink as she gazed teasingly at her mother.

Mrs. Laniston was distinctly out of countenance. "Oh, you two girls!—you will be the death of me. I wish you would try to be more circumspect in the presence of company."

"Meaning Mr. Jardine," Lucia turned in an explanatory manner to Ruth, her face grave but her eyes alight with fun.

"Meaning Mr. Jardine," Ruth turned in an explanatory manner to Lucia, likewise grave but with her face pink and her blue eyes dancing.

Then they both collapsed in a gush of silent laughter, which they half buried in their clusters of grapes.

"Oh, I'm sure I don't know what I shall do with them! I feel like apologising to you for them, Mr. Jardine," Mrs. Laniston protested.

"Oh, don't mind me, I beg," said Jardine, laughing.

"Oh, don't mind him, he begs," said Lucia with an explanatory nod to Ruth.

"Oh, don't mind him, he begs," said Ruth, gravely explaining to Lucia.

125

Then ensued the usual burst of silvery laughter.

"They simply distract me—the two of them;" Mrs. Laniston, after an involuntary laugh, addressed Jardine. "You will hardly believe me, Mr. Jardine, but my Ruth was so good, oh, an angel [the look they cast on one another, while Jardine struggled in vain to listen gravely amidst this foolery], before Lucia came to live with me. And Lucia's father, George Laniston—my husband's brother, you know,—says that when Lucia was at her own home she was a very mouse of a little girl [again that disqualifying look at each other]. And now, together they aid and abet each other in all manner of absurdity and—and—*wildness*—that's just what it gets to, sometimes—just wildness."

"Sad," said Jardine, eyeing the twain indulgently.

They were both munching grapes just now and took no notice.

"They ought to be separated," said Frank, with his capable air. "Offer a premium to the one who gets married first."

"The blessed man would be premium enough," Lucia declared, "if we just could catch him."

"Oh, my dear, think how your voice carries," her aunt hastily admonished her.

"Why, he, whoever he may be, might hear it and come to the rescue."

There was a moment's silence, filled with grapes.

"Mamma thinks that we never see anything," said Ruth, with a very knowing air.

"Didn't he stare?" commented Lucia.

"Who?—the very handsome man that mamma thought Mr. Jardine was monopolising and denying her his acquaintance?" said Frank, with his callow chuckle.

"Oh, no," Ruth's voice affected a dreary cadence. "*He* didn't so much as lift his eyelashes,—his very—long—eyelashes."

"It was the other one then," said Frank, "the bullet-eyed acrobat."

"It doesn't matter in the least, Francis," said Mrs. Laniston, with dignity.

"That manager is really the handsomest man I ever saw," said the discreet Frank. "The clerk of the hotel tells me that he is so considered by everybody. In Duroc's celebrated painting of 'The Last Day,' he is posed as the angel Gabriel. Why, his nickname is 'Beauty'—he goes among his pals by the euphonious appellation of 'Beaut' Lloyd."

Frank had finished his dinner and he was showing some inclination to rock his chair to and fro; he imagined that this was why his mother frowned at him.

"What is his real name?" Lucia asked, unexpectedly.

"Why, child, how should he know?" Mrs. Laniston had risen, and tapped sharply on her niece's shoulder with rather admonitory knuckly fingers.

"Why, Francis passed his exams all right; I should think that he was far enough advanced to be able to construe the hotel register at all events."

"And there he is enrolled as Hilary Chester Lloyd," said Frank genially.

"Not a bad name," said Ruth casually.

"Rather humble for the manager of the greatest show on earth," laughed Frank. "Finest high-dive artist in the world, Captain Ollory of the Royal Navy, Flying Lady, Fat Lady, Snake-eater—eats 'em alive,—biggest boa constrictor, living skeleton, largest Ferris Wheel——"

Lucia's face turned deeply crimson as she listened to this farrago. She did not know why she should blush for the manager—he certainly did not think it necessary to blush for himself. To divert attention from the mounting flush in her face she remarked as she rose from the table, "I'm going up in the Ferris Wheel at any rate."

"And so am I," said Ruth. "I'll snatch that joy while it is within my reach."

The turmoil they anticipated ensued instantly.

"For heaven's sake," Mrs. Laniston solemnly adjured them. "Mr. Jardine, in pity on me let's get them back to the mountains. They will rack my nerves to pieces. The idea— to go up in a Ferris Wheel!"

"It is not an intellectual amusement, nor elegant in any sense, but it is perfectly safe," said Jardine.

"I have been east and west and north and south, yet was I never in a Ferris Wheel," said Lucia, locking her arm in Ruth's as they stood by the table preparatory to issuing from the room.

"I have crossed the ocean, I have visited the Colosseum by moonlight, I have explored—a little way—the Catacombs, yet was I never in a Ferris Wheel," echoed Ruth.

"I have 'swum in a gondola,' I have viewed the pyramids at Ghizeh, I have ridden cross-saddle in the Yosemite, yet was I never in a Ferris Wheel," declared Lucia.

"I have seen the Rock of Gibraltar, I have stood beneath the Eiffel tower, I have visited the Street Fair at Colbury, yet was I never in a Ferris Wheel," Ruth took up the antistrophe.

Mrs. Laniston had less their safety in mind than the staring of the bullet-eyed acrobat, and the fascinations of the long, unlifted eyelashes of the Beauty-man.

128

"If you can endure to stay with them every minute of the time, Mr. Jardine," she consented, conditionally. "Don't trust them to Francis—he is so irresponsible and flighty and young."

She felt very certain that Jardine's gravity and dignity would over-awe any possibility of an approach to familiarity which a lack of knowledge of the world on the part of the rustics, or the irrepressible gaiety of his youthful charges might superinduce.

"I'll take them first to a concert of 'high-class singing,'" Jardine said, and for his life he could not forbear a laughing grimace. "I think the sun is a little too high and too hot as yet for the fascinations of the Ferris Wheel."

Then joined by Frank he accompanied the two out on the verandah and down the flight of steps as once more with their white parasols aglare in the sunlight they took their way through the crowd in the square.

CHAPTER IX

Hilary Lloyd had had his doubts as to how serious a view Haxon might take of his discovery of the moonshining enterprise that had contrived to utilise to its own profit the presence here of the Street Fair. With the return of the morning light and its renewal of courage and hope the possible suspicion of a coalition of these interests seemed to him more remote than heretofore. His own association with the moonshiner's family might perhaps be most naturally interpreted as an accident, a fortuitous circumstance, and the extreme publicity of the appearance of the manager of the show both in the company of the girl and the old grandam would be presumed to imply an unconsciousness, an entire freedom from complicity on his part. All the morning, in a sub-acute process of the mind, he had argued these premises, pro and con. While he laboured to reassure the acrobat, to freshen his nerve, to flatter his composure, to reinstate his pride, so grievously cut down in the episode of the handbill, these mental exercises were hardly pretermitted for a moment. When, however, the perilous feat was once more safely performed and Haxon had been fed, and his nerves recuperated, Lloyd, feeling that the moment for the absolutely essential revelation had arrived and could no longer be postponed, drew him aside and intimated that he had disclosures to make of an importance that necessitated closed doors. Together they ascended the stairs to the room they shared, and even there Lloyd looked out on the balcony and down the cross-hall before he began his story.

"Gosh!" exclaimed Haxon irritably. "What's up? You scare me to death! You're gone bug-house, that's what!"

Lloyd was altogether unprepared for the appalled horror that overmastered the acrobat's every power of reasoning when the disclosure was once made. It was as if the dungeons of the Federal prisons were all agape for him, and he could not escape. For some time Lloyd could only induce him to make an effort for composure by warning him that his gasps, his half articulate exclamations like cries, so shrill and sudden they were, his disordered, hasty strides about the room—he actually fell in one of these, jarring the whole floor of the house—would bring inquiry upon them and a surprise that, unexplained, as it needs must be, would develop into suspicion, and this the briefest investigation would lead to complete discovery of the facts with their trail of false accusation.

Lloyd had expected co-operation and a division of the responsibility of devising a plan of action. He had a fund of excellent common sense. He realised that he was a man of most limited education, of an experience curiously restricted, and he did not flatter himself that he had any special native gifts of perspicacity and logic. He felt the need of help and he had longed for this moment of liberation from the solitary torment of his fears—for the sense of a comrade's support and the mental attrition of a mind fresh to these weary problems. The force with which he was flung back on his own resources stunned his capacities for the time being. The revelation had only increased the danger of immediate discovery in the absolute collapse of Haxon's self-control. Lloyd used argument and persuasion, and finally resorted to menacing warnings.

"You'll give the whole thing away to the authorities before we can have a moment's counsel together and see what we can do."

"What can we do?" cried Haxon, his palms outspread dolorously. "We are caught here like a rat in a trap—we can't get away. God! If I had thirty-five dollars in the world I'd cut and run, and leave you to shift for yourself."

Lloyd eyed him critically.

"Haxon, how can you show so much courage and nerve in that cursed high dive of yours and be such a coward in a crisis like this?" he demanded sternly.

"'Cause why? 'Cause the high dive is biz, but 'tain't my trade to defy the Federal courts for offences I have never c'mitted."

He felt the aspersion on his courage—the lash cut his somewhat thick sensibilities.

"Look here, Hil'ry——" He sat down astride on a chair, facing its back and beating out on its wooden rim the several points as he made them. "If I was in the illicit distilling lay

131

I'd be fixed for the biz, and I'd take my risks along with the profits as cool as I do in the high dive. I'd be where I was known, too,—at home,—an' there'd be some chanst of friends to back you, an' lawyers for hire, an' money at hand—'t wouldn't be at the end of a blue fizzle on the road. But here wheer I don't actually know so much as the name of the clerk of the hotel! I haven't got a fiver to save my life!"

He turned the pockets of his trousers inside out to demonstrate his impecuniosity, and his aspect as he sat thus, his round face pallid, and his hair roached and standing straight in front, might have suggested the ludicrous to another man, but to Hilary Lloyd it only accented and illustrated the stress of the untoward situation.

"I couldn't get a nickel by telegraphing—even if I left the wire to be paid at the other end, for I raised every cent I could scrape to start the show out on the road; and you are in the same fix. An' here are you an' I an' all the men in the company in this strange place, liable to arrest and jail for aiding and abetting in the illicit sale of wild-cat whisky—oh Lord!" His great full voice rose plangent on the air.

"I'll cut your tongue out if you lay it again to them words!" declared Lloyd, in a frenzy of apprehension. He darted to the door and opening it gazed down the cross-halls to detect a possible eavesdropper. He then hastened to the window and looked out on the balcony. There was no one near—no suggestion that suspicion had been aroused. He returned to his chair, reassured, but tingling with the excitement of the disastrous possibility and both angry and dismayed.

"What do you sit there, spouting all that preachment at me for? I know it as well or better than you; didn't I find the thing out and tell you how it stood? What do you suppose I did that for? To hear you spit it all out again?"

"What did you do it for?" Haxon eyed him sullenly.

"To get your help—you are a partner in the biz; you had a right to know."

Haxon looked as if he esteemed it a right with which he would willingly have dispensed.

"You've got my nerve all tore up," he complained.

"That ain't the question—what are we goin' to do about it?"

Haxon, as he still sat facing the back of the chair, took the ends of his pockets in the tips of his fingers and held them out to their extreme limits.

"What can we do—*nothing!*"

Lloyd looked balked and despairing. He had hoped so much, waited so long, with such torturing silence and self-repression for this appeal for the help of his friend and partner. He gazed dubiously at the attitude and face, all illustrative of the idea of absolute collapse, and then he slowly and laboriously gathered himself together. He felt like a pugilist, who, lunging with great force, has caught a heavy fall in the ring. He was game, however, game to the last.

"Well, *I* don't throw up the sponge," he said at length. "That's a trick I've never learned. We can do something! You watch me right close and keep a shut mouth, and sit tight, and you'll see something doing."

He nodded his head determinedly. Haxon, watching him doubtfully, could experience no renewal of activity, no revival of hope. His faculties were completely prostrated. He could only fear.

"Now, go slow," he said, irritably anxious.

"You be bound I will," Lloyd reassured him.

A dull curiosity began to grow in Haxon's eyes that yet winced from the question.

"I have got a right to know. I'm a partner, and what you do will implicate me."

"I've a good mind to roll you on the floor till you're as thin as a sheet of paper," the athlete threatened, "only it's too good a stunt without a crowd. You may bet your immortal soul that nothing *I* do will implicate you or any other man."

"I just wanted to warn you," said Haxon mildly.

"I was warned beforehand," Lloyd protested.

The mental activity, the canvass for expedients that Lloyd had sought to rouse in Haxon's mind seemed now stimulated by the cessation of urgency on the manager's part. A vague sense of being shut out of his counsels was stirring uneasily in Haxon's consciousness—it put out a clutch after the plans in which he would not share.

"Now you take care you don't make no mistake."

"Try not,—for my own sake,—but I'm not infallible," said Lloyd. His interest in Haxon's impressions had evaporated. Since Haxon had neither adequate aid nor well-considered advice to offer, and no fund of courage to recruit and reanimate the flagging energies of his partner, it did not matter how his vague conjecture skirmished about the point of attack and plan of action.

"You be sure you don't get into a hole———" Haxon paused. "You ain't thinking about giving the information to the authorities?" his small keen eyes kindled with the contemplation of this course.

"Certainly not," said Lloyd listlessly. He had drawn off his cuffs that had begun to wilt at the edges and was slipping the sleeve-links of oxydised silver into a fresh pair that, leaning back in his chair, he had reached from the tray of an open trunk.

"But you know the informer gets good pay. The government always pays like smoke." Haxon, now that his speculations, his proffers of plans, his advice were not solicited seemed bent on evolving and laying them before his companion. "We might get enough that way to defray the cost of the company's transportation to New York."

"We'd be much likelier to be laid by the heels for false arrest, for we couldn't prove any illicit distilling or sale, either. Besides, we'd get our heads shot off for playing the spy and informer; that's etiquette in this region."

"You'd better think about that reward, now Hil'ry," the acrobat eagerly urged. "*You* ain't afraid of getting shot, nor nothing else. You're holding back for another reason. There's a woman in the case!"

Lloyd looked up with a certain expectation and a deepening of the roseate flush on his fair, girlish cheek.

"You don't want to inform on them folks on account of that gal. You've gone and got mashed on a mountain singing-gal—the pals all say the public don't fall to her racket not the least little bit."

"Oh," said Lloyd, as if with sudden comprehension—had he thought Haxon was alluding to another woman here? He came visibly back, as from some far digression of thought.

"There's no use talking about that, Hax. I've been all along there—in fact, there ain't a by-path through this tangled torment that my mind ain't travelled since the show opened up. The reward would be paid for conviction, not for suspicion. No man gets paid for suspecting. We couldn't wait till the moonshiners were arrested and convicted in court—eat our heads off in that time, if anybody would credit us for the grub-stakes."

135

Haxon's face fell, so strong a hold had his now unsought plans taken upon him.

"Besides," Lloyd argued, rising from his chair, "our grounds of suspicion ain't firm underfoot; even the authorities ain't sure enough to venture to arrest the Pinnotts. They don't even molest the drunken men that were fairly sprawling all over the town this morning. They'll point the way they have travelled before long. The authorities are waiting for bigger game—laying for the moonshiners."

The terrors of the situation seized Haxon again: The suspicion that the street fair had at least some knowledge of this popular adjunct to its attractions; the obvious fact that it must profit immeasurably by the lures offered a dry town to draw a crowd; the unlucky publicity of the intimacy that the manager of the show had struck up with the old moonshiner and the several members of his family; the incongruity that his daughter had become a temporary member of the company, and had a place on the daily programme, doing a "stunt" that had no value whatever in the public eye, and might thus seem a tribute of flattery to a powerful coadjutor; the certainty that without this recruiting of the moonshine whisky-drinking element in the scantily populated region the fair could hardly have lived through the first day's performance—all were close meshes in such a net that the acrobat could hardly hope to escape thence.

"Oh, Hil'ry—we have worked so hard. I don't see no sense nor justice in our gettin' tangled up this fashion." He bowed his head on the chair back and groaned aloud.

"Now you look here," said Lloyd—he summoned a mental attention and was not disconcerted when Haxon did not lift his head. "You listen to me. I'm going to see this thing through. You just keep your tongue between your teeth and don't bat your eye, and watch me, and you'll see something doing!"

136

His confidence revived Haxon's hopes, though he retained his despondent attitude after he heard the tread of Lloyd's feet slowly descending the stairs. Perhaps it was well for the preservation of his composure that he did not see the deep depression the manager's face expressed while in the solitary transit down the flight, nor hear the half-smothered groan that dropped from his lips. He had wasted much time for naught in hanging his hopes on this futile interview. He was now exactly at the point whence he had started. Time meant money—the increase of the expenses of the show in a ratio with which the gate receipts by no means kept pace. Time meant danger, the continual challenge of disastrous possibilities, and that these were formulating somewhere, somehow, he did not doubt for a moment. He paused when he reached the bottom of the flight and glanced through a window of a side hall that had an outlook in the direction of the sylvan nook where Shadrach Pinnott had planted his staff. He had a vague, indeterminate disposition to make a tour of discovery thither, to satisfy himself—to see, perchance—wild hope—if his suspicions were not merely the result of his over-anxious facile fears. All the world knows that dry towns are only dry in spots, and perhaps the fact that the populace had been so called into the streets by the presence of the show made the pervasive evidences of liquor more obvious. Alack, his first glance from the window proved the tenuity of this reasoning. The farthest man he could see along the street coming from that direction was wiping his mouth with the back of his hand; then amidst a file of ordinary pedestrians two came affectionately clasping each other around the waist, under the firm conviction that four legs can better compass locomotion than two, when all are so unsteady, on the theory of strength in numbers, perhaps. No one took notice, apparently, of the aberrations of this method of progression, but he reflected it would be only the gratification of a morbid anxiety to visit the spot, and his presence there might add an element of curiosity and speculation to a circumstance already unduly suspicious. As he came out into the square he noticed with a sort of melancholy satisfaction how well the show was running in all its various departments, how orderly it was, how mindful of its best possibilities, how cheerful and brisk the performers and spielers, all unprescient, poor souls! It was like a well-oiled piece of machinery, automatic, scarcely needing the eye of the manager. He cast a glance upward at the town clock—it was already time for the afternoon concert; at that moment he heard the tuning of the violins and a booming note from the bassoon. As he entered the tent he remarked that the light within was tempered, mellow, and his artistic taste was refreshed by this—it would aid the effect of the lime-light on the stage which should simulate sunshine amongst the dappling shadows of the peach-tree leaves.

The audience crowded the tent, to his surprise, for this "stunt" had proved no favourite performance with the public, and, since already seen, it had no claims to novelty. Then he realised the cause of this accumulation of spectators; in the best seats in the centre of the place was Mr. Jardine, his jaded, slightly disdainful, thin, grave, thoughtful face easily discriminated among the many that seemed turned out of a mould, custom made, so commonplace they were. The fresh, bright, candid countenance of the young collegian was near at hand, and between the two, radiant in their white dresses and hats, and with their flower-like faces, exquisitely fair and dainty, looking expectantly toward the stage, half amused at their own readiness to be entertained with these slight trifles, were the two belated summer birds of New Helvetia. The entrance of so distinguished a party had already made the "high-class concert" the fashion; the best element of the town was present, and this had been reinforced by the *profanum vulgus* of the street, for whatever the town folks found acceptable the rural wight cautiously sampled, often decrying and ridiculing while secretly approving and imitating. There were many sunbonnets, and snuff-brushes, and big wool hats, and bushy beards, but the dapper townsmen were in greater numbers than heretofore and the Misses Laniston did not wear the only be-frilled millinery that the tent displayed. It was an audience of no mean intelligence, and poor Lloyd realised that were he free from the gnawing wild beasts of secret anxiety and harrowing doubt and actual fear, his showman's heart would have beat high with the determination to stretch every nerve and do his best devoir. Even as it was there was no use in permitting the second violin to enter upon the fugues of the little overture very distinctly sharp to his acute and accurate ear. He had taken a seat near the orchestra, and he suddenly stood up and signed with a wave of the hand to catch the performer's attention. The man turned the screw slightly, and twanged the string. While Hilary Lloyd stood, his head slightly bent, with a face of motionless, intent interest, his hat in his hand, he heard distinctly, besides the violin's keen vibration, the sudden snap of the shutter of a camera. He nodded approval to the violinist, but his eyes followed the camera's sound. Ruth's flower-like face was pink with smiles and Lucia's long, romantic eyes were bright with triumphant daring. The two cavaliers were distinctly disconcerted as their eyes met Lloyd's. It was only for a moment; the manager affected to look over the house, then turning, resumed his seat, and the overture broke briskly forth.

"Lucia," her cousin Frank growled under cover of the music, "you had better mind. You will be led out by the ear, if you don't look out."

139

"I should be delighted to have my ear distinguished in any way, here, where a fine ear is made so conspicuous," she twittered in response.

"But the violins are all in accord now, and that second one *was* out of tune before," said Ruth.

"In printing the film I shall take special pains with so fine an ear," said Lucia.

"You can't fool me," gurgled Frank. "You snapped him because the fellow looked so confoundedly handsome at the moment. You never dreamed that the place was still enough for the click of the button to betray you. There's nothing green in my eye!"

"You two must be a little more careful, if I may venture to say so," suggested Mr. Jardine, who really was somewhat aghast at the camera episode—exceedingly discommoded by the grave eye of the manager and nervous lest some neighbour might have noticed the incident. "Even in a rustic community," he continued, "it won't do to take it for granted that there are no people who know what—er—er——"

"Good manners are," suggested Lucia.

"I beg a thousand pardons—but I did not say that."

"Worse still, you implied it. You rejoice in being enigmatical." Then she turned to Ruth. "Think of poor Mrs. Jardine (when he finds her)—having to pick out his meaning from implications."

"The dear lady (when he finds her)—he will train her to deduce the state of his affections from statistics."

Then they both collapsed behind their white fans, over which they looked at each other with bright eyes, brimful of laughter. The mythical Mrs. Jardine (when he should find her) was one of their favourite subjects of retort when no reasonable justification was at hand, and they spent much time in adjusting and readjusting her traits. Oddly enough, for so sane and grave a man, this folly teased him, which fact afforded them extreme delight.

They were incomprehensible to him in more ways than one, but generally he gave this hardly a languid thought, ascribing it to the idiosyncrasies of the feminine mind, which according to the popular persuasion was adjusted to a peculiar poise. Now, however, he puzzled over the theory of their conduct, which both nettled and embarrassed him. In any metropolitan crowded centre, in any station of fashionable society, he knew from experience that their graceful propriety of demeanour, their air of delicate reserve, their instinct for the right word at the right moment, the soft youthful dignity which they could conserve, were matters for all admiration; he had relished greatly being admitted behind this conventional formal pose into the intimacies of familiar friendship where he saw them as they really were, in their natural girlish relaxation from the conventions of general society. But here was a new phase. They were recklessly conspicuous; they cared naught for the opinions of the rustic crowd—indeed what they did and said was likely to be presumed the fashion of the time and the fad of the day. "I like to be where I know nobody, and where nobody knows me," Lucia had declared, in reply to a covert admonition which he had ventured; "I feel so easy. What is that story of a knight of old who had a magic armour that protected him from sight, and he went through the camps of his enemies all unsuspected. That is how I feel; I feel invisible."

Mr. Jardine had not expected that they would adopt the Colbury standards and sit demurely still, as if conscious, in this little sphere, of the regards of all the world; that they would sparingly converse in the lowest of tones and with solicitude for the effect of their words. They could but be

141

indifferent to criticism and maintain a certain independence in so limited an environment. But it did seem to him that they had reached the extreme of toleration in the episode of the camera. Of course he realised that Lucia had never expected the click of the instrument to acquaint the subject that she had sought and caught his photograph, but in this contretemps she perceived only an amazing jest at her own expense, of a delightful and unprecedented savour. She almost perished with laughter and ridicule of herself and seemed to have no care nor fear of the opinion of the man and this man a stranger, of low station, of most questionable position, who might take bitter offence, or venture some impertinence, or seek reprisal in some wise intolerable to her and her friends. For his own part Jardine was the same in every circumstance of life; formal, civil, conventional, reserved. However the kaleidoscope of environment shifted he did not change, and his standards were unalterable. He sought to reflect that they were both very young; they were like birds, thus freed for the nonce from the frumpish restrictions of the stereotyped dulness of their cage. They were like irresponsible school-girls, liberated from the cast-iron class-room rules; indeed it was not long since both were hard and fast in these restraints; they were like children, thinking no ill, confident or careless of approval, enjoying the passing moment, freighted with scanty opportunity for pleasure though it was, with a zest, a delight, a buoyancy of spirit, a capacity to evolve fun from serious conditions which Jardine could not have compassed at any period of his career. But he realised that there was more responsibility in the office of their chaperon than he had deemed possible when he had assumed Mrs. Laniston's charge and left her to her well-earned rest at the hotel.

Suddenly the tempo of the music changed; the subtle charm of a simple old melody was pulsing on the air and now it dwindled into a vague diminuendo, and then to a pizzicato echo, in the midst of which a clear, brilliant voice sounded singing in the distance. The curtain went up with a rush; the stage was revealed flooded with yellow sunlight and all a-dapple with the shadows of swaying peach-leaves from boughs waving in the wind above. And what was that effect? How could they have such strangely perfect scenery—the purple mountains, the azure ranges of the distance, the blue sky bedight with a cloud all opal and gold, and a river with a crystalline reflex of its splendour. Before the simple expedient of dropping a section of the canvas occurred to their minds a figure, lightsome, airy, featly dancing, bounded into the illuminated centre of the scene. There was one moment of amazed scrutiny—it was like some classic canephora of painting or sculpture; then the eye recognised in the basket-like vessel poised on the head, filled with trailing vines and purple grape clusters, the familiar cedar piggin of the mountains; the antique-draped garb was but the up-caught skirt of the conventional make, but with the yellow folds so craftily held in plaits that they sustained a wealth of the grapes, picturesquely trailing down over a dark wine-tinted petticoat, short enough to disclose ankles and feet of a wonderful agility. The auburn hair, soft, fluffy, rayonnant, was coiled in a knot of negligent charm, and the head was thrown back as the dancer leaped with incredible lightness and grace, catching with one hand toward the lure of a peach on a bough out of her reach, now and then lifting it to poise the basket, singing in a clear, true, sweet voice the lilting measures of the old song. It was a short "turn"; she knew but the single stanza. The effect was like some radiant, transient vision, the fleeting allurement of the senses in a dream, as the curtain suddenly descended, the light went out, and the vibrating echo of the violins ceased.

A moment of silent surprise; then the sound of the clapping of one enthusiastic pair of hands, and presently the tent rocked with a tumult of applause.

"By George—that's great!" cried Frank Laniston, red in the face from his exertions, his hands banging together like machinery. He gazed in sympathy at Jardine, who was fairly startled out of his composure and applauding with a will.

"It is absolutely beautiful, and perfectly unique," he exclaimed.

The two young ladies were trying what resources of clatter the sticks of their white fans might compass as they struck them against the palms of their small white gloved hands.

The man in the old whitish grey coat, whom Lloyd had noticed earlier in the audience, experiencing renewed anxiety lest some inimical espionage might account for his purchase of a ticket to a performance so ludicrous to his taste, sat in the midst of the clamour as still as if he had been carved in stone. The enthusiasm had illumined all faces save his— some subtle shadow of despondency had fallen upon it. He no longer held it half muffled in the high collar and lapels of the big old coat. It was shielded only by the drooping brim of the limp white hat and he presently turned it hither and thither, looking in stunned amazement and a deprecatory, remonstrant, unconscious inquiry at the neighbouring spectators among the crowded benches. The flavour of his secret jest had evaporated—he seemed to find naught to ridicule now.

"Why don't they raise that curtain, I wonder," growled Frank Laniston. "It's as hot as Hades in here, working this way. Bless my soul, won't she accept an encore?"

For the curtain remained immovable. Lloyd, startled by the unexpected endorsement of the attraction he had devised, that had hitherto fallen so flat, gratified by the applause as if it were a personal commendation, flushed deeply red as he sat near the orchestra and with smiling eyes waited too with all the rest for the conventional rising of the curtain and the

144

complaisant repetition of the number. He had left nothing unforeseen in his instructions to the tyro. Clotilda had been fully informed of the nature and exigencies of an encore, and the course proper for her to pursue as the recipient of that great compliment. But, alack, the turn had never received before a hand of applause. In dead silence the rural crowd had heretofore watched the scene and wondered futilely what was the point when a simple country girl, in her old calico "coat," jumped around under a peach tree, and sang a verse of an old song, a thing to be seen on any roadside. Then they had silently filed out and there was an end for the time. Now, however, since there was applause from so experienced and discerning a source, a revised estimate seemed in order. Perhaps a new interpretation waited upon a more æsthetic point of view. The applause was hearty and general, and rose presently to an insistent clamour.

Clotilda, having had no occasion to respond to the plaudits of the public, had forgotten every syllable of her instructions. Lloyd remained yet some moments waiting, like the rest, eyeing the curtain, in the immediate expectation of seeing it rise. The musicians had their instruments in hand—at the tinkle of the bell they would begin *da capo*. But the curtain continued absolutely blank; no sign of the golden glow of the artificial light could be discerned, naught but the ripples of the air, swiftly running over it as the draught from the lowered canvas at the rear struck upon the fabric. Lloyd began to look discomposed, then anxious, then as the applause redoubled its demand he waited one uncertain moment longer, rose, advanced amongst the orchestra, sprang upon the stage, pushed the curtain aside and vanished behind its sphinx-like blankness.

"I never did really believe that he was the manager till this moment," said Lucia, a regretful cadence in her voice.

145

"What did you think he was, a duke in disguise?" chuckled Frank.

"Oh, yes, he *is* the manager," said Ruth glibly, "and this is only the by-play of the real romance staged here. He is in love with that pretty girl, and was fascinated in training her."

Mr. Jardine had fended off the motley crowd from contact with his fair charges as best he might by seating the two young ladies together, with Frank on one side and himself on the other. But there was no protection from the occupants of the seats just in front, and suddenly one of these, a slovenly old wretch, in a dirty, whitey-grey coat and flapping hat, turned and fixed an eager, intent, almost indignant gaze on Ruth's face as she spoke. It was as if she had spoken a thought, a fear in his own mind, and to Jardine's surprise he saw that the face was young—young, but overgrown with the stubble of a three-days' beard, a stiff, dark beard. Wisps of short, dark hair overhung the forehead, as if a forelock were pulled of set purpose half over the eyes; for the rest, the face was dirty, unwashed, one might have thought stained in blotches—a repellent face, with fine, bright brown eyes. They turned eagerly to Lucia as, all unnoting his demonstration, she replied to Ruth's observation.

"I don't think she is so pretty," said Lucia critically. "It is the artistic environment that makes it all so fetching, don't you think, Mr. Jardine?"

He caught but the one word in the uproar of applause.

"Artistic—it *is* indeed! I wouldn't have believed it if I hadn't seen it. That scene has the true poetic glamour; it is as classic as an eclogue of Virgil."

He could hardly speak for the clamour which overpowered the tinkle of the bell, the earliest measures of the violins. As the curtain rose on the golden glow came a sudden hush; the

146

pizzicato of the violins fell as trippingly as fairy feet on the silence; then the sound of singing broke forth in the distance and the beautiful dancing figure appeared. With familiarity one could note new effects, that, however, brought no disparagement. The opal cloud in the scenery had turned to purple, while the saffron cloud had held its glow. Once there was a sudden mutter of thunder and a swift veining of white glister was revealed amidst the hyacinthine tones.

As before, the scene was all too short, the beautiful dancing figure but a glimpse. The curtain came down in a clamour of applause; as this continued it rose after a short space. Clotilda had been schooled anew, and she was a quick study. Nothing could have seemed more perfect, more practised than her manner of smiling, grateful recognition as she came forward to the footlights. She had removed the basket of grapes from her head, but supported it in the round of her arm, half poised against her hip; the other hand lightly touched the masses of grapes held in the folds of her yellow dress, but it was obvious that their artistic draping had been made hard and fast against accident. She bowed with drooping eyelashes, and once more, lower still, she bowed, all rustic grace and diffidence, and then the curtain came down with a rush and the turn was triumphantly at an end.

"Couldn't Lucia photograph her, Mr. Jardine?" cried Ruth. "Oh, how I'd love to have her in my collection."

He hesitated coldly for one moment; then as if suddenly bethinking himself, eagerly assented.

"Doubtless—*doubtless*; you will want her in costume. I must speak to the manager at once."

As he eagerly breasted the crowd, seeking to get in as the spectators streamed out, the two young ladies, amazed by his willing co-operation, which they had by no means expected, stood and gazed quizzically at each other.

147

"A change of heart?" Lucia asked.

"Or a softening of the brain, perhaps," Ruth responded. Then they both turned to note his progress and saw him already in courteous conference with the manager. In fact Jardine had gladly embraced the opportunity to give the impression to this very handsome man of low degree that the highly placed and aristocratic Miss Lucia Laniston was out for snap-shots in general, and was adding to her collection from features of the town, the mountains, the fair, whatever presented itself as of passing interest. This was an inference more creditable and becoming than the possibility that she was greatly struck by the manly beauty of Lloyd's countenance and desired to remember it, to have the likeness to refresh her recollection, and thus caught the exceptional value of his pose at the moment. Jardine did not tell, and he did not think it necessary to tell, that Lloyd's face was the only one she had cared to portray, and that the camera had not been placed in position before and the slide drawn since she had been in town. He thought this an obliteration of the dangerous flattery if the man had been complacent and pleased by the discovery the click of the shutter had afforded him, and a placation of the offence, had he taken umbrage, by the apology suggested in the fact that he was only one of the many victims of the raging camera. He was surprised by the grave and gentlemanly address of the showman. Lloyd might have seemed indeed some man of high grade, were it not for his accent. He would be very happy to oblige, as far as he had any voice in the matter, but he must first ask the "lydy." Most of the attractions of the show were photographed and their portraits were on sale, but this lydy had very recently joined the company, playing only a temporary engagement, in fact, and she had not been photographed at all. Having also his reservations, he did not add that it had not been thought worth while, the reality itself being so incapable of sustaining interest.

148

Jardine, having carried his point, became afraid that he was playing it a little too fine, as the two young ladies approached and he found himself compelled to say, "This is the manager, Mr. Lloyd, ladies, and he is in hopes he may be able to secure the photograph you desire."

Mr. Lloyd raised his hat in a manner to which no exceptions could have been taken by the most exacting critic, and replying, "I shall be with you again in a moment," stepped upon the stage and disappeared.

Mr. Jardine looked harassed; he took out his handkerchief and passed it over his brow. It had been only one afternoon of chaperonage, but he had all the indicia of brain fag. The two young ladies, silent, glanced about at the queer, unaccustomed place; to his jaundiced mind they were measuring its opportunities to furnish them occasion for more mischief. Suddenly beside him the curtain drew up and the beautiful mountain girl stood posed exactly as she had appeared before the audience.

She was flattered that her picture was to be taken—now and again her lips parted over her beautiful teeth in a foolish little grin that annulled every scintilla of poesy in her presence.

"I have tried this sort of thing a bit, myself, and I don't think the perspective will answer unless the lydies are on a level. There is such a—a—mixed crowd outside—will the lydy step on the stage?" suggested Lloyd.

If for no other reason than the dismay on Jardine's high-featured, disdainful face, Lucia signified her acquiescence, and accepting the assistance of the manager's proffered outstretched hand she sprang lightly on the boards. Lloyd's quick intuition interpreted the expression on their several faces, for Jardine had instantly joined her and she felt that she must mask her thoughts if she would not have them read when Lloyd said, evidently in response to the protest in Mr.

Jardine's countenance—"This is quite retired, not at all public now." Then glancing at the three or four people who were yet loitering and staring at the figures on the stage, he called out loudly—"This is no performance. Keep out of here!"

The wondering rustics slowly vanished; only one lingered and as Lloyd's gaze fell upon him he recognised the figure clad in a whitey-gray garb which had so persistently dogged his steps. His voice took on an authoritative cadence.

"Clear out. This is no performance. Clear out, I say!"

The figure turned like a dog that would fain fly at the throat, yet slinks in fear.

"I ain't carin' what you say," the intruder blustered. Then he slowly slouched out, muttering to himself, with the flapping brim of his hat well pulled down over his bright young eyes.

"You will make a lovely picture in that charming dress," Lucia said blandly, as Lloyd stepped here and there, pulling at the curtain to get a better light.

"It's all wore an' tore," Clotilda said deprecatingly. She did not doubt the admiration of the men, but she was all abashed and awkward in this presence of dainty feminine elegance. She scanned the two openly, as if comparing their traits. Then she fixed her eyes sedulously on Lucia. Her face was so out of drawing with this heavy, dully pondering, loutish expression, so incongruous with the poetic charm she had wrought, that Miss Laniston suggested:

"Sing—sing a line or two of that pretty song—sing, and dance a few steps."

The girl lifted her docile head, sprang lightly into the air, her fresh young voice floated out and suddenly the camera clicked.

"That is all, and when I get the pictures out I will come and see you and bring some of them to you. This gentleman tells me you live near by in the mountains. Where is your home?"

"He knows. He'll kem an' guide you," Clotilda easily promised for him.

Lucia turned to Lloyd, with her most entrancing smile. "Thanks, for past and future favours," she said, realising the disastrous storm the unexpected turn of events had roused in Mr. Jardine's conventional soul.

Lloyd bowed in gravest acknowledgment, and as she stepped down from the stage she remarked:

"My first and last appearance on the boards."

"You graced them," said Ruth airily.

But the two men, heavily silent, said nothing.

Lloyd ceremoniously saw them to the door, as if he had been entertaining them in the character of host, and as they departed he lifted his hat with a dignity all at variance with the sudden humorous cry of the spieler close at hand—"He eats 'em—he eats 'em alive!"

Lucia shrugged her disdainful shoulders.

"What an experience! What a place! The incongruities are amazing. I feel as if I were in a fevered dream, or a grotesque fairy-tale."

"You'll ruin those films if you don't look out for that camera," Ruth warned her, but she made no reply and swung the camera as carelessly as before.

CHAPTER X

Mr. Jardine, seating himself on the piazza of the hotel, which overlooked the motley throngs of the square with the salient concomitants of the mushroom spread of the tents, the tawdry ornaments of the vendors' stands, the tall mast of the high diver, the periphery of the gigantic Ferris Wheel with its seats filled with rustics swaying in the slow revolution through the afternoon glow, the business houses of the little town that bounded the space on each side, their decorous, sober, orderly appearance, so alien to the flurry and carnival folly of the streets, had sufficient need of the mild stimulant of his cigar to restore the tone of his nerves and allay the irritation that harassed his mental processes. He was glad of the silence, for so he accounted the freedom from talk whether of accost or reply, despite the varied clamours of raucous voices, the wailing of infants, the whinnying of impatient horses, eager for the homeward journey, and mindful of supper, as the waggon teams stood hitched in rows to the courthouse fence, the braying of the band, the stentorian cries of the spielers, all the unwearied activities of the lungs of the mountebanks. He was glad to be no longer in the seat of the scornful, to be continually objecting, deriding, frowning down the features of the little show; if it was the fad of the young ladies to entertain their idleness with such rubbish, surely for the nonce he might ignore its vapidities, its pitiful poverty-stricken shifts, its sedulous catering to the low capacities of the common rustic crowd. There was much distasteful, even disgusting to a fastidious sense in its exhibitions, but there was nothing absolutely coarse, and not the most remote suggestion of anything vile. It was a clean show, as its handbills insistently proclaimed. It need not have so lacerated his sensibilities, he felt, as the fragrant nicotian solace began its soothing effect. To be sure it was a sacrifice, a poignant trial to his hyper-elegant standards to be with Lucia Laniston amid scenes so unworthy. He would fain meet her, as heretofore, on a plane more in accord with the character of both, among circumstances that elicited those charms of intellect and culture that had won his admiration and respect as her more obvious grace and beauty had captured his heart. In his eyes she united many fascinations, the more remarkable because of her youth. Her solid, unimpassioned judgment, her cultivated taste, her very respectable scholastic acquirements, gauged from even a high educational point of view, of which he had seen many evidences, rendered it manifestly impossible that she should enjoy the exhibition in any serious sense. It merely furnished a surface for that exuberant buoyancy and those fantastic traits which her aunt called "wildness," and which he supposed were the inseparable concomitants of such abounding youth and vitality and joyous spirits. She was alert and energetic, and full of life and mirth, and it was not the fashion of the day, as of yore, to set such a damsel down to sew her sampler by the fire till such time, soon or late, as her cavalier came to claim his domestic paragon. Things were different now. Wider courses of study, much travel, athletic recreations, great liberty of thought and action had resulted in a wider outlook for girls—and, suddenly, he doubted if it made them happier from any point of view. He was remembering the dull depression, the listless disillusionment in Lucia Laniston's face as but now they had walked to the hotel together, and the ladies had sought their rooms for some freshening of attire before starting on the afternoon drive back to New Helvetia. The horses were swift and fresh, and the distance was thus minimised; there was a new moon to enliven the dusk, the roads were very good; the driver, a stalwart young fellow, himself, and Frank Laniston, three men, quietly carrying arms in conformity with the privilege accorded travellers, were ample escort for the ladies, even in these remote wildernesses; but Jardine was a prudent man of a prompt habit. He drew out his watch, and looked critically at the wane of the day evidenced in the skies, bright though they still were, beginning to hope that the usual feminine procrastinations might not so postpone the hour of departure as to render the party unduly benighted.

Chances of casualties, a broken wheel, a horse going lame, a mistaken direction in fording a river, a cloud on the moon, the shattering of the carriage lamps in a blow from a projecting bough, even the unlikely possibility of highway robbers, should not be invested with unnecessary jeopardy and added danger. He was at such a disadvantage in this respect as does not usually harass the guardian of ladies. He was neither husband, father, nor brother, to stand, timepiece in hand, and proclaim the wasting hour, like an irate clock. He could not order the luggage downstairs—packed or unpacked. He could not threaten that he would start on schedule time, regardless if all portable property were left behind. Jardine was only a friend, as yet, benign, complaisant, and in no position to dictate. Yet he wondered, with a vexation which tobacco was powerless to reach, what could be detaining the ladies in their preparations for an afternoon drive through an unpeopled wilderness. If it was a question of toilette its effect was already a foregone conclusion—Ruth had slain her thousands, and Lucia her tens of thousands—unconsciously he was adopting their own exaggerated vein. He could not imagine that anything of consequence hindered their readiness,—only the usual feminine, dilatory aversion to be on time for any vicissitude of life. He began to feel that he must act, yet he shrank from encountering the laggards with admonitions and reproaches. He realised that he had not commended himself by his stiff imperviousness to the simple enjoyments of the "lark" to-day, such as it was, and his disdainful incapacity to enter into its spirit had not bettered it. He was anxious to appear no

154

more as unresponsive monitor, full of warnings, and wise saws, and stiff reproofs. Where was Francis Laniston? Naught was to be disparaged by thrusting him into the jaws of domestic displeasure. Let him make the remonstrance, and bear its resilient blow as behoved his position and relationship. Let the dilatory ladies wreak their displeasure on the urgent Frank! Animated by this inhuman resolution, Jardine sprang from his chair to go in search of Frank. He was interrupted by the sudden issuance of the clerk of the hotel, a young, plump, blond man, wearing an immaculate white duck suit, with short hair in a stiff straight roach above his brow, no eyebrows—thus he dispensed with frowns—a long, blunt nose, a twinkling blue-grey eye, very small and very affable. His whole aspect was not unducklike, and, as he remained all day behind his desk, having no outside vocation to call him from his post, he was very speckless, without even the creases incident to a sitting posture, since he stood at his desk, or perched on a high stool. He might have been expected to creak with starch as his brisk short steps brought him to the encounter.

"Speak to you a moment, Mr. Jardine?" he said, pausing by a chair, and leaning with both hands on its back in his stiff white garments. Many men, however wasteful in general, have some saving grace of frugality. Jennings, the clerk, a most voluble man, was nevertheless sparing in parts of speech, and economised pronouns and conjunctions. This necessitated a reckless expenditure in punctuation— commas, colons, periods, and dashes, but, as his prelections were not destined for type, he did not realise, perhaps, that what he saved at the spile he lost at the bung. "Considerable storm in the mountains. Thought I ought to let you know. Heard you give orders for the horses to be put to at once. See from east window of office. Mountains have been caught up in clouds—so to speak. I tried to telephone to New Helvetia, in interest of your party.—Hate to be alarmist—wanted to find out what weather is doing there. No answer. Central says wire is blown down. Intact as far as Crossroads. Tried Mr. Tackett, the storekeeper there. He says raining there heavily. Big blow in the woods—falling timber—and lightning—thought I'd let you know."

"Thank you, very much," said Jardine, still standing with his watch in his hand contemplating, not its dial, but these untoward complications. "Can you afford us accommodations? I understood this morning that the house was full."

"Thought of that—the ladies have had a room all day—only one—very large, with alcove—two beds—double room. And you gentlemen—we have thought of you—we will offer you little blue parlour—best we can do———"

"And sleep tunefully on the piano, I suppose," Frank interpolated. He had just strolled up, evidently already informed of the quandary, and stood listening, his hands in his pockets.

The duck laughed with a short grating note.

"Folding bed—that handsome cabinet with the Indian curiosities on the brackets—latest patent. The divan is really a sofa-bed, too—you'll be qualified to help us out and be hospitable, if any more single men drop in on us," the clerk said tauntingly.

"Now don't you bank on that. The little blue parlour is my bower, and don't you forget it," said Frank.

The ladies had not come prepared to stay the night, but Mrs. Laniston remembered that in going to New Helvetia in June she had left a steamer trunk here, after her European voyage, filled with heavier wear than would be needed before autumn. According to the accommodating methods of the hotel, it had been received and stored in the attic, and now it was brought down in the nick of time, to the delight of the young ladies, who hoped that it might contain something that they might borrow, in addition to the absolutely necessary paraphernalia for the night. As soon as Mrs. Laniston showed some natural disposition to defend her belongings from these unwarranted depredations, they became "possessed," as she expressed it, to see what she had in her trunk, and, having all the desire in the world to maintain her ascendency and her rights, she declared she would not turn the key until they promised that they would ask for nothing but the loan of a nightgown apiece.

When matters had reached this deadlock, she seated herself in a cane rocking-chair, her bunch of keys in her hand, and her eyes on the pansies that papered the bedroom wall. Both the girls, in the trim pleated skirts of their white linen suits, and their sheer shirt waists,—the two jackets had been folded and laid on one of the beds in the big, cool, clean room,—seemed exceedingly capable of rummaging exploits, and she compressed her lips with resolution as from the corner of her eyes she noted their movements, and their expectant gaze.

"Such fun, Aunt Dora, to try on something new."

"And something blue," murmured Ruth.

"Say, Aunt Dora," said Lucia, sparkling with incredible brilliancy and lustre of delighted anticipation, "do you suppose that little blue messaline waist of yours is in that trunk? I just live to try that shade! I don't want to risk buying anything in it till I can try it on. I believe it would be becoming to me."

"More so to me," said Ruth. "Anything blue suits my blond hair."

"Not that green cast—it throws green reflections on blond hair."

"Girls, this is cruel," said Mrs. Laniston, "to keep me cooped up in this close room, while there is such a fresh breeze on the verandah, and———"

"Mr. Jardine waiting to make love to you; I mean to tell papa." Ruth saucily laughed.

"You needn't stay here a minute, Aunt Dora. Just leave the keys, and go at once," said Lucia, with the eye of a bandit.

"I am fairly afraid to leave the trunk," Mrs. Laniston declared. "You are capable of opening it with a poker."

Lucia glanced around at the utensil as if this expedient had not occurred to her.

"Mr. Jardine must be waiting for you, girls," Mrs. Laniston admonished them.

"I know the reason you won't open the trunk before us, Aunt Dora. Because you are going to lend him and Frank some—some—petticoats! for the night—you know!"

Mrs. Laniston tried to look shocked.

"Lucia, I am surprised," she said.

"Why, I am only talking to you, Aunt Dora. I would not bring a blush to the antique cheek of Mr. Jardine for the world," she gravely protested.

"Much cheek as he has got," Ruth gurgled.

"As for Frank, his brazen athletics have made his cheek a permanent cardinal red, and he could not blush if he would."

Mrs. Laniston broke into an unwilling laugh.

"You two will be the death of me!"

"But what *will* Frank and the other gentleman do?" queried Frank's sister.

"My dear, you mustn't inquire into such matters. Frank told me they would furnish themselves at a clothier's here, where they have ready-made garments for sale."

"It may be indelicate," said Lucia, "but I would rather picture them arrayed in ready-made nightgowns, bought in the metropolis of Colbury, than standing stiffly up on end, dressed in their usual attire all night. It is more humane."

Mrs. Laniston burst out laughing.

"There!" she suddenly exclaimed, rising and starting to the door, throwing the bunch of keys on the floor. "I beg and pray you to let my things alone, and, if you rummage through them, you do so without my consent, that's all."

Her last glance into the room was not reassuring. The lid of the precious trunk was already lifted, and the two girls on their knees before it were diving into its contents, shouldering each other in their eagerness, their countenances alight with keen curiosity and greedy expectancy of novelty.

Mrs. Laniston gave a sketch of their employment when she joined Jardine and Frank on the verandah outside the door of the large parlour. They had drawn forth a wicker rocking-chair for her from that apartment, and here, quietly and safely ensconced, she watched the evidences of storm to the east, as she swayed to and fro, with devout thankfulness that they had escaped its fury.

"How lucky that we did not start half an hour ago," she said. "We should have been in the thick of it."

"I hope you didn't say so to those girls," cried Frank. "They will make it a reason to be behind time for ever more—the dangers they escaped by never being ready!"

A grey curtain of cloud had fallen over the familiar scene to the east. It was null, inexpressive, motionless. It cut off the field of vision. There was no trace of mountain forms, of intervenient valleys and coves. There might seem naught beyond—some prairie country, this, whose low horizon brought down the sky to a level with the plain. Only now and then on the impalpable nullity was a flicker of red fire; in irregular zigzag lines it pulsed, and once and again the thunders of the remote tempest shook the sunbeams here. The gay carnival crowds in the square heeded the storm that burst elsewhere as little as sunshine ever cares for shadow. The contrast reminded her, Mrs. Laniston said, of the indifference of the happy in the world to the sadness of others. Their storms are brewing in the clouded future, to burst sometime, but all unprescient and unsympathising they sport like small insects of the stinging varieties—gnats, and gadflies, and wasps—in the glamour of to-day. "I think happiness, prosperity, give a sense of superiority. No doubt sorrow and adversity discipline the heart and soul and temperament, and form and strengthen the character; but any of us would rather be inferior than perfected at such a cost to comfort. I think the world is less and less ambitious of realising in one's self high standards and spiritual elevation. People only care to be thought fortunate and envied, now—not to be noble, in spite of all that fate can do."

Mrs. Laniston loved to moralise after a fashion. Much feminine club life had liberated a certain facility of expression, and she was an ornament to the rostrum, for she had a good voice, a low-pitched contralto, and a very agreeable and distinct enunciation and intonation, which were natural endowments, but which sounded like the product of training. She had taken no pains to become an impressive speaker, but she rather liked the sense of superiority the reputation fostered, and she had fallen into the habit of analysing her impressions, and setting them in order.

"Gee! wouldn't I hate to have such a rum lot of reflections as all that, just because New Helvetia is getting it in the neck. My! did you see that flash!" said Frank.

"And wouldn't I hate to have such a 'rum lot' of expressions if I was entering my junior year at college, and expected to compete for the medal for oratory," his mother retorted.

Jardine laughed. "Slang is more and more incorporated into the language every year," he said.

"Yes," she assented, "and it is used by a class of persons who were formerly far more exacting. It seems to be considered to impart a sort of rude strength to phraseology, and a shade of meaning otherwise impracticable. It affects to be hearty, and downright, and candid. Whereas it is nothing but slipshod, and out-at-elbows, and a slovenly expression of down-at-heel ideas—sometimes lack of ideas. I think there ought to be some reform, some united action on the part of people who appreciate the art of conversation, the fit phrasing of thoughts of value."

"The Federation of Women's Clubs might get on to it," Frank suggested.

His mother went on without noticing him.

"In fact, Mr. Jardine, all the standards are down. Now, when I was young—it has not been so very many years—it was the extreme of uncouthness for a lady to swing her arms in walking. At present they swing *both* arms, if you please, as if these adjuncts were propellers, and to and fro they work their progress thus along the street, instead of walking naturally and gracefully. I thought for a time that this was a peculiarity of college towns, and of the athletic craze; but you see everywhere the poor wretch, swinging all loose from the shoulder. I have told my girls that I will not tolerate this gaucherie—they try to do it from perversity—but happily they can't remember it always. Then the young men are not

161

more elegant. Things, in the similitude of gentlemen, *whistle* upon the streets!"

"Conscience stricken!" said Frank, with a grimace.

"I don't mean that for you, dear," said his mother. "I should have to feel much more fit than I do to-day to tackle your long list of enormities."

This was as an aside, an interlude. She had a sudden perception of another phase of the subject, and forthwith entered upon it.

"Then, this lack of standard is obvious in matters of far more importance—it enters the domestic circle. I suppose no one ever found housekeeping very great fun, but in my young days nobody ever protested. There may have been shirks, but they hid their misdeeds. Now, there is a clamour of open detestation of all domestic concerns. It began with the caterer; in old times one's own establishment was competent to furnish the refreshments of every entertainment—to have cakes baked or ices frozen out of one's own house would be a confession of being beyond one's depth, and of seeking to entertain more elaborately and making more pretensions than one was entitled to sustain. A household valued its reputation for fine dinners, and elaborate refreshments at dancing parties; people even had specialties that you saw nowhere else, and were sometimes grudging of receipts, and kept some choice concoctions a dead secret. To have additional waiters hired for the occasion—unless indeed it were a ball—was unheard of in houses of good style. Then, when the caterer was fairly established, the expense accounts came in and cut down the menu——"

"Till it got down to the delectable cup of tea and the midget sandwich, with an appetising baby ribbon round its tum-tum," interpolated Frank.

162

"Be still, Francis. In old times every article must be perfection—the heads of families would be bowed in shame if aught were amiss with cooking or service—but now it is all the caterer's affair, even the decorations—sometimes actually the china."

Mr. Jardine was fully ten years Mrs. Laniston's junior, but he was sufficiently retrospective, and his experience sufficiently extensive in days gone by, to make him interested in her animadversions on the present, and her theory of the superiority of the past. He was of a temperament older than his age, and he sympathised rather with the stately methods of yore than the less exacting fashions of the present day. Thus he found it no hardship to moralise on the signs of the times, with his cigar graciously permitted, and his eyes on the far-away storm, with an interlocutor intelligent enough to evolve and present subjects of sufficient interest to titillate his understanding, requiring no exertion on his part, and loquacious enough to discuss them with an ability which did not call for interference, or contradiction, or instruction from him. His was a facile acquiescence, and Mrs. Laniston, accustomed to talk for time, while some factional whips of one of her clubs awaited the appearance of dilatory voters, before a momentous question should be put to the arbitration of the majority, had by no means exhausted the suggestions the outlook presented to her discerning contemplation.

"Now here is another phase that appeals more directly to you than to me, Mr. Jardine. I will venture to say that in the last ten years, since your college days in fact, there has supervened a total change in the popular estimate of youth. Formerly in society it was the young man with the reputation for talent who was in the ascendant. Merely *rich* men had to stand back. You must have known intellectual young fellows who enjoyed all the prestige of achievement, a positive value, merely on the strength of their glowing promise of development. A man was said to be talented—this reputation lifted him into a prominence that naught else could compass. People spoke of him with respect. If a girl desired to marry a man of that sort, yet in college, or new to the bar, it was considered a safe thing even if he were poor—so sure he was to make his mark. Now-a-days they live a life apart as students; a career is not the focus of their regards. Their identity is compassed in their position as back-stop, or stop-gap———"

"Oh, hi!" interpolated Frank.

"———Or whatever it may be called in their insufferable jargon. A young man who goes to college to study, and who does it, is contemned as a grind. Such a thing as taking exercise for health merely in order to be able to study, to clear the brain—like a horseback ride, or a long walk—is antiquated. They exercise for the play—as if their playing days were not over; for the competition—the great children! My Frank there would rather lead the sprinters in the track team than win the medal for oratory———"

Frank did not deny this.

"———And he would be more envied and thought a better man than the medalist."

"If I don't get some sprinting training this fall, they'll shunt me off the track team," said Frank, his face falling with a sudden anxious monition.

"I perceive the same trait in the professions, Mr. Jardine. No longer do you see a politician pointed out as a close and powerful debater, or a lawyer as a cogent reasoner. Why, they used to make all manner of discriminations in a man's mental endowments. One was no lawyer, but a popular speaker—could carry a jury with him against both law and fact; another had no eloquence, nor appreciation of principles, but was grounded in case learning and precedent; another had a splendid choice of words, and a magnetic presence, and a gift of oratory—and the house would be crowded whenever he spoke. Now, they tell me a judge would virtually order such an orator to sit down—ask him to come to the point, or to be brief. They consider all this too flamboyant—spread-eagleism."

"There does seem a great change in recent years," said Jardine, ceasing his thoughtful puffing of his cigar, taking it out of his mouth and looking critically at its ash; "there are now no world-famous orators, very few politicians of real parts, rarely indeed a statesman; the notable lawyers are mostly old men of other days, of other traditions."

"And yet," said Mrs. Laniston, admirably capable of presenting the antithesis, "though imagination, æstheticism, hero-worship, ambition, all the aspirations are dead, this is pre-eminently the age of the fake and the blatherskite. People are capable of credulity, but not of credence. They are superstitious, but they have no faith. The 'isms' of any fantastic sort will flourish, and the churches are empty. The adoption of queer creeds, of fake cures, of quack medicines, of dangerous beautifiers, of impossible methods of learning, of absurd processes of art and illustration, of fantastic devices in edibles would abash the pretended miracle workers of the Middle Ages. You can scarcely buy a yard of genuine goods or a pound of unadulterated food. People don't care for reading as they once did; the art of conversation is dead; nobody writes letters any more—your friends send you souvenir postcards."

She fanned silently a few moments, her delicate, diamonded hand all the more dainty for the simulation of a man's shirtsleeve and cuff, which her plaited linen blouse affected, her eyes fixed on the panorama of storm on the horizon while the air here was so suave that the grey-streaked curls on her brow did not stir with the motion of her rocking. She suddenly resumed, interested in another branch of the subject.

"Instead of the solid business of education, that ought to be as solemn as prayer, the acquisition of knowledge and the mental training for the battle of life being held up as a great opportunity and privilege for the young, it is made attractive, alluring, easy; the fakers have found that royal road to learning. I was dismayed when I had got Lucia and Ruth beyond the geography, and spelling, and arithmetic phase. I said to them, 'Now, if you don't want to learn anything further, you can stay at home, but every day that you do stay at home you shall sew—plain sewing—from morning till night.' Mr. Laniston said I ought to be prosecuted for cruelty to animals. But they developed into quite hard students. They balked just enough to get a bowing acquaintance with needle and thimble. I had my way—I hate half measures. They know what they do know, thoroughly. I can't tolerate incompetence. Unless a thing is excellent in its way I can make no terms with it, no allowance because of partiality or affection. Now, Mr. Laniston loves music, and he knows something about it. But he would sit and listen, with all the delight in life, to Ruth as she bleated out of time and tune— the poor child has no voice and no taste—her talent is for painting. But I stopped that. I said, 'Because her lispings please *you*, she shan't make a show of herself.' And I stopped the lessons. Lucia is altogether different, a fine voice and a fine ear, but she can't draw a straight line. So she had every musical advantage, and I saw to it that she availed herself of them. We had many a battle royal. 'The sons of harmony came to cuffs,'" she quoted, with a laugh.

The accession of Mr. Jardine's interest was so apparent when Mrs. Laniston spoke of Lucia that she might have been tempted to continue the subject, for she made a point of

166

deserving her reputation as an agreeable woman, had not the young lady in question suddenly issued from the door of the hotel. Her cousin Ruth was following, and, after a glance of inquiry, they smilingly took their way along the verandah toward the door of the ladies' parlour, where the party sat. The eyes of both were intently fixed on Mrs. Laniston, as if in anticipation of some effect, she scarcely knew what. Suddenly she remembered the plundered trunk, left defenceless at their mercy. Mr. Jardine was devoutly grateful that they had seen fit to remove their hats. He was priggish, even old-fashioned in certain persuasions, and the sight of a young lady at table, on the verandah, at the piano, all day, in a hat, was at variance with his taste. He had no idea that the hats had disappeared because of an incongruity with adjuncts, very lately assumed, of the white dresses. The jacket of Lucia's gown had been laid aside, and she now wore, in lieu of the plain white linen blouse, one of fine white Irish lace. It had dainty elbow sleeves (Mrs. Laniston still conserved a plump arm). It had a belt, a stock collar, and at each elbow a knot of delicately tinted ribbons of a sea-shell pink, with rainbow stripes of faint blue, brown, fawn, and a thread of red. Nothing could have better accorded with the fair, fresh complexion, the brown hair, in a luxuriant pompadour roll, half crushed down on one side of the forehead, the long, romantic, dark grey eyes, with their drooping black lashes. He could not imagine why they should be received in such cold silence by this woman, with her evident motherly doting on them both. Ruth was a bit the more showy; she had confiscated a bolero of alternate lace insertion and lilac ribbon, and she had found a lilac ribbon for her blond hair. Mrs. Laniston had a moment of wonder as to where that blue messaline waist could be— certainly it had not been in that trunk! Since she remained silent, Mr. Jardine's manner was marked with an accession of humorous cordiality as he rose and placed chairs for the two.

"And what are the commands of your ladyship for this evening?" he said, looking admiringly at Lucia.

"The Ferris Wheel, of course!" she exclaimed, with enthusiasm.

He could have fallen on the spot. He had ignored the Ferris Wheel, and he had rested supine in the fatuous conviction that she had forgotten it. He was indescribably tired of the street fair. Its inanities would have been insupportable to a man of his type in its best estate, but hampered with the thousand sensitive points that beset the escort of a lady in an amusement utterly beneath her pretensions and custom, so remote from her comprehension that she was as if on another planet, made heavy draughts on his amiability, his endurance, even his *savoir faire*. He hardly knew how to meet the unprecedented problem it presented in the interest of his fair charges. If he had had his way neither should have shown her face in so motley a throng. But he was exacting, a bit old-fashioned, and had not even Mrs. Laniston's philosophy that would give them a little line in matters of scant importance that she might more easily curb them when circumstances required this. They would soon tire of a harmless folly, but a monotony of dulness could not be maintained. The prospect of further experiences of the street fair strained the tension of his equanimity almost to the breaking point. He could scarcely endure the thought how nearly they had escaped it all; a little more—but for the causeless delay of their preparations—and the "hack," with its strong, fleet horses would have been at the door. To be sure it would have whirled them into the midst of the mountain storm, but the thought of wind and lightning, thunder and torrents of rain was less abhorrent to him at that moment than the recurrence of the trials of the "show."

"Oh, yes, indeed!" Ruth chimed in. "How glad I am we couldn't get off—we would have missed the ride on the Ferris Wheel, the cream of the whole correspondence."

It was a relief when he discovered that they had no intention of sallying forth for that enjoyment until after the early supper of the little hostelry. There was a possibility that something might occur in the interval—rain, wind, earthquake, he hardly cared, so keen, so nettling was his irritation, and his desire to obstruct their fell purpose, to keep them within doors, decorously spending the evening in conversation with their own exclusive party, or, so long as the little blue parlour remained open for the general use of the guests of the hotel, a quiet game of bridge, in its quasi retirement. Mrs. Laniston and he were often partners at this delectable pastime, and the two girls delighted to combine their science, luck, even chicanery, against them. The delay restored his equanimity for the nonce, but his look of annoyance had been so palpable that Mrs. Laniston thought a remonstrance in order, when she could speak aside to one of the young ladies.

"I wouldn't insist on the Ferris Wheel," she said to Lucia, as they walked through the ladies' parlour; the verandah had become unpleasantly crowded; the evening intermission had supervened at the fair; the wickets were closed; the lamps were not yet lighted, and the sunset glow was dulling into twilight. However removed from the normal estate of mankind, the living skeleton and the fat lady must eat, rest a bit, quench their thirst, and sigh against the ridicule of Fate. It was one of the unadvertised features of the show, considered amusing or pathetic according to the individual temperament of the spectator, that the fat lady, who, poor soul, had not her nerves under the best control, burst into tears, ever and anon, and her mountain of flesh shook and trembled with sobs. She had an æsthetic mind, and was

169

sensitive to ridicule and the wonderment of the crowd, and would fain have been beautiful and admired rather than have filled her purse with gold. She needed a respite to bathe her eyes and readjust her tawdry finery, and hearken to the consolations of her attendant. The boa constrictor, gorged, had coiled up, and was lost in the torpor of digestion and the recuperation of sleep. The spielers had cast aside their horns; one or two were in the drug store, busy in swallowing the unpalatable vaseline for their throats; the Ferris Wheel was empty and still for the nonce; the rural visitors of the more prosperous class who could sustain the added expense of the hotel, detained also by the storm in the mountains, were trooping up the steps and sauntering along the verandah. Their ladies were ensconced in numbers in the rocking chairs of the large parlour. It had occurred to Jardine that the garden walks were probably solitary and attractive at this hour, and he suggested repairing thither. As the party emerged into the fragrant flowery paths, Mrs. Laniston continued her aside to her niece.

"I fancy Mr. Jardine considers the Ferris Wheel undignified."

"There is no question of dignity about it," said Lucia coldly. "It is the simple amusement of a simple little fair. If we see fit to break the monotony of our detention at New Helvetia by visiting a countryside *fête*, new to our experience, and so far interesting, and by participating in such a degree as pleases us, it is not an appropriate subject for his criticism."

Mrs. Laniston was struck with the justice of this observation. "But don't be too independent," she admonished the young lady, for Mr. Jardine was a very good match from a worldly point of view.

"I do not need his assistance to preserve my dignity," she retorted. Thus she walked on with her head held very high, and an added stateliness of carriage that comported well with her fine height and her slender, willowy figure.

170

The sunset glow was still reddening among the dark, luxuriant shrubs. In the few locust trees the wreaths of honeysuckle vines, that clambered up to the lowest boughs and festooned the space from one to another, were in the fall blooming—all the world was pervaded with that sweet reminiscent fragrance of spring. There were late roses, too, of an old-fashioned kind, pink and white, and one, "the giant of battles," had dark-red velvet petals, and an odour as of an exquisite distillation of all the hoarded sweetness and sunshine of summer; it furnished a rich note of colour to Lucia's brown hair, where it clung with its thorns and leaves with as artless an effect as if it had been blown thither by the breeze, coming more freshly now from the dusky reaches of the east. The sky was still perceptibly a faint blue, but here and there the crystalline scintillation of a white star trembled, and the red was fast dying out of the west. As the party, two by two, paced slowly along the pleached alleys, Jardine became aware of a change in Lucia's manner toward him. In one instant every other consideration was annulled. With absent, reflective eyes he meditated for a moment, fumbling mentally for the cause. Then, with the quickened divination of a lover, he surmised the betrayal of his disaffection, and Mrs. Laniston's politic admonition. He did not realise that she prudently considered his eligibility, but only that she feared that it might not prove agreeable to go about pleasuring in a humble way with an escort who openly scorned the simple diversion. Despite Mrs. Laniston's bland graciousness, he was indignant that she should have interfered. His fastidiousness had fallen from him as if he had never entertained so finicky a disdain, as it seemed to him now. Rather than displease Lucia, than incur her resentment, he would have taken a turn on Ixion's wheel— the safe and healthful revolution of the monster circumference glimpsed over the hotel roof was, indeed, a minute sacrifice to afford her the girlish fun, the simple

171

pleasure she found, like a child, in simple things. It was her unspoiled taste, he now said to himself, her fund of good humour, her indulgent, uncritical attitude toward the humble folk, that could forbear ridicule, and share their pleasure in little things—all added a grace to her metropolitan experience, her travel, her culture; she saw good in everything, because she saw the reflection of her own warm heart, and her own pure mind.

Jardine was not unskilled in casuistry. It would have been his instinct to cast himself on his knees at her feet, and beg her forgiveness, if so much as the glance of his eye had offended her, but he knew that confession fixes the fault in mind, and a fault that is condoned is not so obliterated as one that is, in effect, denied. There are some affronts that will not be expunged by pardon. To be tired of her amusement, to question her dignity, to repine at escorting her wherever she might list to go, to scorn the subject that interested her—he would not throw himself on her generosity with this score against him. He would annul, disavow, disprove the impression. He suddenly turned, as he walked slowly along with Mrs. Laniston, and, standing in the path, impeding the progress of the two young ladies, he looked straight at Lucia with warning eyes.

"Now, I don't want to say anything disagreeable," he cast down his glance at the dial of his watch which he held in his hand, "but that wind from the east is freshening very considerably. It may bring rain, and you two may risk your ride in the Ferris Wheel if you postpone any preparations you may have to make till after supper."

He was quick enough where his interests were concerned. He caught a swift upbraiding glance that flashed from Lucia's eyes to those of Mrs. Laniston, who looked embarrassed.

"Why, you are not complimentary," cried Ruth. "Don't you see we are already bedizened to the best of our ability."

"Won't you need your hats?"

Having worn them when they were so little appropriate, surely, he thought, they would not sally forth without them to ride in that queer, uplifted procession of passengers in the Ferris Wheel, as if they had dressed for the occasion.

"No, indeed, we *can't* wear them," cried Ruth. "They are not suited for lace; we are wearing lace, and they are embroidered."

She looked at her mother with such arch audacity that Mrs. Laniston could scarcely refrain from giving her a box on the ear.

"I was in hopes they had forgotten that miserable Ferris Wheel," said Mrs. Laniston, turning toward Jardine.

"Oh, why?" he exclaimed disingenuously. "Let them exhaust the attractions of the fair."

"Well, since you will kindly look after them," Mrs. Laniston's craft matched his own, "I have no inclination, myself, for the 'wild wheel, that lowers the proud.'"

"Oh, that is Fortune's wheel; this is Ferris's wheel—altogether a different make; warranted no vicissitudes," cried Lucia, all her gay self again, and Jardine drew a breath of relief, for he felt that he had made a very narrow escape of encountering her resentment.

Perhaps he doubted that the Ferris Wheel was exempt from the vicissitudes of the wheel of fortune, for, shortly after the conclusion of supper, he hurried them out upon the verandah, saying that the wind was rising and he would not risk them on the machine if its force should increase.

CHAPTER XI

Clotilda Pinnott had not been very definitely sensitive to the dull disfavour with which the public had received hitherto her song-and-dance. In her own mind she accorded it scarcely more appreciation. She perceived, of course, that the other artists enjoyed a boisterous enthusiasm of applause, the snake-eater, the winged lady, the high diver, and their confrères, but their meed of praise seemed but just, since the merits of their respective turns were so great in her primitive estimation. Singing and dancing in her rustic garb were but everyday matters, and she sustained no great mortification that her turn should be regarded with scant interest. She had not lost her relish for the performance, however; the praise that Lloyd accorded it was sweet in her ears, though she secretly thought him a fool to care for such folly. It brought him near to her the only moments in the day when he had been accessible. And this had been both a surprise and a grief; she could only see him at a distance, coming and going, absorbed with a thousand anxious details, she knew not what, nor wherefore; she had fancied that at the street fair he would be continually at her side, for the love of the beauty of that face and form he extolled so enthusiastically, that joy in the endowment of voice and motion he had found so poetic. Only a few moments before the turn did he appear, stepping lightly on the stage behind the drawn curtain, his hat on the back of his head, his face, of which she dimly appreciated the beauty of contour and chiselling, hot and moist, flushed and a bit anxious; giving a word of direction here and there to the "supes," charged with the management of the simple scene; critically surveying her as she stood ready for the rising of the curtain. He always spoke gently to her; she vaguely realised that he was sharply disappointed by the public reception of the attraction, and that he sympathised with her in the downfall

174

of her presumable hopes. She cared for naught else, when his eyes kindled as he surveyed her in the rising glow of the lime light.

"You're a peach!" he would exclaim, "and don't you forget it! The fools out there don't know their heads from a hole in the ground!"

The joy of his approbation surged through her whole being as she looked shyly at him while he stood at gaze, his hands in his pockets, and his hat on the back of his head. Her cheeks blazed under the rouge, laid on for the broad effects of the lime-light; her eyes shone with a radiance that embellished and vitalised her youthful beauty; she trembled from head to foot in a quiver of humble adoration, of gratified vanity, of the ecstasy of loving and believing herself beloved. Once he noticed her agitation.

"I thought you were going to pull through without a touch of stage fright," he said casually. "Don't think of the house—soon over."

"Reg'lar buck ager," Tom Pinnott remarked. One or another, sometimes several of the Pinnott men made a point of being present at the performance, and there were persons at the street fair unsophisticated enough to believe that it was the discovery of the Thespian genius in their household, and their pride and solicitude in her achievements, that had brought the Pinnott family as a unit down from their mountain fastnesses to attend the fair. But these credulous wights hailed from the furthest coves, and had never indeed heard that whisky could be procured by any means save by placing in a designated hollow tree a jug, with a half dollar mortised into a corn-cob stopper, and after an interval returning to find the money absorbed and the jug gurgling with tipsy delight. That the ardent could be found in a store or a saloon, or dispensed at a lunch stand was an idea that, unassisted, could never have entered their minds.

175

"Fust time," continued Tom Pinnott vivaciously, "I ever tuk sight at a buck running on a deer path, by a stand, my finger shuk so on the trigger, an' my aim war so contrarious that the bullet glanced out to the middle of the ruver, an' the beastis war humpin' hisself along so fast that he beat it thar, an' it tuk him right a-hint the ear, and killed him. Left ear, 'twar."

"Skiddoo!" said Lloyd, laughing slightly at this veracious chronicle. "Clear the stage! The public is too well used to liars to want to hear you. Now, Heart's Delight! listen for the orchestra, and mind you go on at the third beat of the fourth measure, or you'll get thrown out. Count! Count!"

On this immemorial day, when in the storm of applause that thundered upon her disappearance and clamoured for her return, she stood in the little nook that served as wings, stunned, stolidly surprised, overwhelmed, forgetful of all she had been taught to observe for this contingency, she did not shiver, nor tremble, nor sob half hysterically, till he found her there.

"What did I tell you?" he exclaimed, elated, full of pride in the success of the unique attraction he had devised. But she apprehended a reproach.

"I furgot—I furgot! An', oh, I'd ruther die than spite you so! Lis'n—lis'n——" as the gusts of applause came with a roar. "They sound like painters an' wolves of a stormy night in the woods."

"I told you they'd catch on! I told you how 'twould be. Now look out. The third beat of the fourth bar—count—count—now go'n!"

When, still recalled, and she was to go on for her simple bow of thanks, she cared naught for the audience; she saw only him, the man who had found her fair and gifted, had opened vistas of undreamed-of splendours, and had brought an

176

undiscovered world to her feet; she saw not the world, only him, and the pleasure in his eyes, and the pride and success to which she had ministered.

It was indeed a strange transition for the mountain girl, whose vicissitudes had been hitherto the incidents of the wood-pile and the cow pen. Perhaps only the physical freshness and vigour appurtenant to a life so stagnantly calm enabled her to sustain now the strenuous rush of sudden excitement. She felt more sensibly the dull reaction when all was at an end for the day. Lloyd had quickly left the tent when the experiment in photography was concluded, and the party from New Helvetia had returned to the hotel. Clotilda, looking after him with a keen jealous pang, was surprised and somehow consoled to perceive that he had not followed them thither. A check on the inrush of pride and gratification in her heart had ensued on the appearance of the two young ladies with the camera; but he had indifferently gone his way, and they had retraced their footsteps. Gradually as she slowly strolled along the road leading out of town and toward the encampment of the family, these two fluttering, flouncing white butterflies were less insistently in her mind than the details of her own great triumph, so tardily, so hardly won. "Heart's Delight!"—he had never before called her this and it seemed so apt, so dear a phrase; that it was slang, and absolutely without meaning, never occurred to her for a minute. She felt a great glow of satisfaction. How she had justified his faith in her—his admiration of her talents, her beauty and grace. The echo of the applause—no longer suggestive of the howling of wolves—sounded anew in sweetest flattery through the spaces of memory. Those elegant strangers, the sojourners of New Helvetia Springs, were as naught before the crowd in comparison with her, the central figure, dancing to dulcet music on the stage, all illumined with a burnished golden glow. Her lips curled as she remembered the sudden pang of jealous prescience she had experienced—so fair they were, so daintily bedight, holding themselves with such delicate hauteur and distance, embodying a superiority which she could not imagine and only vaguely felt. But how should she fear a contrast with aught? She remembered his descriptive phrases, not one of which she understood, but they were words of poesy and music on his lips, applied in enthusiastic admiration of her. An oread she was now, fresh from unimagined heights; and now a dryad, escaped from a tree; and once more the most ethereal bacchante that ever wreathed a vine. She conned them again and again as she strolled on. Sometimes she lifted shining, happy eyes to the river, red with the sunset, and here and there white with foam where a half-submerged boulder or a ledge of rock broke the currents into silver. Sunset lingered along the mountain tops and she hardly needed to mend her pace to be sure to reach the encampment before dark. Nevertheless, she looked sharply about her now and then, with vague apprehension. She met few wayfarers, now making their way into town; most of the inebriates, prominent last evening at the street fair, were sobered by this time, and the effects of strong liquor would not again be apparent until later. There was an interregnum in the sway of the Bacchus of the "moonshine." She could not formulate the uneasiness that possessed her, and once again she resolutely turned her mind to the recollection of her triumph, the manager's delight, the poetic justice that had so amply overtaken the cavillers who had derided and belittled the stunt. And still— suddenly she turned and looked behind her. It was an instinct, nothing more; the vigilance of an unnamed, causeless fear. The long red clay road stretched out here straight by the riverside for nearly a quarter of a mile. Silent, still it was, overhung on either hand by the heavily foliaged boughs of great forest trees. A waggon that had passed her a moment since was yet creaking its lumbering course toward the town, and the odour of tar on the hubs was discernible on the soft air. Nearer was the solitary figure of a pedestrian, an old man, to judge by the thick stick with which he supported his steps. At the distance she only noted the long grey coat and a limp broad-brimmed white hat. Turning, reassured, she walked on, conscious of the suave air, redolent of the scent of the forest, the freshness of the river and the pungency of the mint and water-side weeds; a bird—it was a thrush—was singing in the drooping boughs of a great beech; a star was whitely scintillating in the blue sky, seen in the space limited by the tops of the rows of tall trees on either side of the avenue. Suddenly a step sounded just behind her and a hand fell on her arm.

The scream on her lips was framed only in dumb show; her voice was paralysed by sudden terror. It was hardly annulled when her wondering gaze recognised the face—the young eyes under the flapping brim of the old white wool hat; the alert, trig, young mountaineer in the semblance of a slovenly, unkempt, hirpling old vagrant. There was something very sinister in the metamorphosis, and it may be doubted if ever heretofore she had heard of a man in disguise, still less found occasion to discern the traits of the fraud. She gazed with a fascinated horror at him, her cheeks blanched, her white lips still trembling, her eyes dilated and wildly shifting.

"I tole ye ez how I'd see you uns at the Fair, Puddin' Pie," Eugene Binley said, essaying a smile, but it was rather a grimace, for his mood was rancorous. He was ill at ease, too, agitated, suspicious, ever and anon looking over his shoulder, as if he feared an unheralded approach.

"But ye said *I* wouldn't see you uns," she gasped, finding it still difficult to breathe. "And," she spoke slowly and significantly, "I wisht I hadn't—I wisht I hadn't."

The solemnity of her voice evidently increased his discomposure. But he laughed in a husky, raucous undertone—a sarcastic, unpleasant laugh.

"Ye'd feel freer to go flyin' round with a strange man, ye never heard tell on, ef ye 'lowed thar warn't an eye spyin' on ye."

She flushed indignantly. "I ain't been flyin' roun' with no men. An' I'll take Tom ter witness ter it," she said defiantly. Five brothers are a small standing army, if occasion should require. She was ashamed of the threat, and even more ashamed of him, as she noted its salutary effect. There was a distinct change of policy in his tone; he would avoid recourse to disparaging insinuation.

"Wa-al, what hev ye been doin'?" he demanded, and quickly again glanced around.

"Dancin' an' singin'—what I kem fur," she replied sullenly.

"And, oh, Lord, what a fool ye let them showmen make o' you uns," he groaned. "I wuz ter the tent an' seen ye—an' my sakes! I blushed ter the soles o' my boots fur ye!"

Her face flushed. "Let go my arm," she said in parenthesis.

He released his hold and stood in his old man attitude, leaning on his stick and looking at her with those dismaying young eyes that had a strangely daunting effect in their incongruity, like some frightful thing in a dream, trivial and all devoid of terror to the waking sense.

"If you uns hed been ter the tent terday," she continued, "ye mought hev saved some o' them blushes fur yer own misdoin's—ye need 'em." And she tossed her head with a bitter smile.

"Gosh, gal—warn't I thar! I sot right in front o' them town gals an' men from New Helveshy an' hearn 'em plottin' an'

180

plannin' ter make a puffeck laughin' stock o' you uns, by clappin' an' stampin' an' makin' a c'mmotion, ez ef ye war doin' wonders. My cracky, Clotildy, what ails ye not ter sense that thar couldn't be sech a power o' diff'unce 'twixt terday an' yistiddy. Ain't the turn, as ye calls it, the same?"

Her satisfaction suddenly wilted. The logic of his proposition appealed to her solid sense. It was indeed a sudden, causeless, and most radical change. Her heart sank; her nerves, strong, normal, unstrained as they were, vibrated under this heavy stress; the tears welled up suddenly into her beautiful eyes, a moment ago so happy and lucently clear. Was the ovation indeed a burlesque, a scheme to try her foolish capacity for vainglory to the utmost; she remembered with a keen pain at the heart a certain light tinge of satire in the tone and manner of the young lady they called Ruth.

Then she remembered Lloyd, and his satisfaction.

"Wa-al—ef they all wuz ter make game o' hit, an' me, till they draps dead, every one, I'd think 'twar smart an' fine an' a good turn, kase that thar showman tole me so, an' I b'lieve him, every word."

He looked at her intently for a moment, as if he was minded to wring her neck, and canvassed within himself how to most effectively lay hold. Then he flung back his head with his mouth open in the dumb show of laughing extravagantly, the youthful demonstration seeming a great lapse from the personality of the old man, causing her to step back with a gesture of repellent distrust. She recognised him perfectly, yet she was constrained to look at him as at something uncouth, uncanny, strange.

"Wa-al, that's one o' the dernedest enjyments the town air gittin' out'n the street fair—the way that man makes you uns puffawm, 'lowin' ye air doin' so fine, an' till terday they didn't hev the heart ter jine in makin' game o' you uns."

Again that stricken look on her face—the facts so bore out the semblance of the interpretation his malignity had devised. And of herself she had no art to judge. It seemed indeed to her a slight thing to so arouse enthusiasm, ardour—the humble sporting beneath the orchard tree. But even against her own conviction she could not doubt Lloyd.

"He hev gin his word on it, an' it air a true word. An' I b'lieve him."

Binley was raging inwardly, but he controlled the surging tempest for a time. He could hardly have mastered his emotions in a good cause, but enmity prevailed mightily within him. And he loved the girl in his way, and jealousy consumed him like a fire.

"When a gal wants ter be fooled, it's powerful easy ter make a lie seem like the truth," he moralised. "Look hyar, Clotildy; every woman that man hires, but you uns, air dressed up finer than a fiddle, the flying lady, an' the fat lady, an' all. But ye dances in yer shabby old everyday clothes! Lord, child, they talked all over town an' the cove bout'n it."

Again the cogent reasoning, the recurrent shock to her faith! And this she knew was the fact, for Lloyd himself had come to the camp and detailed the gossip; had expressed the doubt he had, lest his ardour for the fitness of the rustic turn had rendered her liable to criticism.

Still she believed in Lloyd against the confirmation of her own knowledge. "I know that man ain't a liar," she averred. "He's good an' he's true. He wouldn't fool a—a—frawg! He hev gin his word, an' I b'lieves him. Ef 'tain't a good stunt it's kase he dunno what a good stunt air."

There was a momentary silence of tremendous import to him. Both felt that the forces of the crisis were accumulated to an outburst.

"Look-a-hyar, Clotildy," he said in a low, tense voice, "you uns hev done fell in love with that thar showman." He brought out the asseveration with the force of an accusation.

It was not maidenly, and she blushed for the scandalous candour which she felt an admission involved, but she had contended and refuted and denied till the unwonted mental exertion had taxed her endurance—she was glad to be rid of sophisms—to stand on plain fact.

"Yes, I be in love with him, ef that's what you want to know," she said.

"But ye air promised ter me!"

"That war afore I seen him," she declared.

"An' ye'll keep that promise, by Gawd," he vociferated, "else that thar showman'll find out what sorter stunt the trigger o' my pistol can do."

The significance of the threat steadied her nerves and roused her flagging faculties. This was a desperate man. By blood already his hand was stained. In the rude experiences of the primitive mountain folk she knew that often one such crime was followed by another, a sort of desperate precedent rendering facile the consecutive deeds, till here and there a man could be found proud of his record of slain foes, the deeds, more or less foul and unprovoked. The law was slow; the place was remote; time wrought continual changes; and at length public sentiment accepted the criminal and in a measure condoned the crime—as if, when matters went awry, another murder might be expected as one of his little peculiarities.

She cared for naught now but to divert Binley's mind, to regain her sway, such as it was, to obliterate her confession of love for the showman. She broke out laughing suddenly with so natural a tone that it might have passed for genuine mirth with any but a jealous lover.

"Wa-al, sir, Eujeemes Binley!" she exclaimed—at the mention of his name in her clear, vibrant young voice he glanced apprehensively over his shoulder, reminding her of the cause he had to seek and to maintain disguise—"ye air too easy fooled yerself ter be laffin' at me fur bein' made game of. Do you reckon ef I was in love with the showman I'd bleat it out like that!"

In his turn logic played a deceptive part. But for his ever-vigilant jealousy he might have been convinced.

"That thar showman ain't never said a word o' love ter me,"—she noted the incredulity in his face,—"barrin' complimints on the stunt, an' sech. I ain't goin' ter dance fur nothin'—got ter hev sa-aft sawder from the public, or somebody."

Still he was silent, standing in the middle of the red clay road, leaning on his stick like an old man, with his fiery young eyes looking up at her from under the flapping brim of his old white hat.

"But that don't mean I be in love with you uns, Eujeemes," she said severely. "I ain't thinkin' much o' you uns, like I uster do. I be in no wise pleased with you uns."

He was doubtful; influenced, but not overcome.

"I dunno why," he said sullenly.

"Kase ye 'lowed ter me whenst we uns fust took ter courtin' ez when ye killed that man ye shot 'twar plumb desperation—else he'd hev killed you uns in another minit."

The crisis, the emergency had sharpened her wits. Heretofore he could never bear unmoved a reference to this incident, that had changed all the currents of his life. She noted that he did not wince now. Her heart sank as she drew the obvious conclusion—he was no longer sensitive to the imputation of crime, the terror of conscience. He only lowered at her and stolidly listened.

"You used ter say you even wisht it had been you uns, 'stead o' him; it was jest an accident you got the drap on him fust."

His silence was inexpressive; he waited the application of these reminiscences.

"Ye useter say ye war no hardened crim'nal; ye acted in self-defence, as the law allows."

He did not even nod his head in acquiescence. He silently stared at her, as she stood very definitely outlined against a thicket of young willows on the bank, in the soft evening glow which was so golden on the river, so deep a daffodil tint in the sky, that she might have suggested to a cultivated imagination some bit of emblazonment or brilliant enamel painting, in her saffron gown and red petticoat, and with her rich auburn hair piled high on her delicate head. She had not the great clusters of fruits, for these were daily renewed, but now she plucked at the artistic draped folds of the yellow skirt in nervous embarrassment, keeping silence as a great hooded waggon rolled by, coming into town, laden with a farmer's household, frantic to see the fair, and reaching their journey's end with the dusk. The passengers looked curiously at the ill-assorted pair as they jolted past, but the team consisted of two strong mules who mended their pace as they approached town and fodder, and they were soon dwindling in the distance.

"You uns useter say ye was so sure ye war clear o' the sin o' murder in the sight o' God an' the eye o' the law that ye war

185

willin' ter leave it ter men—ef only ye could be sure they'd act fair by ye!"

Still he awaited the gist of her recollections.

"An' I believed ye—else I'd never hev allowed ye ter talk love ter me. I know some folks see a differ in brawlin' an' slayin', an' ain't keerin' fur sech. But ter my mind blood is hard ter wash out."

"I dunno what you uns is drivin' at?" he said at last, goaded to seek to stimulate the climax.

"Ye'd know mighty well, ef yer mind warn't so perverted. They war lies ye tole me. Ye shot a man in a quar'l, for puer spite; an' hyar ye air ready ter shoot another fur puer spite with no quar'l. Ye hev got a crim'nal heart an' a bloodstained hand, an' they will never be jined with mine on no weddin' day, that we uns useter look to see in the good time comin'."

She tossed her head resolutely more than once as she sounded this knell to his hopes, but her dilated eyes were fixed eagerly upon him, as if she doubted the policy of so stringent a measure. She knew the man even better than she had thought. He stood unsteadily, shifting his weight from one to the other of the great slit boots he wore on his shapely feet; he hesitated, fumbling dully for a protest, while his thoughts evidently reviewed the successive reminders which had culminated in this untoward declaration.

"Ye knowed all the facts whenst ye promised ter marry me, Clotildy," he reproached her. "I never hid nuthin'."

"Ye couldn't hide it; the talk o' the mountings, like the buzzards o' the air, war a-peckin' an' a-circling 'bout yer crime. A body jes' needs ter look out'n the winder to know suthin's foul an' rotten, an' that's death an' a bad deed."

His eyes shrank from meeting her stern gaze.

"I dunno what ails you uns ter go ter railin' at me that-a-way, Clotildy. I ain't no wuss'n I was whenst ye promised ter marry me, ef we could git yer dad ter agree ter it ennywise."

"I 'lowed the killin' war a plumb misfortin', an' no willin' fault. But hyar ye air, willin' ter dip yer hands in human blood the minit ye air crost—oh, the devil's grinnin' at ye from out his home in hell!"

She held up her hands at arms' length and drooped her head toward her shoulder, as if to evade the view of the frightful image she had suggested. He was insensibly, perhaps, more moved by her dramatic pose and the subtle influence of her agitation than repentance or fear or even credence in her crude personification of evil potency.

"'Twar jes' fur love o' you uns, Clotildy. I jes' said the word," he averred, quite conquered. His voice dropped to a dulcet cadence; his eyes plead with her.

"But ye meant the word; ye meant murder!" she shrilled out. "The deed was done in yer heart, a'ready—a'ready! Cain! Cain!"

"I swar it warn't, Clotildy," he urged vehemently, coming close to her. But she fended him off with both hands outstretched, with face averted, as she had evaded the grisly sight of the leering Satan she had limned in a word. His eagerness to recover her favour, his ardour, were redoubled by the obstacles she interposed. It was all that was left, to him,—so had his world narrowed,—hunted, proscribed, endangered, doomed as he was. He felt its value more in being thus dramatically snatched away from his grasp than if absence had dulled it, or it had grown chill in the lapse of time. He was moved to protest, to clutch at it anew, to stay the ethereal winged joy before it might rise beyond his reach.

"I swear ter you I was jes' talkin' ter be a-talk-in'," he declared. "I never meant him harm. I—I——" he could

187

scarcely find words to frame the lie, so ready were his lips for threats and cursing at the very thought of his rival.

"The truth is far from yer heart," she declared. "Now, *now*, this minit, yer shootin' iron is in yer boot leg, an' it's loaded with every ca'tridge it can kerry."

She pointed down at his left foot, and its uneasy movement was like a confession of discovery.

"Why, Clotildy," he lowered his voice mysteriously, "that's kase I mought meet up with—" he glanced over his shoulder, as if expecting to view an apparition of far greater terror to his quaking senses than the materialised horror of the principle of evil—"the sher'ff, ye know———"

"No sech fool ez ter use it, ef ye did," she sneered. "Ye know ye'd only make matters worse."

"Then I mought meet some o' that man's kin," he suggested.

"Air you uns layin' fur 'em?" she asked, "an' they don't even live in the county."

"Naw—naw," he muttered, at a loss for a subterfuge.

"What did ye kem hyar fur, in them scarecrow clothes?" she gazed contemptuously at him, her disgust for their unkempt condition, their rags, their dirt, which was suggested rather than seen, delineated in high disdain in every feature of her face.

He was pitiably conscious of his unpicturesque plight, and yet he had been proud of the completeness and efficiency of his disguise.

"You uns know I couldn't come lookin' like myself, Clotildy, though I'd mighty nigh ruther be drowned 'n let you see me 'pear so—so—common."

His humility might have been expected to disarm her.

188

"You kem hyar never expectin' me ter view you uns," she said sternly. "I 'member yer words an' how secret ye looked whenst ye said 'em. Ye kem hyar ter spy on me an' him—an' ef ye 'lowed I liked him most, ye'd draw that shootin' iron out yer boot that ye loaded a-purpose. That's what ye kem hyar fur, lookin' like the scum o' the yearth—ez ye air."

He flushed to the roots of his hair, shame for his poor habiliments so mastered him. He felt all in fault that he had revealed himself. He had not that control of his faculties, the possession of the situation, the normal ascendency of the man's mind over the woman's that he would have grasped under any other circumstances. He had only acquainted her with the dangerous secret of his presence here; with his jealousy, and his fell determination of revenge for the heart reft from him; with the fact that he went armed in search of the sweet opportunities of vengeance; with the identity of the malefactor in the event of a deed of violence, of some mystery of disaster. And for what? To receive her faint-hearted denials of her fickle faith; to be rated and upbraided as never before had he heard her—heard any of the submissive mountain women—lift her voice in arraignment of a man's deeds; to have her deliberately take back her promise, or as an alternative dictate terms; he felt that some hard compact was in contemplation. Yet this was his only resource to retrieve his mistake in revealing his identity, and if her terms did not suit him he too could keep or break a bargain. Nevertheless he did not dream of the condition when he said:

"Clotildy, believe me fur wunst. I jes' kem ter see you uns, honey-sweet. I pined so fur the sight o' ye—the sound o' yer voice. I resked all—the sher'ff, the jail, the man's kin—all, ter kem ter view ye, as all mought—but me—hid out in the wilderness. Believe me fur wunst, sweetheart. I only said it bekase I love ye so."

189

She hesitated, he thought, in a relenting mood. She came close to him and laid her hand on his ragged coat sleeve. She gazed up into his eyes under the drooping hat brim.

"I will—I will believe you uns," she said, "ef ye will do one thing."

He looked a keen, eager inquiry.

"Take that loaded shootin' iron outn' yer boot leg, an' leave it hyar with me," she hissed between her set teeth.

It was little the demonstration of a languishing, love-sick girl, seeking to protect her lover's safety against his own impulsive imprudence. But her histrionic intuitions, great as they were, had yet their hampering limitations. She was a presentation, rather, of some warlike feminine spirit, a Bellona, who, having conquered in a hard fight, inexorably dictates the sacrifices of the capitulation.

For a moment, so taken by surprise he was, he could find no words for answer. Then he broke out with oaths so crowding on his tongue that his utterance was for a time but an inarticulate mouthing of profanity.

Still close beside him she eyed him threateningly. "I hed hoped never ter lay my tongue ter sech a word," she declared, her eyelids narrowing. "But ef ye won't abide by my proof I'll believe the wust o' ye. I'll b'lieve ye threatened him in dead earnest. An' I'll gin the word who ye air to the sher'ff afore that star draps a-hint the rim o' the mountings." She lifted her eyes to the lucent splendours of the evening star, just slipping from a roseate haze to the tips of the firs darkly cut and finial-like against the clear horizon. Then once more she gazed sternly at him.

He cast one furtive glance up and down the vacant road. Then he stooped and drew a long glittering weapon from the leg of his shapeless boot, pulled high over his baggy trousers. But he did not place it in the hand she held out eagerly. His eyes blazed with a light far more dangerous than the stern, steady, menacing gleam of hers, for it was the intemperate rage of a jealous lover, of a desperate gamester, losing all on the turn of the dice, of a duped and overreached schemer. He had hardly space for a step before him, to be taken of his own free will; he was driven, hounded, pursued, brought to bay.

"I'd be justified ter shoot ye dead, hyar in the road, Clotildy, an' before Gawd, I'll do it," she heard him gasp.

The dusk was deepening about them. She could scarcely discern the expression of his face, but she could see that it shone with thick drops of moisture that had sprung from every pore; he was in a cold sweat of excitement; his hand trembled as he held the weapon. There was a moment of intense suspense; the low rune of the river sounded its rhythmic measures through the solitude; the mighty forests did not stir, save once there came that strange, long-drawn breath, the sylvan sigh of the dreaming woods. A bat on noiseless wing went by with its sudden, shrill, mouse-like cry, as it almost brushed against the two still, silent figures; the star dropped down out of sight. Then she heard the metallic click once and again as the hammer of the pistol was drawn to full cock.

"Say yer pray'rs, gal," he hissed. "Before Gawd, ye hev goaded me ter this! Say yer pray'rs!"

She saw the weapon flash in his hand; there hardly seemed so much reserve of light in all the landscape, with the blurred sheen of the river, and the cloister pallor of the pure, aloof sky, and the deep glooms of the encompassing woods. "Say yer pray'rs," he growled again.

She could hardly imagine such terror as possessed her; her heart had dissolved; her hands, her feet were numb; her brain seemed as if paralysed; the roof of her mouth was dry and her stiff tongue clove to it; to her it was as if other lips framed the words, but she noted the thick falter of the voice when she said in tones near to tears:

"God will purtect me, 'thout waitin' ter be asked. The spar's don't pray, an' he heeds thar fall. But 'tain't the time fur prar'r now, nor murder, nuther. Ye dassent shoot me, Eujeemes Binley—it's too nigh the camp on one side, an the town on t'other. The crack of your pistol would help my blood to cry from the yearth till the neighbours, ez would roam the woods this night, would git ye fast an' sure by the scruff of yer neck. Hurt me, ef you dare! Ever'body would know who done the deed—an' why!"

The words seemed inspired, so definitely they broke the power of the threat. She was not helpless; she was not alone. That infinitely potent and turbulent force, the rage of a roused community, that she had prefigured as her avenger, terrified him as no other possibility might. He had skulked from the deliberate law, and from the busy officers, charged with its many behests, but he could never evade the neighbours, when every man was ready to usurp the functions of justice and the appointed minister of vengeance in the feuds of the community. He began to realise his precipitancy; the noose was drawing about his own neck. He regretted infinitely his outbreak; his ill-considered, intemperate threats against Lloyd; could he not have worked his will without even revealing his presence here? The man could have been shot in a crowd as if by accident, presumably by some silly, drunken lout among the spectators, or even by the accidental discharge of a weapon, he argued within himself. His alibi could have been easy to prove by the Pinnotts, themselves, if indeed his agency could have been suspected, for they had left him in the cave in the mountain, afraid, because of his previous troubles, to come

192

to the Fair. Some less obvious fate might have been devised for the interloper—something that would better perplex and disconcert investigation. He had relied too implicitly on his hold on this girl's heart; he had loved her with too confiding a devotion. But since he had lost her—yet perchance with this inter-meddler out of the way she might turn anew to him, as of yore—he would not sacrifice himself gratuitously.

He suddenly broke into a hollow, raucous peal of laughter, so at variance with his look, his attitude, his threats, that the girl nervously set both hands against her ears to shut out the sinister dissonance.

"Lawk-a-day, Clotildy," he mocked at her, "yer head is in an' about turned with yer play-actin', an' song an' dance, an' stunts, an' sech. I'm jes' a-funnin', seein' ez how I kin play-act, an' do stunts, an' sech, too. Toler'ble well, I reckon, seein' ez ye thunk the demonstration war genuyine. I wouldn't git myself tangled up in a snarl with shootin' that thar showman fur ten dozen sech flimsy leetle cattle ez you uns. An' I wouldn't harm a hair o' yer head fur a whole county o' sech ez him. Ye hev got a right ter a ch'ice 'mongst men. Make it ter suit yerse'f. Gawd knows I don't want no gal ez ain't powerful glad ter git me. I kem ter the Fair kase I war so dad-burned lonesome in the mountings, an' I war sure ez nobody would know me in this hyar rig—all the old clothes I could find in yer dad's roof-room. But you uns 'pear ter be a toler'ble long-headed leetle trick, an' I do b'lieve I be safer 'thout the pistol, like ye say, than with it. Hyar, take it—take it—ef ye want it! Wait—it's full cocked." His face changed visibly, even in the dusk, at this evidence of the deadliness of his pretended jocosity. "Thar now, it's half cocked. But handle it keer-ful, an' keep it out o' sight. Ef enny war ter ask ye whar ye got it 'pears like 'twould be a toler'ble awkward lie ye would hev ter tell!"

The revulsion of feeling, her astonishment at this sudden change, the amazing transition from mortal terror to the assurance of safety, so overwhelmed her faculties that for a moment in the reaction she was not far from fainting. She seemed more overwrought than in the instant of the immediate expectation of death. She leaned back against the bole of the great beech tree above her head; she was glad to brace her feet against the projecting roots; her face was white in the dusk; she could even feel the cold as the chill quivers ran over it. Yet never did she lose the grasp upon the pistol. She felt as if she had the whole earth in her hands, so dominant was her sense of power. Not for a moment did she credit her scheming lover's protest of innocent intention—he had meant to slyly, treacherously kill the man, and now it was impossible. He could not with his bare hands slay the stalwart athlete; he could not buy a weapon, he had neither the money, nor the courage to dare the suspicion this might provoke; he could not borrow it, for who would trust aught of value to so irresponsible an old vagrant as he seemed. Lloyd was safe, and she felt a sudden revivifying joy in the fact that it was she who had saved him.

There is no more invincible persuasion in the mind of a man than the overestimate of his hold on a woman's affection. With Lloyd out of the way, Binley argued, she would soon forget the showman, and her old lover would easily find his place anew.

"'Member, Dumplin'," he said with a tender intonation, odious now to her sensitive nerves, "ye promised ye'd b'lieve me ef I'd leave the shootin' iron. I kem hyar fur nuthin on yearth, precious dear, but ter see yer sweet eyes, an' kiss the hem o' yer frock."

He reached out his hand as if to lay hold on a plait of the draped skirt, but she shrank back in disgust and repulsion.

194

"Don't—don't," she said sharply. Then, to mask her aversion, "Somebody's kemin' now. Thar will be travellers soon, to an' fro to the town, an' it'll be remarked how long I stood hyar talkin' ter a ole rag'muffin. Somebody might suspect 'twould be more natchural ef he war a peart lookin' young man. 'Twould be better ef we war ter part."

She began to walk slowly along—she was languid, feeble—holding the pistol hidden in a fold of her dress.

"Time's slow, till I see you agin, Honey-sweet," he called after her, as he stood and watched her progress in the chasm-like rift the red clay road made in the midst of the dense forest.

"Time's forever, till I see you agin," she declared. Her gait suddenly gathered speed, and she fled like a deer, like the wind through the shadows, and was lost in their midst.

He stood, his face still looking toward the spot where she had disappeared, even after the iteration of the impact of her swift feet upon the ground had ceased to sound. He was silent as he listened, but at length he turned with a contemptuous laugh that yet partook of the characteristics of a malignant snarl. He shook his head to and fro with the prophetic triumph of an unspoken thought. Then he began to retrace his way toward the town, and though there were none to observe him, he leaned heavily on his thick stick, after the manner of an old man, walking with one step longer than the other, apparently feebler in one limb. He kept his head bowed as he approached Colbury, only now and then lifting it to gaze out from beneath the flapping brim of the old white hat, as the town gradually came into view, nestled—as it were—in the heart of the great hills. They loomed darkly, indistinguishably, above it at this hour, and the grey and purple mists were vaguely visible, outlining ravines. The courthouse tower arose with an impressive architectural effect in the dim night. Stars in the vague sky

195

struck indefinite glimmers from the long shining steeples of the churches. Below trees interposed, but he could discern a sort of halo of illumination among the roofs that was the exponent of the kindling lights heralding the evening attractions of the Street Fair.

CHAPTER XII

The lights of the Street Carnival were all broadly a-flare in the purple dusk when the Laniston party once more issued forth into the square. The stars, now in scintillating myriads, shone white from a remote and richly dark sky; across it in tattered fragments thin tawny clouds were flying before the wind, stragglers from the routed armies of the storm. The young moon, golden as it tended toward the west, but with a vague, veiling, pearly tissue, illumined the upper atmosphere and showed even the bending of the tree tops of the nearest forests as they crouched before the blast. There was a suggestion of solemnity, of silence, of the great latent forces of nature, of the unresponsive, insoluble problems of creation when one glanced off to that benighted landscape under the voiceless moon. But the sordid purlieus of the little square rang with the spielers' solicitations, the hucksters' cries, the wild clatter of the merry-go-round, whizzing gaily to the music of the band,—every saddle was bestridden; every chariot was occupied with the philandering rural youth, who saw no incongruity in being obliged to shout soft nothings to each other amidst the grinding of the machinery, the blare of the band and the clamour of voices as loud as their own. The Flying Lady was a-wing in her tent, its outer aspect suggesting a great illuminated mushroom; and from a similar semblance close at hand issued the heart-rending howls of Wick-Zoo, that made many a rustic shiver now with fascinated fear, and with reminiscent horror at every casual recollection far away in his mountain home for six months to come. At every turn was this glow of canvas, the lamps within shining through the translucent fabric, and threading their way amongst these tents Mr. Jardine and his two fair young charges came presently to the base of the frame of the great wheel, its periphery reaching high up above all the glare and sound, the glow of its infrequent electric bulbs seeming to enstar the dim purple dusk.

The wind had freshened considerably, but it was no deterrent to those who would fain try the revolution, for only three of the settees were now vacant, and while the earlier comers were poised, gently swinging high in mid-air, the obliging custodian of the monster was affably ready to receive the price of admission and accommodate as many passengers as could find places. The contrivance had long been a trite feature at all shows and street fairs and pleasure grounds catering to the amusement of the humbler populace, but to Mr. Jardine, who did not frequent entertainments of this description, it was as astounding a novelty as to any backwoods denizen of Persimmon Cove. Its method of operation was of course obvious at the first glance, but he asked several questions of its custodian as he stood with the young ladies at the wicket below and passed in the price for its giddy pleasure, and if he had not been thus occupied he might have been pleased to observe that while they were submitted to the critical gaze of the jostling crowd, arrayed with so special a daintiness, their jaunty bravado wilted a trifle and their ready laughter had frozen into an icy dignity of demeanour. It might seem difficult for a lady in an Irish lace blouse and a crisp white linen skirt, determined on an ascent in a Ferris Wheel in a rough country crowd, to maintain the aloof, pale hauteur of a princess, but Lucia's aspect in the light of the sparse electric bulbs and the flickering torches was calculated to thus impress all privileged to gaze upon her. There was a respectful silence pervading the crowd for a few moments after they had reached the spot, but the interests of self are predominant, and after a modicum of patience Mr. Jardine was unceremoniously urged.

"Does the wind affect the safety of the machine?" he asked solicitously, gazing aloft as well as he could through the slender steel spokes to where the topmost laden settees were swinging back and forth, seemingly with added impetus in the stiff breeze.

"Not at all, sir," said the functionary, as in a parenthesis, while he counted the change, "twenty-five, thirty, thirty-five."

"There is no danger?"

"Ef ye air afeard, old man, jes' stand back an' lemme git a chanct," a country youth admonished Mr. Jardine.

"Lord sakes, stranger, take yer place, an give we uns the next turn," an elderly mountaineer suggested.

"Them folks up thar air gittin' twict the wuth o' thar money in all this wasted time," a grudging soul opined. And the rest of the crowd pressed sensibly forward.

Jardine had never been so unceremoniously addressed since he was born. But the two young ladies, who laughed on such slight provocation, were enabled to preserve an impassive gravity now, which fact he observed with a feeling of grateful relief, for he was conscious of the ridiculous plight of his elegant personality. He went on with as deliberate a dignity as if he were aware of no interruption, albeit acutely conscious of a score of eyes eagerly fixed on his face.

"No danger of the wind obstructing the revolution, and preventing the descent of passengers?" he concluded his query.

"Not at all, sir—forty, forty-five, fifty, fifty-five—that's O. K.—I think you'll find your change correct, sir. Take this seat."

Jardine moved forward with a young lady on each arm—suddenly, as he was about to induct Lucia into the waiting settee, he stopped immovable—"Why," he exclaimed, addressing his charges, "where is Frank?"

The patience of the wheel-man was overstrained. He had collected the price of admission, and if Jardine did not care to make the ascent no money would be refunded. He was now keen to sell the passage in the last remaining settee.

"Take your places, sir, and let these gentlemen come forward," he said peremptorily.

But Jardine still looked over his shoulder and said again to the young ladies, "Where is Frank?"

"'Where, oh, where is good old Francis?'" sang a wag in the group. "'Safe in the Promised Land.'"

There was a guffaw of appreciation from the bystanders and it ameliorated for the moment the temper of the crowd, which had shown a nettlesome rancour. It was still pressing forward, and a dirty, horny hand offered over Jardine's shoulder the money for the same seats. "There air fower o' we uns—ef he won't ride let we uns go up?"

"Why," exclaimed Jardine wonderingly, still looking over his shoulder expectantly, "Frank promised to get some cigarettes at the hotel and then overtake us."

"Take your places, sir," the ticket-seller insisted. "I can't keep the wheel standing still all night while you collect your party."

At that moment a call came from above, and all gazing up through the barely seen spokes and fellies of the great wheel to where the loftiest chariots seemed to swing vaguely among the stars and the swift scud of brown and white clouds, perceived how the oscillation was increased by the atmospheric disturbance. The pause, too, had grown monotonous, the air was becoming cold, and one of the passengers summoned the official below to continue the revolution and bring the descent into progress.

"Take your places, sir, or I will give them to the next comer," declared the custodian of the wheel.

There was a scuffle in the crowd for the first opportunity. Jardine, but for very shame, would have yielded the places and relinquished the money, yet he could not allow his escort of the ladies to this coveted pleasure terminate so disastrously. How inefficient, he reflected, how superannuated he must seem to them, how preposterously he had contrived to mismanage this humble little outing on which they had set their whimsical hearts. How cordially he would have welcomed an opportunity to slaughter with his own hands the marplot Frank! How willingly he would have deprived him of the pleasure of making the ascent in this choice company by leaving the recreant and proceeding at once.

"But I can't," he said in perplexity. "We have taken two of the settees—four seats. One of the settees would be inadequately weighted with only one person—its balance would not be kept—it might not be safe. I must wait for the gentleman whom I expect every moment."

In vain the ticket-seller protested that the equilibrium of the settees did not depend upon the weight or number of the occupants. But the wind had now grown so chill that he looked up with anxiety and deprecation at the stationary wights high in the wheel, who were threatening to make complaints to the municipal authorities for their detention thus out of reason and against their will, and demanding an

200

immediate descent and release. Then he said, for he had a gift for expedients and was an excellent man of business:

"We can't wait no longer, sir. If you think the wheel ain't safe with only one passenger on the settee jes' let this gent take a seat alongside o' one of the ladies, and that will sure make the balance all right," and he summoned forward with a nod the wag who had chanted the inquiry concerning "the good old Francis."

He was a slightly built, common young fellow, arrayed in a cheap plaid suit, a steel watch chain, a straw hat, and he was chewing a straw as if it were his daily provender. He had a flat face, sandy hair, a good-natured small grey eye and no eyelashes to speak of. He stepped forward with nonchalant alacrity. He had evidently been selected as the most responsible looking person available, and the only reason that Jardine did not faint upon the spot was that his attention was stimulated by the sudden offer of a substitute even more distasteful to his prejudices.

"Do you think that with this wind more avoirdupois is necessary?" Lloyd's voice broke upon the air. He had come up during the discussion and was a witness of the speechless horror of Jardine, who might have involved himself in some unpleasant dilemma with the crowd had he declined, and who could not of course accept the expedient. "Well—it is up to the show folks to make these things satisfactory to the public as well as safe, and if the gentleman will consider me a sufficient makeweight I'll undertake to balance this settee."

He forthwith cut the Gordian knot and broke the deadlock by handing Lucia to the waiting settee with a grace as definite and a manner as gravely deferential as if the role of squire of dames were in continual rehearsal in his repertoire. He seated himself beside her before Jardine could protest, and as they swung off together into the air the next settee came within reach and there was no course left to Jardine but to assist Ruth to her place, and follow in the regular rotation of the wheel.

Jardine had never esteemed himself an elderly lover; in the conventional walks of life in the city of their respective homes there had seemed no disparity whatever in their ages. Now the variance in taste, in temperament, in the outlook at life, in the pursuit of excitement, in sheer endurance, was definitely asserted. The sensation, as the settees rose elastically with the revolution of the wheel, was nauseating to his well-conducted stomach. Then, as they paused and swung, pendulum-like, to and fro, while the lower seat was filled and other passengers were liberated, the posture, the situation was revolting to his priggish sense of dignity. He fairly dreaded the upper dizzy reaches of the circumference, and naught but the coercion of the circumstances could have constrained him to the ordeal. He maintained silence, however, remembering the rural fling "old man" and desiring to betray no sentiment of discomfort to the delighted Ruth, who sat beside him gurgling with gleeful laughter, and uttering little disconnected exclamations of half-feigned fear and a real sense of jeopardy.

When, rather than incur Lucia's anger, Jardine had lent himself to the absurd pleasuring, on which the two girls seemed bent, he had no conception of such a turn of circumstances as should relegate her to the care of another, a stranger, and of all people in the world, the manager of an itinerant show. He scarcely knew how he should face Mrs. Laniston after this signal demonstration of his incapacity to discharge so simple a duty as devolved upon him in the escort of the two young ladies—she could never be made to comprehend the pressure of the situation. He sought to comfort himself by the realisation that after all the wheel was but a public conveyance, and for a lady to sit beside a strange man in this vehicle was not a matter of more pronounced familiarity than in a street car or a railway train, an episode of daily occurrence. In this point of view the rural wag would have been more acceptable to his predilections than this extraordinarily handsome man, with the manners of a gentleman and the calling of a strolling faker. Lucia would never seem aware of the existence of the one, whereas the other had after a fashion been brought to her notice; they had asked of him the favour of photographing the dancing-girl, though as an excuse indeed for having been detected in surreptitiously photographing the manager. The two had on that occasion exchanged sundry formal observations, and it would be but natural that some conversation would ensue upon being brought thus accidentally into this renewal of association.

The wind blowing so freshly into their faces almost took away their breath, and now and again, hearing naught from the other couple, Jardine hastily glanced up at them, thinking that it was the gusts that annulled the sound of the exclamations, silvery and joyous, with which Lucia in this novel and coveted amusement must be regaling her incongruous companion as they rose together in their swing ever higher and higher toward the stars. But the electric bulbs showed her face very quiet and grave; her dress gleamed like "white samite, mystic, wonderful," against the purple dusk; she was silent and to his great gratification the manager sat beside her as uncommunicative as if he had been a part of the machine, essential to its utility, like one of the dummy horses of the merry-go-round. A very well-conducted young man, Jardine thought, with a fervent thanksgiving that matters were no worse. He had feared that the incongruity of a simulated flirtation with so inappropriate a subject, might attract her eager quest of amusement and her mirthful disposition to horrify and tease her aunt. He formulated an apology in his inner consciousness. He said to himself that he ought to have known her well enough to realise that her innate sense of propriety would conserve all the essential decorums, even in these circumstances so conducive to unconventionality.

But it was not a conventional observation that Lucia saw fit to address to the manager, as he still sat silent, and it surprised him beyond measure.

"Do you think this is a suitable business for you?" she asked, her manner stately and almost reproachful, her voice low but icy, her beautiful head turning slowly toward him, and the light of those magnetic eyes seeming to shine through his very soul.

Lloyd had not been silent from any realisation of the difference in their station, any humble acknowledgment of the superiority of her world. He could not speak, his heart beat so fast; his proximity to the goddess that she seemed abashed his every thought. Her beautiful dress, her dainty hands, the exquisite pose of her head, the soft flutter of her lovely hair in the wind, each made its own bewildering demand for homage. He was in the thrall of an appreciated bliss, so perfect, so unexpected that it almost overwhelmed him. He had never dreamed that he might be so near heaven as thus alone with her. And yet until to-day he had not known that she existed. He could scarcely realise that she could turn her head and look into his eyes and speak directly to him—it scarcely mattered what were the words. The day had been hard; the dangers that menaced him were great; the difficulties that pressed him down were heavy; and suddenly, in a moment, he was translated into elysium. Swinging so elastically in the wind—the medium of the air a purple dusk, the river molten silver in the moon where the reflection of the splendid cresset glanced upon it and the rest mystery, the mountains vast imposing barriers against all the sordid world beyond, the town but a bevy of flickering lights below, and above the pure white fires of the constant stars—they two were side by side, while she, the ideal loveliness, she spoke to him!

"Beg pardon," Lloyd said, catching at the necessity of reply.

"Do you think this is a suitable business for you?" she repeated.

He stared at her for a moment amazed, hardly comprehending. Then recovering himself he made an effort at appropriate rejoinder. "The business ought to be better of course," he said. Then he hesitated doubtfully. His heart could but expand toward her, though his sensitive nature must needs feel the topic intrusive. "You see—we were misinformed. A town of this size generally has an outlying population that makes up a toler'ble payin' crowd. We *are* playin' to very little money. Business is poor—and that's the truth——" he paused abruptly, for she had blushed so deeply in embarrassment that he felt that he was altogether beyond his depth.

"Oh, I don't mean the financial returns," she said, beginning to falter. She hardly knew, she said to herself, what she would be at. Why should she have fancied that this man would understand her—why should she upbraid him with a calling below his merits? Certainly she did not understand herself.

"Oh—beg pardon," he said, obviously confused, gazing searchingly at her in the electric light. Her face was pale, a trifle agitated, grave; her eyes—they looked immortal, they were from the beginning of the world, for all time to come— the beautiful eyes, with a thought—was it pity, was it sorrow, was it faith—what was it in their depths?

"I meant—I meant," she hesitated, realising that she must follow her suggestion through—that there was no opportunity for withdrawal, for recantation, "I meant that it seems that you ought to have a better kind of business."

"It is a mighty good business for the money that is in it—it is the best show for the investment that ever was under canvas," he protested with sudden fervour—he was loyal to the merits of his funny little show.

It was all out of the question, she felt now—one of her sudden mad impulses—but an explanation must needs come. She would not for the world decry the little exhibition, on which he had lavished such whole-souled labour and thought and eager solicitude. Besides she had her object which she could hardly interpret even to herself. Her lips curved suddenly in the sweet smile that was wont to embellish them; her eyes flashed with her ready laughter. He was looking eagerly, intently at her. But her ridicule was genial—she was laughing with him rather than at him. "I'm not saying a word against the greatest show on earth nor the high-dive artist, nor the snake-eater, nor the beautiful dancing oread; but I shall never see you again, and I thought I would tell you something that occurred to me to-day."

The swing moved gently to and fro; the wind came fresh and free and fluttered her white draperies; she gazed far off, far off amongst the purple mountains; in the valley beyond a foothill she could see a red spark of light, so high they were now, at the very summit of the circumference, the light from the hearthstone of some humble home. The golden moon still showed in a deep indentation of the horizon line. Mists hovered about the lofty domes of the range. The stars sparkled aloof in the dark blue sky.

Still he looked intently at her and her words came with difficulty: "Our party could not believe that you were the manager of this little show—not because it is a poor show, but—because—you—you seem different."

Oh, would the wheel never turn! What was she saying, and why—why—should she say it? What madness to be thus isolated between heaven and earth so that she must face out

206

to the end the inexorable statement that she had so foolishly begun.

His coolness somewhat reassured her. "Oh, you mean that I look above my business," he said quietly; "that is, this was the opinion of your party."

"Yes," she replied in grateful renewal of confidence, "Mr. Jardine said that you looked like a gentleman—according to his interpretation, of course, I mean."

"I hope, for his sake, that it is a just interpretation," he said with a constrained, inscrutable smile. "It works overtime, that word 'gentleman'!"

"So often I have heard of a hint shaping a life," she went on to explain her meaning more clearly; "I thought that if it should occur to you that others esteemed you capable of better things it might be an inspiration to you to achieve them."

"Much obliged to Mr. Jardine," he said equivocally.

"Your associates in the show are so accustomed to you and to themselves that probably they do not perceive the difference."

"Real or imaginary," he interpolated.

"So I thought I would tell you," she faltered, at a loss, now that the disclosure was at an end.

"Now, Lydy, I want to say one thing to you—and mind, this is straight goods—I thank you on the knees of my heart for what you have said and how you have said it. I make no mistake about that. But you are young, and maybe you don't know that it is a deal more important *how* a man does a thing than *what* it is that he does. I can think of worse things, in *my* interpretation of 'gentleman' than being a showman— a good showman, giving full value in exhibitions and entertainment for the money. Now, I wonder if Mr. Jardine ever thought of a lawyer, who neglects his clients' business 'cause he's lazy, or busy about his own affairs;—or a preacher, who does the Lord's job for the money he finds in it;—or a fortune-hunter who gets a rich wife to take him off his own hands;—or a politician who buys his popularity— all these are 'gentlemen' only in a superficial appraisement. Now, I'll tell you where Mr. Jardine's view ain't in it—he thinks because I'm put up in a sort o' ornamental case that I look like a gentleman—but the Living Skeleton, who is an educated man and right rich for a freak, but who ain't put up in any case at all scarcely, Mr. Jardine would never think of for a gentleman. It won't do to trust to externals—Mr. Jardine surprises me for a man of his large experience."

She gazed searchingly into his face for a moment. She could descry no lingering suspicion there that she had used Mr. Jardine's name as a stalking-horse over which to fire her own opinions. It was a delectable deceit, but she knew that he would have forgiven the liberty—poor Mr. Jardine!

"If ever I was to find a better trade, Lydy, I'd take it with psalms of thanksgiving. But until I do I ain't goin' to shirk the show because I look like a gentleman. The main stunt is to act like a gentleman, and I think we are all up against that."

A silvery voice called out in the night to Lucia, and looking backward toward Ruth and Jardine she saw that their swing was moving upward one degree, and that they had reached the very summit of the circumference. With the consequent descent of one degree in their turn Lucia and Lloyd were now on a lower level. There seemed no appreciable difference in the height, however, as they gazed over the landscape; the wind still rushed down from the mountain with a pungent odour of dank leaves and a fragrant moisture from where the rainfall had been heavy; the clouds still in broken ranks fled tumultuously across the enstarred sky; the

misty moon was slipping down behind the purple ranges—
the burnished rim was visible for another moment and then
was gone; the square was yet filled with people, and now and
then a wild, raucous yell or loud voices in drunken
altercation gave token that the mysterious inebriates were
again astonishing the streets of the dry town; several of the
tents were no longer illumined, the day's work being over
for the "freaks" and the flying lady; the merry-go-round had
ceased to whirl and whiz and the band was playing
sentimental airs on the grass in front of the courthouse.

As the swings of the great wheel swayed, gently pendulous,
in the breeze-filled purple night above the flaring orange-
tinted lights of the Carnival below everything seemed jovial,
contented—a successful day drawing serenely to a close.
Suddenly from the swing on a level with the manager's lofty
perch a missile shot through the air; it passed in a straight
line below the swing where Jardine and Ruth sat at the
summit of the circumference of the wheel, and whizzing, as
if flung from a sling, it struck Lloyd's head just behind the
ear and fell, a compact boulder, as large as a man's fist, on
the ground below.

Lloyd, bent half double by the force of the unexpected blow,
swayed forward, struggled violently to regain his place, lost
his balance, and like a thunderbolt fell from the swing, while
the frenzied pleasure-seekers, all safe enough, screamed in
sheer dismay at the sight.

It might have been far worse. To another man the fall from
such a height would have meant certain death, but with the
presence of mind and the trained strength and elasticity of
the professional acrobat, the showman mechanically
gathered renewed control of his muscles, caught at one of
the steel spokes that upheld the structure of the wheel, and
thus arresting the precipitancy of the descent turned a
somersault in mid-air, another and with still another came to

209

the ground amidst a tumult of shouting and applause from the crowd assembling from every side of the square.

They seized upon him instantly, noting his half-fainting condition, and carried him bodily to the corner drug store, where the prescriptionist hastily administered restoratives and medicated the wound in an inner room with the door locked, while awaiting the arrival of the physician. The manager was in no condition to be questioned, he stated to a policeman who was early on the scene.

With an augmented sense of the importance of the disaster the officer, the only one on duty in the small municipality, returned to the wheel with the intention of taking the names and addresses of all in the swings at the time of the attack.

There had been a panic amongst the occupants of the swings; loud and frantic shouts for liberation, for the turn of the wheel, had predominated even over the clamours below in the square. The wheel was as aversely regarded as if it had been the instrument of torture of old by the dizzy wights who clung to their places uttering frenzied appeals for release, for they feared indeed that there was a madman among them. In obedience to the reiterated cries for extrication from their plight the wheel had been revolved as rapidly as practicable, and although the order of precedence among the settees was retained, the position in the periphery at the time of the disaster could not be established, and it was now impossible to say whence had come the stone so quickly flung in the darkness during the rotation of the machine. A number of the swings had already been vacated as soon as the ground was reached, and the occupants of others, to evade testifying or suspicion, leaped out when at a safe distance from the earth and disappeared, mingling indiscriminately with the crowd. Jardine noticed how many of the settees passed by the wicket already empty as the revolving structure brought them within safe descent and he imperatively motioned to Lucia in advance to vacate the swing as soon as the pause at the ground made it possible. The occupant of the swing behind Jardine did not await the stoppage; he was a countryman in a long greyish coat and a wide white flapping hat, and he leaped to the ground in the shadow with a nimble temerity which Jardine thought altogether inconsistent with his slit boots as if bunions troubled his feet, his thick stick, his bent figure and hobbling gait as he made off through the shadows which the intense electric lights served to deepen about the stand. Once he turned and looked back and catching a far glimmer of the light on his half-obscured face he showed two rows of strong white teeth bared in a grin of extreme relish.

Haxon was on the scene in a few minutes, wild with anxiety and asking hither and thither how the disaster had happened. "Where's my partner—if my partner is killed we are all ruined," he declared.

For Lloyd had not divulged his plan of action to annul false suspicion and to evade the aspect of collusion with the moonshiners who had so craftily utilised the presence of the street fair to profitably pursue their illegal traffic.

Haxon showed so definite a determination of detection and reprisal that Jardine, gripping his charges each by the elbow, propelled them through the darkness toward the hotel, demanding through his set teeth by way of explaining his vehemence, "Do you two want to be witnesses in a police court?" But indeed, they were tractable enough as they sped as swiftly as he dared set the pace, that they might not seem in flight, through the half-deserted square, past the vacant hucksters' stands, the shadowy, lifeless tents, the vague equine figures of the merry-go-round, stiff and silent in the claro-obscuro, cutting across the courthouse yard and coming at last to the hotel verandah, almost vacant at this hour.

Lucia was so trembling, pale and shocked that he could not forbear saying, "I hope—I do hope, that this will be a lesson to you," when she burst out laughing; and when Ruth, scarcely less agitated, declared, "For my part I hope, I do hope that that handsome Mr. Lloyd is not killed," Lucia burst into tears.

CHAPTER XIII

Frank came in presently and joined the group, for until the hour for retiring they were monopolising the little blue reception room as a private parlour. He had encouraging news of Lloyd. "He's all right," Frank cheerily averred. "His head has got a lump on it as big as a hen's egg, and it aches to beat the band. The doctor says, though, it is not serious. The stone glanced aside, didn't hit him squarely. If it had he would have been a deader by now. Ought to have seen 'Captain Ollory of the Royal Navy' fairly blubber—he is a good-hearted old kid."

"But what was the motive of the attack?" Mrs. Laniston asked, enjoying every item of the sensation, without the jeopardy and the shock.

"Nobody can imagine," said Frank.

"Some intoxicated wretch," said Jardine disgustedly—he felt as if he would like to be disinfected, fumigated, because of the moral effluvia of such low company—he had never been in such a crowd before in his life.

"A drunken man can't sling a stone with a steady hand like that," said Frank. "I *did* hear," he added with a sudden after-thought,—"that old Shadrach Pinnott's son, Tom—who my informant said was as drunk as a 'fraish b'iled ow*el*,'—ain't that a lovely expression for a lovely state?—declared that the man who threw the stone was a lover of Tom's sister, Clotildy Pinnott—sweet name!—and was jealous of the manager fellow who had taught her to sing and dance in that dinky, dainty way. The manager is dead in love with her, too—so the discarded lover chews the rag, and holds the bag, and hurls the bolt."

Lucia, who had ceased her tears as she listened, pressing her handkerchief once and again to her eyes, as she was thrown, half reclining on one of the sofas, now began anew to sob nervously, and Jardine looked anxiously at Mrs. Laniston, as if commending the demonstration to her attention and ministrations. But Mrs. Laniston was eager for the news— she had had a dull evening at the hotel.

"Nefarious business," she commented.

"Of course," declared Frank. "Intent to commit murder. The man tried to kill Lloyd. If the manager hadn't been a ground-and-lofty-tumbler once in his career—he seems to have been some of everything—all 'round athlete—he couldn't have broken his fall by throwing somersaults—he would have been killed by the fall from such a height."

"But consider the frightful danger that Lucia was in, mamma," cried Ruth. "A little swerving to one side and the stone would have struck *her* head instead of his."

Frank's boyish red face grew grave and dismayed.

"Was the man in the settee beside Lucia?" he asked aghast, hearing this detail for the first time.

"But, for God's sake, don't mention it," said Mr. Jardine testily, rising from his chair and taking a nervous turn through the room. "If this miscreant should be captured and a trial ensue, it would be a most disagreeable, almost derogatory thing for her to have to give her testimony in

213

open court under these circumstances. Don't—
don't mention it."

"Certainly not," said Frank formally. "I shall bear your injunction in mind."

No one can so bitterly object to schooling as he who stands in need of it. In reality this phase of the possibilities had not occurred to the youth, and he fully appreciated the value of the warning. But he deprecated the tone, the possessory manner in which Mr. Jardine was playing the role of tutelary deity to the family. The interest of the subject, however, overpowered his rancour, and after a momentary pause he went on with an indignant sense of offended dignity. "But how in the name of all that is stylish did the manager of the Street Fair happen to be escorting Lucia?"

"Because," said Ruth, with a deep satirical bow and a manner of punctilious ceremony, "*you* were so polite as to decline to escort her."

"My child!" remonstrated Mrs. Laniston, aghast. Then turning to the delinquent, "Why, Francis—how is this?"

"Frank gave us the slip—he promised to meet us," Ruth with true sisterly candour was bent on fixing his remissness upon him.

"I would have given up the project," Mr. Jardine felt it incumbent on him to say. "But we had waited a good while and the crowd was very impatient; and when the manager proposed to take the place it was on the score of balancing the swing, and really it seemed a little too pointed and conscious to decline—the wheel being a public conveyance, so to speak."

"And besides, he didn't give you time—he didn't anticipate a refusal," said Ruth. "He selected Lucia in preference to me, thank goodness! I wonder that, when he was attacked, Lucia

214

did not fall out of the swing—it shook like a leaf in the wind."

"Francis should have been with you—I thought that was what you went out for—to escort your relatives," Mrs. Laniston fixed rebuking eyes on him.

"Oh, I did—I did," Frank's repentance was always most complete and disarming. He had no nettling reservation of justification. His square, rosy face was crestfallen and concerned. "I simply forgot! I stopped for some cigarettes at the cigar stand in the bar-room—or rather where the bar ought to be—and there were a lot of country fellows there, spinning yarns of bear-hunting and trapping wolves in the mountains—I stopped to listen—quaint characteristic stories—and I had no idea of how the time was passing. I am awfully sorry, Lucia. But my apologies do no good now."

"You needn't apologise," said Lucia good-naturedly, though she could not cease to sob as she spoke. "I was not in the least hurt—only considerably scared—and if you had joined us in time I should have missed the most sensational incident of my experience."

"It is not a little mortifying to me that I should have been the cause of it—and of your appearing in public on so conspicuous an occasion escorted so inappropriately, to say the least of it."

Frank was of the opinion that Jardine was in fault—he should have called the excursion off rather than consign Lucia to such escort. He should have brought the young ladies back to the hotel, if anything more were involved than their foolish, childish desire to swing in the big wheel. As Frank sat solemnly gazing at the toes of his white shoes, one hand on each knee, he was resolving that he would submit this view of the case to his mother as soon as he could have an audience with her free of Jardine's presence. It did not in

215

the slightest degree, he felt, mitigate his own remissness in failing to appear, but surely Jardine need not have carried out the plan at all and any hazards. And having satisfied his conscience to this extent he began to seek to minimise the most nettling and derogatory phases of the incident, as it personally concerned his relatives.

"I don't believe the point that he was acting as escort to Lucia will be brought out at all," he said. "I noticed in the drug store that when 'Captain Ollory' asked Lloyd how in h-h-heaven he happened to be in the Ferris Wheel he merely answered that he went to balance one of the swings which apparently was not sufficiently weighted to be satisfactory. And the matter seemed to pass."

Lucia drew herself into a sitting posture. The nervous shock she had undergone showed in her pallor and the dark circles under her eyes. Her dainty lace blouse, with its elbow sleeves revealing her fair, beautifully proportioned arms, the knots of faint-hued ribbon, her delicately arranged hair, all seemed incongruous with the piteous aspect of her tearful eyes and the pathetic downward droop of her lips.

"I think that was very considerate of him, especially in view of the state of his wound—don't you, Aunt Dora? He might easily have overlooked that point."

"Or he might not have appreciated it," Mrs. Laniston assented.

"Yes, he would appreciate it," said Frank, wagging his wise head. "I tell you now, that fellow is as delicate-minded as any girl. He has got very popular here too—the town folks were fairly gushing over him in the drug store. If that rascal were caught they'd make him squeak, you bet your life. He would see sights."

Mr. Jardine was not an imaginative man, but before his mental vision was a dull night scene of dusky purple atmosphere, veined about with white lights, and hirpling away in the shadow was the figure of a grey-coated old man, suddenly turning over his shoulder a malignant young face with a grin of glistening white teeth.

Jardine gave an abrupt start, for it was as if this recollection had become visible to others, when Frank, still sitting in his pondering attitude, a hand on either knee, and his florid face bent down, said without preamble—"I wonder if any of you noticed this afternoon at the 'high-class concert' a fellow with an old whitey-grey coat who looked in the back like an old man and had a young face, if you could catch a glimpse of it under the flapping brim of an old white hat."

"Yes, indeed," cried Ruth excitedly. "When I said the scene was merely a by-play and the real romance was when the manager had fallen in love with the girl he had trained so beautifully, this man, who was sitting in front of us, turned and looked straight into my eyes as if he would deny it—as if he could destroy me for the suggestion."

"I noticed that too," said Lucia. "That is what made me remember him when I saw him again to-night—in the same old whitey-grey coat and flapping white hat. He was in the wheel with us—in a swing alone—just behind you and Mr. Jardine."

"Ladies—ladies—let me beg of you—I must insist that you do not pursue this line of thought!" Jardine admonished them. "You do not want to convince yourselves, that your consciousness may convince others——" he paused dumbfounded. He was himself advancing the matter. He was formulating their conclusion, inchoate as yet—he was putting it into systematic words.

"Oh, Mr. Jardine," cried Ruth with the cadence of discovery, and rising to her feet, "*you* think that this man was the criminal—that it was a case of jealousy."

"No—no—that is precisely the impression I do not wish to give," Jardine protested. "I am sure I do not know, and I have no right to accuse or suspect anyone."

"Well, *I* know," declared Ruth recklessly; "the whole matter is as plain as a pike-staff. I saw a perfect inferno of wrath in his eyes when I said that the manager was in love with that beautiful mountain girl. And when we were photographing her I noticed that she looked at Mr. Lloyd with adoring eyes. He has taken her away from her mountain lover, and these primitive people have primitive reprisals. Mr. Lloyd has paid the penalty for his easy fascinations."

"Ruth, you must not run on so," Mrs. Laniston admonished her, after having listened with interest to the end of the cogent speculations. "For heaven's sake, how ill Lucia is looking," she broke off suddenly. "You are tired, Lucia; you need rest, my dear, after all these excitements. Come—we must say good-night." She rose rather wearily herself, and stood for a moment while the others reluctantly came to a standing posture and gathered themselves together in a group.

"It is really quite necessary that we should not put mere suspicions into words—very unpleasant consequences might ensue," Jardine ventured. He noted in the mirror over the mantelpiece how anxious, and patient, and sharpened was his face. He had already felt that his dignity had never been so seriously compromised as in the events of the day, but this possibility was of far more importance.

"You are very right, Mr. Jardine," Mrs. Laniston assented. Then turning to Ruth with an admonitory air, "Really, I think that we have had quite enough of undesirable publicity and sensation. You might presently find yourself swearing to your fancies in court. You must heed Mr. Jardine's very sensible warnings, for which *I* at least am much obliged. [Ruth wheeled about and made him a pretty little mirthful

218

bow of smiling acknowledgments.] You might actually swear a man's liberty away with your foolish impressions. This is a serious matter and you must rein your tongue."

"I am mute; I am mute," Ruth declared gaily, "and here is Lucia with not even a word to throw to—to Wick-Zoo."

"I can say good-night at least—and thank you very much, Mr. Jardine," Lucia remarked languidly. She was as pale, she seemed as fragile as the lace she wore. He accompanied them along the verandah to the foot of the staircase, and as their white draperies rustled up the flight into the shadowy dimness of the upper story he turned away with a practical anxious solicitude, characteristic of a husband or father rather than a lover, wondering if Mrs. Laniston realised the seriousness of a nervous shock, and if it would have been too intrusive to suggest calling in a physician to prescribe. This trend of thought led to the alternative of a stimulant rather than a drug. A glass of wine could do no harm, and he hurried to the office with the intention of sending up a bottle of the best that the town afforded with a plate of wafers or crackers of some delicate sort.

The duck-like clerk dashed his hopes with a single quack. "Dry town, Mr. Jardine," he reminded the guest jocosely.

Jardine remembered his brandy flask. He had left it, well filled, at New Helvetia.

"This is really a case of necessity," he said, and then checked himself abruptly. The circumstances of the nervous shock it would not be well to unnecessarily detail.

"Mrs. Laniston ill?" asked the clerk, drawing his visage into such an expression of respectful sympathy as might do homage to one of the valued patrons of the house. "Sorry, indeed. Would be glad to provide the stimulants. Interests of house prevent. Law strictly enforced. Sorry, indeed."

Then a sudden new thought seemed to strike him. "No law against tipping you a wink." He began to laugh very much. "I wouldn't tell such a thing to the young man, Frank—of course. Promising boy. Confide in your discretion. Distinguished stranger in town. Retiring disposition. Dispenses for a consideration. Holds forth in seclusion. Best of reasons. Follow the first tipsy hill-billy you see. Meet up with something. Surprise you. Purest liquor in the world. Absolutely unadulterated." The duck smacked his bill together and quacked forth a laugh of the most wicked relish.

As a matter of curiosity Jardine had been given the opportunity more than once at New Helvetia to sample certain spirits said to issue from no bonded still. There hung about this beverage a wholesome home-made flavour, or perhaps its extraordinary strength and its colourless limpidity imparted a persuasion of its purity. He was easily convinced of the value of the commodity, but he only doubtfully thanked the clerk and walked forth on the verandah, his ardour very definitely quenched.

He had made for Lucia Laniston this day sacrifices of inclination and conviction altogether disproportioned to the trivial matters that had constrained them. He would not have believed himself capable of so much self-abnegation as they had involved. He could have done greater things that were in accord with his tastes, his habits, his sense of the appropriate, with far less strain upon his generosity. It seemed to him now that he had indeed reached the limit. To be recommended to sally forth to seek a moonshiner's lair!—he was amazed and affronted that the clerk should have ventured such a suggestion. Then he reflected that he had said that it was a case of necessity, and not even the drug stores were privileged to keep the ardent stuff for medical purposes.

It was indeed a case of necessity, he said to himself, remembering the transparent pallor of Lucia's face, the nerveless flaccidity of her cold little hand as he had held it in his grasp for one moment in the good-night leave-takings. He loved her in a plain, home-like, hearty fashion. He would have been constant himself, and unreceptive to little variations of sentiment in her; he would not have entertained captious and suspicious theories as to minutiæ of tone and word and manner; he would not have sought unhappiness in analysing his own affection and the degree of responsive warmth it awakened had she once accepted his devotion and promised her love in return. He would have believed placidly in her and continued altogether confident in himself. He was solicitous for her well-being, her health, her happiness in a reasonable sense. Had he been sure of her heart, her approval of himself, he would not have hesitated to deny her all the fantastic follies that had no real value as amusement and that had served to make the day a nettling penance to him, as it should have been to any other sane being. But any valid pleasure, any opportunity of worldly advantage, any cultivated and appropriate enjoyment—he would have strained every nerve to afford her these. The idea that she was neglected, that her aunt did not realise the shock she had endured, that she was suffering for aught that he could procure and he alone—he clapped his correct hat on his priggish head and started out into the night.

It was dank and cool; the winds were still astir in the upper atmosphere, for the clouds raced continually athwart the densely enstarred sky. The town, stretching away in straggling streets along the hillside, was dark save for the lamps at regular intervals; here and there an upper window shone above shrubbery and vines, the chamber of some late patron of the Street Fair or perchance a sick-room. The square was almost deserted; the business houses were dark, presenting the blank front of their shutters to the passer-by; only the drug store was yet alight and groups of loiterers congregated here, more than one exhibiting the unsteady footsteps in which the hotel clerk had recommended his patron to walk for the nonce.

These wavering steps set a languid pace along the quiet country road for a considerable distance. Trees grew close on either hand but there were few dwellings; they were dark and silent, with one exception where a frantically barking dog dragged a block and chain around a dooryard, unaccustomed to be thus accoutred by night, and possibly restrained to avoid harassing the unusual number of harmless wayfarers along the highroad. The stars gave sufficient light to show the direction of the thoroughfare and the eccentric gait of the guide whom Jardine had elected to follow. There was a footbridge visible spanning the river; many a broken stellular reflection flashed from the dark, lustrous surface, and the foam of the rapids was assertively white in the claro-obscuro. Jardine had a sense of anxiety lest the feet of the "hill-billy" in advance were too unsteady to carry him safely across the narrow structure. But he presently descried him meandering cheerfully along on the sit, he had paused and clung fearfully to the hand-further side, although at one point, when in tran-rail, and cried aloud in thick, drunken accents that he was falling—he was a goner—he was a goner!—"Tell Polly Ann how I died—how I died—how I died!"———All the solemn rocks and all the impressive dark solitudes echoed and re-echoed the serio-comic mandate, till even after Jardine had crossed he noted a crag that was still rehearsing the words as if in conscious mimicry.

There seemed no goal to this night jaunt, and Mr. Jardine was beginning to feel a fool in his own estimation—a catastrophe he dreaded, for he was fain to think well of himself—when he met two or three hilarious, roaring wights coming townward singing with more uproarious mirth than melody—"A leetle mo' cider, too, an' a leetle mo' cider, too."

He was glad of the darkness that precluded their notice, as they passed, that he was of a different type from that proclaimed by their accent. But as he turned a sudden curve of the road obscurity no longer protected him. He must have been instantly visible even at the distance in the flaring fires of an encampment which sent far-reaching red pulsations through the woods and across the dark waters of the river. A dozen torch standards, after the manner of the lights of the street fair, showed rude tables whereon barbecued meats, salt-rising breads, and home-made cakes and pies were dispensed at prices which no doubt undercut the charges for such refreshments in the town. There were two barrels, brazenly displayed, placed close together with a small plank, shelf-like, from one to the other, holding glasses and a big blue pitcher. In the background was a stanch waggon, of which the white canvas hood was no mean shelter from the weather had one needed it; two or three of the dogs were now asleep on the straw beneath it. An old woman, a younger one, with an infant in arms, and a girl of eighteen, perhaps, grouped about the fire gave a touch of domesticity to the scene. Naught could seem further removed from the suggestion of law-breaking and defiance of vested authority. An eating-stand at a distance from the town, to escape the municipal tax on a lunch counter, and yet catch the country custom, to make some small profits on the occasion and see the Carnival—what more candid? Jardine felt pierced through and through with the vigilance of the eyes focussed upon him as he advanced in the light. And never was there more virtuous indignation expressed in voice and manner than was shown by an elderly man with a bushy red beard and a pale stolid face and a brown jeans suit, standing at the refreshment counter, as Jardine came up and proffered his request.

"Brandy—or whisky? why, stranger, we ain't sellin' whisky and brandy. It's agin the Fed'ral law 'thout ye air able to pay a tax and hire a spy to watch you. And it's agin the town law, bein' a dry town. We uns hev got a good supper cooked an' some powerful ch'ice apple cider hyar though. We uns got a fine orcherd in good bearin' this year, but we wouldn't even sell a bottle o' cider—we sell by the drink—thar ain't no money in it cept' by the drink."

And when Jardine had declined this refreshment the old woman beside the fire rose and came forward and earnestly essayed to sell him one of the home-made baskets. She was most voluble as she recommended her wares. "They ain't no cur'ous baskets like them Injuns make over ter Qualla-town, stranger," she said. "They ain't no quare shape with some kind o' spell in the weavin'they tell me that *them* baskets kin be read like a book by them ez hev got the key o' the braid. But I ain't one as would want some onholy witch-like savage saying ter be in use round my fireside, a-repeatin' a spell or a curse on me an' mine ever' time it was handled in the light. Now, hyar is a reg'lar, homefolks, sanctified, Christian basket, ez don't mean nuthin' but a quarter of a dollar. That's all the magic there is about it. It's good and solid and roomy, stranger, an' yer lady would find it so convenient to hold chips around the hearthstone. Try it, stranger—jes' twenty-five cents."

Jardine was ashamed to refuse altogether any expenditure of money and presently he was trudging along the road to Colbury with the basket in his hand and a fund of information as to the ingenious methods in which the moonshiners were successfully defying the Federal law. Had he been known to the distillers, or perhaps had he merely demanded a drink he would have been served with the brush whisky in one of the primitive gourds, since the evidence must needs have gone down his throat at the stand, and few men would have sought the informer's reward at the risk of the informer's fate on the testimony of a recollected flavour, which is hardly proof in any court. That the two barrels indeed contained cider was obvious by the fragrance—the more fiery liquor was in some secret receptacle not so easily seen and seized, secured perhaps when the moonshiner turned back to the spring, which he did more than once to rinse the gourds in the waters of its branch.

Despite the appearance of an invincible security, however, Jardine was forcibly reminded of the pitcher that goes to the well; he saw clearly in the future the inevitable consequences of the extreme daring of the old moonshiner, rendered unduly venturesome by long immunity and prideful faith in his own ingenious craft. The idea struck Jardine's mind, with a most unpleasant collocation of circumstances, that the Street Fair must profit largely by this extraordinary opportunity to the inebriates of the whole surrounding region. Since the closing of the saloons in Colbury the poorer class, by far the larger, must needs be constrained to purchase in the quantity by shipment from some city, or in default of the price for this luxury, or the hindrance of distance and ignorance, be reduced to the absolute despair of temperance. Doubtless for the facilities of boozing by the drink they had flocked into Colbury by scores, where in the close vicinity the flowing bowl might be drained for a nickel, and the moonshiners might justly have considered themselves entitled to a share of the profits of the show since their powerful attraction must have added so largely to the gate receipts. He shrugged his shoulders mechanically in the effort to shake off the suspicion which he had begun to entertain. The Street Fair was so obviously playing in hard luck; was so pitifully inadequate as an exhibition, in his opinion; its financial resources were evidently so limited that this phenomenal opportunity of recruiting its exchequer rendered it peculiarly liable to a charge of collusion with the moonshiners, in the estimation of almost any man seeking the solution of the problem of so many inebriated spectators of the show on the streets of a dry town. Only the appearance and manner of Lloyd caused him to doubt his conclusion, and then he wondered at himself that the endowments of unusual personal beauty, a thing valueless in a man, absolutely apart from character or station, a gift, an accident, together with a grave and gentlemanly address, which was also a fortuitous circumstance, should weigh with him for an instant where an itinerant faker was concerned. In this development of the situation he was infinitely nettled that this man, the manager of the show, and doubtless the prime mover and responsible agent of this unlawful whisky traffic, should have been brought into any association with Miss Laniston, however casual and temporary. He ground his teeth with indignant contempt that it was possible that she should ever exchange a syllable with such a man, should be seated beside him in the Ferris Wheel in the midst of an attack upon him, stimulated by jealousy or whisky or both. Jardine was not a profane man, for oaths are ever bad form, but between his gritting teeth he cursed Frank Laniston again and again that his callow folly should have left his position vacant by her side, and open to the possibility of such a contretemps.

Jardine canvassed almost in a state of nervous panic the probability that these facts might be remembered by the police should the camp of the moonshiners be raided by the revenue force and the manager of the Street Fair be implicated. Even if no more should result than a casual mention in such an investigation it would be an indignity insupportable in his estimation. And should the miscreant who attacked the manager be discovered would not her testimony be required to establish the facts? The tormentingly acute divination of the two young girls had fixed on the culprit, he was convinced, and should some unwary word from them lead to his discovery a prosecution would involve to them as witnesses the most annoying and derogatory conspicuousness. He hardly knew how he could answer to his friends, their respective fathers, that while in his care, assumed of sheer good-will though it was, such social inappropriateness could be permitted to supervene. They were not at the end of this miserable tangle—and he felt greatly to blame. Yet with no authority, a disregarded advice, a thousand hampering constraints on speaking his mind candidly, how could he do more than he had in protection, and counsel, and care? He wished to high heaven that the Laniston Brothers were not so intent on turning the trick in the late advance in the price of cotton, and would give their personal attention to the precious interests of their families. He was conscious that by this collective term he meant only Lucia, and he was fair enough to admit to himself that under the chaperonage of her aunt, and with the companionship of her cousins, male and female, and the volunteer tutelage of a friend of the family, an experienced man of the world, George Laniston was amply justified in thinking his only daughter safe enough, and well out of harm's way.

So perverse were the circumstances that Jardine thought that even his own excursion to-night might be subject to misconstruction—and he hedged immediately on the chance. As he had not succeeded in his quest there was certainly scant utility in seeming to have patronised the moonshiners. There was no great change in the aspect of the town as he entered it—a torch a-flare here and there among the tents; the street lamps shining at regular intervals; the drug store alone alight among the silent business houses of the quadrangle; the gas ablaze in the hotel office, and although, so short was his absence, the duck was off duty he

227

still lingered in the room lighting a thick cigar at the little lamp for the purpose on the counter.

"No go," said Jardine—he had earlier thrown away his basket.

The duck raised astonished eyebrows. "I'd resent that. Personal. Listen, will you?"

A voice mellow, clear, floated in from the street—singing in beatitude—marred only by hiccoughs, and now and then a wild involuntary wail off the key. "We won't go home—we won't go home—we won't go home till mornin',—till daylight doth appear."

When silence ensued the duck said significantly: "All the rope they want—hang themselves—don't even run them in. Visitors soon. Official."

CHAPTER XIV

The next morning when Jardine issued early forth from the little blue reception room, where he had tossed sleepless almost throughout the night on the folding cabinet bed, he paused on the verandah, staring in stultified amaze. Not a tent was visible on the square, not a huckster's stand. The great circumference of the Ferris Wheel no longer vexed with its incongruous periphery the august mountain scene which it had framed. Not a spieler's horn could be heard, nor an echo of the brazen melodies of the band; the wooden horses of the merry-go-round seemed to have galloped away in the night. There was not even the mast for the high dive, nor the reservoir that broke the fall of the leaping acrobat. The street fair had vanished, like an exhalation of the night in the beams of the morning sun. Jardine might have doubted his senses, save for the crowds of wondering rustics

228

that wandered dolefully up and down the pavements, disconsolate, disappointed. Now and again groups paused before written notices pasted on the door of the courthouse and of the post office, and at the distance seemed to discuss it, and then moved aimlessly away, making space for other groups on like errands. Another placard was at the main entrance of the hotel, also under frequent consultation by drearily strolling groups of the more prosperous class of country folks. It was of course impossible to decipher it at the distance, but as Jardine moved toward it he was accosted by the duck-like clerk, seated in the office window opening on the verandah.

"Complete surprise, ain't it?" said the clerk jovially. "Jig's up."

"The fair is gone?" asked Jardine futilely.

"Do you see any fair?" quacked the duck. "I don't."

"Isn't it very sudden?" Jardine demanded.

"Liked to broke my neck," declared the clerk hyperbolically. "Left on the morning train."

"What's the reason for it?" Jardine asked, looking again toward the posted notice.

He was experiencing the most intense relief. All the troubles that had infested his consciousness were annihilated. The vanishing of the street fair was like awakening from a nightmare—a deep sense of gratitude contended with a feeling that his troubles had been unreal, overstrained, gratuitous.

"Oh, they give the plain facts—straight goods—honest fellow, that Lloyd. Couldn't pay expenses any longer—only made their transportation in three days. Disbanded show, and lit right out."

229

He had jumped down on the inner side of the office, then turned anew to the window, as if with a sudden thought.

"That fellow, Captain Ollory—keen to get away—never saw a man so rattled! Here in the office last night they had it out—*one* of them had to stay. *He* wouldn't—he'd have walked to New York first—said so—perfectly wild!"

Jardine looked for a moment as if he had beheld a Gorgon's face—his own seemed petrified.

"Then that manager—that rascal Lloyd is here yet?" he asked.

The clerk seemed disconcerted.

"Hard phrase, Mr. Jardine." Then he hesitated as if he thought he had said too much. It was no part of his duty as clerk of the Avoca House of Colbury to censor the guests' criticism of each other. "Poor business, but no man could behave more fairly. Lloyd wanted to go, but gave up the preference. Ollory seemed possessed to get away—Haxon, I should say. And there was not money enough for both."

Jardine could hardly control his irritation, the revulsion was so great. He had just been liberated from all his fears and anxieties to find himself suddenly enmeshed anew. It mattered little indeed that the foolish, sordid, futile paraphernalia of the fair had been removed, if the point of danger in divers interpretations, the man himself, remained. As he stood by the window, frowning down in deep absorption at the floor, silent, forbidding of aspect, cold and formal as always, the clerk resumed, somewhat at a loss.

"Lloyd, too, seemed frantic to be off," he said. "He could hardly resign himself."

He laughed a little at the forlorn plight; it had to him its ludicrous suggestions. "'Sent for, but couldn't go,'" he quoted gaily.

Jardine made no answer; he was reflecting that both men had doubtless the best of reasons for quitting the country; he hardly questioned that they were amenable to the Federal law in some measure for conspiring with the distillers for the sale of illicit liquor, and reciprocally profiting thereby through the enterprise of the street fair. The manager was obviously the responsible individual, the principal, and his apprehension would rebound with all its conspicuous derogations upon the personnel of Jardine's own select party. Since one must needs remain, it was a thousand pities that that one could not have been the innocuous Captain Ollory.

He did not speak, and the clerk had an unpleasant fear that he had offended him, for the sake of a phrase, forsooth, in the disparagement of the most absolute stranger, for whom the duck in reality did not care a single quack. He waxed suddenly very genial and confidential, and Jardine, who under other circumstances would have resented the gossip as familiar and intrusive, was an eager listener—absurdly enough he had so much at stake in the personality of this man Lloyd.

"'Twas as good as a play," the clerk laughed, "in the office late last night,—a much better play than any they bill—when they counted out the money—had it in my desk. All couldn't get off. Ollory wanted to leave Wick-Zoo, too, but it seemed the wild man had money of his own. They paid him with a due bill, ha, ha! Ollory wanted to leave the Fat Lady; he said she was too fat to be disturbed—I don't know whether he meant mentally or physically—and Lloyd—he's a funny fellow!—he swore he wouldn't mention such a thing; she was a high-toned lady, if she was a bit stout! He declared he never would run off and leave a part of his company stranded, least of all a woman, and one, by her infirmity, helpless to shift for herself—*he's* not a bad egg, Mr. Jardine!

231

When Lloyd saw it must fall between himself and Ollory—Ollory had the money in his paw; he grabbed it as soon as it was laid on the counter, and to do him justice he counted out only the transportation—and Lloyd had the bag to hold, he tried to raise the money for his railroad fare on a personal valuable that he's got. Told him nobody here did pawn-broking. Tried me."

"Why didn't you lend it to him?" exclaimed Jardine suddenly, seeing a way out of the difficulty. It had never occurred to him to pay the man to go, lest he implicate himself in he knew not what—though money was no object in this connection. But it was indeed grievous to perceive a means of extrication so simple, so near, and cast aside.

"Didn't know how valuable valuable might be," the clerk laughed. "Step in here, Mr. Jardine. Show it to you. Left in safe."

It was a thing of which Mr. Jardine would never have believed himself capable as he stepped through the window and addressed himself to appraise a valuable which an unknown man had left in the custody of an hotel safe. But he made up his mind, however worthless the trinket might be, to advance to the clerk the necessary sum, to be loaned through him, without mention of the source whence it came. Anything to be rid of the incubus of the showman!

His face changed as the clerk touched the spring of a small leather case. There, reposing on a bed of faint blue Genoa velvet, so faded as to be near green, was a ring set with a large pigeon's blood ruby; a row of very white diamonds was encrusted into the dull gold of the setting, but the red stone was held up in claws, and was visible throughout.

Jardine had a sudden monition of caution. These were gems of price, doubtless stolen! He could not—he would not involve himself further in such a matter, whatever æsthetic

232

discomforts, whatever mortifying publicity incidents of far less moment might occasion Miss Lucia Laniston. Every throb of his impulse was still. He was once more the cautious man of the world.

"Worth the money?" the clerk queried curiously.

"Worth forty times the money," Jardine calmly responded. If the Avoca House should oblige a guest by lending money on good security it would rid him of his dilemma, and affect him no further. But beyond this he promised himself he would not be urged by his adoring, worshipful reverence for the pellucid aloofness and unapproachableness befitting a young girl, that lent her the dignity and remote charm of a star. There were sordid matters to consider in this world, and the responsibility of trafficking with stolen goods was one of them.

"But look here; these rubies are sometimes what you call doublets, ain't they? Just a sort of veneer of the real thing over glass."

"This is no doublet," said Jardine, taking the gem into his hand. "This is a genuine and very perfect stone of a very rare type—the pigeon's blood ruby."

As he looked at it he was impressed with the antique aspect of the ring; the setting was in gold of several different tints— green, red, yellow in two shades. He had not given much attention to ornaments of this order, but he knew that this method of setting was antiquated, not to say antique. He thought of the incongruity with the sordid little show—the high dive, Wick-Zoo, the Ferris Wheel. More than ever the conviction that the gem was stolen took possession of him. He suffered suddenly a qualm of conscience. He felt that the clerk was of limited experience and needed a warning. He ought not to be suffered unnecessarily to lose his money and involve himself.

"It is so fine, so rare, and so valuable that I am very sure it must be stolen. I don't say by whom, or when."

"Oh, Mr. Jardine," said the clerk, quite self-sufficient. His cheek reddened. He was blushing for the imputation. "Don't you think you are quite a little *too* suspicious?"

"Perhaps—perhaps! At all events you are warned," said Mr. Jardine, as he walked past the safe, around the desk, and out of the office by the door, rather than informally through the window as he had entered.

The clerk looked after him with no very friendly eyes, then he snapped the old ring in its dingy leather case, and locked it in the safe with Mr. Jardine's careful warnings. The value of the jewels ascertained he was prepared to lend the amount of transportation upon it; should he not be repaid he would profit enormously, and he was altogether willing to take the risk that however in the vicissitudes of his life the showman had come by the ring it was honestly owned.

Before the hack started for New Helvetia—it was indeed standing in front of the door—Frank came fuming up into his mother's room, where she, his sister, and his cousin were putting on their hats, preparatory to the journey. The young girls were fresh and bright again in their white dresses, which had, indeed, been sent to the laundry to be pressed and now showed as unwrinkled and perfect as if the stiff linen skirts and dainty little embroidered jackets were donned for the first time. The embroidered frills of their lingerie hats shaded, yet did not shadow, their fair faces, which showed no trace of the fatigue and excitements of yesterday, save that Lucia seemed a bit pale, and her eyes were larger and more appealing than usual. They were putting on their long silk gloves, now and then turning to eye each other from head to foot, for they entertained an enthusiastic mutual admiration, and were wont to point out a hair awry, or a line out of plumb with a serious rebuke, as of sacrilege.

Mrs. Laniston was not ill-pleased to be getting back to New Helvetia, but she regarded the outing as a highly successful break to the monotony. She could not enter into Mr. Jardine's sentiments in reference to the little fair; she had noticed his impatience with its grotesqueness and shortcomings, and in the privacy of the domestic circle had commented adversely. Did he think it was the Paris Exposition? she had demanded sarcastically of her daughter and niece. There is a sort of leniency of judgment peculiarly becoming to the highly bred and highly placed. Mrs. Laniston realised, for example, that the little village hotel was not the finest type of house of entertainment in all the world, but one was fairly comfortable there, and she seemed courteously unaware that there was aught better or more pretentious in New York or London, so long as she was under its hospitable roof. To be easily entertained with the best attainable was an instinct with her, and when Frank, his boyish face red and his scanty frown drawn above vexed and troubled eyes, paused with his hands in his pockets, complaining, "I do declare, that fellow Jardine bullyrags the life out of me," she was predisposed to be her son's partisan, and to discriminate against some ultra-fastidious prejudice of Mr. Jardine's of the sort which, if regarded, would already have destroyed every vestige of pleasure which the humble little outing could afford. She whirled half around from the bureau, where she was standing before the mirror putting on her wide black hat, holding it with one hand, while with the other she thrust a hat pin tentatively back and forth through the structure, seeking to find a steady grip in her masses of grey-blond hair.

"In the name of pity!" she ejaculated, gazing inquiringly at him.

"Ye-es," he whined, "anybody would think I was born yesterday, and couldn't find my way to the hall door there."

"Well, what is it now?" she asked impatiently, with another thrust of the hat pin forceful enough to seem to the uninitiated very dangerous.

"Well," he pushed both hands far down in his pockets and took an aimless step to and fro, his red face overcast and crestfallen with the sense of being thought a fool, and such a realisation of his own immaturity as prevented the recouping satisfaction of a full faith in himself. "I found that that fellow Lloyd would be here a little while waiting for remittances—it seems the whole show came very near being stranded, and, like the captain of a sinking ship, he is the last to leave. Well, it seemed no great absurdity to me, as he is a first-class, all-round professional athlete, such as I am not likely to meet again in a hurry, to ask him to give me a few lessons in boxing. I'm *bound* to have exercise, and a punchbag is such a lonesome fool!"

Mrs. Laniston evidently did not see the point as yet. The hat adjusted at last, she began to pull on her black silk gloves over her rather bony jewelled fingers, gazing the while into the mirror, to which reflection he addressed his appeal.

"Do you see anything extraordinary in that project?"

"Except the expense of coming from and going to New Helvetia," she replied a little wonderingly. "I always did think the monopoly of that hack line ought to be put down. The charges are extortionate—it is practically impossible to go back and forth as one might like to do in excursions about the country if rates were reasonable."

"Why, that is what I told the fellow—that I could better afford the price of the lessons if he were waiting at New Helvetia, instead of here in Colbury."

"And then?" Mrs. Laniston was very dense; she did not yet perceive the point.

"Then Lloyd inquired as to the hotel rates at New Helvetia, and when he found they were lower at this season than the charges for transient guests at this place he said that he had no objection to going to New Helvetia—that it would be a change for him, and that he was fed up with Colbury."

"See here, Frank, you are developing a gift for oratory. Why don't you come to the point, if there *is* any point?" Mrs. Laniston, who herself could hold forth so volubly and with such a flow of well-considered words, admonished him.

"Why, it seemed such an advantageous arrangement; he said, first off, that he could give much better value for the money. He could coach me, too, for the track team—it seems he was once a short-distance sprinter—free of charge. He said we could just run up and down the roads for fun, if they were as good as I said. And then we could have a few bouts with the foils, once in a while—he took a prize for fencing once in an athletic contest—showed me the medal. And I'm getting so fat!" Frank's voice rose to a dreary plaint. "I was perfectly scandalised this morning when I stepped on the public scales on the other side of the square——"

"We understand," murmured Ruth. "Where they weigh the other prize calves."

He looked at her with a little grin of appreciation, but, absorbed in the subject, went on without retort. "I shall be ruled out of every athletic event at college this year. Whereas, if I train down, and have this splendid coach to get me fit I may be able to take my place on the gridiron just as if I hadn't been away; it's only a substitute playing with the Eleven now."

Mrs. Laniston's mind quickly reviewed the situation. So long as athletics did not interfere with scholastic grading, her husband and she had agreed that they were to be encouraged. Frank had neither the tastes nor the application of a student, but he possessed a good mind, and a very sound conscience. Since his parents desired he should have a collegiate education, and take a degree, he read with great diligence, and they sugar-coated the pill by endorsing the college athletics, and giving him all the outdoor sport that was craved by his physique, abounding in vitality and vigour. It was a compact in some sort, unacknowledged, but very definitely appreciated, that he should grind and toil, and assimilate a thousand ideas for which, so far, he had neither use nor liking, and pass his examinations creditably, and that he should be unmolested to play as he would.

"Yes; it seems an excellent arrangement for the purpose. Mr. Jardine is a man of very judicious conclusions, but I can't imagine his objections in this instance."

"Simply threw a fit! I told him that Lloyd and I had signed up a little contract, for I want only to promise to pay for the boxing lessons. I couldn't, out of my allowance, undertake to pay for *all* that fellow could teach me—he could teach me something of value for every wink of my eyelids. And Lloyd chimed in, too, and said it was best to have it understood, for we would probably be lonesome, and spend the time playing—with Indian clubs, and dumb-bells, and wrestling—and we had better set down what was to be work, and what was to be pastime."

"Come to the point, Frank! You *are* long-winded!" his mother admonished him. She had sunk into a chair, and, as the two girls were ranged side by side on the sofa, he stood before the family in the guise of a domestic orator, and made a desperate bolt at the main statement of his disclosure.

"Threw a fit! Adjured me not to compromise the dignity of the family!"

There was a feminine chorus of exclamations.

"Crazy, ain't he?" said Frank. "I told him a few lessons in boxing couldn't compromise the dignity of any family that had any dignity. He said I perversely misunderstood him. For a fact he did. Said it was the *person* he objected to. Emphasised *person* as if he would like Lloyd better if he went on four feet, like Wick-Zoo, once in a while. I asked him what was the matter with Lloyd. Said that on account of my folly he had had an opportunity to ride with Miss Laniston in the Wheel."

"Well, upon my word!" exclaimed Mrs. Laniston.

And the two young ladies grew breathless and round-eyed.

"It was his own fault—he should have called off the event; he could have said that he was waiting for me; his party was not complete. I did not dare suggest this, though. I declare I have had to eat enough humble-pie this morning to destroy my appetite forever." And Frank drew out his handkerchief, and, with a long-suffering air, mopped his shining, roseate, fresh face.

"I think it was very ill-judged in Mr. Jardine to bring the mention of Miss Laniston into the matter," said Mrs. Laniston, her delicate features flushing with irritation.

"In my humble mind that was the only impropriety committed," said Frank. "But of course on account of my youth, and being a sort of standard fool, I did not dare to say so. But I did pluck up enough to state that we could not consider Lloyd's riding in the Wheel with Miss Laniston in any sense except as a convenience to her, to weight the machine, and we could not base any action on any other hypothesis."

"You were very right," said his mother heartily, and Frank, encouraged by this infrequent and unexpected approval, took heart of grace to continue, fetched a long sigh of relief, and once more mopped his face with his handkerchief.

"I said to Jardine that there had been no presumption whatever in the man's conduct, and that the suggestion was offensive to us."

"Very well, indeed," said Mrs. Laniston. She was thinking that Frank, after all, was not so incompetent as a squire of dames, and was realising how the contortion of the circumstances in Jardine's mind would affect George Laniston, should he hear that version.

"But you won't believe that he wouldn't accept the situation. He called me a boy, and of course I had to submit to that. He said the showman had noticed our family at table—he had been offended to observe it. As if, in this free and enlightened country, people should fall on their faces, with their faces in the dust at our august approach. I reminded him that the bullet-eyed man stared at us, and that it was *we* who stared at the manager, who is liable to that sort of thing, for he has got the face of a god or an archangel— told me, when I asked him where was his photograph in the show collection, that he had promised Duroc, the painter, not to be taken till his great picture, 'The Last Day,' is finished. Lloyd is the model for the angel Gabriel in that, and he says it's great, though he thinks the horn makes him look like a translated spieler."

"But about Mr. Jardine———"

"Mamma, I think I am the most put-upon fellow that ever lived. That great Jay stopped Lloyd as he passed and told him that I was a minor, and incapable of making a contract—in my presence, mind you; *in my presence!*"

"Why, Frank!" exclaimed Mrs. Laniston, amazed and offended.

"Oh, he did it in a sort of innocuous way—he's very crafty; said I'd been telling him about the arrangement, and then, as if jocularly reminding me of a disability, said that I was a minor, and the contract invalid. He slicked it over and smoothed it down. I think he could smooth down the Great Smoky Mountains, if he should try his hand on them."

"And what did Mr. Lloyd say?" asked Mrs. Laniston, very seriously annoyed and indignant.

"Really, he seemed the best-bred man of the two. He said he would consider my word as good as my bond—the contract was merely a memorandum, as between us two, determining what exercises should be considered business and be paid for, the rest being merely amusement and voluntary. He passed it off easily, but I felt extremely out of countenance."

"I must say Mr. Jardine takes a good deal on himself," Mrs. Laniston said, holding her head very high, the colour mantling her cheek, "and his standpoint is very unreasonable. That you should not hire the services of an athletic coach, because he took a vacant place beside Miss Laniston, in order to weight the machine and make it safe, there being no one else for the purpose in the party, he being the manager and owner of the apparatus, is more than preposterous. We must take no notice of Mr. Jardine's assumptions that there was anything derogatory in the matter. We will treat the man like any other stranger. And now let us get back to New Helvetia where, thank a merciful providence, there is somebody besides the wearisome Mr. Jardine!"

The approach to New Helvetia ushered Lloyd into a new experience, despite his wide wanderings in many ways. The trails he had followed had not sought seclusion; a full population, showward bent, was the desideratum of his journey's goal hitherto. He had scarcely realised that there was so lonely a region on the face of the earth as the dense and gigantic forests through which the smooth, hard, red clay road led. The scarlet oak, the sumach, and the sourwood on exposed slopes to the north had turned red, and flaunted gorgeously against the blue sky. The foliage of hickory now and again appeared at sudden turns, a clear translucent yellow from trunk to topmost twig. Here and there great grey crags showed through boughs still green and lush, that yet held the summer captive, loath to let it go. There was a stream that kept the road company, as if apart they might be affrighted in the vast unbroken wildernesses, and now it showed a miniature cataract, clear as crystal, fringed with foam, leaping down great broken ledges; and now it brawled, widening into marshy tangles by the wayside; and now it ran over rocks, and flashed and frothed like rapids; and now it showed stretches of smooth golden flow above a bed of gravel, with here and there the sudden silver glinting of a water-break. He watched it with a sort of fascinated revery, unconsciously marking its moods and garnering its spirit. Occasionally a gap in the woods showed the mountains, vast, endless, austere, dominating all the world, and he appreciated that the road was continuously rising by gentle degrees to higher and higher levels. The horses were fleet and strong; the roads only fairly good, for in some localities the rain had converted the red clay into mud of a most tenacious character; elsewhere the downpour had come with such force as to beat the ground hard. Here they bowled swiftly; the driver, evidently, had a monition toward atoning for the interval when they toiled and bogged through the sloughs. There had been a delay at the last moment; a new passenger presented himself who could not be ready to start till one o'clock, and, though Mr. Jardine had protested that he had chartered the hack,—in the phrase of the region,— the driver declared that the orders of the line required him to take up all the custom he could gather before it was necessary to leave town in order to make the run before dark. The episode had greatly irritated Jardine, but he found a certain consolation in the fact that the presence of this representative of the general public, so to speak, exerted a repressive influence on the exuberance of the two young ladies. The incidents that had marked the trip down were not repeated—the pauses to alight and gather wild flowers; the shrieks of delight over some lovely vista of the stream and protestations how dear it would be to wade in the shallow crystal flood, floored with golden gravel and great solid ledges of moss-grown rock; the determination which could not be gainsaid to visit the shaft of a mine, worked for silver, in a primitive way, hard by, where a windlass was in operation. Lucia unexpectedly stepped into the swaying bucket above the abyss of ninety feet, holding her skirts tight about her, and ordered the men to lower her, that she might look into the intersecting tunnel. "I'll bring you luck," she declared. "I'm a mascot!"

"Shure I niver knew till to-day, leddy, that anny o' the fairies had emigrated from Oirland, their native land," said an old Irishman, as she alighted from the bucket, relinquishing, with pretended reluctance, the descent which her aunt with some precipitancy forbade; the compliment in a rich brogue, and the flattering twinkle of the eye had set Jardine wild, but Mrs. Laniston had laughed pleasantly, and had descanted elaborately, after they were in the stage once more, on the national gift of blended blarney and poesy that tips the tongue of an Irishman, of whatever degree, wherever found.

Now all was changed. Strangers were fellow-travellers. Placed with Mrs. Laniston on the back seat of the "hack," the young ladies had relapsed into the inexpressive, sedate demeanour which they assumed so easily when subjected to the gaze of the outside world. It might have been different, thought Jardine, if only Lloyd—who had unluckily acquired a quasi acquaintance—had been added to the family party.

The person who thus reconciled Mr. Jardine to the fact of his creation and appearance on this occasion was himself disposed to take little note of the personnel and conditions of his environment. He was a tall, portly man, with a strong, handsome, rather round, face, a florid complexion, and round, somewhat staring, eyes; middle-aged, soberly dressed, and extremely reticent. Beyond an undeveloped feint of a bow to the assemblage in the hack when he entered the vehicle, he accorded none of them a moment's notice. He had the front seat beside the driver; each of the other two seats held three passengers, Jardine being between Lloyd and Laniston, and controlling the very scanty conversation, taking the word whenever an observation was ventured by either. This line of tactics greatly nettled Frank, who, being unable to appropriately return it in kind, relapsed into a marked silence. Lloyd was apparently not aware of its significance, for he responded pleasantly, though monosyllabically, but indeed Jardine permitted nothing more.

When they reached the foot of the mountain, however, and the driver paused to breathe the horses, the men alighting to lessen the burden for the steep ascent, the stranger, who had presumably been profiting by the platitudes with which Mr. Jardine had beguiled the journey, did not select his company as solace in the long, stiff tramp. On the contrary he attached himself to Lloyd, and together they were soon well in advance of the straining team, while Frank and Jardine walked on either side of the vehicle and talked to the ladies over the high wheels. Here, out of sight and beyond the participation of the mere outsiders, Mr. Jardine was pleased to unbend, and be most affable and entertaining, for he did not include in the scheme of creation such objects as the driver—the mere furniture of life—a stalwart young mountaineer, walking nimbly beside his team, holding the reins in his hand, and calling out admonitions and encouragements. As he could not, afoot, use the brake Frank found occupation and utility in "scotching" the wheels with a big stone, or locking them with the chain, generally used to impede a too rapid descent, whenever the team was halted on the steep acclivity for a few minutes of breathing space.

Lucia, with her quick faculties, was well-fitted for a duplicate mental process. She smiled appropriately when Jardine made his neat little points of mirth, or nodded serious acquiescence, when his remarks seemed of weight. In reality she gave him only the most superficial attention, barely enough to discern the trend of his talk. Her interest was concentrated on the two pedestrians ahead, and once more she wondered how the showman should look such a gentleman. The road curved and doubled in innumerable turns to evade slants impossible to the straining horses. Looking upward one could see it here and there in the breaks of the thinning foliage, suggesting unwound coils of brown ribbon. The wind came fresh and free, laden with the sweet dank odours of the fallen leaves, the exquisite freshness of the mountain heights, and all the bouquet and tang of the wayside herbage. It brought the words of the two pedestrians, now passing them on a higher level, and visible above a mass of broken rock.

"Late in the season to visit the mountain resorts," the elder man observed.

"They are usually closed by this time," Lloyd politely responded.

"I suppose the yellow fever in the South detains their patrons."

Then they both trudged silently on.

The horses were once more urged forward; in their improved speed Jardine and Frank both fell behind. The driver, who had no possibility of comprehending the many finical delicacies which racked Mr. Jardine's prepossessions, kept up the pace till he had passed the two passengers on ahead, and when next he paused in the shade to rest, the stanch team, sweating at every pore, they presently overtook in turn the stationary vehicle, and stoutly marched past, without a word or glance for the occupants.

"Fine water at these springs?" suggested the stranger.

"So I hear, but I am new to the place—never was here before," Lloyd replied.

His fine figure was especially marked, the perfection of strength and symmetry, as he went swinging past, his hands in the pockets of his light fawn-tinted suit, his hat tipped slightly over his eyes, a spray of the jewel-weed, which he had caught up by the wayside, in his buttonhole, keeping step with his portly companion, who was content to pound over the ground anyhow, regardless of grace, as a man of his weight must needs be.

Jardine, all blown, and panting, and eager from his hasty pull after the hack—he and Frank had sought to shorten the distance by a cross-cut through from one curve to another, and hindered by brambles and obstructed by boulders, had found it hard travelling—had noticed, too, the figures on ahead, and had heard the words as the wind wafted to him the casual talk. He had taken off his hat, and was wiping the traces of his exertion from his brow with his fine white cambric handkerchief.

From time to time the elder stranger fixed the eyes of a very close and keen observation on his companion. He was evidently interested, even inquisitive.

"You hardly look as if you need the waters for your health, sir," he said.

"I am particularly fit, just now," said Lloyd. But he made no advances to gratify the curiosity of his new acquaintance. His reserve struck Jardine with a peculiarly sinister suggestion. Did the showman fear this stranger, and why? He remembered his own conclusion, that the street carnival had been involved in the sale of the moonshine whisky and that the manager as representative was personally liable. A new fear fell upon him like a thunderbolt. This stranger was doubtless a detective, an emissary of the revenue department, who was tracking and shadowing this man till he had grounds sufficient for the arrest. And Frank Laniston—the callow fool!—had brought upon him, upon his own family so ill-flavoured and derogatory an association. Nothing had supervened like this—the detective might arrest the creature at any moment, and had the authority to call on him, and Laniston, and the driver as a *posse comitatus* to assist him in apprehending and securing his prisoner. What else could bring a man of this type here, at this season, an evident stranger to the locality, when the sojourners of the Spa had flitted home, and business was booming in the cities, and only a few old habitués of the place, a mere handful, lingered, extending the summer, to avoid the yellow fever in the South.

As these thoughts surged through Jardine's mind he followed the vehicle with so disordered and exhausted a step, although he was of a stanch, wiry, and tough physique, that Mrs. Laniston called out to him, inviting him to ride for a while, saying there was quite a level stretch of road ahead, and the additional weight would not harass the horses here. He so far collected his faculties as to express his thanks, and protest his comfortable state, and then fell back to contemplate the horrible possibility. Good God! what would people say! In what fantastic guise would they imagine he disposed of himself, to come into such a plight. He, too, kept an eye on the two figures in advance, and he gave strict heed to their words, as in detached fragments they floated back.

Evidently Lloyd thought a counter-query was in order.

247

"They say the waters have wonderful medicinal qualities. Do you expect to take them?"

"Me—no, no, sir. No, indeed. I am here on a piece of business, important business. Out-of-the-way place."

He seemed not only to Jardine, but to Lloyd, to cast a singularly sharp and wary eye upon the figure at his side. In fact he was obviously scanning the contour of the showman's face for some moments, when he suddenly said:

"If it is not an impertinence, sir, may I ask your motive in visiting New Helvetia?"

"Business, too, in a way," said Lloyd. "I am a coach for that young gentleman beside the hack."

"The classics?" the stranger asked respectfully.

"Oh, Lord, no!" poor Lloyd burst out explosively. "Excuse me, but I'm an athletic coach. He wants to train down for the gridiron—and he needs it, too—going all to fat."

Once more the long keen scrutiny, from which Lloyd visibly winced; his cheeks reddened; his hot, hunted eyes gazed straight ahead; his step flagged. Nevertheless he held his ground and kept his self-control.

"And is this coaching your regular profession?" the inquisitive stranger persisted.

"I have no regular profession," Lloyd hesitated. Then, gathering his nerve with a mighty effort, he boldly risked absolute candour. "I have done many stunts in the athletic line. Performed in circuses and shows; sung a little, too——" with a wry contortion of his perfectly chiselled lips, for he knew what good music is, and he loved it. "But lately I have been trying to make some money on my own account. I have been the manager of a street fair——"

248

"Oh, fool, fool, fool!" Jardine apostrophised him, between set teeth.

"A good, clean show it was," continued Lloyd, "some unparalleled attractions; finest high dive I ever saw. But we went to pieces here—got stranded—and———"

The wind carried away the words, and as Jardine, still muttering, "Fool—fool," looked up, he saw the tall, portly figure stop short, lean forward, and clutch the manager excitedly by the arm. The next moment the foliage intervened. Suddenly there rose on the air Lloyd's voice, pitched high, in wild agitated exclamations, and the deep, steady, bass tones of the stranger. Then was silence, and the forests received them, and the tourists below saw and heard no more.

CHAPTER XV

To Jardine's infinite relief these two of his fellow-travellers did not reappear. Lloyd evidently had had the grace not to resist to the extreme of coercion, and thus had spared the ladies, and indeed Mr. Jardine's own delicate sensibilities, the indignity of being even remotely concerned in so sordid a scene. He hardly wondered whither they had gone, when the hack, with Frank and himself once more seated within with the ladies, rattled up to the door of the hotel at the New Helvetia Springs, for the officer would naturally be expected to hurry his prisoner to some wayside log cabin, and there await transportation to Colbury. It would have been a needless expense, as well as a gratuitous affront to the ladies and gentlemen at New Helvetia, to introduce amongst them so offensive a personality as a Federal prisoner.

The wide piazzas surrounding the hotel and overlooking a craggy precipice and a vast expanse of mountain landscape seemed spacious, rather than deserted. A group of ladies, mostly elderly, handsomely gowned, though accoutred with little knitted shawls, and here and there a "fascinator," against the chill, rare air of the evening, sat in rocking-chairs, surveyed the majestic prospect, and talked of many things, contentedly awaiting the white frost which should set them free and fleeing from the mountains. Many doors, already illumined with lamplight, stood open, casting great parallelograms of golden radiance on the shadowy floor without. No sign of the habitation of man, not a spark betokening a lamp-lit window or a glowing hearth, showed in all the stretches of wooded ranges, with dark and sombre valleys between, barely distinguishable now, with a river here, and a silent presence of mist there, and a sense of awful solemnity and infinite loneliness brooding over all. Perhaps the impressive and austere aspect of nature without rendered the fire of hickory logs, burning on the broad hearth of the large office, of so genial and friendly a suggestion. Before it a number of great rocking-chairs stood ranged in a semicircle, and here, too, sat guests, much at their ease. It was a coign of vantage from which one could observe all that went on in the great deserted hotel—the clerk at the desk was on the remote side of the spacious apartment and the fireside group need not be hampered by the very inconsiderable business that he was called upon to transact in these dull days, out of season. But the main staircase, a large pretentious structure of double flights, was in full view, and everyone coming and going paused for a word. The two intersecting hallways met in the office; the great bay-window, formed by the ground floor of the tower, was contrived at one corner of this apartment, and, overlooking the finest prospect to be seen for many a mile, was always occupied—by loiterers at gaze in the mornings with some trifling work of crochet or battenberg, and by a table of bridge at night. A pleasant place, a peaceful haven— and Jardine looked unwontedly benign and condescending as he received his key at the counter from the clerk, and responded affably to that functionary's "Glad to see you back, Mr. Jardine."

The hotel at New Helvetia had an effect of palatial dimensions in its wide, unpeopled, vacant expanses in the shrunken state of its patronage. The immense logs, flying long, broad pennants of red and yellow flames, and supported by glittering old-fashioned brass andirons, sent a rich illumination far down the spaces of the big dining-room. The glossy hard-wood floor glistening in the sheen gave a suggestion of expense quite spurious, for there was little other timber available in the building of New Helvetia. A few round tables were set near the genial glow and the high white-painted mantelpiece. The other tables had been removed, and there was a most comfortable sense of absolute monarchical possession in having such vast apartments at one's own disposal. There was a pervasive atmosphere of privacy, of seclusion. The place was difficult of access, and the usual touring population had never found it out. Year after year the same high-grade patrons came and went; their fathers, and in some instances their grand-fathers, in days agone, had likewise flitted to and fro, and drank the waters, and danced in the ballroom, and flirted on the piazzas, and played at the lawn sports and the games of cards fashionable in their time. There were white-haired couples in the dining-room this evening who had turned each other's heads, blonde or auburn then, on the moon-lit verandah there, or beside the spring of magic beneficence, or strolling beneath the trees of the grove that could have shown many rings of added girth and many feet of lengthened growth since those enchanted hours.

251

It was a decorous, pleasant scene, almost home-like, yet with an agreeable community geniality and informality, as now and again groups at table exchanged comments with other groups half across the room. It might well have been a shock to Mr. Jardine strolling in to tea, freshly attired, thankful to be once more in his accustomed niche, surrounded by "nobility, and tranquillity, burgomasters, and great one-yers," even if the sight had involved no other associations, to perceive at one of the tables, sitting in this bland glamour of firelight and mellow lamplight, and the radiance of the moon which poured in through one of the long uncurtained windows, the two strangers, erst his fellow-travellers, whom he fancied he had quitted forever in the ascent of the mountain. Both were freshly groomed, quiet, and gentlemanly of demeanour, sustaining without show of consciousness the covert observation of the other occupants of the room, who were all mutually acquainted, even to the earliest sprout and the latest twig of their respective family trees. It was naturally a point of speculation what could have brought these two strangers, thus out of season, to the remote resort of the New Helvetia Springs.

One glance at Lloyd's face and Jardine's keen perceptions were satisfied that he had experienced some great excitement, some nervous shock, an agitation from which he had hardly yet recovered. His companion's aspect was unchanged, placid, powerful, but otherwise null of facial expression.

Jardine hesitated, his hand still on the knob of the door. The head waiter had briskly crossed the shining floor, with a flourish drew out Jardine's accustomed chair at a table near the fire, and stood blandly awaiting his patron. Jardine hardly heeded. He was formulating in his mind such an explanation of his suspicions as it might be consistent with prudence to detail to young Laniston—a warning, lest he continue even

252

for an evening, an hour, this derogatory association—or would it not be better to remonstrate plainly with the officer on the indecorum of his course in bringing such an association upon respectable, unsuspicious people?

The choice did not long remain possible to him. A side door opened suddenly and Frank Laniston, fresh, roseate, all handsomely bedight, for he was of the type that loves and beseems fine clothes, entered with an elastic step, and a gay greeting as he passed the table of the strangers.

"Got here, eh—all in one piece, I see—lost you on the road," and then he took his seat at his own table, bowing and smiling rosily to the greetings he encountered, and, with a half audible sigh of pleasant anticipation, he unfolded his napkin.

"Fi-i-ne." He exclaimed presently, in the interval, while his order was filled, replying to an inquiry from across the fireplace as to the outing to Colbury.

Jardine, once again coerced by circumstances, could only traverse the room to his waiting chair, and respond with his usual sedate and appropriate urbanity to the questions as to his enjoyment of the excursion. He kept a furtive, but stern, eye on the strangers, with little result, save that he observed that the portly man ate a somewhat elaborate and well-selected meal almost in absolute silence, giving his whole attention to the matter in hand. Lloyd, on the contrary, ate little, and was as silent. He seemed distrait, perturbed, preoccupied; now gazing drearily into the flashing flames, and once, for a long interval, with lifted face watching the beams from the unseen moon, falling through the window, the rays all differentiated like the fibres of a glittering skein, the more distinct because of the background of the dark foliage of a great oak without.

When a sudden alert attentiveness usurped this apathy of reverie, Jardine, too, looked up sharply. Lucia Laniston was entering the room. The unique character of her beautiful face, the poetic, indescribable charm of her eyes, the high intelligence and nobility of sentiment that her presence expressed, despite her extreme youth, all seemed curiously independent of fashion and superior to its behests. She might have been appropriately garbed in some severely simple and classic design, apart from the modiste's creation, exclusively her own. But naught was further from her desire—naught could more definitely accord with the prevailing mode than the costumes she affected. As she came forward the long, straight folds of her chiffon gown, worn over a shining silk of the same tint, accented her height and her slenderness; the gauzy material was of a sage green, embroidered here and there with a pattern of a Persian design in terra-cotta, and darker green and a thread of gold; it had sleeves to the elbow, but was cut low and square over a beautifully modelled, but somewhat thin, neck, and, in what she called "the region of the bones," was a delicate little necklace of five emeralds placed at intervals on an almost invisible chain whereon glimmered here and there a very small and very white diamond. Her soft light-brown hair was dressed high in fluffy puffs, and as she paused, waiting a moment and glancing over her shoulder, her cousin Ruth came in, her dress duplicating this costume in lilac.

To Jardine's consternation, as they took their seats, Lloyd gravely and circumspectly bowed to both. After they had ceremoniously returned the salutation, Jardine observed that each cast a swift, searching glance at Lloyd. They, too, saw that which had not been in his face before. Mrs. Laniston now joined the party, deceptively arrayed in what she called her "old black Chantilly," which seemed a very fine lace dress as long as its wear and tear were obliterated by the black satin beneath, but a sorry sight it might have been over white silk, which it had been designed to cover in its palmy days. It was quite good enough for New Helvetia, out of season, and, with the twinkle of a diamond lace-pin, and the flutter of a fan of inlaid pearl, not even her nearest neighbours knew how they had been cozened of a toilette of distinction. For it was rather a point at New Helvetia to maintain all the flattering delusions of a sojourn of pleasure and free will, rather than an enforced detention, and all the formalities of dressing, and dancing, and playing tenpins, and cards, and tennis were continued as long as the covey of summer birds could muster the numbers to sustain the diversion. Jardine suddenly bethought himself of this, and not to be forestalled anew he leaned backward and touched Frank Laniston, as he sat at the next table. Frank turned instantly, and leaned slightly to one side to hear the communication, made in a very low tone under Mrs. Laniston's voluble description of her experiences addressed to the occupants of the neighbouring table on the left—charming ride—somewhat fatigued—quaint little town—enjoyed the fair—how the storm must have frightened you, lightning terrific at such an altitude—must have been terrible—glad to escape it——

"Frank," said Jardine seriously, "for God's sake let's have no dancing this evening, no german——"

Frank's patience had worn well, but it had now waxed thin. He was no longer tucked up under Jardine's arm, so to speak, and off on their travels. New Helvetia, familiar to him since infancy, was like home, and he felt independent. He was not "looking for a row" with anybody, but, if one were forced upon him, there was no longer an obligatory association—there was elbow-room here—Jardine and he could move apart, each going his own way without embarrassment, or an open esclandre.

"You needn't adjure me," he said with spirit. "I am too tired to put one foot before the other. *I* don't want to dance."

"But don't let the others———" Jardine began.

Frank Laniston had his own theories of the becoming. He had thought it well enough that Jardine, in escorting the young ladies under circumstances so unusual, should have special solicitude touching the decorous and the appropriate. But he felt, if he might venture to criticise anyone so assertively *au fait*, that Jardine was not infallible in his management, as the swing episode intimated, that he was prone to magnify any awkward little contretemps, and by much pother make something out of nothing. A man with feminine relatives is susceptible to a certain sensitiveness in their behalf, impossible for a man not so connected to appreciate. In Mr. Jardine's persuasions concerning these matters of propriety he overlooked one point—that he, himself, committed a solecism in mentioning them to Frank in this connection. The mere discussion was an offence in young Laniston's estimation. He would not longer suffer it.

"You are afraid that Lloyd, my coach, might get into the german—say as a rover?" he asked, with the infinitely exasperating, callow sarcasm, his big white strong teeth gleaming in his rosy square-jawed face. "Why, I don't know whether *he* can dance the german at all. I should say that a tight-rope fandango was more in his line."

Jardine turned without another word, and at all the white-draped tables the amicable plying of knife and fork continued, unaware of this provocation to a breach of the peace.

After tea Jardine lighted his cigar at the counter in the office and strolled out on the side piazza, puffing at it in a very ill frame of mind. He needed its solace, and the sedative influence to his nerves, after the vexatious incidents of the evening, and the perplexity that beset him as to how he should proceed—or indeed, with no seconding from this young cub, whose position as a near relative of the ladies authorised interference, what could he do? Of course Jardine realised that his solicitude in these troublous complications was entirely on Lucia's account, but he said to himself that any ladies of his acquaintance placed in a position so menacing to their dignity, with such inadequate protection as the shallow-pated Frank Laniston could afford, had a claim on his good offices to spare them a discreditable episode.

He paced to and fro in the chill air, pulling hard at his cigar and glancing now at its light wreaths of smoke, and now at the illuminated disk of the moon, riding high above the infinite solitudes of the mountains. He heard the wind stir in the leaves far below on the slope; he marked how the great ranges against the horizon fended off the world; he listened to the impetuous dash of the mountain torrent in the ravine leaping down the rocky abysses on its way to the valley. But as yet there was no flicker of light from the windows of the ballroom, a long, low building in the extremity of the west wing, remote from the more inhabited portion of the hotel that the sound of revelry should not reach the old, the invalids, the slumberers in the bedrooms. There was no vibration of the tuning of the fiddles or banjos, for the regular band had gone, and the music of an humble sort was furnished by several of the negro waiters, musically endowed and hired for the occasion. It seemed really as if the guests might not intend to dance to-night, their limited number being so reduced by the defection of the exhausted excursionists. From the front piazza, which extended along the whole façade of the building, came the sound of joyous young voices, and it occurred to Jardine that perhaps the youthful element might content themselves with promenading to and fro in the moonlight till the increasing

257

chill of the air should drive them within to the fire blazing so ruddily on the broad hearth of the office.

He walked to the corner and stood for a moment, his cigar in his hand, casting his eye along the length of the piazza. It was much as he had expected. In the white sheen of the moon a young couple here and there slowly strolled, idly chatting. The columns supporting the roof were duplicated in shadowy pilasters that extended the effect of the colonnade. The bare boughs of a locust tree, always the earliest denuded by the autumnal blasts, were drawn on a clear space on the floor with the distinctness of a line engraving, and the dense foliage of a great oak close by cast a deeper gloom within the railing because of the clear lustre that elsewhere suffused mountain and valley, and sward and pillared portico. The parallelograms of light earlier cast on the floor from the lamp-lit windows and doors were now annulled by the lunar brilliancy, obliterated. Indeed he might scarcely have discerned from where he stood the position of the office door had not the light, elegant form of Lucia Laniston with its lily-like suggestions, suddenly issued from it, one hand holding up the sheer draperies of her dress, the other furling her fan of dark green ostrich tips. His heart throbbed at the sight of her; then he stood as one petrified.

For a man, who was leaning smoking against one of the pillars, suddenly threw his cigar over the balustrade into the lawn, and with perfect assurance approached and accosted her as she stood glancing about in loitering doubt.

"Miss Laniston," Jardine heard the words, for Lloyd's enunciation was very distinct and his voice carried well, "you spoke to me very kindly last evening—and I should like to tell you about something, sad and wrong and irrevocable in the past, and a very strange thing that has befallen me to-day and changed all my prospects."

258

Jardine woke to sudden life. He strode along the piazza and joined the two before the young lady had framed her reply.

"Good-evening, Miss Laniston," he said imperiously, taking no notice of the presence of Lloyd; "I hope that you are not too fatigued for a stroll on the piazza to enjoy this balmy air. Let me show you a charming view of the moonlight on the cascade. The stream has risen so since the storm that you can see the falls from the end of the piazza at the west wing."

He could not believe his ears. "Later, perhaps—thank you very much—but just now I am engaged."

She summoned Lloyd with a glance, and catching up the fleecy overdress with one jewelled hand, while the silken skirt below shimmered blue and shoaled green in the moonlight as it trailed, she paced slowly along with him in the opposite direction, and Jardine noted the sympathetic cadence in her voice as she invited the colloquy with a question.

Jardine was furious, on fire, not from jealousy, for he could not stoop to recognise rivalry from this quarter, but with the sense of the subjection of the highly placed and finely endowed woman whom he loved to ignoble association, which because of her youth and inexperience she knew not how to discern and repel, and from which by reason of the incompetence of her guardians and his own lack of authority she was altogether unprotected. He would not be still—he would no longer supinely submit. He turned into the office of the hotel animated with an intention that would brook neither denial nor delay.

In the summer this large apartment was almost entirely relinquished to business and to the masculine guests who were wont to wait here for the distribution of the mail, to read the in-coming newspapers, to discuss the phases of politics and public events they suggested, and pending all to

259

smoke interminably. Though the number of habitués was so wofully decreased the autumn wrought an added cheer in the presence of great, alluring, genial fires and the change of feminine intrusion. Now it was almost given over to the ladies, but neither politics nor tobacco had been tabooed. Games of hazard for stakes had always sought more secluded quarters, and naught could better comport with the sentiment of the refining influences of woman's presence than the game of chess at which two elderly worthies sat, their eyes fixed on the board, as motionless as if they had been stricken into stone. A group of four ladies and gentlemen were deep in the allurements of bridge at the table in the bay-window. Several guests languidly swayed in rocking-chairs before the fire, aimlessly chatting. Among these was Mrs. Laniston cutting the leaves of a new magazine and theorising ably on the perishable impression of periodical literature. Frank Laniston was hooked on by the elbows to the counter, while he gazed up the staircase ever and anon, expecting the descent of a very young lady whose mamma had required her to procure her long red cloth coat before she ventured out with a party bound for the spring. The elderly stranger, fraternising with no one, had deliberately lighted a cigar after observing that the practice of smoking here was permitted, and sat in the chimney corner, very much at home, composed, observant, evidently enjoying the luxury of the fire and satisfied with his surroundings. He took his cigar from his lips and fixed his great, shiny, hazel eyes on Jardine with very much the air of being interrupted, before the stare of surprise effaced every other expression of his large, handsome florid face.

"I want to know what you mean by this?" Jardine said without preamble or disguise. His voice was tense and low, but so obviously freighted with passion that the bridge players paused in amaze.

260

"What—what?" sputtered the portly guest, seeming to collect himself with difficulty, and not till Jardine had repeated the question was he able to speak coherently. "Mean by what, my good sir?"

"Mean by letting that fellow go at large?" Jardine hissed out. He stood erect at a little distance leaning on the high back of one of the vacant rocking-chairs, and as his hands now and again quivered, responsive to the surge of excitement in his mind, the chair swayed slightly, and then was still again.

The portly guest stared with unavailing intentness, as if he sought with the physical eye to discern the mystery. Then he looked around at the group as if they, knowing Jardine, might be able to explain him. But they remained silent in blank astonishment; even the automata of the chess table turned dismayed and startled faces, and the knights and castles and pawns had surcease of their schemings for the nonce.

"What fellow?" gasped the stranger, seeming to doubt his senses. He burnt his fingers with the lighted end of his cigar in inadvertent handling, and he let it fall to the hearth unheeded.

"That fellow Lloyd—what do you mean by letting him go at large?" Jardine reiterated his question.

"My God, sir—he is perfectly sane—do you suppose that *I* am his keeper?"

"No, I do not—I most certainly do not suppose that you are any such thing," Jardine replied with a significance not to be mistaken.

The portly stranger was recovering his composure. Under other circumstances he might have thought that Jardine was himself mentally unbalanced, but he had already noted him on the journey that day with the keen observation that little

261

escaped, and he was aware that there must needs be other methods of accounting for his demonstration.

"I will tell you what I suppose that you and he are," Jardine declared. He had utterly lost his own self-control—he was tingling with the long-repressed irritation, vented at last and utterly beyond his power to check.

"Let me warn you, sir," said the newcomer, with a certain menacing dignity in his look, "how you dare asperse either that gentleman or myself." Then with a sudden, sinister, chuckling laugh, "He is more than capable physically of resenting any injury, and I tell you now that if you slander me I will have the law of you."

This utterance stirred the group.

"Permit me to remind you, Mr. Jardine, that ladies are present, and that this violence, now and here, is unbecoming," one of the chess players observed. He was an ancient bachelor and solicitous on the subject of the claims to delicacy of the fair sex. He thought this suggestion would induce the feminine members of the group to retire, when the men could have their difference out as best pleased them. But every woman sat immovable, absorbed, interested in the outcome. They had not achieved their enlarged liberties for naught. Not a soul thought of retiring from the scene—if ever they had known how to faint they had forgotten the accomplishment.

There was not an appreciable pause and the crisis was acute. One of the bridge players rose to the occasion, while the others stared petrified and round-eyed. He was a tall, lank, blond gentleman, bald and clean-shaven. "I think, Mr. Jardine, you must be under some mistake." His hand in the game was a dummy, and already lay exposed upon the board while the other players still clutched their cards tight. He approached Jardine thinking that by some miracle he might

262

be intoxicated, and keenly eyed him as he spoke. "This gentleman—both, I am sure, are strangers to us all. I beg— in fact, I *insist* that you say no more."

"Then, let him tell us who he is," Jardine persisted with a vehemence that amazed the coterie, "and why he has this Lloyd in his custody."

"My good sir, let me recommend you to discipline your tongue," said the stranger hotly, "or I warn you again that it will get you into trouble."

Jardine's expression of disdainful contempt was so definite that it constrained a reply.

"I never anticipated such a 'hold up' as this, I am sure," the portly guest remarked satirically. "We *are* strangers to all present, and I can't imagine why anyone here should take such a vital interest in us—flattering, very, but most uncommon."

"I desire you to observe," said one of the gentlemen who had been idly swaying in a rocking-chair, aimlessly chatting, till stricken motionless and dumb with amazement, "I desire you to observe that this intrusive interest in your personal affairs is manifested by only one individual. We do not ask nor desire to know anything concerning them."

There was a general civil murmur of unanimity.

"I assure you we have nothing to conceal," the stranger said with a sort of large, jocular scorn. "I am a lawyer—a member of the Glaston Bar. My name is George Conway Dalton— here is my professional card," he handed it to the blond bald bridge player, who received it reluctantly and civilly avoided looking at it. "I came here to ask Mr. Lloyd to execute a power of attorney to enable me to act in some property interests in which I have already been of counsel, and to acquaint him with the fact that he is a beneficiary under the will of a relative from whom he expected to receive nothing."

CHAPTER XVI

Jardine, after one moment of stultified amaze, felt as if the floor were sinking beneath his feet. In the sudden revulsion of his rage his head whirled, and he saw the room and the people go round and round in concentric circles. But for the chair he grasped he might have fallen. He was grateful that the interest produced by the announcement so superseded the surprise which his demonstration had occasioned that for a time he escaped notice, and was afforded an interval for the recovery of his composure.

"I am well acquainted in Glaston," one of the coterie observed. "I have never had the pleasure of meeting you there, Mr. Dalton, but I have often heard of you from my relatives, the Rickson family. Happy to make your acquaintance," and he offered his hand.

Some further informal introductions and atoning hand-shaking ensued with the discovery of mutual friends, all a trifle conscious and awkward, however, and there was a very general feeling of relief when Mrs. Laniston, perceiving the "lapse into barbarism," as she called it, at an end, broke into vivacious comments with her tactful perception of the least nettling phase of the disclosure.

"How perfectly delightful—such a romantic incident—an unexpected legacy—a windfall. But—since from the nature of the case it must be to a degree public—may I ask were not you two strangers when you met to-day in the stage?"

Mr. Dalton, in younger and slimmer years might have been an acceptable "ladies' man." He beamed with most responsive urbanity upon Mrs. Laniston, and was quite willing to permit a little harmless gossip to annul the impression of the violent methods by which the announcement had been elicited.

"I had not the most remote idea that he was the legatee. I had been looking for him—advertising in fact in every medium that I thought might meet his eye for the last four months. I heard by an accident that he was in Colbury as the manager of a little street fair."

There was a distinct sensation among the heavy-weights, financial and social, upon this mention. A sort of dismayed surprise usurped the genial satisfaction in more than one face in the coterie. Mr. Dalton seemed rather to rejoice in the effect he produced, to shatter thus their well-bred nerves. He looked around the circle, expansively smiling, before he went on: "When the train came in this morning I found that the Fair had collapsed, closed, and departed. Not disposed to a wild-goose chase I sent telegrams in every direction which I thought he might take. I concluded to await results, and preferred a sojourn at the Springs to the little town."

"The subtleties of the professional legal mind are past fathoming, I know," said Mrs. Laniston. "But I cannot understand by what keen insight, by what unclassified faculty of discrimination you could say to yourself as you toiled up the mountain beside an absolute stranger '*This* is the legatee I am hunting for.' Why, among your fellow-travellers, did you select this Mr. Lloyd, instead of Mr. Jardine or my son Francis Laniston?"

Mr. Dalton twinkled appreciatively as he listened to this. "I have a mind to appropriate those compliments, madam— you have doubtless heard that the profession is not overscrupulous in taking advantage of a concession. But the fact is that the young gentleman's extraordinary personal

265

appearance first gave me a clue to his identity. His mother took a fifteen thousand dollar prize in an international beauty show."

"Oh," ejaculated Mrs. Laniston, fairly taken aback. She had had it vaguely in her mind that the manager was not really what he seemed, and was about to protest that she had had the discrimination to discern this from the first, inquiring who was "that distinguished-looking young gentleman."

Mr. Jardine had thrown himself into the rocking-chair on which he had been leaning, feeling that he had done all that he could, more than his unfounded suspicions justified, and seeking to recover himself of his excitement and nervous strain. At this disclosure of the showman's antecedents he raised his eyebrows in sarcastic disdain. After all the Lanistons were free agents, and if they deliberately chose association of this type—why, they were not for him nor he for them.

Mrs. Laniston vaguely lifted her eyes to the window opening on the verandah; to see Jardine not in attendance on Lucia gave her an unwonted sense of something awry, but the next moment the interest of the gossip annulled this impression, and she was listening to Mr. Dalton, who, having exhausted his relish of the survey of the flinching group, went on with animation.

"And she was as good as she was pretty—which is saying a very great deal! She provided for her aged parents permanently out of her prize money, sent a consumptive brother to a hospital where he was cured, to be drowned afterward on an ocean voyage. I fancy she bought much fine dry goods and frippery; in effect she distributed the sum in a year or so, contentedly relying on her slender salary as a dancer—they tell me that despite her beauty and grace she was an indifferent dancer—till she met this young fellow's father, who straightway married her."

Mr. Dalton had reached the limit of his capacity it would seem to sustain the public interest. So genteel a circle was not entertained by a biography of this sordid character. The bridge party, albeit with a civil effect of listening, had begun to play out the interrupted hand, though the owner of the dummy sat sideways in his chair and still turned an attentive face. Mrs. Laniston, fluttering the leaves of her magazine, was vaguely disconcerted. She could hardly be said to have her two charges in mind in this connection—she had no reason to think that the young showman would presume to speak to either of them. Jardine, a contemptuous satiric smile on his jaded face, sat languidly listening.

Mr. Dalton, perhaps, had already found a field at the Bar for his gift of marshalling facts, approaching with an ever-increasing velocity of significance the climax, but a chancellor, or a *puisne* judge, or even a jury was better fitted to resist the shock of sudden surprise than the idle summer birds in their relaxed mental attitude.

"Now," he continued, "the father was of a different sort; he was a young man of the very highest social connections. Moreover, he was talented, well-behaved, studious, very young—only in his junior year at college—heart-rending infatuation. His family investigated the facts and when they found that the marriage was really valid they cast him off without a moment's hesitation, absolutely, irretrievably. I never shall forget Judge Lloyd's dismay——"

"Judge Lloyd?" exclaimed several voices in different keys of sharp surprise.

"You surely don't mean Judge Clarence Jennico Lloyd of Glaston?" said the gentleman who had connections in that city, and was familiar with the status of its principal people.

"The noted jurist?—I do! He was considered a hard man, but he was a very just one. This happened in his palmy days, when he was very rich as well as esteemed far and wide an ornament to the judiciary. The family could trace a long and proud descent and they carried their heads very high. The judge could not tolerate such a mésalliance. He persisted in considering the woman a designing baggage and tried to buy her off. He bid very high—that was before his financial reverses."

Mr. Dalton swayed his big head to and fro, his eyes alight with the fires of reminiscence as the scenes of nearly thirty years earlier were re-enacted in his memory. "And yet from his standpoint he was quite right. They were very strict religionists, those Lloyds—Methodists, or Campbellites, or what not—they thought it a mortal sin to attend even a Shakespearean performance at a theatre. Judge Lloyd did not know one card from another—and was proud of the fact. I remember that once I tried a case in his court that involved a gambling transaction—his cousin Charles Jennico was of the opposing counsel—but that's neither here nor there. Judge Lloyd had other children then—boys and girls—he could not bring them into such association—he could not justify such an example."

"Jennico—isn't that a name down your way, in Louisiana, Mrs. Laniston?" one of the chess players suggested.

"I was just thinking," said Mrs. Laniston, her surprised eyes on the fire, her thin, jewelled fingers still keeping her place in the magazine. "There is an inconsiderable plantation called the Jennico place just beyond the bight of the bayou. The proprietor never lived there. I always understood that the owner was wealthy—but it is much neglected and in need of repair."

"It belongs to this fellow now," said the lawyer comfortably. "What sort of a house is on it, do you know, madam?"

"Not much of a house—a six-room frame, I think—there is not much land, but it is of good quality."

The lawyer, identified with his client's interests, nodded his head, smiling as if in personal gratification.

"I have some curiosity, Mr. Dalton," said one of the chess players, a soul dedicated to problems, "to know how such an unexpected windfall would affect a man. How did the young fellow receive the news of his good fortune?"

"Almost stunned at first—dreadfully taken aback;" the lawyer laughed and then grew grave.

"He had some points besides the money interests to claim his attention, you see. The *danseuse* and her highly bred and refined husband had very hard luck. Her earnings were poor, and he could not get employment in any appropriate way on account of the impression which his marriage gave to people of position. He was naturally supposed to be such a man who would make such a marriage. He tried all sorts of things, unsuited to his training and traditions. He was a ticket-taker, an advance agent, doorkeeper—had a classical education and wrote theatrical advertisements and puffs for newspapers—had no conception of the dramatic afflatus, wrote a play or two, heavy as lead, warranted to fall flat. He succumbed to ill-health, and then his father, having lost several children—all but this one and the eldest, Robert— and being much softened, offered to take this son back, excluding the wife of course, but paying her a handsome pension; this was refused. Time went on; the situation waxed worse continually; the judge then offered financial assistance unconditionally. But it came too late; the son died— presently his wife died also, and the grandson, then almost grown, doing a 'ground-and-lofty-tumbling turn' in great glory in a circus company went his way, chiefly on his head. He was lost sight of for a time, for Robert Lloyd, an admirable man and considered to have excellent business judgment, having made several most fortunate speculations, went beyond his depth, was caught in the undertow and dragged to ruin, overwhelming with him Judge Lloyd himself—I never could understand the tangle of Robert Lloyd's affairs. In the confusion of the financial wreck no one remembered this boy—the friends of the family thought the outcome well enough. The boy in his risky vocation must soon break his neck; and thus the unlucky episode of the beauty-prize winner in the Lloyd family would be definitely terminated. But, luckily enough it proved, the old gentleman once saw this grandson. Have you met him—this young fellow?" he broke off suddenly, addressing one of the chess players.

"No, I have not," the gentleman responded a trifle stiffly—street fairs were not in his line.

Mr. Dalton smiled benignly. "The most winning personality—yet with a quiet inherent dignity all his own, the most disarming amiability—and a face that you might wander through a hundred exhibitions of painting and never see equalled for a certain sort of charm. I don't wonder at the award for the fifteen thousand dollar prize—ha, ha, ha!"

"What is it that the court says when counsel becomes prolix—Be brief, sir—be brief," suggested Mrs. Laniston, laughing nervously. She was surprised to find herself eager, expectant. "Your story is too interesting to bear digressions, Mr. Dalton."

"Thanks—thanks greatly," Mr. Dalton beamed.

"Well, the circus roaming around the country gave an exhibition in the neighbourhood of Charles Jennico's summer residence near Glaston, where Judge Lloyd was visiting. He and Jennico were first cousins, and after his financial reverses the judge, who was as proud as Lucifer, scarcely went anywhere else. And this youngster, a man grown he was then, had the hardihood, or the good feeling, or the curiosity—or nobody knows what actuated him—to deliberately call on the old man. 'I don't want a thing in the world of you,' he said. 'But I know that my father owed you much, and I owe you much for what my father was to me. I came to pay my respects—to get the glad hand, that's all.' Judge Lloyd never opened his lips to me on the subject of this visit, but he was taken by surprise, the young man being ushered into the library, and Charles Jennico was sitting in the bay-window—he used to laugh and cry together when he rehearsed the scene. The judge, he said, was like a man in a dream at first. Then he began to beseech this stranger to come and live with him like a son without conditions and without restraint. 'But I could not become a dependent on you,' the boy said. 'It would be like a robbery of your old age. I have heard of your financial reverses or I would not have come. I know that you are broke.' And though he put it thus bluntly the judge did not wither him with a look. He said that he had influence—without depriving himself he could provide the youngster with respectable employment. 'You have no idea of my ignorance, grandfather. What you call respectable employment for me would have either to be a farce or a gratuity. I can do real work, such as it is, where I am and eat my own bread.' Judge Lloyd argued that he could secure money for his education. He had friends who would be glad to oblige him. 'It would go hard with you to ask a favour for yourself, sir—you shall not sue for me.' The old gentleman then urged him to consider what he would lose—he should have every advantage, he should travel. 'Grandfather,' he said, 'I have stood on my head in every capital of Europe—what I should be tempted to do would be to stay with you, quiet, resting, for I am fed up with stir and racket.' The whole thing captured Charles Jennico's fancy. He said that he had never expected to hear Judge Lloyd come so near a confession of arbitrary injustice, as

271

when he said how cruel had been the past, and how he feared that he had allowed a subservience to artificial standards to embitter and impoverish and shorten the lives of the youth's parents. 'You were just and true from your standpoint,' the boy sought to comfort him. 'A father has a *right* to his son's obedience'—the old judge used to repeat this phrase; it justified his course to himself. 'And yet my father was right, too, from his standpoint—I can't judge between you. I don't blame either for what is gone. I would willingly live with you in my father's place, but I must make and eat my own bread and play the man. You made a great mistake about my mother, though—you never knew my mother. She was It! She was the whole team! She was the Pearl you threw away, worth all your tribe!' And Judge Lloyd said that he believed it now that he had seen her son—he wished he had seen her first. And then the two, as competent fools as ever lived, fell on each other's necks and wept and parted."

"Tut, tut, tut—what a pity," said the bald-headed bridge player, oblivious of the words of his partner until she twice repeated, "Shall I lead, partner," when he caught himself with a galvanic start and responded, "Pray do."

There was a pause while Mr. Dalton eyed the fire reflectively, puffing at his cigar, which had gone out while he talked, requiring to be rekindled.

"What so won upon me this afternoon was the manner in which young Lloyd received the intelligence. He did not seem to remember or care at first that his financial miseries were now at an end—although he has been at his wit's end for money as he told me afterward; in fact, that he had not enough to pay for his transportation with the rest of the troupe or show or carnival or whatever the organisation is called, and had even tried to pawn his mother's engagement ring which had been indeed his grandmother's engagement

272

ring—an heirloom in Judge Lloyd's family, a thing with a legend, more or less mythical, I suppose."

Jardine thought of the gems he had seen in the safe of the hotel in Colbury, but he kept his own counsel.

"Of course the detail of the circumstances brought back to him that day of parting, and he told me that when he had first heard of his grandfather's death without another word between them he had deeply regretted his refusal to live with him in his father's place. He thought he had been too sensitive as to his independence—too afraid of grafting. It would not have been for long. He could have been the solace of the old gentleman's reverses and his age. He was wild that he had denied him aught—the only time that they had ever seen each other! His grandfather had been good to him that day, he said. And there," said Mr. Dalton with a whimsical wave of his cigar, "I had to wait and postpone the details of business communications while he leaned up against a tree in the woods and sobbed like a child because his grandfather had been good to him that day when he had offered him—so late—the boon of a life of precarious dependence in lieu of his free agency and a certain means of livelihood. I was touched, I must confess, I was very much touched. He has a rare nature, this-ground-and-lofty tumbler."

Mr. Dalton had not observed the usual legal reticence concerning a client's affairs. The nature of the case, the will and other matters of record, would give publicity to the mere facts, but he was solicitous, since the details had of necessity been elicited here, that the personal character of the harlequin legatee should be put into evidence, and receive from all the respect which he felt to be its due. No better method could he have found to disseminate the impression he wished to create than these reminiscences addressed to a symposium of idle gossips. Their craftily titillated interest

273

kept them still loitering around the fire after the card and chess tables had been abandoned as the hour wore late, and when Mrs. Laniston began to ascend the stairs to her apartment she noted, glancing back from the landing, that a group of gentlemen with freshly lighted cigars were drawing closer round the hearth continuing the subject with its cognate themes.

She had so unusually prolonged her loitering about the office fire to-night that she found that her son and daughter had returned from their mild diversions with the other youth of the place and were awaiting her coming in her room.

Frank was busy with some boxing gloves and was directing with a very exacting air precisely how some stitches should be set in the puffy awkward bags which had somehow become ripped. His sister Ruth, with her thimble and waxed thread, had placed the kerosene lamp and her workbox on the little table and was patiently repairing the damages according to his directions to the best of her ability.

"Ruthie, how close you do put your head to the lamp-chimney," her mother exclaimed in irritable warning. "Do be more careful, child. In another moment you would have singed your pompadour. Where is Lucia?"

Ruth lifted the endangered rouleau, stared around a moment, as if she expected to see her cousin here. "Why, she came upstairs with me—" then suggesting, "She must be in our room, I reckon," went on with her work as before.

Mrs. Laniston, proceeding into the adjoining apartment, found that it was not lighted, save by the moon, pouring the white rays through the windows, the shades being still up, and the shutters open. Outside was the limitless wilderness of the mountains, purple and dusky against the light indeterminate blue of the sky. A few stars, large and whitely lustrous, scintillated at vast intervals, but the moon was supreme, and the white mists in the valleys shimmered with opalescent suggestions of delicate tints. Far away the sudden shrill snarling cry of a catamount smote the air, then all was silent save the rush of the torrent in the valley. For a moment it seemed that no one was in the room; then Mrs. Laniston perceived that Lucia was seated, half kneeling, close by the window, very still, very silent, and she was sure that the girl had been weeping.

"Want anything?" asked Lucia, in a voice that yet betrayed tears; then she put her elbows on the window sill and more deliberately addressed herself to the contemplation apparently of the night.

"Lucia—chilly as it is! What are you doing at that window? You'll catch your death of cold."

Lucia in a muffled voice muttered something about the air being quite balmy, and remarked that she had been already most of the evening promenading on the verandah.

"Why," said Mrs. Laniston, stolidly amazed, "Mr. Jardine was in the office the whole time."

"We are not the Siamese twins," said Lucia dully.

"Of course not. Who were you with, most of the time?"

For there still remained at New Helvetia a number of squires of dames, eminently available for germans, and verandah promenades, and sentimentalisings in the moonlight.

"I was with Mr. Lloyd, all the time." Her voice quavered as she anticipated the note of surprise, and reprehension, and dismay in Mrs. Laniston's rejoinder. It sounded instantly.

"Why, Lucia! That showman, Lloyd?"

"I could not very well avoid it—and I didn't want to avoid it," she said rather doggedly.

Mrs. Laniston had a monition of George Laniston's ultra particularity in social matters; then she had a saving recollection of the standing of Judge Lloyd.

"Oh, poor fellow! I suppose he wanted to boast a bit of his legacy. It seems he comes of good people on his father's side, and has been remembered in a codicil, or something."

"He did not mention the legacy, except that he did say as it would make his connections a matter of newspaper notoriety he did not mind speaking of them. He said he would not do this ordinarily, for in a man in his humble business it would seem boastful, and he declared that he was more proud of his mother, and her generosity, and her struggles, and her courage, and her life of sacrifice in the care of those dear to her, than of every Lloyd that ever stepped."

And the proud Miss Laniston burst into tears—not the first she had shed that night over the pathos of the ci-devant dancer's woes.

"Why, Lucia," Mrs. Laniston exclaimed, irritably, "I am surprised that you should be so weak."

Lucia had no desire to be strong; she continued to weep without reserve.

"She was lovely—lovely; I can see it through all he says of her, and how bitterly she blamed herself to be the cause of her husband's and son's abandonment by their fine relations. She would have been willing to give them up, to go off anywhere, in any poverty, so they might have the position, and luxuries, and advantages of the station to which they were born. But they clung to each other and to her, as anybody might know they would!"

And once more the hot tears came.

There was a moment's silence in which Mrs. Laniston canvassed this unprecedented difficulty.

276

"And now he reproaches himself that afterward he did not go to his grandfather. He is wild about it. He says his grandfather was right from his standpoint, and he was old and forlorn, and yearned for the arm of his son's son to lean upon. He is stricken with remorse, and he has no peace. No—he didn't talk at all about the legacy."

Mrs. Laniston gathered her forces for a desperate *coup*.

"Lucia Laniston, listen to me. You are not falling in love with that man, for of course you couldn't consider so ignorant a person, with so frightful an accent and choice of phrases. But you are allowing your imagination to become involved."

"Oh, no, Aunt Dora," Lucia murmured. But Mrs. Laniston kept on.

"It is not becoming for you to sit here on the floor in that nice dress—and there is no earthly process by which those delicate fabrics can be cleaned—and weep your eyes out about a stranger's mother. No matter how lovely—and she took an international prize for beauty—she was a circus girl, or a ballet dancer, a position that in itself it is impossible to ignore or forget, no matter what he or anyone else may say. I am glad, since his father was one of Judge Lloyd's sons, that he is to be redeemed from that awful calling; it seems that he will own that small Jennico plantation near us in Louisiana, and the little six-room frame house on it. I suppose he will farm there, and maybe some people will receive him on sufferance—such an uneducated man, my dear! Of course I know if he were really rich he could go where he pleases, and the best society would pull caps for him, and he could marry whom he chooses. Don't think I am sordid, dear. *I* don't make these conventions. They are the inexorable law of the world. But consider, my dear, what—once in New Orleans, or St. Simon's Island, or Jacksonville—you would think of such a cavalier. You know I have never been hateful and stiff with you and Ruth. I have let you have all the good time you could with propriety. I think this young fellow's prize-beauty makes him very fetching, and his 'lydy,' isn't the awful address it would be on any other tongue; and his suddenly inheriting a bit of money is like a romance. But life is made up of commonplaces and realities, dear, and a girl who lets herself dream in the moonlight must wake at least to a very sordid day. Your papa wouldn't forgive me if I didn't warn you, dear. Love must be founded on respect; a man must be in a position for a woman to look up to him, to defer to his experience and judgment, and superior information and education. A woman cannot lead a husband by the hand."

"You take too much for granted, Aunt Dora," Lucia interrupted, a trifle angrily.

"A man with a past like his would reveal a thousand amazing tastes and prejudices and views, the like of which you never heard. You would spend your life in teaching, and combating, and obliterating. And the little six-room frame— seems to me it has a little garden in front, with turfed flower beds, raised in stars, and hearts, and triangles. If cotton doesn't pick up somehow you can't expect much from your father till his death—I hope for your sake, as well as his, that's a long way off. He is a young man, comparatively; he may marry again. I want you to make a comfortable match, and be easy and happy. Ruth's prospects are so good in her engagement to Philip Trumbull—I wish I could make her write more regularly to that man—she is so idle!—and I couldn't bear for you to be less appropriately placed."

"I haven't asked him to marry me, Aunt Dora," Lucia said suddenly in her natural manner, "and I can assure you that he has not made the slightest intimation tending that way."

"Well, so far, so good! Get up off the floor—that stuff pulls so, and just see how your knee is straining it. What a moonlight night!" she exclaimed, rising and standing before the window. "What a mystery on the mountains!"

CHAPTER XVII

The morning broke with abounding good cheer. It was impossible not to respond to the revivifying matutinal influences. The vast solemnity of the austere mountain ranges filling the universe seemed more impersonal. Some stupendous, resplendent work of art might thus affect the senses. Only a keenly receptive temperament, the impressionable, plastic mood, might embrace its insistent meaning, its eloquent message, its redundant appeal to every vibrant, sensitive pulse. One saw the reality, yet put it aside, postponed it, like the great facts of life and death, and the momentousness of eternity, turning instead to the cheerful trifle of the hour. And perhaps it was enough to breathe such fresh balsamic air, to hear the sonorous periods of the lordly wind sounding over cliff and torrent, while all the poly-tinted leafy forests bent in obeisance; to see with the shallow outward eye the variant tints of blue, from the dark blurred efflorescence on the nearest slopes to the translucent sapphire of further ranges and thence to a hard, clear, turquoise blue, and so to a faint, vague azure that one could hardly discriminate from the sky line; and above still, the silent great, white domes, where, although so early, the snow had fallen. Even the shadows were but simulacra of winged joys, as the white dazzling clouds sped through the sky, while their similitudes followed swiftly below over the mountain side and the valley, racing for some unimagined aërial goal. The air was full of woodsy fragrance—the odour of sere leaves, the pungent aroma of mint and of water-side weeds, the balsamic breath of fir and pine. Keen, too, withal;

the group gathering around the hearth in the office comprised all the adult guests in the house, save a few loiterers, still lingering at the breakfast tables nearest the fire in the great dining-room. Now and then juvenile parties came thundering down the stairs with golf clubs or tennis rackets, rushed through the office, and were gone, banging the glass doors to imminent fracture, or the hearth-side was recruited by the laggards from the breakfast table bringing a whiff of cold air from the transit through the hall. Ruth and Lucia were rubbing their pink hands, and shivering in their boleros of dark red and light blue cloth respectively, worn over their sheer lawn morning dresses, to the wonderment of Jardine, who could not comprehend why, if they were cold, they should not wear warm cheviot gowns, unmindful of the unwritten law of truly orthodox Southern women, who would fain cling to their white lawn attire till the snow falls. Lloyd's theatric discrimination had already appraised the effect of their Dresden belt ribbons, and high stocks, the one in red and brown, the other blue and pink. He bowed to them with distant gravity, but his face had a suggestion of happiness which had not heretofore characterised its quiet composure. His peculiar appeal to popular favour had been all the more effective because of the romantic history of good fortune detailed in his absence last night, and there had been some very hearty hand-shaking in the casual introductions around the fireside this morning. All the house looked with a joyous prepossession upon the newly found legatee and a sort of vicarious pleasure. They were even prepared to find a certain quaint zest in his "outrageous profession," as one irreconcilable old prig called it.

"Did you have a fine bout with the gloves?" asked a clean-shaven gentleman, taking his cigar from his smiling lips. His expression just now was as benignant as a bishop's, but he was broker at home.

Lloyd was a trifle embarrassed; he did not know how much of the lawn had been in view from his interlocutor's point of observation.

"Oh, Mr. Laniston will get so he can stand up, after a little."

There was a laugh around the circle, and Frank's pink cheeks grew very red.

"Why, Francis," exclaimed his mother in genuine amazement, "I thought you were a champion boxer!"

"Oh, I've got it in for him, good and hot," Frank sputtered, over his cigarette.

"Did he down you?" asked the broker. "Really?"

"I fell over somehow, every time he crooked his little finger."

"I'll get him so that he can stand up," said Lloyd patronisingly.

"There's all the difference in the world between a pastime and a profession," said the broker. "We see that in the market—a little flier once in a while—and a plunger."

"But will you continue this profession, Mr. Lloyd?" the prig fixed him with such a scandalised expression in his prominent, lashless eyes, that it amounted to an intentional reproach and affront.

Mr. Dalton seemed to resent it.

"He has something better to do." He laughed prosperously, and stroked his moustache.

"He was signing cheques for half an hour this morning," continued the lawyer. This boast was not in the best taste, but Lloyd had so far won upon him that he was both sensitive and belligerent in his client's behalf.

The showman was pained, and winced visibly.

"Just some little things I wanted before the fairy gold melts away," he said, laughing but disconcerted. He had begun to entertain great confidence in Mr. Dalton, but bruiser though he was, he could not appreciate the lawyer's faculty for putting people down.

Mr. Dalton took from his pocket a great sheaf of letters, ready stamped for the mail.

"And I had better post these while I think of it;" he began to sift them apart, and one by one slipped them into a slit in the counter where a box lurked for their reception.

"The first expresses filial piety, and endows a bed in a hospital in his mother's name. The second orders a monument to the memory of his parents."

Mr. Dalton looked around with a triumphant eye, evidently bent on "rubbing it in."

"Then comes the discharge of just debts. James Tunstan."

"That's Wick-Zoo," said Lloyd, suddenly forgetful of the public display of his affairs. He looked with a laugh of extreme relish at Frank, who cried hilariously, "Oh, hi! the wild man!"

"And John Haxon."

"Captain Ollory," Lloyd interpreted, still smiling, half regretfully; the street fair seemed now some tender reminiscence of many a year agone.

"I can't persuade my young friend to sever his connection with the greatest show on earth," Mr. Dalton laid the letters on one knee and glanced around the circle with an expression of disapproval and exasperation. "That is, he doesn't propose to manage it personally or to perform, but he still remains a partner, and intends to finance it. With all

282

its faults, he loves it still!—and Haxon succeeds to the managerial—er—er—er—ermine."

"Why, they'd go to pieces without me—to everlasting smithereens!" exclaimed Lloyd excitedly. "And it's hard to get a place in a company to break your neck in!"

"But I understand they went off and left *you*," said Dalton.

"Somebody had to stay, and I was the captain of the ship."

"But, Mr. Lloyd, think of the unpleasant personal publicity," said the priggish gentleman. "They will advertise your name in this connection and make money out of it. That's what they'll do—make money out of it. They will use your accession to fortune as a sensation, a card to draw people to the show."

"Exactly what I wrote to Haxon—work it for all it's worth, and quit sousin' in that old tank of yours that will break your back and drown you some day! I'll keep that show going—straight goods; it kept me going many a day."

Mr. Dalton mournfully shook his head, and the priggish gentleman, too inquisitive for good form—but he was justified in some degree by the uncommon circumstances—demanded:

"Then you contemplate a different occupation for your own life, I suppose?"

"Yes; I'm fed up with knocking about the world. I want to be quiet for a change. I'll go to my own house," he paused, and shook his head a trifle sadly. "Sounds funny to me! I don't understand farming, but I'll see if I can catch on. I like animals, but they're wild generally; the lions and panthers and such fellows always get to know me almost before I notice them. Maybe cows and mules *would seem* tame." He laughed a little.

"Professor Gordon B. Lancaster," read Mr. Dalton from another stamped and addressed envelope, "—thought I'd mislaid his letter; desiring if possible to secure his company and services."

"Ah, to read with Mr. Lloyd," said the priggish gentleman, a look like a benediction in the lashless orbs, such satisfaction beamed from them. "Yes—yes; you are still young enough to prepare for a collegiate course."

"But I don't contemplate that," said Lloyd, very calmly; "I'd fizzle out at that. This gentleman, if he accepts, will seem to the world to be my secretary, but in private life he will be my tutor, and live with me in my house."

Mrs. Laniston looked bewildered.

"But I should think that would be more expensive than a regular university course."

Mr. Dalton smiled and beamed, and tapped the letter against the sheaf he was sorting.

"A good bit of money goes with the real estate. Mr. Lloyd thinks he can afford to put himself on a level in culture with his station."

"Very praiseworthy," said the prig.

"I haven't the proper foundation for the classics," explained Lloyd. "I propose that this gent shall read with me. Hist'ry is the racket I care most for. When I performed with a circus company I travelled with through Europe, I saw enough to excite my wonder, and I jus' wondered, an' wondered. Now I want to *know*. And the poets and general literachure! My father used to read a great deal of such stuff when his health had disabled him, and I am going to travel right along the road he took, and read the words he read, and dream the dreams he dreamed. I never had the time before. I'm strong on the common rudiments—readin' and writin' and arithmetic."

"A very fair accountant," Mr. Dalton commended the meritorious attainment.

"Oh, yes; kept the books of the company."

"'Greatest show———'" suggested Mr. Dalton, dimpling.

And the impresario had the grace to laugh good-humouredly, though he flushed, too.

"Now here are two letters to the department stores," said Mr. Dalton, who for some reason seemed bent on exploiting his client, who in his inexperience and his absorption in the strange developments of his affairs, apparently saw nothing unusual in the trend of the conversation.

"They've not got stamps," he exclaimed excitedly, "That'll never do. They must get off! Can you accommodate me?" to the affable clerk. "Thanks, much."

"They are both orders for dry goods?" said Mr. Dalton.

"Oh, no; this is for the hydrostatic bed for the Living Skeleton. That poor man's bones, that he lives by, torture him. The feather beds, and the flock beds, and the mattresses are simply fierce. And he is stingy, yet he is tolerably warm in this world's goods. And he is an educated man. But he always stuck at the expense. Now he has got it."

Lloyd chucked the letter into the slit with extreme satisfaction.

"Stop—hadn't you better ask some lady about the number of yards for that gown, Mrs. Laniston, for instance, before you mail that letter?"

"If you will be so very kind." The *ci-devant* showman turned toward Mrs. Laniston with that distinguished manner which she had first observed in him. "It depends, of course, on the

285

size of the person. It is a gown for the fat lydy. She is sensitive, and suffers dreadfully from the public. But she is a very nice lydy! I think she would like to be beautiful, and as she has so few pleasures I thought a surprise might tickle her. So I ordered sixty yards of silk—the heaviest and best quality."

"Oh, oh, I should think that would be ample," said Mrs. Laniston, decorously able to preserve her gravity.

But Ruth's dimples could not be hid; she was all pink now, and smiled alluringly.

"What tint—Mr. Lloyd?" she asked.

"Alice blue," he replied, quite solemnly, and Ruth's suppressed laughter burst out uncontrollably at the idea.

His eyes had a suggestion of reproach, as he looked at her, but Lucia's face was grave, deeply flushed, pondering, pained.

"Hard life, to be a freak," Lloyd said; then as if for tabulation of correspondence by Mr. Dalton—"One dozen pink sandals for flying lydy. She has so much trouble presenting fresh soles to the public, and dingy ones show so."

"And now, your grand relative, Thomas Lloyd, Esquire."

"Do you visit him in Glaston?" the habitué of Glaston asked with an added infusion of respect.

"No, sir!" said the ex-showman, with his first touch of stiffness. "*He* visits me at my house."

"Mr. Thomas Lloyd wrote to request the honour of a visit, and I brought the letter," said Mr. Dalton; he still had the air of exploiting a case and marshalling his points, one by one, before a judge or a jury. "It seemed an agreeable arrangement to me, but Mr. Lloyd saw the matter in a different light. He is a man equipped for *tours de force*, and he seemed to think it best to make the mountain come to Mahomet. So we telegraphed his refusal and his counter invitation last night, and received a long distance telephone of acceptance this morning. Now Mr. Lloyd writes to name the day. It seems he is not leaving New Helvetia immediately."

"I hope you don't inconvenience yourself on my account— our little contract," said Frank, with solicitude.

Lloyd showed sudden embarrassment.

"No—no——," he said, his fine face flushing, his candid eyes faltering. "Not on your account. I know you'd release me. I'm tired of hustling round; and—I like the place, and I've a little leisure now."

Mr. Jardine hearkened to this in prophetic displeasure. His pride, his self-respect, had been cut down by the part he had played in the esclandre of the previous evening, and yet he could not reproach himself with precipitancy. He had vainly sought to evade, to shake off this dangerous, this derogatory association, since the incident of the Ferris Wheel. The crisis was forced when he had seen the woman he loved and admired and respected unsuspiciously promenading the moon-lit verandah in this showman's company. The fact that he proved to be the scion of a family of standing, and that he had been lifted from vagabondage to competence by the provisions of a will did not in any small degree annul the objections to his career and the suspicion, which Jardine felt was justified, of recent complicity with the moonshiners in their unlawful traffic. Jardine's inherent caution, however, was rendered more conservative by the circumstance that the fellow-traveller had proved to be a lawyer, rather than a Federal emissary, and was charged with a mission of honour and service to the object of his suspicion instead of espionage and arrest, as he had fancied, and he was devoutly thankful that this ludicrous mistake of identity was not definitely elicited in his impetuous and uncharacteristic outburst last night, when he had demanded an explanation. The sensational outcome with its elements of romance, so alluring to the average mind, had served to obliterate at the time Jardine's own extraordinary conduct, and although it had recurred to the memory of more than one of the group, since the excitements had subsided, they had hesitated to mention it. Jardine was not a drinking man, but intoxication only might serve to account with simplicity for the demonstration. His was a nature of almost austere reserve and his presence had always a certain distinction and dignity difficult to disregard. Most of those present after the breaking up of the party last night, lingering to finish out their cigars, had reconciled themselves to the ravages of their curiosity, and there was a sentiment of gratitude as to a public benefactor when the broker suddenly accosted Jardine.

"By the way, Mr. Jardine, you treated us to a fine sensation to-night. Were you acquainted with this lawyer and his lucky client, or whom did you suppose them to be?"

"A case of mistaken identity," said Jardine easily, but with the certain aloof composure that became him so well. "I beg you won't refer to it. I could not discuss it—very embarrassing. Good-night." And he turned away.

In the days that ensued Mr. Jardine's gloomy expectations seemed hardly likely to be justified. Mrs. Laniston had taken the helm with a strong hand, and the sway that she could maintain when she would was amply manifest. The two girls were continually under her wing, and the old routine of their occupations was re-established as before the outing to Colbury. Jardine once more found himself her partner at bridge against Lucia and Ruth, whiling away long hours of rainy weather, while Lloyd was smoking and chatting or playing billiards with some of the other gentlemen, with whom he had swiftly become cordial friends, or deep with his lawyer in business correspondence, or out exercising with the stalwart Frank. Mrs. Laniston was not so radical in her management of the situation as to attract attention, not even indeed from the persons most concerned. Now and again Lloyd, all unsuspicious of her effort at avoidance, entered into conversation with the two young ladies in the group by the office fire, and their chaperon had not a word or glance to check them. She even smilingly surveyed the scene when more than once he joined them in the procession of young people who, in wraps and rubbers, essayed a constitutional tramp, trudging up and down the wet and windy piazzas while the persistent rain steadily fell without and the rest of the world had vanished utterly in the clouds. But these occasional incidents occupied inconsiderable fractions of time, and counted but scantily against the long hours that Jardine spent in their society, at cards, or driving in the woods, or reading aloud to them, while they sat at their crochet-work in the bay-window, an improving book, of which Mrs. Laniston had expressed her desire that he should give them his views, in marginalia, so to speak, which were somewhat in contravention of the conclusions of the author. Mr. Jardine entertained a conviction not only that he read well, but that his thoughts did not suffer disparagement in contrast with the expositions of the text.

It was not altogether with a good grace, however, that Jardine fell into line under these tactics. Mentally he revolted at every concession, even slight and apparently obligatory, to evade an awkward discrimination against Lloyd. Jardine could tolerate no half measures, and the errors of this policy he deemed amply demonstrated one morning of brilliant sunshine when all the guests were assembled in the hotel office awaiting the arrival of the stage from Colbury.

When the stage came in with the mail, but with not a single passenger, there was a general diversion of the attention of the group around the fire. Letters were opened and read, the recipients now frowning over unwelcome information, now with hard-set teeth and firm jaw, as the eyes scanned the lines, in prophetic refusal of a proposition as yet hardly presented. Only once or twice was there a gleam of pleasure, so awry does the world go with most of us, so do anxiety and disillusionment, and actual disaster predominate. The composite expression of countenance of the group after opening the mail was a reluctant and grudging thanksgiving that matters were no worse. The columns of market prices and stock quotations in the newspapers came in for serious and silent study, and the politician, who had congressional aspirations, pondered long and deeply over the reports of the returns from certain local elections, of moment to a possible canvass.

Mr. Dalton and his young friend had retired to the bridge table in the bay-window, where the man of law explained and expatiated upon certain business interests of which his correspondence treated. Now and again Lloyd's eyes wandered to the verandah outside where Lucia and Ruth were rapidly walking to and fro in the sunshine, their sheer, crisp, white skirts waving in the speed of their motion and their chilly hands tucked under their elbows in the sleeves of their blue and red boleros. Jardine noticed that they smiled graciously upon the two gentlemen in the bay-window as they passed. They came in presently, all aglow, announcing their intention to make up a party for the bowling alley.

"Mamma says the ground is too damp for tennis," pouted Ruth, glancing at Jardine, expectant of partisanship and counsel.

He had been saying to himself bitterly that it was not his capacity for self-sacrifice in Lucia Laniston's interests that was limited, but the possibilities. Her aunt had been present throughout the scene of the disclosure of identity and otherwise knew as much of the man as he did, for his suspicions could not have been safely suggested, and he had no means of proving their truth. He was amazed to find that his anger against Lucia Laniston, his disapproval of her headstrong folly, had not diminished the strength of his attachment, for the qualities she had displayed throughout the Street Fair episode were precisely the traits with which he had least sympathy—unconventionality, girlish impetuosity, a lack of solid judgment, a flighty fun that no sane man could enjoy, a wild relish of fantastic novelty, and the evening of their return a flout at a friendly monition and a defiant persistence in her own course. He loved her, it was clear, and he had an infinite patience where she was concerned.

He merely bowed with silent acquiescence in the proposition to wile away the time with tenpins, but Mrs. Laniston broke out with inexorable negation.

"No—no bowling alley to-day. The roof leaks like a riddle and the building is sopping with dampness and as chilly as a vault. What *are* you two thinking of?"

Lucia's countenance clouded with disappointment.

"We can't sit moping by the fire all this magnificent day, Aunt Dora," she plained.

For his life Jardine could not refrain from coming to the rescue.

"What do you say to a brisk gallop in the sunshine? The horses are in fine fettle."

"The very thing!" cried Ruth.

"I just *live* for the saddle!" declared Lucia, beaming with pleased anticipation.

291

"What a help he'll be to Mrs. Jardine (when he finds her) in making up her mind!" said Ruth, in explanatory wise to Lucia.

"How astonished Mrs. Jardine will be (when he finds her) at the way he can hit it off when he does let himself go!" said Lucia, in an affected aside to Ruth.

Jardine laughed with genuine good humour. It had been so long since he had encountered this fiction of "Mrs. Jardine" that he was heartily glad to hear of her again, and was disposed to think them and their ingenuity in manufacturing her views very fetching.

"Shall I have your saddle put on Admiration?" he asked of Lucia, for two of the horses were his; the affection of the liver which he had, or fancied he had, was presumed to be benefited by horseback exercise, and as Mr. Jardine had no affinity for martyrdom he had brought his own excellent mounts with him. On occasions like this he sacrificed his own pleasure and rode an animal from the livery stable which, however, kept very passable stock, especially since the hard driving and riding of the season were over and the horses had had time to recuperate.

"Oh, do, Lucia," cried Ruth. "I'm afraid of Admiration. He's dear, but he dances so on his hind legs."

"He's perfectly safe," said Jardine, "only a little spirited."

"And so fast! I lo-o-ve him!" declared Lucia.

"And will you have the mare, Rosabel?" he asked Ruth, respectfully.

"Oh—won't I, though!" she said, dimpling.

"And the rest of us will have to put up with the livery stable nags," said Frank, oblivious of the fact that Mr. Jardine had not invited him to join the party; indeed Jardine had contemplated taking the two girls on a decorous morning canter, riding a livery stable nag between the two, and had by no means proposed an equestrian party. Still, the suggestion had grown out of the taboo of tenpins and tennis, and it was natural, with his cubbish facility for blundering, that Frank should not think the project at all exclusive. Indeed, the idea that it was to be a general outing of the youth of the place was shared by others as well, and one of the elderly gentlemen, the broker from New Orleans, turned with a sudden inspiration to Lloyd, who had completed his business with Dalton and now waited to pass through the group.

"Let me warn you against the livery nag. I have an extra good saddle horse here, and shall be much complimented to put you up."

He had been greatly attracted by the young fellow's face and manner; besides Lloyd might be soon seeking investment for his money, and there was no telling when he would want to buy or sell stocks. Fair words go as far in the brokerage business as any other.

Jardine was amazed and incensed at Lloyd's ready acceptance, and the broker, turning to the telephone, was the first to cry "Hello" to the livery stable.

It seemed a fate, the most mischievous of complications, that Jardine's effort to save his lady-love the ennui of a dull day should presently place her beside the man of all others whom he wished her to avoid—handsomer than ever in correct equestrian costume—"possibly his gear as a ringmaster," Jardine thought, with a sneer—and riding like a centaur. The broker's horse was a stylish, well-bred brute, and his very proximity seemed to stimulate Admiration to sudden bursts of competitive speed. Both mounts were hard to hold, and Lucia had never seemed half so beautiful, so spirited. Her dark-green riding-habit enhanced her fairness.

She wore the regulation high stiff silk hat on her fluffy brown hair, with a shimmering white silken veil twisted half about it, and half about her throat. Her high white collar and shirt front in their mannish effect and a dark-red four-in-hand tie were her special pride. Her airy poise on the side-saddle seemed to Lloyd infinite temerity and a great sacrifice to feminine bondage in convention, for he was accustomed to see "lydies" ride cross-saddle, but she appeared to have much confidence, and maintained a secure seat. Erect and fearless she now and again looked over her shoulder to invite Ruth's bright-eyed sympathy from the distance. For Rosabel could not canter in the same class; sleek and gentle and fleet enough, she was ideal for a lady's use, and Jardine jogged on his hired nag beside her. Jardine had jockeyed, as one may say, to throw Lloyd with Ruth Laniston, and himself join the two ahead. But Lloyd had taken his place beside Lucia's rein, and persistently kept it. Frank was soon losing ground. He could not maintain the pace, and Jardine presently to his immeasurable chagrin found the brother and sister beside him while the fleeter steeds carried the couple ahead on and on—out of sight.

For a time neither drew rein; the sandy road, beaten hard by the late storm, was ideal. The foliage of the forest trees all along the vast slopes was freshly washed and resplendent. The illuminated yellow of the maples and hickories might have dispensed with the sun in its wonderful clarity of tone; it seemed to glow with inherent light. The red of the sourwood and the sumach and the scarlet oak contrasted richly. Down in the valleys, glimpsed whenever the road skirted the mountain's verge, one could see that the deciduous trees were still green, but on these lofty levels no foliage showed verdant save the fir and the pine. The wind itself seemed hardly more swift than the racing steeds; the clouds, dazzlingly white above the endless blue ranges, challenged their speed, scudding before the high aërial

294

currents above even the bare domes, the "balds" of the mountains.

Now and then as the riders skirted a precipice they caught sight of a swift torrent, leaping down the mountain side, in cataract after cataract. Once Lloyd checked his horse to mark how the great vine that climbed from among the roots of a giant poplar on the slope below to its topmost branch, was laden with grapes; on a level with the road sat the cub of a bear in their midst, feeding on the fruit, pausing to gaze at them with a quaint ursine stare.

The horses snorted and sprang aside, and he laid his hand on her bridle as they passed along the narrow precipitous way. It was somewhat too narrow, too precipitous for this breakneck speed, and perhaps but for his peculiar insensibility to danger in equine matters he might earlier have checked it.

"We had best go slow along here," he said. "The earth is soft with the rain, and it might cave. Step lightly, my friend," he addressed the animal. But when they came on good rock-ribbed footing he did not mend their pace.

"Yes, we will go slow," she said, "and wait for the others."

"I don't care for them to overtake us," he said. "I have something in mind I want to say to you."

She looked confused, agitated. Her flush rose to the roots of her hair. She turned upon him her beautiful eyes—was it appeal or was it a gentle compassion that looked out at him inscrutably. Then she turned them hastily away.

"Don't say it," she exclaimed. "Don't say it!"

"You know already what it is—and why should I not speak? You want to spare me?"

She made a gesture of assent.

"I am not very easy hurt; that's one value of the hard knocks I've had; I'm equal to taking my punishment. I hardly hoped—how could I? But from the moment I saw you there on the piazza of the hotel in Colbury I knew the difference 'twixt prose and poetry. The world's been set to music since; sometimes it's sad, and sometimes it's sweet, but it's all singing rhymes. I loved you from the minute I heard your voice—but I did not begin to say my prayers to you till that night in the wheel; oh, you seemed so kind, so good, made in a special creation, unlike all in heaven or earth—not an angel—'cause you are a woman; not a woman—'cause you are a blessed saint! Oh, I lived to see you, and in all my troubles I'd only have to think of you, and though I never expected you to speak to me again my heart would be light—light!"

He broke off suddenly.

"Oh, I distress you;" for her head was bent low and he saw the tears falling from her eyes on her little trembling riding gloves. "And you are so kind; you wanted to spare me."

"No," she said, suddenly, brokenly; "I wanted to spare myself, for, oh—oh, I care as much as you—and more; *more!*"

She could not look at him, but she knew that his face was irradiated.

"Then—why—*why* can't we be happy together? Say it again! I can't believe it!"

"No—no——" She was calming herself, sorry and dismayed that she had said aught. She had lost her self-control, and was struggling hard for composure.

"You mean that your friends would object? I would not have spoken a word, but for this change. I told you that if I had a chance for life on a better scale I'd take it. I have the means to make your life comfortable; I could not, I would not have asked you to make any sacrifice. Ought you to let your friends prevent our marriage if you care—if you really care?"

"It is impossible—the sorrow of my life, but impossible!" He gave a sigh of perplexity.

"You think I am—or rather my life has made me—so unacceptable?"

"I am so artificial," she sobbed. "I should not be easily contented."

She thought of the little six-room house just across the swamp and beyond the bayou, near her aunt's handsome country place in Louisiana, and tried to see herself there—in a rocking-chair on the porch, or planting seeds in the turfed, star-shaped flower beds.

"You are no more artificial than a lydy of culchure should be," he asseverated. Then ensued a long pause during which she glanced at him as, with a frown of doubt and perplexity, he looked far away at the horizon line, and she winced to note his grace and perfect pose in riding, realising the tawdry life which this apotheosis of equestrianism comprehended and represented.

"If you care," he said, "and God bless you for the word, will we be happy apart?"

"Oh, no! no!" she said, with a gush of tears. "A great joy has knocked at my door, and I can't open to it, but must bar up, and draw the bolts, and—how can I be happy?"

He turned in the saddle and looked sternly at her.

"Are you promised—to—another? That Mr. Jardine, perhaps?"

She rejoiced to see the fires of jealousy fiercely kindling in his eyes. She burst into a peal of laughter.

"Oh, poor Mr. Jardine," she cried. "To be jealous of poor Mr. Jardine!"

"Then, why—why—?" he asked impatiently.

"Can't you see that there would be no happiness for us together? We are of different worlds. I couldn't endure to see you give up your standards—and yet I could not abide them. The distance between us would widen, not close. I have no instincts for the simple life, and you would have no interest in the artificial."

Once more the dark and dreary little farmhouse came within her mental range of vision.

"You would not know what I relinquished, nor I what you sigh for. You keep up your connection with your roving company for *their* benefit, and I honour you for your generosity—but I would prefer a more selfish man, with more regard for the sneer of the world."

"And you care for that—the sneer of the world?"

"The world would think I had quite thrown myself away."

"H-a-rdly—ha-a-rdly. The world noses out a little money mighty quick!"

"All your training, won with such pain and toil, is something I can't appreciate; tawdry and odious with a personal application, a stumbling-block and an offence to me; and all I have been taught and have striven for is beyond your ken."

"All I know is I love you; and all I care for is that you have said you love me!" he declared resolutely.

"And I should never have said it, but I have a confidence in you beyond my faith in any other mortal. I wanted you to know it, and keep it hidden in your heart, though we part forever."

"For my life I can't see why."

"It will be bitter, but that knowledge will help us to live through it."

"Oh, we will live through it—like the survivors live through death. The sun shines on graves all over the world, but the mourners go about the streets."

She burst into sobbing again, holding up her handkerchief to her eyes. Suddenly she lifted her head.

"They are coming—they are coming! Do I look as if I had been crying? Oh, I don't want them to know—it's like a sacrilege for them to know! There! there is a man coming along that path. What is that in his hand? Let us ride forward and stop him, as if we had been questioning him."

She drew the white gauze veil over her tearful eyes, and her cheeks all pallid from weeping, and together they rode forward to hail the mountaineer who had stopped stock still on beholding them. And from the long reaches of the road, like the footsteps of approaching doom, they heard the iterative tramp of hoofbeats, every moment growing louder.

CHAPTER XVIII

As the distanced equestrian party came within view of the two in advance they perceived that Lloyd was riding forward toward a young mountaineer who stood at gaze in the path which intersected the somewhat more definitely marked main road. They could hear Lloyd's cheery, vibrant voice as he called out to him:

"Where does this road lead?"

The man responded in somewhat surly wise, eyeing, gloweringly, the dashing apparition of the young horseman, springing up so suddenly in the midst of the woods, for

Lloyd's appearance, thus well mounted, was doubly effective.

"Why—it jes' leads round an' round about 'n the mountings." He spoke as if constrained to elucidate a self-evident proposition. His large brown eyes, which had a special lustre of surface, not depth, seemed vaguely familiar, and somehow inimical, to Lloyd, who started as he heard Lucia speak, although her voice was too restrained to reach the mountaineer's ears.

"Look, look! it is an old acquaintance of ours," said Lucia, wheeling her horse to accost the laggards in the rear. "It's Diogenes. Don't you see the lantern in his hand? It's Diogenes! What distinguished people one does meet in the Great Smoky Mountains!"

The young mountaineer shifted his gaze to the approaching group for an instant only; then he fixed his intent eyes once more on Lloyd's face.

He was a fine type of his class, well built, tall, with a peculiarly trig, trim effect. He wore no coat, and his shirt of blue homespun showed how slim, yet muscular, was his body, and his long boots, drawn to the knee over his trousers of blue-jeans, encased legs of which every movement suggested activity. He had a large brown hat, the brim in front turned up, and showing a jagged, ill-cut fringe of hair that resembled an old fashion of ladies' coiffure, called a "bang." He was as surly, as ill-conditioned, as unattractive of aspect as a panther; his handsome traits appealed as little to one's liking.

Lucia's airy, debonair manner bespoke the blithest spirits. "Oh, joy! Diogenes is looking for you, Mr. Jardine. His quest is successful at last. You are the honest man! You know it *must* be you, for we are all aware how politic poor Frank is."

For the first time Mr. Jardine deigned to mention Lloyd. Heretofore he would not so much as glance at him. But he could not resist converting her pleasantry into a slur, and barbing the point. "And is not Mr. Lloyd a competitor for distinction as an honest man? Am I alone?"

Lloyd discerned the acrid taunt in the smooth tones and flashed a fierce glance into Mr. Jardine's bland and smiling countenance.

"Oh, my, no," exclaimed Lucia unexpectedly. "How can you ask? Didn't Mr. Lloyd fake up Wick-Zoo as a wild man— shall I ever cease to shiver when I think of his blood-curdling howls—when he is really as tame as—as—as you? And didn't Mr. Lloyd make out that he was nobody much, and nothing, when he is the grandson of Judge Clarence Jennico Lloyd, one of the most distinguished jurists of the day, and is a representative of one of the oldest and best families in the South. Oh, Diogenes wouldn't light his lantern to examine such a patent fraud as we have discovered Mr. Lloyd to be."

Jardine's thin cheek was flushed, but his tact enabled him to carry off the "slugging," as Lucia's retort featured itself in Lloyd's triumphant consciousness, as jauntily as a man well could.

"But really why is he going about here in the sunshine with that lantern in his hand?" Jardine pressed his horse forward, and spoke to the mountaineer. "What are you doing with that lantern, my man?"

The mountaineer turned his head slowly and looked up at Jardine with so sinister an expression of countenance that Ruth was moved to a subtle affright.

"Why does Mr. Jardine speak so—so discourteously to an inferior?" she said discontentedly.

"Because he is that kind of hairpin," said Frank lucidly.

"Well, it isn't nice; mamma always insists on special politeness to humble folk."

"You will have a harder hunt than Diogenes, if you look for mamma's precepts and practice in general action," said the loyal Frank.

There was something so incongruous with the inimical, tigerish glow in the mountaineer's eyes, and the youth and comeliness of his face, that his sharp retort seemed whetted to an edge.

"Doin' with it? Totin' it—can't ye see?"

Frank laughed out gaily, with an applausive cadence. "But *why*, partner? You understand that we are from the New Helvetia Springs—strangers—going around to see what we can see, and we are asking a million questions of anybody that will have patience to answer them. And we can't make out any good reason for you to carry that lantern out here on this sunlit mountain."

One might think it impossible to look at Frank's gay, pink, dimpled face and not be mollified. But the lowering, glum disaffection of the yokel's expression remained unmitigated. He continued silent, vouchsafing no response, while his eyes travelled from one to another of the faces of the group, successively studying their lineaments with no friendly result. There was a pause of embarrassment disproportioned to the trifling cause that provoked it. To break the awkwardness a few words were interchanged amongst the riders.

"Had we not better move on?" suggested Jardine.

"Give Lucia a little time to rest," said Ruth. Then to Lucia, "How fast you must have been riding! You look pale with fatigue."

"Oh, I'm not tired at all," said Lucia, flushing suddenly. "You can preach hygiene nearly equal to Aunt Dora. I'd be a poor stick if that little canter could make me pale."

"Mebbe thar's no use fur a lantern on top the mounting," the mountaineer spoke so suddenly that more than one of the group started in surprise. "But how about the inside o' the mounting—ain't much sunlight thar."

"What! a cave?" Frank asked interested.

The mountaineer nodded. His face now had a slow, pondering expression. He was evidently following out a line of intricate introspection. When he looked up again, he seemed a different creature.

"Finest cave you uns ever seen," he said. The gleam of his white teeth gave his face an unexpected geniality. "It's all plumb white inside, an' shines powerful in the light of the lantern. Thar ain't a room at the New Helveshy Springs ez fine, nor in the hotel at Colbury, nuther."

These instances expressed the limits of his comprehension of magnificence, but the incongruity passed unremarked in the interest of his disclosure. Ruth and Lucia instantly began to clamour.

"Oh, couldn't we go to see it?" one cried.

"Oh, what a novelty!" exclaimed the other.

"Is it far?" asked Lloyd, a little doubtfully.

The man's eyes had been so charged with rancour, with a sense of burning wrath as he had encountered their gaze, that Lloyd had been reluctant in the presence of ladies to elicit words from him. Lloyd could not, of course, imagine any reason for this, save the unassuaged hatred that the poor of a certain type entertain for the presumably rich and favoured, without regard to individuals or circumstances.

But the reply was as suave and courteous as the man's limitations rendered possible. "Thar air two openings ter it. One's a mile away, but thar's another clost by. I never know'd about it till one day las' spring. I war huntin' hyarabouts, an' viewed a dark hole 'mongst some rocks, an' crope in. I fund the place was a part of a cave I knowed afore. The door ter it is ever yander nigh the valley. I hed some matches in my pocket, but I was feared ter trest 'em fur. So I fetched a lantern, an' went plumb through ter the other eend. It's a s'prisin' sight."

"Could you guide us in a little way—so that the ladies might see something of it—what is best worth seeing?" said Lloyd. "We will pay you for your trouble, and your loss of time."

The mountaineer was standing near the showman's horse; he cast up his eyes reflectively, and presumably named a sum of money, for Lloyd replied:

"That seems pretty stiff, but we will pay you that, if you have enough candle, or oil; let me see?" and he took the grimy lantern gingerly between his gloves.

Jardine, tingling with irritation, was constrained once more to address Lloyd directly. Frank Laniston, he said to himself, was such a boy, so plastic to every impulse, that he could do more, perhaps, by allying himself with this man.

"Don't you think this rather risky?" he asked distantly.

"I can't judge without investigating," Lloyd replied, with that quiet dignity which accorded so ill with his bizarre profession. "I thought I might go in the cave a reasonable distance with the guide, and, if it seems safe and worth while, the ladies might venture a short excursion."

"Why *surely*, Mr. Jardine." Even the ultra-amiable Ruth had reached the point of irritation expressed by emphasis.

"What could be more reasonable?" said Lucia, also with the countenance of reproach.

Mr. Jardine often felt at these crises that such a degree of popularity as he enjoyed with them was hardly worth conserving, but he made many sacrifices to prevent its impairment, and he was glad now of an opportunity to recede gracefully.

"That's a very good idea. I had not thought of a reconnoitering expedition."

They set out at a moderate pace, to enable their guide to keep abreast of the horses. The direction necessitated a divergence from the main road, a circumstance which aroused in Mr. Jardine a degree of anxiety and suspicion. He looked about him sharply, fixing landmarks as well as he might in his recollection—the situation of a great dome, the horizontal summit of a range, a high precipitous cliff, looking far away over a hundred minor ridges and valleys, a green abyss intervenient among steep slopes, as dank, as lush, as luxuriantly leafy as if summer had fled for hiding in this lonesome dell. But the incidents of the way were repetitious; he could not have discriminated the difference in the outlook now before his eyes, and the one which a sudden turn had served to obliterate. The path grew more narrow, less distinctly marked; it was necessary to proceed in single file, so closely did the dense rhododendron boughs press upon the dim outline of a trail. Presently all outlook was shut off by the redundant evergreen growth, almost meeting above their heads, the jungle of indefinite extent, and, but for this slender line betokening a foot-passage, impenetrable. Jardine was as courageous as a reasonable man need be, but he felt as if he had been foolhardy when he considered the down-looking, ill-conditioned aspect of their guide—like that of an implacable and surly cur—the fact of his gold watch, and those of his companions, the

305

diamonds on the daintily gloved hands of the ladies, the well-filled purses of the men. They were indeed easy victims to highwaymen in this remote and inaccessible wilderness, and he wondered futilely how he could have so submitted his judgment to a lady's unthinking whim. As to Lloyd's indifference, he was a man experienced only in towns and town ways; he either did not realise what he might be encountering, or he was so used to jeopardy in his fantastic profession that needless risks seemed the normal incidents of life.

Of all his anticipations Jardine least expected to be led to a veritable cave, instead of an ambuscade, and his spirits rose incalculably when the voices of Lloyd and Frank sounded in the van, proclaiming their arrival at the spot.

It was a wild and lonely place; the sunshine filtered through the red and gold foliage of the trees with a lucent glister, as through stained glass. The rhododendron jungle clustered about, and fenced off the world impenetrably. A high slope on one side was bestrewn with gigantic boulders; great fragments of a fractured cliff towered above, and amongst them was a vertical crevice of irregular shape, some eight feet in height. It looked black, uninviting, sinister; but there were moss-grown ledges hard at hand, and a dimpling, swirling rill ran down the declivity and was lost in the great lush ferns. A breath of exquisite freshness and blended perfumes pervaded the air, and a steady current, outward set, was perceptible from the mouth of the cave.

"The horses can be picketed here, and doubtless Mr. Jardine will be kind enough to look after you two while we are gone," said Frank officiously.

"But why don't you wait also," asked Mr. Jardine, by no means relishing the exclusive charge of five fine horses, to swell the booty of the highwaymen, should he be molested.

306

"Surely Mr. Lloyd does not have to ascertain if the excursion is safe for me," said Frank bluffly. "Either you or I have to stay with the girls, and I thought you could entertain them best. They know all my patter from 'way back."

"Oh, certainly," said Mr. Jardine frigidly; "with pleasure."

Despite his irritation, his preoccupation, he noticed the sudden, acute disappointment on the mountaineer's face. His jaw dropped, his fierce eyes stared, disconsolate, doubtful; he was all at once crestfallen, stumbling, slow. Had he expected only Lloyd to venture with him into those bleak abysses? Why should he deprecate the company of the stalwart young Laniston? The inference was too plain—they made two to one. Any false dealing, any foul treachery was now impracticable. Still Jardine could not refrain from remonstrating with Lloyd, so imperative was his persuasion of some strangely inimical element.

"Mr. Lloyd," he said, with more geniality than one would have thought it possible for him to show, "let's call this thing off. We have made a mistake—a serious mistake in contemplating it. I have my reasons which I will tell you without reserve at our first opportunity. We will pay this man all the same, and consider the money a forfeit. But I beg of you—I am a serious man, no trifler—let's call this cave excursion off, right here and now."

His appeal seemed to impress Lloyd, but Frank Laniston broke out into his gruffly callow remonstrances, and the two young ladies set up a plaintive duet of reproach.

"Lloyd may back out, if he likes," said Frank, "but I will let no such show as this escape me."

"Oh, Mr. Jardine, how you shilly-shally," cried Lucia. "You agreed there was no objection if Mr. Lloyd would reconnoitre the place."

"Oh, Mr. Jardine, how you willy-nilly," cried Ruth. "You will have it that there's death and destruction in every earthly thing we propose. A serious man! Yes, as serious as the grave."

The two girls flung about in mock despair, and finally subsided, their arms interlocked, on one of the mossy ledges.

"I submit to Fate," said Lucia, "if nobody will take me in to see this cave I reckon I shall never have another chance."

"I submit to Fate," echoed Ruth. "If nobody will take me in to see this cave I shall try to lead him a life, the rest of my natural existence!"

And she fixed her eyes on her brother.

"Oh, come on, Lloyd," laughed Frank, in his gruff, callow fashion. "It's up to us."

And he plunged toward the entrance of the cavern.

The mountaineer turned and looked at Jardine with so insolent a triumph, so scornful a relish, as he stood disregarded and disconcerted, that the force of his inchoate anxieties and suspicions was redoubled. The trio disappeared, the lantern glimmering feebly in the light of the day, but casting a stronger glow in the black mouth of the cave, and suddenly shining like a star, seen through a crevice higher in the wall of rock.

Jardine seated himself upon a boulder near the two young ladies. He lifted his hat to bare his head to the breeze, for the sun had waxed hot, and he took out his white handkerchief and mopped his brow wearily. He did not lift his lashes, but absently regarded his riding-boots, now and again flicking them lightly with the whip in his hand. He knew that the eyes of both were fixed, beguilingly, upon him. He was angry with them, and he did not wish to be easily placated. But he did not evade their blandishments.

"Don't you know," said Ruth to Lucia, "that he is just hoping and praying that Mrs. Jardine (when he finds her) will be like neither of us."

"And don't you know," said Lucia, in an aside to Ruth, "that he will just dedicate himself to teaching Mrs. Jardine (when he finds her) not to be headstrong and hard-headed, as we are."

It were churlish to resist their fantastic amende, and he raised his eyes with a positive plea of anxiety in them.

"If you would only consider my views!" he urged. "If you would but trust to my larger experience! It sends me frantic for you to endanger your precious lives. I *have* done—I am willing to do everything for your pleasure that is safe for you. I don't consider my own taste. I *love* to be at your service. I care for nothing so much as your happiness. I think I have shown this, and I ask in return but one boon—that you do not run your precious selves into danger—that——"

But they desired to hear no more from him on this theme.

"I shall tell Mrs. Jardine (when he finds her) that she is not the first!" cried Ruth, dimpling; "that he made love to *both* of us!"

"The jealousy of Mrs. Jardine (when he finds her) will never know surcease, when she hears he calls both of us 'precious,'" echoed Lucia, with mock solemnity.

Then they collapsed into their silvery laughter as they sat on the mossy ledge, and guyed him.

His remonstrances were obviously futile, but before he had time to attempt another Ruth spoke, suddenly serious.

"You know I have practised drawing faces so much—the individual features from the flat, and the whole countenance in the life class—that I have become just dead letter perfect in the discrimination of human physiognomy. I don't pretend to discern character, and all that sort of thing—to set up as a second Lavater—but a face with any distinctiveness that I have once seen I recognise on a second view."

Jardine felt a sudden premonition, as of discovery—a sudden inexplicable sinking of the heart. He looked at her intently as she paused, leaned aside, plucked a tiny flowering weed from a niche in the rock, and turned it in her gauntleted hands. Lucia, one elbow on the ledge behind her, gazed indifferently into the great encompassing stretch of the woods, where in the illuminated air there was a continual wafting down of the rich, glinting, yellow leaves.

"I thought I knew that young mountaineer the moment I saw him," continued Ruth. "And now I have placed the recollection. He is the young man who sat in front of us at the song-and-dance turn, disguised as an old man. I knew his eyes, and that slight rise in the bridge of his nose, breaking the insipidity of contour—very good shape."

Lucia was erect, looking at her with startled eyes. "Sure enough?" she said.

Ruth glanced at her with a laughing rebuke of the slang phrase. "Sure enough!" she assented.

"Why, that man was in the Ferris Wheel that night!" exclaimed Lucia. "And I am morally certain he slung a stone, or iron missile of some sort, and knocked this Mr. Lloyd out of the swing. Why didn't you tell him?"

"It only came to me a moment ago," said Ruth. "Besides, you know Mr. Jardine and Frank thought that idea was just our notion—the vapourings of semi-idiots."

She glanced with pink and beguiling smiles at Mr. Jardine, expecting his complimentary protest. But he was too seriously ill at ease to respond. He, too, had realised the belated recognition, realising as well that it was unconsciously at the root of his objection to the cave expedition, and his strong, though undefinable, uneasiness. He was thinking that if the mountaineer had had the motive and the venom to attack the manager, his vindictive rancour would not have been allayed by the ineffectiveness of his assault. He doubtless would make another attempt, and this with his unsuspecting victim at his mercy in the recesses and dangers of an unexplored cave. He remembered the guide's patent dismay when Frank Laniston joined the party, and he began to take comfort from the fact that the incident was evidently unpremeditated, and that the man was unable to cope with odds. If Lloyd and Laniston had but the discretion to keep together, as indeed they needs must, for the paucity of the means of light, no disaster might befall them. True they might be led into difficult and remote labyrinths and left—the lantern extinguished—to wander till they fell into abysses, or perished with hunger.

He caught himself sharply. What fantastic folly was this? The whole theory was based upon a girl's romantic version of a fall from a foolish, mechanical contrivance—heaven knows how inefficiently constructed—and a fancied resemblance to a face seen only twice before, each time in a dim light, and apparently half eclipsed by a disguise.

He breathed more freely. He had never before had to reproach himself with morbidness. The whole idea was doubtless nonsensical. Even if it had any foundation in fact, the party outside—himself and the two girls—would be a check on treachery of any magnitude. The guide had not means at hand for such wholesale murder as the destruction of the two young men would necessitate; evidently he was not armed, or he would not have flinched, crestfallen and dismayed, when the muscular Frank Laniston had joined the manager. The report of their disappearance, and a search party from the hotel and the neighbourhood might rescue them, if abandoned to the tortuous depths of darkness, or ascertain their fate, if treacherously misled into abysses and over precipices. Despite his careful reasoning of a moment before, he had come back to this horrible possibility.

Suddenly he sprang to his feet. Frank Laniston, the lantern in his hand, his blond hair damp and limp over his forehead, his teeth chattering with cold, his shoulders shrugging with shivers, plunged out of the entrance with the wild cry:

"Come on! Hurry up! Finest thing yet! Great! Perfect palace of wonders! Don't waste a minute!"

He caught Lucia by the wrist, and she shivered at the touch of his cold hand, as he turned, and together they dashed toward the entrance he had just quitted.

"Stop, Laniston, I want to tell you something," exclaimed Jardine insistently.

"Some other day," called back Frank, between his chill teeth.

"But I must—I will speak to you!" began Jardine.

"I have left that man and Lloyd in the dark, waiting. The mountaineer didn't want me to take the light—said it burns faster in motion. He wouldn't stay alone—said he's afraid of harnts—ha! ha! ha! And we couldn't make him come back, said it's bad luck to turn back. So really I can't stop to listen to you. I can't leave them there in that awful blackness longer than I am obliged to. If you are coming—come on! Follow the lantern!"

"I insist—I insist," cried Jardine, advancing with long strides in their wake over the rocky ground, finding it impossible to overtake them. "I insist that you do not take Miss Laniston!"

312

Frank was infinitely affronted. He stopped short and ceremoniously referred the matter to the lady.

"Are you coming, Lucia?" he asked.

"Yes, yes!" exclaimed the girl, grasping his arm, and pulling him forward. "Oh, don't stop! Let us hurry. Oh, get the light back!"

"Always the pluckiest ever!" said Frank.

They both were running. Jardine made another frantic effort to remonstrate and stop them, as he dashed after them.

"You don't know about that guide!" he called out. "We think he is——"

"I will tell him!" cried Lucia over her shoulder. "Don't stop him. He must get the light back!"

Seeing the utter hopelessness of his effort Jardine desisted, and retraced his steps to the mouth of the cave, where Ruth stood waiting. Lucia did not so much as cast a glance backward, but Frank paused once to look over his shoulder at the two in the shadow of the rocks.

"If you two are coming, follow the lantern—if not, you'll look after Ruth, Mr. Jardine? Thanks, much."

Jardine was very doubtful of his best course. If he and Ruth joined the party none of them might ever be heard of or seen again. Yet he realised the value of the strength in numbers. Still the fact that two were without the cave to report the disappearance of the others, should they not return after a reasonable interval, was a check on the possible malevolence and treachery of the guide.

"The lantern will be out of sight," Ruth pouted. "Shall we follow them?"

"To tell you the truth I distrust that guide," said Jardine. With women he seldom resorted to candid speech, and an appeal to their intelligence and judgment. But he resolved to be frank now, though he marked how her cheek paled, how her eyes dilated. "I think that if he has any sinister intentions our remaining on guard here, so to speak, will be a check upon them. They will be rendered impracticable for fear of our report of the entrance of the party into the cave, and their failure or delay to return. Now I propose that we wait here, say, half an hour, and, if we hear nothing of our friends in that time, we will mount our horses and gallop for help to New Helvetia. What do you say?"

"Yes, yes, by all means! But, oh, why, why did we let them go!"

"We couldn't help it," said Jardine rather bitterly. He was not wont to be so frustrated and set at naught. He was a man of consideration in the ordinary associations of life. Never had he suffered such disparagement as at the hands of these youthful feather-pates.

"But they will probably come out all right," he added, "in a little while, and you and I will have the pleasure of figuring as alarmists and cowards—afraid of the cave."

"What a wild country—what wild people," Ruth shuddered.

"We will give them half an hour," suggested Jardine, drawing out his watch to consult it. "And if they do not rejoin us in that time we will raise the countryside."

She assented rather dolorously, and sat down on the ledge as before, while Jardine resumed his place on the boulder, near at hand.

The wind blew freshly through the odorous woods; the gold leaves shifted down in showers; the crystal rill went purling over the moss, and, as her watch which she held in her hand ticked away the minutes, she looked eagerly ever and anon at the dark crevice-like entrance to the cave, listening vainly, hoping to hear her brother's boisterous, boyish voice.

CHAPTER XIX

Lucia, hurrying along beside Frank as he sturdily strode through the gloom, swinging the lantern to and fro to apprise the explorers, waiting in the darkness, of his approach, felt that wings could hardly be swift enough to convey to Lloyd the warning of his peculiar and imminent danger. And, yet, it might be even now too late! She was appalled at the thought of his risks alone in the depths of an unexplored cavern, without a light, without a landmark, without a clue to his station in the subterranean labyrinth, his only companion a strange, half-civilised man, who had once already, at great jeopardy to himself, slyly and treacherously attempted his life. She marvelled at Lloyd's foolhardy temerity, and then—and the thought redoubled her speed—she realised that he had no vague intuition of the secret of his peril, she was sure that he had not for a moment recognised or distrusted his guide.

She hardly felt the chill of the rare air; she cared naught for the rough footing; now and again she stumbled and clutched at Frank for support, but instantly pressed on, unwearied, fevered, alert.

Naught so sinister as the unutterable blackness was ever presented to her imagination. She stared wide-eyed at the palpable-seeming glooms of the vast halls, made visible by the dim glister of the little lantern. Things of evil omen, winged, unseen, whisked by her head; once a bat struck her full in the face. The place seemed alive with these creatures, and, now and again, as she heard their strange, uncanny squeak, she started violently, all her nerves jarring.

315

"We shall soon be beyond the bat zone, Lucia," said Frank kindly, remembering the universal feminine horror of the genus.

His voice, so hearty and cheery in the outdoor world, seemed strangely hollow, unnatural in this environment, echoing far away, and coming anew in a different key, and startling her with the conviction of terrible, unseen beings, conferring apart in the unimagined distance, speaking her name.

"Oh, not a word—" she whispered, "on your life, not another word," and she clung to him terrified.

He burst out with his boyish, rollicking laughter, and all the cavern was filled with mocking merriment, raucous, horrible, as if the cachinnation of invisible fiends repeated his tones, resounding anew, now here, now there, now far in advance, now close behind them, and, even at last, when all seemed still, again an elfin mimicry.

Frank checked himself; he saw that her terrors were genuine. The feminine ideal had always figured in his unsentimental appraisement as a marplot; he was beginning to be afraid, from Lucia's heavier drag on his arm, the dilation of her eyes, the tremor in her voice, that such courage as she had summoned for the enterprise was already failing her, and that he would shortly be adjured to turn about and retrace their way, and restore her to the glad outer air and the pleasant surface of the earth. He said naught further, and when she had begun to fear that they had missed the trace, although he had told her that for a certain distance there was no break in the right-hand wall, and they could not go amiss as long as they kept in touch with it, she heard a faint halloo in the night, as one might hear in a dream. When Frank responded vociferously, it came anew, and stronger still.

Suddenly she saw, across a vast expanse of utter darkness, like the face of the deep when the earth was without form and void, the outline, as it were, of a promontory growing slowly into being; a faint flicker of light—it seemed star-like in contrast with the deep gloom—revealed two moving creatures poised there, which she presently recognised as human beings. One, she was sure that it was Lloyd, had struck a match, and from it had kindled a bit of wood—it was his forlorn little cigar-case of imitation lacquer, which he extravagantly sacrificed; he expected to have better things after this! While the stolid mountaineer looked on, Lloyd once more called out blithely to his approaching acquaintances, and distinguishing the voice which she had feared would never sound again, she burst into tears.

Frank, all tingling with the ardour of adventure, with the excitements of extreme jeopardy, with the interest of novelty, felt a surge of resentment toward her as an inopportune spoil-sport. The spirit of discipline was strong within him.

"Well, upon my word, Lucia Laniston," he said severely—and a hundred distant voices were repeating, "Lucia Laniston! Lucia Laniston!" while she hung upon his arm, vaguely flinching from the echoes and seeking to stop her ears. "I'll never take you with me anywhere again, as long as I live! There is no danger. What are you crying for—answer me that?"

And the darkness conjured her—"Answer me that?"

"Oh, Frank," she whispered: she could not speak aloud for the echoes—even the sibilance that followed her words made her now and then shrink away and look back. Then she put both hands on one of his shoulders, and stood on tip-toe to bring her lips close to his ear, "We must look out for that mountaineer. We have recognised him at last—both Ruth and I. He is the man whom we noticed in disguise at

317

the concert where that girl sang and danced, and who afterward tried to kill Mr. Lloyd in the Ferris Wheel!"

"The devil he is!" exclaimed Frank, stopping short, disconcerted and dismayed.

"The devil he is—he is—he is—he is the devil!" The echoes reiterated the words with a distracting distinctness, and she put her hand over Frank's lips.

"The next time you speak—whisper," she admonished him. "I expected,—Mr. Jardine expected that he would kill Mr. Lloyd while you were gone."

"It must be that he has got no pistol," Frank surmised decisively. "And that's strange, for these fellows all carry their 'shootin' iron' in the leg of their left boot. That's the only reason, I dare swear. By sheer strength, he couldn't. Lloyd could throw him from here to New Helvetia. He doubtless expected to take Lloyd by surprise, and suddenly push him over into an abyss, and didn't get the opportunity. He saw enough of athletes at the carnival to know he would be outmatched in a fair fight. Treachery or a pistol was his only chance. But why on earth did not Jardine tell me?"

"He tried—he tried—but you wouldn't wait a minute—you wouldn't hear a word."

Even in the dim light Frank's face showed crestfallen, dispirited, mortified.

"I'm sorry you came—but we must make the best of it. See here, Lucia, when we join them, do you get close to Lloyd and very quietly tell him—don't choke him, like you did me; you've pretty near strangled me, clutching me by the collar that way—but whisper the facts to him. Very quietly, mind you. We mustn't excite the suspicions of that miscreant. Our safety may depend on his thinking that we do not recognise him. Let Lloyd know, and walk with him, and I'll keep right along with Mister Mountain-Man. We will only make a feint of seeing the cave—just to avoid precipitating some rascality—and take the first chance to get out of this as soon as possible."

When they reached the waiting explorers, who being without adequate light could not come to meet them, Lucia was no longer walking with her cousin's arm, but following, as he preceded her, swinging the lantern. The way had grown rough and unequal; sudden unexpected descents made the walking difficult amidst the jagged edges of the crag and fragments long ago fallen from the roof; climbing the acclivity, on which they still stood, she was now and again fain to clutch at a projection of rock to assist her steps, and, although she was rarely light and active, and kept up well with Frank's long stride, he carefully handled the lantern to afford her all the light possible. It seemed to Lloyd, however, that she needed more effective assistance, and, as soon as their proximity made it possible, he advanced to meet them, as the crafty Frank had anticipated, and offered her his arm. Frank turned for a moment, surveying this arrangement, as if he had not expected it; then, addressing the mountaineer, but still keeping the lantern in his own hands, he said bluffly, "Come on, old Sport—we'll take the lead. Guide us to that marble palace we were thinking of buying when we turned back."

"It has got marble palaces beat to a frazzle," Lloyd chimed in enthusiastically.

She noted with a pang, half gratulation, half grief, that he asked no questions as to the others. He had no curiosity as to their reasons for declining the excursion. He seemed not even aware of their absence—to him all had come since she was here. She felt the strength of his support, his sure-footed agility, and moved on swiftly and easily on his arm. But she could not, by lagging, find an opportunity for her confidential whisper. When sharp, jagged rocks intervened in the path, and she slackened her pace, the mountaineer seemed to observe it immediately, and accommodated his gait to theirs, although, once or twice, Frank, forging on with the lantern, the way being obvious, a canon-like interval, between great, beetling cliffs, left them so far behind that Lloyd called a halt.

"Remember Miss Laniston," he admonished the youth. "You are not walking for a purse." Then, jocularly, "That lantern is not your personal property—it doesn't look well for you to make off with it like that."

Somehow, on Lloyd's arm, Lucia forgot to be afraid. The terrible glooms had a certain gruesome picturesqueness that no longer appalled her. She could look up into the infinite vaults of the darkness, and her hope, her soul, no longer fainted within her. The lantern, like a tiny star, lucently white, with a rayonnant halo about its focus, showed vast, rugged, crag-shaped forms looming indistinctly in these undreamed-of subterranean realms, and now the path skirted an abyss of unimagined depth, and now toiled up an ascent, mountain-like in its vague immensity, but she had no tremors, no thought of regret for the bland outer air, and the bliss of the candid sunshine. She trusted implicitly to him. She knew that he was ignorant, all untrained mentally, sadly neglected, hardly used by Fate, but she relied on the inherent strength of his judgment, his fine, bright, native intellect, his optimism, his simple valiance in the fight of life. She did not doubt that she would have presently an opportunity to disclose the facts to him, to communicate her warning, and she was sure that he would instantly know the best course to pursue, and that he would have the courage and the dexterity to make it effective. She realised his high moral qualities, so rare in these days that they seemed like a special gift. His unselfishness would take due account of her, of

Frank—his magnanimity would even spare the murderous mountaineer, unless, indeed, their safety, their lives were the price of his.

So restored, indeed, were her faculties, that she was the first to note the sudden responsive light, as the far-reaching gleam of the lantern struck out the glitter of calc-spar. "See there!" she cried. "What is that?"

"We are coming again to the palace, I do believe," said Frank, as if surprised.

"Wa-al," observed the surly guide, stopping short, "warn't ye lowin' ez ye wanted ter go the same way? I kin show ye other ways—ef so be ye'd like ter travel 'em; a short cut ter nowhar."

Frank was conscious of having expressed unintentionally, in his surprise, his lurking suspicions, and his answer was not readily forthcoming. But Lloyd discriminated the note of offence in the guide's voice, and sought to re-establish harmonious relations.

"That is all right—just what we want to show the lydy," he said cheerily. "But I don't call it the marble palace," he continued, addressing himself directly to Lucia; "it is the 'Hall of Heroes'—you will see why directly,—and, oh, what a stage-setting it would make."

Even now the darkness began to shimmer with vague transient white gleams suggestive of apparitions, of gigantic human forms. At a word from the guide, Frank strode ahead down a steep declivity, and, pausing at last, stood in the centre of an oval-shaped apartment, glimmering white, with here and there a sudden crystalline sparkle. The lofty ceiling rose above like the interior of a dome.

The mountaineer waited with the other two, as if he felt that since Frank had usurped the lantern he might also assume the functions of a cicerone and exhibit the wonders of the cave. Lucia began to realise with a sinking heart that the mountaineer having decoyed Lloyd here for the purpose of wreaking now his frustrated vengeance, would not for one moment permit himself to be separated from his prospective victim. She once more grew anxious lest it would be impossible to speak to Lloyd apart, and began to scheme, to devise, rather than await, an opportunity to warn him.

Young Laniston, placed at a disadvantage which he had not anticipated, although he did not regret his manœuvre to keep possession of the precious light on which all their lives depended, hesitated for a moment—then he addressed himself to the methods by which the mountaineer had earlier displayed to the explorers the beauties of the sequestered place.

He took up from the ground a long pole with a short prong or fork at its end. He lifted the lantern high on this, and like a miracle the splendours of the underground scene burst forth. The walls were white and sparkled with calc-spar. The wondrous forces of nature, tirelessly building through the ages these unseen, unimagined, weird splendours, were still at work, and though great stalactites hung down from the lofty roof like a hundred chandeliers, the continual drip from these ponderous pendants, of the waters charged with lime, had not yet built up from the floor the stalagmites to form the columns in which they would one day meet. These stalagmites, now in process of development, had taken on strange, fantastic shapes. At the distance it was like a hall of glittering statuary. Lloyd pointed out, with all the zest of discovery, the similitudes which his keen imagination had discerned in the rugged rock. Now he discriminated a statesman-like figure, erect upon a column, gigantic, majestic, a scroll in his hand; here a great, rugged pedestal,

322

where the waters had been received in a wide depression, supported an equestrian soldier mounted upon a rearing charger; his fancy descried an aboriginal group, a warrior— he was insistent on the distinctness of his plumed crest— with his tomahawk uplifted, his victim a-crouch at his feet; he pointed out Neptune, on the rocks, his trident in his hand, a dolphin sporting at his feet.

Somehow, all the vanished wonders of the world were lurking here, awaiting the magic touch of imagination to give them form and grace and bid them live anew. The mountaineer, impervious to these impressions, walled up in his limitations, seemed to listen stolidly, uncomprehendingly, as Lloyd, discoursing all unsuspicious, all undismayed, gaily discerned poems in the stones, and music in the dropping of the water, for they could discriminate the sound of the ripple of a rill, somewhere in the darkness, from the staccato fall of the drops from the stalactites, building ceaselessly the majestic architecture of the cavern.

"Listen, listen," said Lloyd smilingly, one hand uplifted, "was there ever anything more harmonious than that tinkling interlude with its appoggiatura of drops that comes always *a piacere* after the solemn, hesitating tones of the *tema?*"

The foreign phrases suggested a chance to her despair.

"Do you speak Italian or French?" she asked.

"No—nor English, either, I'm afraid. Wish I did," Lloyd replied, looking down at her, his face illumined in some stray shifting gleam of the lantern. "The only consolation is that I have not much to say anyhow. A few words will express my thoughts."

"Say," exclaimed Frank, from the centre of the floor of the Hall of Heroes—"it is as cold as Greenland down here, and as damp as a marsh."

323

"And it goes through you, this damp cold," responded Lloyd. "It isn't like the dry cold at the entrance of the cave." Then to Lucia, "Did you notice how dusty it was there?"

"Well, say," exclaimed Frank, "have you seen enough of this?"

Lloyd submitted the question to Lucia, who assented with feverish eagerness. Then he shouted to Frank, "Suppose we get a move on us. I'm about fed up with this place."

As Frank retraced his way to rejoin the others, the precious lantern once more dangling from his arm, he pondered anxiously as to his next step. He knew, partly from the position of the group, and he thought that he could divine from the intonation of Lloyd's voice, that Lucia had not been able to exchange a word with him out of the hearing of the mountaineer. Hence, he was sure that Lloyd was still all unconscious of his danger, and thus cut off from his advice and co-operation, young Laniston felt peculiarly helpless, yet laden with responsibility. While in certain traits of his adolescence he represented a type of the callow undergraduate, he had an appreciation of his own inexperience and limitations that indeed did much to annul them, and rendered him almost as cautious as a man versed in the mutations of human affairs. He hardly knew what to do, and hence he was slow to act. He thought at one moment that he would call Lloyd aside and disclose the facts, thus bringing the matter to a crisis. But this, he reflected, might precipitate the lurking treachery, whatever deed it was that the man had in contemplation. At length he determined that, with the shifting of the personnel of the conference, he would call the mountaineer aside, thus giving Lucia one moment for her whispered confidence to Lloyd.

"Come here, my friend," Frank said, stopping short and looking straight at the guide and then down at the light, "Come and see what is the matter with this lantern."

His face, all thrown into high relief by the light shining upward upon it, placid, and smooth, and roseate, gave no intimation of the unrest in his mind, and even a suspicious man might easily have been caught by the lure.

But the saturnine mountaineer resisted stanchly. "Nuthin' the matter with it," he retorted. "But I tell you now, ef ye fool with that thar lantern an' git it out'n fix, you will be in hell fire a good spell 'fore yer time comes—that's whut!"

"Look out, man—bridle your words in the presence of this lydy—or I'll cut your tongue out," Lloyd spoke abruptly, with such sudden fierceness that the mountaineer started aside.

The stalwart Frank, knowing what he knew, could have fainted at this provocation to the lurking menace. With desperate eagerness he sought to re-establish such poor pretence of an *entente cordiale* as had heretofore existed. "Have patience with the speech of the country, Mr. Lloyd. The thoughts of a plain man are plainly expressed, hey, my friend?" he said jovially, clapping the guide on the shoulder.

It was but a momentary diversion, but in that restricted interval Lucia whispered to Lloyd, "He is the man who attacked you in the Ferris Wheel."

Lloyd looked surprised for a moment—startled. Then he responded, laughing a trifle, "You must be mistaken. The doctor thought the hurt was from the fall—not a blow. He had no motive. I never saw him till to-day. I haven't an enemy in the world."

"He was in disguise," Lucia whispered.

"Oh, that, indeed." Lloyd looked down at her with a doubting but lenient smile. "If ever I have to go on the road again, I'll get you to write me a play!—you are a prodigy at plots—I can see that!"

Lucia was on the verge of collapse—fit to fall. For the sake of this moment she had controlled her fears, and tried to the limit her powers of endurance, and followed into this abyss the guidance of a known traitor. She had risked her life in this cavern of darkness and despair whence she might never issue, that she might tell Lloyd that his own life was in danger—and for naught! She could not appeal to his fears—for to fear he seemed impervious.

And so he thought she had come, simply because she wanted to see the cave—the folly of it! And he would never know that she loved him and his safety better than her life—and indeed why should he know this, when she would have none of him, and his bizarre past, and his humdrum future with his "bit of money" and his little dingy home of a six-room frame house on a small plantation! He had already offered her these values—which she had rejected, though she loved him, as she had already told him—why should he know how much—how much!

She hung heavily on his arm, so had the elasticity of her gait failed her, and almost at once he noticed the change.

"This is too much for you," he said considerately. "You are tired. Look here, guide," he called out peremptorily. "Get us out of here now—the shortest way."

The mountaineer, after his sullen manner, made no comment, but set out at once at a fair pace, preceding Frank, whom he still permitted without protest to carry the lantern. Young Laniston, crestfallen and very considerably dismayed, sought to lessen the distance between them, some twenty feet, by spurting in a fast walk, whereupon the guide broke into a jog trot, keeping the interval exactly the same.

"Hold on for the light," exclaimed Frank, realising that Lucia must needs be distressed to keep this pace or fall hopelessly to the rear. He relapsed into his former gait and at once the guide relaxed his speed in exact proportion. "You had better wait a bit," said Frank, ignoring that aught of unpleasantness had happened; "you will fall into a crevice if you don't mind."

He sent a shaft of light flickering on ahead, but sullen and sinister the man made no response, still steadily preceding them into the dense glooms, his figure barely glimpsed by the lantern's fluctuating light as they followed.

Frank's alarms were now very definitely excited. He could not understand the change in the man's policy in leaving the post which he had so steadfastly maintained in Lloyd's immediate proximity. He had either relinquished his scheme or he was now proceeding to put it into execution. Frank was mindful too of the malignity with which the mountaineer pointed the fact how his caution had overshot the mark by retaining the custody of the lantern. Much good would it do them if the guide, evidently curiously familiar with the place, should contrive to distance them altogether, or dodge behind one of the buttresses of the cliffs of this underground world, and so hiding leave them to find their way out of this labyrinth without a clue, or perchance, wandering in eccentric circles, perish finally of cold or starvation. It was impossible for them to recognise any landmark of the dread Plutonian scene—black night on every side, save dusky outlines of crags and chasms, the tiny white focus of the lantern with its fibrous halo failing in deep glooms, and beyond, the dim shadow of a man, trotting steadily—how well he knew his footing!—to lose sight of whom were certain death in this world of Erebus.

"If I only had a pistol, even without a cartridge in it, I'd stop that light-heeled fellow," Frank said indignantly, but in a low voice, over his shoulder to the two who followed close upon his steps.

"Don't be frightened, Miss Laniston," Lloyd reassured Lucia. "We shan't lose sight of our precious guide. I could run him down in two seconds. And if necessary I will just snatch you up in my arms and overhaul him forthwith. I'd do it now, but it is best to give him line, and see what his intentions really can be."

The next moment a chilly sound rang through the silent cave and all the unfortunate explorers started with a nervous shock. In another instant they recognised its character. It was the hooting of a screech-owl.

"That settles it," exclaimed Lloyd with a joyous sense of relief. "That shows we can't be very far from the outside. The owls hide about near the entrance of a cave in the daytime—then they fly out at night like the bats."

Lucia tried to share his hopefulness; she looked about with eager expectancy. "But I don't see or hear any bats," she said.

"They will no doubt put in an appearance before long," Lloyd answered. "There is the owl again."

She shivered at the blood-curdling, ill-omened cry, despite its fortunate augury to them.

The shrill, uncanny notes of the screech-owl again trembled repetitiously on the thin, rare air, then the low, sinister chuckling of the bird ensued, so true to life, so perfectly imitated that the cry had been several times repeated, after considerable intervals, before they perceived that they had heard no owl—that the mountaineer now and again paused as he hurried on in advance and standing still mimicked the creature's ill-omened cry with a perfection of similitude that might have deceived the senses of more practical woodsmen than they professed to be. The stoppage gave the explorers time to gain on their strange guide and as the shrilling rang out once more the source whence it emanated became obvious.

Frank, looking over his shoulder at the others, showed a startled, dismayed face and Lloyd with a strange, unaccustomed thrill about his heart, felt that a crisis impended. Their thought was the same—they were following a madman, or he was signalling to confederates ambushed in the hope of booty, or he was masking the noise of their approach by this, a familiar sound.

Lucia suddenly spoke, a joyous break in her voice that was nevertheless like a sob. "I see a faint light in the distance— we are truly nearing the exit." She looked up at Lloyd through tears in her eyes. He felt her hand grow light on his arm, her step quicken at his side—so does hope control the nerves, the muscles.

But it was his turn to doubt. He had what is called "a head for localities." The entrance which he remembered had for a distance longer than the light of day could be glimpsed a straight blank wall on one side, without an aperture or a break, which fact had made it possible for Frank Laniston to go and return without a guide. Whereas here there were vast spaces of void darkness on either side, the path was damp and slippery in places, and he could smell the breath of running water, and hear the vague susurrus that echoed the murmur of its flow. There it had been as still as death, but for the whisking of the almost noiseless wings of the disturbed bats and now and then their weird mouse-like cry, and dust, dust, dust, was over all the dry precincts of the way. He suddenly spoke his conviction. "That is undoubtedly light," he said, "but this is not the way by which we came into the cave."

The guide caught the words and paused abruptly. He showed a change anew. He seemed suddenly metamorphosed from the malignant, tricky gnome, fleeing from them as they approached, or the madman aping the bird's cry of evil presage as he threaded the endless labyrinth

329

of this subterranean realm. He was now the simple prosaic yokel whom, of their own free will outside, they had hired as a guide to explore a cave as a bit of pastime in a pastoral day.

"Waal," he remonstrated, doggedly sullen as at first, "didn't you uns say ez ye wanted the shortes' way out; this is the shortes' way."

"But I expected of course to go out at the same place—I wanted the shortest way to that exit," said Lloyd sternly. "You know that our horses are not here."

"But only a leetle piece off," the fellow remonstrated. A real owl began to rive the dark still air with his keen shrilling, and anon his low tremulous chatter. The guide paused to listen to the sound and then went on. "I thought she mought rest outside whilst I went to lead down her horse-critter." Once more he paused to listen to the scream of the owl. The whole place echoed and re-echoed its sinister chuckle. "But now I kem ter study 'bout 'n it I misdoubts it be too steep fur she. Jes' step for'd, stranger, an' see. It be jes' round the turn."

Before Frank could warn Lloyd, before Lucia could utter a word of remonstrance, before Lloyd himself took an instant's thought, he dropped Lucia's hand from his arm and stepped around the great buttress of the cliff, the mountaineer at his side.

Lloyd's figure was suddenly defined in a great glare of artificial light and what he saw the others only knew afterward. Descent was obviously impracticable. Sheer down, but only some twenty-five feet, lay a vast replica of the white cavernous hall they had quitted, with stalactites and stalagmites all a-glitter; but here was habitation, movement; strange, troglodytic figures, with skulking black shadows, shifted about amongst the columns; prosaic suggestions environed the great vats and tubs, barrels and

330

sacks of grain, the metallic glimmer of a large copper still, and the open door of a furnace, the fire flaring to a white heat. So silent had been the approach under the normal cavernous sound of the owl's shrilling that not one of the moonshiners looked up as Lloyd looked down. Only when the guide, impatient for the catastrophe, uttered a sharp, short call did they raise their eyes. Lloyd, dumbfounded, instinctively stepped backward, and at this moment Frank, eager with curiosity, flung the lantern forward as he moved, and thus the shadow of the guide was projected from the darkness on the floor below.

It was the boast of Shadrach Pinnott that he had not missed his aim for thirty years. It did not fail him now. He saw the form of a man standing at gaze in a niche in the wall which vanished suddenly from view; then a shadow fell from the niche across the floor below. With a nice calculation of the station of the figure that threw the shadow he fired and the rocks reverberated with the sharp crack of the rifle like the musketry of a battle, and intermingled with it all were the repetitious echoes of the death-cry of the victim.

The body of the guide, as, mortally wounded, he fell forward, slid downward into the moonshiners' lair. The next moment the door of the furnace clashed and all was darkness and silence. Lloyd and Frank, realising that the height on which they stood and the doubt of their numbers and personality precluded pursuit for a time from the distillers on a lower level, made the best of their way with the lantern, carrying the half-fainting Lucia with them, toward the direction in which they had entered, so far as their recollection might serve. How they would have fared in their dazed and exhausted condition, what disastrous fate might have befallen them they often speculated afterward. But it was not long before they heard the resonant halloos of the searching party summoned by Jardine to their rescue, and only the detail of the extraordinary treachery and fate of their guide saved them from very trenchant ridicule, in that land of sylvan prowess, for involving themselves in a trap whence they must needs be extricated by raising the countryside.

CHAPTER XX

Mr. Dalton, hearkening professionally to the adventure, took charge of the legal aspects of the matter in the interests of his client. He notified by telephone the local officials of the death of the guide, and also by the long distance wire the marshal of the district of the probable location of the still, and in each communication offered on the part of Lloyd and young Laniston to be prepared to give their testimony whenever it should be required.

Then, since caution is always concomitant with conscience in a certain organisation, he proposed that the summer sojourners should depart New Helvetia forthwith.

"There is no use in mincing matters," he said. "These moonshiners are very desperate men. They may make an effort to prevent this direct and irrefutable testimony against them from ever reaching the ear of the authorities, Federal or local. For a while they may not know who Mr. Lloyd was, as he appeared judgment-wise in the niche, like the miracle of the writing on the wall of the palace of Belshazzar. But the rescue party will of course spread the details far and wide through the countryside, and the lives of both Mr. Lloyd and Mr. Laniston might be much endangered in lingering in this sequestered place. In fact this wild region is not now safe. I am not an alarmist, but I should recommend indeed the immediate closing of the hotel and the departure of all the guests from New Helvetia at this very critical juncture."

There were grave faces contemplating the glowing log fire in the great chimney-place of the hotel office as he talked. Few people relish the role of scapegoat. The idea of becoming a sacrifice to a possible mistake of identity for either of these formidable witnesses, the billet for the bullet of a distiller's rifle fired from the ambush of the shrubbery of the lawn one of these dark moonless nights, seemed far from a fitting sequel to the placid summer pleasuring at New Helvetia. There was also the possibility, unpleasing indeed to anticipate, of the incendiary destruction of the hotel, with all its guests, to make sure of the witnesses in the holocaust, to shield the crime of the murderous distillers. The personality of the adviser went far to commend his counsel, and the fact that the host ardently seconded the proposition made it manifest that the owner of the hostelry was not without fears for his property and person. A short consultation resulted in the resolution of the guests to quit the place early the next morning, no one caring after dark to encounter in addition to possible attack by the wayside the dangers of the precipitous mountainous road in the descent from the heights.

The night was already coming on, clouded and drear; the white cumuli so gaily racing with the wind through the blue matutinal skies had grown grim in heavy grey tumultuous threats of storm. The wind was still astir amongst the tossing cumulose tumult and falling weather seemed hardly yet imminent, but when Lucia, refreshed by rest and sleep under the influence of bromide administered by her aunt, joined the group in the office, the gusts were beginning to dash torrents of rain against the great black windows, all adrip, and the shouts of the riotous powers of the air filled the outer voids of mountain and valley and the utter darkness of the moonless night.

Mrs. Laniston had deemed it better when the girl returned that afternoon from the ill-starred jaunt, exhausted and half hysterical from fright and horror, that as scant regard as possible should be accorded her nervous agitation. She urged Lucia to exert her will-power to throw off the influences of the disastrous day, even its recollection. The evil results upon her mind and physique would be best nullified by slipping with as slight jar as might be into the normal routine of life.

"Think of it no more, dearest Lucia," she said pettingly. "Wear your prettiest gown and come down to tea. If you lie here and brood over this to-night, you may not to-morrow be able to quit the subject."

But Lucia found naturally enough the theme still rife about the fireside in the office. The question of transportation, the problems of conveyances and horses had already been settled, partly with the aid of the hotel stables which were usually available only for pleasure trips, a Colbury livery establishment having the monopoly of the general travel; but on this occasion every vehicle and horse at New Helvetia were brought into requisition, so eager was the proprietor to be rid of such a source of danger as his pleasant guests seemed now likely to prove. An arrangement was made by telephone by which the Colbury livery stable was to send up additional vehicles for baggage and servants, and the business interests thus satisfactorily concluded, the minds and conversation of the group reverted forthwith to the sensation of the day and the solution of details of mystery, not altogether comprehended in the jejune accounts that had at first reached the hotel.

The views of Mr. Dalton, by reason of his profession and his close association with the chief actor in the sensation, commanded much respect and were very generally adopted.

"I take it," he was saying as Lucia entered and Lloyd rose and offered her a chair—the lawyer glanced up from where he was comfortably ensconced with his cigar in a rocking-chair before the blazing fire, "Good-evening, Miss Laniston—I trust you are fully recovered from the ill effects of these unlucky excitements—I take it that the man met the horseback party merely by accident, and having some deep and murderous grudge against Mr. Lloyd——"

"Someone in the rescue party," interrupted Frank, "when the body was found and identified, was saying that his sweetheart had thrown him over, and that he suspected that it was the influence of her foolish admiration of Mr. Lloyd, whom she had seen at the Street Fair, where she danced."

"And that's arrant nonsense," Lloyd instantly asseverated. "She did a song-and-dance turn, like any other coryphée, and had no more consideration for me than the Flying lydy or the Fat lydy who perform in their own interests."

"At all events," Mr. Dalton said, "this Eugene Binley thirsted for your blood. He was unarmed—which surprises me very much——" Mr. Dalton fitted the tips of his fingers accurately together as he pieced out his bits of evidence— "really surprises me. These mountaineers, if to all appearances without weapons, usually carry what they call a shooting iron in the leg of their long boots. He could not kill a professional athlete like Mr. Lloyd in a fist-fight; he could not probably get an opportunity to push him when off his guard into an abyss—though this is what I think he contemplated when he refused to accompany Mr. Laniston back for the ladies or to wait alone."

"That idea occurred to Mr. Jardine—after we had remembered seeing the man in disguise at the Fair and in the Ferris Wheel," said Ruth, who, being far more phlegmatic than Lucia, and having been tortured by fears for her relatives rather than physical hardships and the sight of a hideous deed, had readily recovered her equanimity when their safety was assured. "That's why we gave them so little time to return before we rode off and raised the community as we went."

"This man's plan was well laid and evidently was evolved almost on the spur of the moment." Mr. Dalton continued his research into the motives of the deed. "He bethought himself that the moonshiners would not stay their hand should a presumable spy be detected looking in upon their illicit still. Thus he led Mr. Lloyd to their lair within their view. He must have had a grudge at the moonshiners too, for he had provided himself in Mr. Laniston and Miss Lucia with witnesses to the nefarious deed. What a precious shifty rascal this was—committing a murder by proxy!"

"A wonderful escape for Mr. Lloyd," said Mrs. Laniston. "And where do you go, Mr. Lloyd, from New Helvetia?" She was seeking to change the subject on Lucia's account. The young girl was looking very pallid, though delicately lovely in a gown of white voilé over white silk. She wore a belt of old gold brocade which had as a clasp a fine old topaz, a bit of the antiquated jewelry that recent fashions have caused to be delved out of old cases and brought to light in new settings. This had been a great brooch, and three other stones, similar but smaller—once the ear-rings and bracelet-clasp of the same set,—were now mounted in a "dog-collar" of filigree gold about her delicate neck. In her hair Lloyd noted a cluster of golden-rod, a relic of the ride to-day.

"Where am I going?"—Lloyd repeated the question—"as soon as I can get away from the coroner's jury I shall go to my own house—I am due there on the tenth at any rate."

"To receive your cousin Mr. Thomas Jennico Lloyd, I suppose?" said the gentleman who was well acquainted in Glaston and who had manifested much interest in the transformed showman.

336

"And his wife and his daughter, Miss Geraldine Lloyd."

Mrs. Laniston looked bewildered. "But isn't this rather early to go so far south? The danger from yellow fever is by no means counteracted by these light frosts in the upper country."

The gentleman who had connections in Glaston surveyed her in surprise. "Why, there has never been a case of yellow fever to originate near Glaston—they feel no apprehension whatever."

"Mr. Lloyd's home-place is within a few miles of Glaston," Mr. Dalton explained.

In common with most talkative women Mrs. Laniston could not silently await developments. "Oh—I thought his home was near us—in Louisiana—beyond the bight of the bayou."

"That——" said Mr. Dalton, with undisguised disregard, "why I understand that that plantation has only a little house on it—a neglected place, too. I think that Mr. Jennico only took it for a debt."

"Mr. Lloyd's home-place, the old Jennico place, near Glaston, is one of the finest country seats in the whole South," the gentleman who knew Glaston said, with almost local pride. "It is positively baronial. I should think, Mr. Lloyd, that you would be very happy to own it."

Lloyd smiled, his eyes on the fire. "I saw it only once," he said.

"Yes—yes——" exclaimed Mr. Dalton delightedly, "the time you called on your grandfather, Judge Lloyd, when he was visiting there. Ah ha! you took no notice whatever of the plump little gentleman reading the paper in his easy chair in the bay-window—and listening to every word. Charles Jennico always had more curiosity than any woman! He had intended to leave all his property to the eldest grandson of

337

his friend and cousin, Judge Lloyd—this Thomas Jennico Lloyd. 'But by George, I made up my mind then that I'd divide my estate evenly between the two grandsons,' he told me when he gave me his instructions to draw up his will. He said, 'I wouldn't do anything then; I wouldn't interfere with the young cock's independence—I honoured him for it. But I never saw anybody who would grace wealth better and I made up my mind that he shouldn't eat the bread of carefulness all his days.' And that's how our young friend came to be the residuary legatee and devisee."

The priggish gentleman, who was of the type who grudges a fellow-creature nothing so much as self-satisfaction, remarked with sour emphasis: "Your Street Fair colleagues, Mr. Lloyd, will have marvellously little trouble in advertising themselves with your accession to fortune. The newspapers are beforehand with them already. You are spread all over the New York papers,"—and he turned a sheet trembling and crackling in his hand as he unfolded it, and read the following flaring headline:

"A Windfall. From Mountebank to Millionaire."

Mrs. Laniston could not forbear so sharp an exclamation of surprise that Mr. Dalton turned and looked interrogatively at her.

"Why—we have made no secret of it," said he. "I mentioned that a good bit of money went with the real estate."

"Oh," Mrs. Laniston explained, faltering and flushing, "I had no idea that it was as much as that." Then recovering herself as best she might she continued, "I suppose I received that impression because I had heard you say that his grandfather, Judge Lloyd, was so reduced in fortune."

"Judge Lloyd left nothing," said Mr. Dalton. "This fortune comes from Charles Jennico, a very distant relative who was

338

a childless widower and much attached to Judge Lloyd's family."

Lloyd's eyes were fixed discerningly upon Mrs. Laniston for one moment, with that infrequent sternness that was yet so definite in his face. He wondered if the girl's course toward him to-day had been prompted by her influence. He reflected that Lucia had shown,—she had said indeed,—that she loved him. And yet she would not tolerate his suit. This he felt sure was the work of the cautious chaperon, under the mistake that his affluence was but a most limited competence. Doubtless she had subtly argued, urgently constrained, really overwhelmed the young girl's mind and preference, for independent and self sufficient as Lucia affected to be she was in reality docile to authority and in any matters of importance easily controlled, as he could see, by the judgment of her aunt, whom she loved and respected and trusted.

Mrs. Laniston could not disguise her dismay when once more Lucia and she were together in the upper story of the hotel. The apartment seemed bare and wintry as the storm beat upon the resounding roof and gables of the building, and the infinite stretches of the tempestuous clouds, above the vast purple mountains and the untenanted valleys, showed in the occasional broad flashes of the lightning through the uncurtained windows, as the summer birds rifled their temporary nests and made ready for their flitting on the morrow.

"Oh, Lucia, Lucia, my dear," wailed Mrs. Laniston. "I have made such a terrible mistake! I have destroyed your splendid chances—for you loved that man, and but for me you would have married him."

And Mrs. Laniston sat on the side of the bed in the sparsely furnished fireless summer room and wrung her hands in wretchedness.

Lucia's face was wan and wistful as she stood tall and slim and beautiful, in her sheer white dress with the shimmer of the silk beneath it, against the background of the dark window with the fluctuating view of the tempestuous landscape without. She held in her hand the golden-rod that she had drawn from her hair and she looked like the personification of the departing joys of summer.

But she had taken strong control of her nerves and she held it.

"You meant for the best, Aunt Dora," she murmured. "All that you said is true—as true now as then."

"But, oh, child, money makes such a difference—opportunity, travel, splendid environment. The incompatibility I feared, the bizarre influences of his past life, his language, his opinions, his manners, his lack of education would all be condoned by the world in a man of great wealth. And, even without it, you loved him." After a pause, "Lucia," Mrs. Laniston pleaded tremulously, "can't you try to lure him back. It would do no harm to try."

"I will not," cried Lucia with sudden passion. "I would not—for all his fortune—have him to think that it made the difference to me."

Mrs. Laniston could not herself have attained such dignity of poise, but she had a dreary satisfaction that Lloyd could perceive no suggestion of change in Lucia's manner wrought by the revelations of the magnitude of his windfall, no token of relenting in the scanty association that remained to them during the journey and the final parting.

His detention in Colbury was slight. In that short dazzled bewildered moment when he had looked down upon the still in the cave he had not recognised any face or figure among the distillers. No facts could be adduced against the Pinnott family in connection with the moonshining evidently

340

practised in the cavern, and he was not sorry that they should go scot free despite his suspicions. Clotilda had obviously lost little in losing her lover, but it was because of this he thought that she seemed dazed and dull and dense to him when he told her of his windfall and bestowed upon her and the old crone and Daniel Pinnott's wife and child such gratuities "to remember him by" as he fancied might please their taste. Then he was gone and she heard of him never again.

Mrs. Laniston did not lose sight of him. She was wont to scan with pangs of self-reproach the reports of the social world in the newspapers, and bitterly noted the fulfilment of her prophecy how easily it might reconcile itself to peculiar antecedents and endowments when the wealth was commensurate—and in justification of this mundane appraisement it might be urged that the prestige of family distinction was great also. In the shortest imaginable interval Lloyd became noted in the social whirl; he was a patron of the theatre and the fine arts; a great devotee to outdoor sports, master of the fox-hounds, prominent in the country club and at the horse show, and he soon grew interested in the turf as an owner of fine racers. His attractive personality, and his inherited claims to fine social position speedily made him a favourite in certain high and exclusive circles. He became, so to speak, the fashion; his traits were admired and imitated; his sayings were repeated; his every movement was chronicled; and when it became bruited abroad before many months that he was about to marry his cousin's only child, Miss Geraldine Lloyd, his popularity rendered it a matter of very general satisfaction that the great Jennico fortune, which had been divided in his behalf, was once more to become a single interest to his further advantage.

When this news came to Louisiana Lucia Laniston was moved to take her way in a solitary walk down toward his little neglected plantation which she knew lay beyond the bight of the bayou near the swamp. The narrow path kept the summit of the levee along the Mississippi River, the great embankment covered with the thick mat of the Bermuda grass,—the still, deserted plantation fields on one side, the crisp sere stalks flaunting here and there a flocculent lock, "dog-tail" as the ungathered remnant of the cotton is called, and on the other side shining pools, where the encroaching river was creeping up into the area of the "no man's land" between the protective levee and the treacherous current. A lonely region this; she met no living creature, and as she, herself, swiftly walked along the embankment, her tall slim figure in her gray cloth dress with her gray chinchilla furs— the only note of vivid colour being the red wing with the grey ostrich plume in her hat—might have been visible a long way off, had there been any observer in view. When she quitted this path she followed the quiet country road, along its many windings to Lloyd's little plantation, a pilgrimage of final farewell to a cherished thought, and stood at the padlocked gate, and looked long at the little humble unpainted house, which was without a tenant now. The soft bland air of the Southern winter was about her; the sheen of the sunlight had a glister like spring; the eternal green of the hedges of the Cherokee rose and the never-dying foliage of the live oak above the roof aided the illusion. She had never regretted his millions, but looking over the gate locked against her, she saw herself as once heretofore rocking in her chair on the porch of his house, and again, with blowsy hair and red cheeks, planting lily bulbs in the high turfed flower beds of fantastic shape, and she knew that she had had then as now a vision of happiness.

So definitely was Lloyd present to her thoughts that as she turned and saw him standing on the border of Bermuda grass that fringed the road, she did not start with an appreciation of the reality of the apparition,—it affected her

342

only as the continuity of her dream. It was indeed the surprise in his face, the embarrassment of his manner, the searching questioning look beginning to grow intent in his eyes as he lifted his hat that brought her suddenly to the recognition of the facts of the moment.

"You are not surprised to see me here," he said, ill at ease, flushing, consciously malapropos,—it was as if presumptuously recognising the fact that he must have been predominant in her mind at the moment.

"I was thinking of you." She regained her self-possession by a mighty effort, as she offered her hand. "We have heard the news. I am glad to have an early opportunity to congratulate you."

His mobile eyebrows went up at an acute angle of amazement. "Oh," he said at length, as if suddenly bethinking himself, "that happy man's name is 'Boyd'—not Lloyd. The similarity is giving us no end of confusion,—the gossips are all off the track. No, no," he added, "for myself I have nothing more serious on hand than a cruise in the Gulf,—my yacht is lying-to for supplies across the bend." He turned and glanced out at the great Mississippi, at high water resembling some vast lake, it stretched out so far, and the vermilion sphere of the sun, slowly sinking, made a great sheen of red glister on its murky rippling expanse. They could both see the smoke rising from the funnel of a yacht lying below the point where a fringe of pecan trees cut off the view, and a noisy bevy of green parroquets flitted in and out in search of nuts. "It struck my fancy, while waiting, to come ashore and view my possessions here."

He had thrust his hat back on his head and she winced as his look of critical, supercilious disparagement wandered cynically about the dreary, shabby, neglected little farmhouse.

343

"So this is the palatial home which you thought I had done you the honour to offer to you," he said, smiling ironically.

"Oh, don't—don't guy it,"—she cried with a sharp accent of pain, remembering her visions.

She had not kept the control of her nerves; she was consciously embarrassed and flushing painfully. She felt his intent eyes on her face, and she averted her own and looked up at the sunset aglow on the tiny panes of the blurred cheap glass of the windows.

"You thought little enough of it once," he said hardily,—he had acquired an assurance, doubtless through much adulation, which kept him from the fear of misapprehension,—"even after you had learned that it was not to be a home of poverty,—yes, indeed," he continued with an accession of bitterness, "you took pains to convince me that even wealth was powerless to commend me. I am not sensitive—but there was no need to turn and turn the knife in the wound."

He gave a short, angry sigh. "Well,—it is all over. I never meant to persecute you with my protestations again. I knew then that Mrs. Laniston urged you to reconsider,—that she would leave no stone unturned. I never expected to see you again,—and yet it is a melancholy pleasure,"—he looked at her with a sad smile in his eyes,—"and I take it mighty kindly of you that you don't deride the little place that you thought was the home I offered you."

"I love it," she cried with a gush of tears. "I have never regretted it but once,—and that was every moment and all the time, since I let a word of counsel,—a well meant word though it was,"—she hastily stipulated, "close its doors upon me."

He was at her side in a moment. "Then tell me why— *why* were you afterward so cold, so silent, avoiding even a casual glance?"

"Lest you might think that the discovery,—the wealth,"— she faltered.

"Don't put that into words," he interpolated sternly. "I will not forgive you even an imaginary aspersion of your motives."

They had turned away from the padlocked gate, but they were together and there was no shadow of misunderstanding between them. As they took their way up the embankment of the levee in the direction of her aunt's house, revolving their plans for the future, Lucia glanced over her shoulder, then turned and with her wonted airy grace she kissed her hand to the dingy little cottage, so sombre and meagre beneath the gorgeous sunset sky.

"*Au revoir*, little home," she cried, her voice ringing out joyously in the silence. "I shall set up my staff here for a time at least. It is the trysting-place of Happiness, and all its dreams come true."

For she had romantically stipulated that their honeymoon should be passed here, where she had seen herself in visions so simply happy.

Lloyd looked at her, his eyes shining with a new glow. Then he, too, fervently kissed his hand toward the cottage and echoed her words.

"*Au revoir*," he said, "a low lintel, but that door will be the portal of Paradise."

THE END

COMMENTARY & BIOGRAPHY

Charles Egbert Craddock was the pseudonym of Mary Noailles Murfree (1850–1922), an American author celebrated for her vivid depictions of Appalachian life and natural landscapes. Writing under a male pseudonym, Murfree earned significant acclaim during her career, particularly in the late 19th century, when regionalist fiction flourished. Her works, including *The Windfall* (1907), combined a keen understanding of human nature with a profound appreciation for the rugged beauty of the Southern mountains.

Biography

Born in Murfreesboro, Tennessee, into a wealthy and educated family, Mary Noailles Murfree was exposed to literature and culture from an early age. Her childhood was shaped by frequent travel, which introduced her to the Appalachian region that would later inspire much of her fiction. After suffering a bout of paralysis as a child that left her physically disabled, Murfree turned to reading and writing as a source of solace and creative expression.

Murfree began publishing short stories in magazines such as *The Atlantic Monthly* in the 1870s, initially using her pseudonym to avoid the biases against female authors prevalent at the time. Her first collection, *In the Tennessee Mountains* (1884), gained widespread attention and solidified her reputation as a skilled regionalist writer. Over her career, Murfree published more than 20 novels and collections, blending realism with romanticism to portray the lives, dialects, and struggles of Appalachian communities.

The use of the pseudonym Charles Egbert Craddock added an element of intrigue to her career. Readers and critics assumed the author was a man until 1885, when Murfree revealed her identity during a meeting with her publisher. This revelation did little to dampen her popularity; instead, it underscored her talent and the depth of her commitment to authenticity in her work.

Literary Commentary on *The Windfall*

The Windfall (1907) is a lesser-known but quintessential example of Murfree's artistry. Set in the Appalachian Mountains, the novel tells the story of complex human relationships set against a harsh but majestic natural environment. The plot centers on a family inheritance—the titular "windfall"—that becomes a source of conflict and transformation for the characters. The narrative intertwines themes of greed, justice, and redemption, showcasing Murfree's ability to blend human drama with a richly atmospheric setting.

The novel highlights Murfree's hallmark traits: her detailed descriptions of the Appalachian landscape and her use of authentic regional dialects. Murfree was a master of local color, and in *The Windfall*, she vividly portrays the mountains as more than a backdrop; they become a character in their own right, shaping the lives and destinies of the people who inhabit them.

One of Murfree's strengths in *The Windfall* lies in her exploration of moral and social issues. She delves into the effects of poverty, isolation, and community dynamics, painting a realistic yet sympathetic portrait of Appalachian life. Her characters are often caught between tradition and change, reflecting the broader cultural tensions of the late

19th and early 20th centuries. The inheritance in the story serves as a metaphor for the struggles between materialism and integrity, a theme that resonates deeply in her body of work.

While praised for her ability to evoke place and atmosphere, Murfree has also faced criticism for her use of stereotypes, which some argue simplified Appalachian culture for urban audiences. Nonetheless, her works, including *The Windfall*, are significant for their historical and literary value, offering a glimpse into a time and region often overlooked in American literature.

Legacy

Murfree's contributions to American literature were instrumental in shaping the regionalist movement. Her work, including *The Windfall*, paved the way for later authors like Willa Cather and Eudora Welty, who also explored the interplay between people and place. Though her popularity waned after her death, Murfree's novels remain an important part of the canon of Southern literature, celebrated for their vivid depictions of Appalachian life and their unique perspective on human resilience and morality.

References

- Rubin, Louis D. *The History of Southern Literature*. Louisiana State University Press, 1985.
- Harris, Sharon M. *American Women Writers: A Critical Reference Guide*. Greenwood Press, 2000.
- Murfree, Mary Noailles. *The Windfall*. Houghton Mifflin, 1907.
- Pizer, Donald. "Local Color in American Literature." *American Literary Realism*, vol. 15, no. 3, 1982.

Made in the USA
Monee, IL
05 December 2024

72553195R00193